FINDING Chaz

BY ANISA ASHABI

Cover artwork by Tina Butts.

Publishing Services provided by Paper Raven Books LLC

Printed in the United States of America

First Printing, 2022

Hardcover ISBN: 979-8-9862897-1-7

Paperback ISBN: 979-8-9862897-0-0

Dedication

For Kian, whose support of me and love for these characters make this book as much his as it is mine.

The Backstory

If my life were a TV show, Chaz Humbert would be the bad guy. Not Casanova bad. Not James Dean in *Rebel Without a Cause* bad. Just plain bad.

Fat, creepy, and depraved, Chaz looks the part of a stereotypical sex offender as much as he plays it. From his dated haircut to his Members Only windbreaker, everything about him screams "stranger danger." Trust me: if you're a girl and you saw him coming your way on a quiet street at night, you'd run screaming in the opposite direction.

But sadly for us girls, Chaz loves the chase. When prowling the halls of the high school, he usually isn't too selective with his targets. If I'm standing by my locker, it's a safe bet Chaz will materialize within seconds. Of course, I don't let him get away with anything. Depending on his level of offensiveness, I'll either fire something right back, laugh it off, or punch him if he gets handsy. That said, I'm not his only victim. Wherever freshman girls may roam, Chaz is forever underfoot, if not under*skirt*. While most boys our age are at the point where they can talk to girls without awkwardness, Chaz is only interested in deviance. Whether he's snapping bras, snapping pics, or deliberately landing on top of me during PE, he never takes a day off. By the time I graduate high school in 2010, I will have endured 2,191 days of uninterrupted sexual terrorism.

Chaz first emerged in sixth grade. We were all new to middle school that year, but my family had only been in town a week, and I knew no one. The first day, I was sliding into my chair when my foot bumped something large, spongy, and alive. Peering beneath my desk, I jerked back and shrieked. A boy shaped like a bowling ball was crouched directly under me, looking up my shorts and grinning like the Cheshire Cat. To this day, if I ever feel too lazy to double-check my front door's deadbolt before going to bed, Chaz's first greeting floats back into my subconscious.

"Humbert," he purred. "Chaz Humbert. We're going to have a lot of fun together."

"Fun" with Chaz was beyond abnormal. First, I had him in homeroom, but then suddenly he was in two, three, and four of my classes. Week one, he asked me out. Week two, he began stalking me. Figuring he was trying to get a rise out of me, I stopped reacting, so he kicked it up, and by the end of the month, Chaz was flying out at me from dark corners of the school with a lacy thong stretched across his face. Near the end of the year, someone drove a remote-controlled car into the girls' locker room with a video camera taped to the roof, and while a couple girls took it to the office and implicated Chaz as the driver, he never took the rap.

After Chaz humped my backpack during homeroom one morning, I'd had enough. I excused myself from class and went directly to see the school counselor, Ms. Stein. Upon arrival, I was surprised to see a girl sitting on the couch, her eyes red-rimmed and puffy. I recognized her from a few of my classes.

"I'm so tired of it," she mumbled, her blond curls framing her face. "He gets away with everything."

My interest was piqued. Straining my ears, I tried my best to hear the rest of the conversation.

"He snapped my bra strap twice during the fire drill," she sniffled. "Then, during culture week, he pulled up his kilt and flashed me as I was walking to class."

"Wow," Ms. Stein said, shaking her head. "That's nuts. I'm so sorry, Hanna. I'm going to see what I can do, but I'm quite surprised. I have several students I've had to keep an eye on, but I can't say I've gotten any complaints about Chaz Humbert."

"Ms. Stein," I interrupted, forcing my way through the door.

"Excuse me," she replied sharply. "I'm with a student."

"I've been having problems, too," I said. "With him."

"With whom?"

"Chaz Humbert."

"And tell me, who are you?" Ms. Stein gave me a look.

"Roxie Nazari," I said. "I left class to see you. Here for the exact same reason she is."

"Well, I'm not sure about…"

"Sexual harassment," I cut in. "Unwanted attention of a sexual nature. Stalking. Following. Pressure for dates. Inappropriate touching."

The previous afternoon, I'd spent my bus ride flipping through the ethics section of my planner and, to no great surprise, found everything Chaz had been doing to me punishable under school law. I listed off several more reasons why Chaz should be in a straitjacket before sitting down on the couch next to the girl.

"I can't do anything about it, and he refuses to stop," I concluded. "I was told to come here for help."

"I'm sorry. What was your name again?" Stein asked, addressing nothing I'd just said.

"Roxie. I'm new here."

"Well, Roxie. I'm more than happy to meet with you later."

"It's no trouble," I said quickly. "That's all I came here to say."

"Okay, then," Ms. Stein replied. "Well, thanks for stopping by."

"And," I continued, feeling brushed aside, "what she's saying sounds a lot like what I'm saying. That creep is out of control."

"Well, let's not start name-calling," Ms. Stein said firmly.

I gaped at her. "Are you serious? I just came here to report the same thing. I don't know this girl, and I'm not lying about Chaz. He's dangerous and a freak!"

"Enough!" Stein snapped, holding up a withered palm. "I said I would look into it, and I'm happy to call him in, but that's all I can give you. Now, if you'll excuse me—other students are waiting." She rose to get the door, but I beat her to it, wrenching it open and slamming it shut behind me.

Not feeling like returning to another useless classroom session, I loitered by the water fountains, complaining to no one in particular.

"What a crock!" I griped to the vending machine. "She's supposed to help."

"I know."

I spun around to see the girl from earlier. "He's been bothering me since the start of the school year."

I raised a brow. "You too?"

"Oh, yeah." The girl managed a smile. "I'm Hanna, by the way."

"Roxie," I replied. "I think you're in some of my classes?"

"Yeah," Hanna said. "A few, I think."

I made a face. "Which is how you know Chaz."

"Everybody knows Chaz," Hanna sighed. "At least every girl. I don't know what to do. I've told the teachers, Ms. Stein, the principal. Nobody cares."

"Yeah," I said. "Doesn't seem like it's going to do squat. I'm going to be late for class, so I've gotta run. It was good talking to you, though."

"See you next period?" Hanna asked hopefully.

"Totally." I laughed. "You, me, and Chaz."

And we did see each other. From that day forward, Hanna and I started hanging out together in class, at lunch, and after school. By the end of sixth grade, we were inseparable. School days could be exhausting, but at least somebody else shared the burden that was Chaz. Our friendship cemented by a situation far too many girls face, our relationship wasn't based on common interests or extracurricular activities, but survival. The years went on, and Chaz's obsession with us remained constant. By the time we entered the ninth grade, I knew it was time for drastic action.

Chapter 1

"He didn't."

"He did!" I insist. "Stephanie wasn't there, but she knows people who were. She never lies."

Hanna shakes her head. "So he…?"

"Rollerbladed after girls wearing a strap-on." I rub my eyes, trying to dislodge the imagery. "He had this little pink nub sticking out of his fly, and he just went rolling around trying to stab them with it. Freaking sick."

"He's ill," Hanna agrees. "Something's, like, medically wrong with him."

I raise my eyebrows. "And you've only recently figured this out?"

"No," Hanna says. "I'm well aware. But that's a little much, even for him."

"How so?" I shrug. "Oh and get this. The entire time he was cracking these sick puns like 'I'm about to finish' or 'track *meat*' in a weird accent. He did it Saturday during the relay."

"With a strap-on around his hips?" Hanna frowns. "How did he not get caught?"

"Like I said: it was inside the pants." I gag. "Concealed carry."

We're on the bus home on Friday afternoon. Petra, the psychotic bus driver in charge of our route, forced Hanna and me to sit up front with the first graders after catching us scarfing down a packet of Oreos in direct violation of her "no eating" rule. I'm not upset, though. Ten more minutes and we're out of here. Plus, in the midst of the chatter of the younger kids, there's less of a risk of being overheard. And I've got important business to discuss with Hanna.

"It's time," I say slowly. "Let's get him."

Hanna furrows her brow. "What do you mean? Like, entrap him? Show some damning evidence? Yeah, I'm totally with you there."

I roll my eyes. "No. We're way past that. I mean *get* him, get him."

"Look, I agree Chaz is way out of bounds," Hanna says, knowing where this is headed. "I hate him as much as you do. But we can't do anything that could get us in trouble. Now that we're in high school, it's just not worth the risk."

"A little trouble never hurt anyone," I counter. "Detention isn't even that bad. I was just there last week, and The Swindler sent a corn dog and a Sprite my way for a couple bucks. The cool kids hang out there, and sometimes they bring in hot seniors to help you do homework." I grin. "Sold yet?"

"Hot seniors?" Hanna raises an eyebrow, a smile playing across her lips. "Could be fun."

"You see?" I say. "Life is like a river. Pools come after the rapids."

"Okay, Rumi," Hanna laughs. "You still didn't answer my question."

"What question?" I scrunch my face at her. "Getting into trouble? Getting caught? It won't happen."

"And what if someone gets hurt?" Hanna demands. She lowers her voice. "You know, like last time?"

"What happened last time?"

"When we egged Jenna's house!" Hanna hisses. "Don't you remember? They had to bring the pressure washer and everything."

"So?" I chuckle. "Jenna told people I was turning tricks for lunch money. I couldn't just let that slide."

"That was it?" Hanna asks. "That's all she did? You said it was really bad and that Chaz was involved. I don't even remember what you told me; you say so much bullshit every day I can't keep track."

I shrug. "Nothing happened to Jenna. It was her grandma who fell off the porch. We never got caught."

"She went to the hospital! And we were technically responsible." Hanna shudders. "Are you even listening to me?"

"Of course," I reply, putting in an earbud and choosing a rap song I know Hanna can't stand. "Collateral damage. We'll make sure it doesn't happen again. Deal?"

Hanna's mouth twitches the way it does when she's torn between a tempting scheme and being perfect. "Fine," she finally agrees. "But I get to choose this time. I don't want to end up serving time in the state pen once we turn eighteen."

"Yes!" I punch the air. "This is going to be awesome." Ecstatic, I rip the earphones out of my iPod and start rapping along with Ice Cube, only to receive a lukewarm reception from the rest of the bus riders. I try to get a few sullen sophomores to join in, but they stare at me blankly and resume huffing something out of a paper bag.

I flop back into my seat, the wind gone from my sails, and realize we've reached our stop. Taking Hanna by the arm, we stand and barrel toward the front of the bus.

"Halt!"

I tentatively face Petra. "Yes?"

She flares her nostrils. "Was that you causing a ruckus on my bus just now?"

"Um." I stall for time. "Well, I was, like, really excited about something, and it was…"

"Wonderful!" Petra cuts in. "On my bus, we've got rules: sit down, pipe down, and don't cause a fuss. You broke all three today."

"I know," I say. "Please just let this one go."

"Okay," Petra agrees. "I'll let it go. You ain't banned."

I smile gratefully. "Thanks."

"Just suspended! See you in a week."

I open my mouth to inform her she can't do that, but Hanna pulls me away before I get the opportunity. With a belch of black smoke, the bus lurches forward and roars away from my street.

***

Even when early, I cannot show up on time to save my life. If tardy slips worked, I'd have learned my lesson years ago, but to this day, I have yet to be in the classroom before the bell rings. I'm already behind schedule on Monday morning when Chaz spots Hanna and me in the commons and rushes over to us.

"Whoa, whoa," he crows, dropping his voice to a low growl. "It just got hot in *here!*" Beginning to unbutton his shirt, he looks over at us and grins. "Let's cool down. Together."

"I'm cold, actually," I say, trying to keep my voice even. "But you know who isn't?"

Chaz looks at me hopefully. "Hanna?"

"Nope," I say. "The cheerleaders."

"They're in the gym right now," Hanna chimes in, following my lead. "Training. For basketball season."

I nod. "In bikinis."

"Really?" Chaz gasps.

We both confirm.

"Well, I'm out," Chaz announces. "Greener pastures await. Later, hos."

As the creature flies out of sight, Hanna and I slap a high ten.

"Good one." She smirks. "That should keep him busy."

I grimace. "For now."

"Did you do your homework?" Hanna asks as we begin walking towards home economics. "That worksheet was due today."

"Can't remember," I lie. "I might have. If it is, it should be in here somewhere. I might've already dropped it in the tray."

Hanna shivers. "How could you not know? I can't imagine."

"I'm sure you couldn't," I mutter. "How much time we got until class?"

She holds up her phone to display the time. "We're late."

We crash into our chairs right as the bell stops ringing. Of course, Mrs. Fullerton, the teacher, notices this.

"Roxanne?"

I groan. "Yeah?"

"It's 'yes,' not 'yeah.' Teenagers!" She sniffs. "Roxanne, did you turn in your original recipe for homestyle fried chicken?"

I stretch my legs out underneath my chair. "I'm vegan now."

Hanna laughs, and Fullerton scowls. "Well, I hope you turned something in, but I'm sure you didn't, knowing your track record."

"I did," I answer, annoyed. "Check the tray."

Fullerton shakes her head in disgust and suddenly becomes distracted by a stain on her blouse.

"Would you look at that," she sighs. "And to think I just got it back from the cleaners."

"That's *such* a cute blouse," Jenna Carmichael simpers before Mrs. Fullerton can take a breath. "I have to buy one. Where did you get it?"

I'll get to Jenna later.

"Why, thank you, Jenna." Fullerton beams as Hanna and I roll our eyes to the backs of our skulls. "I bought it at a thrift store in Minneapolis many years ago. So I'm not sure where and if you can find another." She turns to the rest of us. "Class, today we're going to watch a short film on being a smart consumer. Some of us could do with a little education in that department. Derrick, would you mind turning off the lights?"

Like Mrs. Fullerton, the movie is dated, useless, and terribly boring. I hope we're not getting quizzed on it because forty minutes in, I still don't know what it's about. Once Derrick killed the lights, I pulled my hood up, grabbed my iPod, and let Kurt Cobain serenade me into further depression. While we're filing out of the classroom at the bell, Mrs. Fullerton stands by the door and intercepts me with a bony arm.

"Stay," she commands. "Hanna, you hurry along."

Hanna shoots me a look of pity before leaving me on my own. Mrs. Fullerton motions for me to sit on one of the cold metal seats by her desk.

"Roxanne," she begins, squinting at me through her round spectacles. "We have some things to discuss."

"Sure," I say, fighting back a laugh. "What's up?"

"I'm going to cut to the chase," Fullerton says. "You need to step it up."

"What do you mean?" I feign confusion. "Step it up how?"

"I want you to begin respecting the assignments I hand out and put effort into your work. I've seen you fooling around and distracting others most of the time. That's not okay in this class."

I frown, this time genuinely confused. "I don't like anybody in this class besides Hanna. What are you talking about?"

"You know," Mrs. Fullerton says, studying me. "And I'm not going to repeat this. Grades are coming up. This isn't middle school. Your grades count here."

"Totally," I say. "I agree. I'll step it up."

"I checked the tray," Fullerton sighs. "Your assignment wasn't there. Neither was the last one. I don't know what to say."

"I did them," I insist. "But if you say they aren't there, I'll print both of them and bring them tomorrow."

She heaves another sigh. "Fair enough," she says, though I can tell she thinks that's anything but fair. "And what are your plans for the future? You know, in life?"

"Uh." I try to think of an answer that'll get me out of here. "Doctor. Lawyer. A feminist? I don't know. I don't really think I need to learn how to cook if I'm fighting the patriarchy, right?"

Mrs. Fullerton shakes her head and sighs. "You are dismissed."

***

School's out, and I've got a stack of homework in addition to the pile from yesterday I didn't do. And it's not totally my fault. The school, understaffed and hopelessly disorganized, rarely updates its website despite the fact teachers claim their assignments can be found online. I turn to ask Hanna to see if she has any clue where to find tonight's English assignment when Chaz swoops out of nowhere and wedges himself between the two of us.

"Bunnies!"

"Eat one," I snap, shoving him off me.

"Party tonight?" he offers. "Two girls. One tub. No suits needed." He caresses his lumpy body in an attempt at seduction.

"Nope." Hanna flips her hair. "It'll be you and your hand."

"Funny." Chaz smirks. "And when you two change your minds and show up, a two-piece is too much," he reiterates. "No swimsuits. Just birthday suits."

"Yeah, well. Make sure to keep food, water, and a coffin by your front door while you wait," I say. "It ain't happening. Now move. We got to ride the bus."

Chaz shrugs and cups his groin. "Why don't you ride me, instead?"

Hanna flips him off, and we keep walking.

"How rude," Chaz tsks. "So distasteful. My car's parked out back if you change your mind."

"Your car?" I snort. "You mean that oxcart your mom drives? With the dent and the handicapped placard?"

Chaz's eyes sparkle. "You know my car? You actually care."

"No," Hanna says, rolling her eyes. "Vans are what weirdos drive. And you need room for all the little girls you've abducted."

Before Chaz can respond, we run towards the back lot and step in line right as the last passengers start to board. As Hanna and I step onto the bus, I suddenly recall Petra's declaration and put my head down, hoping she won't notice me.

"Off." She shoos me with both hands. "See you next week."

"This is my only ride home," I beg. "Can't we stay? You won't hear a word, I promise."

"Not my problem, hon," Petra gloats. "Find another way. Forget to tell your parents?"

"They're dead."

The lie rolled off my tongue before I could stop it, but the more I think about it, it isn't completely off-base. My father died almost four years ago, and my mom works all the time, so I hardly see her. Why does Petra the bus driver need specifics?

"Oh, darling," she gasps. "I didn't know. You poor thing. Go on, sit up here by me."

I produce a grateful smile and sink down in my seat. Hanna flops down beside me and refuses to look at me.

"Now, Roxie," Petra begins, craning her neck to look at me. "I get it if you don't feel like talking about it. But who do you live with?"

"My brother," I say. "He's eighteen."

At least that's true. My brother, Nick, really is eighteen, but can hardly be considered responsible. I'm basically raising him, in case you're wondering.

Digesting my response, Petra redirects her attention to some middle schoolers having a tinfoil war towards the back of the bus. I lean back in my seat and brainstorm more lies in case Petra wishes to talk further. But more importantly, why can't I stop lying? Any other time, I'd come clean and confess, but I can't because Petra's now staring at me in the rearview mirror and smiling earnestly. If I tell her now, she'll hit the ceiling.

As the bus slows to a crawl at my street, Petra stops me up at the front.

"Roxie," Petra says, locking eyes with me. "If you ever need anything or need help...just let me know, okay? Growing up without parents is tough. Life is hard enough, but trust me, growing up orphaned? Let's just say I understand."

My stomach lurches. "Thank you."

***

As I charge through the front door, I'm met by the sweet aroma of spiced bread. Feeling snacky, I kick my shoes off and slide towards the kitchen, wondering what tasty treat awaits me.

"Yo!"

"In here," Nick calls. "Baking."

"What's the occasion?" I ask, stepping into the kitchen.

"A girl in my culinary class," Nick responds. "She's new, and I'm trying to impress her. Nothing says 'interest' like a slice of homemade pumpkin bread, am I right?"

Turning to me, Nick's front is almost completely covered by my mom's tabby-cat apron. A burnt oven mitt obscures his left hand, while his right hand holds a wooden spoon coated in orange batter. Unable to help myself, I start laughing. Pouting, Nick strikes a pose, and I quickly snap a picture for Hanna.

"Who's the girl?"

"Gabriella Svenson," Nick replies, tossing the spoon in the sink. "She's doing an exchange year from Sweden. She's nice. She's funny. And she's super hot."

"And you think you can win her heart with baked goods and a form-fitting apron?" I ask. "That's the game plan?"

"It's my only hope." Nick runs a hand through his shaggy locks before looking up at me. "You're a girl. How do I get her to notice me?"

I stare at him blankly. "We've been over this. Dress normally, cut your hair, and don't act like a freak when girls come around."

Nick furrows his brow. "Freak, huh? I'll need some examples to back up that claim."

"Costco," I say at once. "On Sunday, right in front of everyone, you air-guitared and moonwalked at the sample stand. That's what I'm talking about."

"What about it? Biscotti excites me." Nick lowers his eyes. "Okay, so what do I do? Feather my hair and play cover songs at the local coffee shop? Be in touch with my emotions? Act my age? That's not who I am. What'll she think when she uncovers the real me?"

"I didn't say to lie," I insist. "I said change up your image. A little."

"But I don't want to change my image," Nick protests. "My image is tight! You're telling me to turn into an indie poetry dweeb who acts mature and comfortable around women. I'm incapable of all those things. Plus, I can't lose myself looking for a girlfriend," he concludes. "A girl needs to love the real me, not a myth."

"How did we get to that?" I snort. "I never brought up indie poetry. Just be a—I don't know—subdued version of what you are now."

"Calm it down a little," Nick says, nodding. "That I can do."

"Good," I say, grabbing him around the waist and trying to wrestle him to the floor. "Because what girl in her right mind wouldn't want a pumpkin-bread-baking, accordion-playing, wannabe gangster?"

"Right?" Nick laughs and shrugs me off. "Enough about that. How was school?"

"Dog shit," I reply. "Nothing new."

"Chaz again?"

I make a face. "He wanted Hanna and me to come 'party' at his house."

Nick chuckles. "Well, are you going?"

I shriek. "As if!"

"I'm actually kind of curious," Nick says, untying his apron. "How does a juvenile sex offender party? Like, who's on the guest list? Blowup dolls? Children? Victims of human trafficking?"

"I don't want to know," I say. "But I'm sure you can score an invite. Chaz won't care what gender shows up as long as it's warm and willing."

Nick shudders. "Despicable."

"That he is."

"What time does Mom get home?" Nick asks me. "Tonight?"

"Why?"

"I gotta clean this up," he says, gesturing to the batter-encrusted pans laying in the sink. "Then cook dinner. Then clean that up. And then get started on homework." He wipes his forehead. "Growing up sucks."

***

Seven-thirty and I'm stuck on the second question of tonight's algebra homework. I stared at it for ages, hoping if I invested enough time looking at it, it would magically solve itself. Fortunately, Hanna's online, and, as of right now, I'm begging her for assistance.

"Please," I whine into my headset. "Just give me the answer."

"Come on," Hanna encourages. "Think. You've already got three-quarters of it. It's basically done."

I force attention, then desist. "You know I can't grasp abstract concepts," I say. "It's hereditary. Neither can my mom. Or Nick, for that matter."

"My mother can barely read," Hanna shoots back. "But I can. Genetics aren't an excuse. Come on. Don't shut down."

"I'm not," I huff.

"Try applying yourself," Hanna says. "Like, for once."

"Jeez." I crease my forehead. "Way to bring out the zinger."

"Okay, sorry," Hanna says. "You're right. That was rude."

"It's all good," I say. "But if you really want to make it better, all you gotta do is—"

"Not give you the answer!" Hanna exclaims. "Come on, Roxie! You can do this."

"But there's still eight more problems to do," I moan. "And then I have to show my work and double-check my answers. God, I hate math!"

"I know," Hanna says sympathetically. "And it shows. You don't work hard. You never pay attention. You either distract me from my work or sleep through class. How do you even pass?"

Cramming. Plagiarism. Cheating on exams. These strategies are how I manage to not flunk out of school.

I smile. "Insider knowledge."

"Why don't you go to the morning study session tomorrow?" Hanna suggests. "The trig teacher, Mr. Evans, runs it."

"You know how it'll go," I grumble. "I'll walk in late, be surrounded by overachievers, and end up feeling stupid. I'll inevitably fight with the teacher. I'll get yelled at. Then I'll go to detention. It's the same story every time."

"And you'll go in with a positive attitude, and that won't happen," Hanna says. "Because I'm going with you."

"Really?" I bounce in my seat. "Great! Now let's talk about something interesting."

Hanna laughs. "Okay."

I'm about to answer when a webcam chat request pops up on my screen.

"Hey, Han," I say. "Do we know anyone named 'Biggie Johnson?'"

Hanna chews her bottom lip while scrolling through her contacts. "I don't think so."

Curious, I click the answer button in the lower right corner of the window. "I'm taking it."

Chaz Humbert stares at me from the screen of my laptop. He's alone, standing in what looks to be an office or rec room because there isn't any furniture behind him. His hair appears to be covered by a pink stripper wig like the one Natalie Portman wears in *Closer*, and although he's draped in a muumuu and his face hidden by dark glasses, there's no doubt who it is. As I take a closer look, I spot a small remote clutched in Chaz's plushy right hand.

"Welcome," he announces, "to the Chaz Show."

With that, he shrugs off the robe, aims the remote into the distance, and stabs the play button. Now nearly nude, Chaz is barely covered by a doll-sized pair of briefs. Justin Timberlake's "SexyBack" is pounding into my eardrums, and to the beat, he starts dancing.

This perverse performance is unlike anything I've ever seen. Never have I been nauseous, terrified, and transfixed simultaneously, but Chaz has managed to change that in one take. A dervish of testicles, moobs, and flesh, he's sailed into his nonconsensual performance with libidinous fervor. Paralyzed, my eyes fuse to my screen, and, as Chaz drops to his knees and caresses his chest, somebody calls my name.

"Roxie?" Hanna asks, sounding worlds away. "Roxie, are you there?"

"Yeah," I say quickly. "Yeah, I'm here."

As Chaz climbs onto his desk and violently pistons his crotch towards me, I'm struck with an idea.

"Uh, Chaz," I say as I take a couple screenshots and save them to a file. "You've got the wrong handle. Did you want to reach Edgar? He'd definitely crank one out to this. Redial."

Edgar Yarbrough, another oversexed freak and social tapeworm, is Chaz's closest companion and partner in perversion. Whenever I can, I try to spread the word that Edgar and Chaz are lovers as a clapback to their harassment. Of course, it's pure speculation, but with us kids, you can start a rumor with just about anything.

Chaz, though out of breath, stays in motion. "I give you the delicious gift of my body in all its glory, and you have to ruin it by implying it was intended for another?"

"About that." I hover my cursor above the end call button. "Do me a favor and keep your gift to yourself. It's small."

And before he can respond, I click out of the chat and nearly pass out.

***

"No."

Until now, Hanna and I never got the chance to debrief about Chaz's late-night visit. I've just finished giving her the details, and more than half a day later, I'm still trying not to vomit.

"I swear on my life," I say. "And if you think I'm crazy, check these out." I reach into my backpack and retrieve the hard copies of the screenshots I printed last night. Rolling them into a tube, I pass them to Hanna, who unrolls the first one and gasps, her stare becoming more incredulous as she thumbs through them. Shaking her head, she packs them back up and hands them to me. I stick them in the front pouch of my backpack and zip it up.

The bell rings, and everybody rises to leave. I wait while Hanna organizes her stuff so that the two of us can step out in sync. As we pull up to our lockers, Hanna presses her lips together, staring at me intently.

"Are you thinking what I'm thinking?"

"What?" I say. "That we've got a case? Proof? That maybe they'll finally take us seriously this time?"

"They've got to," Hanna insists. "He's right there in full view. You can't deny it."

"We'll do it then," I say. "Looks like our luck is finally turning around."

"Never thought I'd see the day," Hanna agrees. "Let's put Chaz on record."

The second we knock, Mr. Mercer, vice principal and bench press enthusiast, tears it open.

"Girls," he begins. "What brings you in this morning?"

Hanna shrinks a little, but I step forward. "Last night, I received a video chat request from someone with the screen name 'Biggie Johnson.'" I suck in a breath. "I accepted it against my better judgment, and Chaz Humbert came on my screen, wearing an unacceptable amount of clothing." Retrieving the evidence, I jab my pointer finger at Chaz's screencapped pelvis pulsating in my face.

Mr. Mercer slides his thick glasses down his nose and inspects the photos. "Oh, my. Yes, I see."

I close my eyes, not wanting to miss a detail. "Ever since we were sixth graders, Hanna and I have been sexually harassed and bothered by Chaz. No one helps us. It says in the school handbook that this type of harassment won't be tolerated. Well, I've reported every incident involving him, and this is still going on." I stare at Mr. Mercer, trying to judge his reaction. Hanna looks over at me and nods supportively.

His expression unreadable, Mercer produces a handkerchief, blows several blasts into it, and stuffs the gluey wad back into his pocket. I try to remain expressionless, even though I'm about to gag. Trying to read his thoughts, I stare at his face to see if any of this has sunk in, but I can't even guess what he might be thinking.

"Sit," Mr. Mercer says, gesturing towards a couple of wooden chairs facing his desk. "State your names for the record?"

I hug my arms to my chest. "Roxie Nazari."

"Hanna Gilbert," Hanna says, her voice a little louder than normal.

He types something into his computer. "So. It's come to my attention that you both have a problem with Charles. And have for a while?"

"We do," I say at once.

Mercer rubs his nose and stares at the printout again. "What makes you so confident this is him?" he asks. "This, uh, person, is wearing tinted glasses. The hair's clearly not a fit. It isn't a video, so there's no audio or continuous motion. I don't know what to tell you."

"It's. Him!" I seethe, punctuating each word with a venomous glare. "He found my web handle. There was music, and Chaz stripped. Why don't you bring the creature in to ask him yourself?"

Mr. Mercer gives me a tight-lipped smile. "Why don't we?" He hits the intercom. "Charles Humbert, please report to the vice principal's office. Thank you."

Hanna and I sit motionless in our chairs, waiting for whatever's coming. I cross my legs and put on my most composed expression. Chaz arrives minutes later. When he spots us, he blanches, then hides his discomfort with a big, phony smile.

"Roxie! Hanna! What's going on?" he laughs uneasily. "You got called in here, too?"

"Charles," Mr. Mercer says sternly. "Sit down." Chaz obeys, pulling out a chair next to us, and sits stiffly, without looking at Hanna or myself.

"I've got two very upset girls here saying you contacted Roxie last night and stripped over the webcam. I'm going to ask you right now, and I want the truth. Did you do that?"

Chaz rubs his ear as if he misheard Mercer. "Wait, what?"

"There are screen grabs," Mr. Mercer continues. "Why don't you have a look? Roxie, show him."

"These." I stand up, retrieve the envelope, and begin fanning the prints out in front of him. Chaz gulps and twitches but recovers smoothly.

"What gender is it?" he asks, examining the photos. Mercer snorts. "I don't strip, and I don't send pics of myself. Ever." He's trying to feign disbelief, but I can taste the fear coming through his voice. Mr. Mercer, however, isn't as perceptive.

"I don't know what to tell you, girls," Mercer says, throwing up his hands. "I'm sorry you had to see that, Roxie, but to accuse another student? That takes a lot, you know. Charles denies it, I personally don't think it was him…and we can't exactly ask him to strip for us, can we?" He sounds disappointed. Hanna and I are not.

"That said," Mercer continues, "this school takes sexual harassment extremely seriously. If I hear of any more nonsense, at school or outside, there will be consequences." I can't be sure, but it sounds like a subtle warning. Chaz nods and looks down at his shoes, and I wonder for a second if Mercer actually does have an idea of what goes on. Maybe he doesn't like Chaz and is on our side. Perhaps other girls have come forward with complaints recently. From what I've heard, Mercer's been eyeing the position of principal for some time, and there's no better way to snag it than by cracking down on wayward students. But, as usual, he switches to the tired monologue we've all heard a thousand times before.

"In the meantime, if any more problems come up between you kids, I'm glad to step in. And remember, my door is always open."

Chaz grins and bobs his head. "Got it, Mr. M. But I don't have any problems. Glad we could clear everything up."

Mercer gives him a curt nod. "Miss Nazari, for the future, I suggest you think twice before you accuse." He pauses. "This thing you guys have going on…if it continues, I'm going to call your parents. Everybody's parents, so we can finally put this to rest and get on with the school year."

Chaz is the first to exit. Hanna and I leave next, but as we turn the corner on our way back to class, he steps in front of us and sneers.

"Make sure your laptop's charged," Chaz laughs as he saunters away. "Part two's in the works."

Chapter 2

Clambering up the porch steps, I stumble through the door and drop my things in the foyer. School was unbearable. All day, Chaz was on a victory high, and Fullerton got on my case when I forgot to raise my hand. To top it off, Petra slid me a business card for a therapist who specializes in troubled teenagers, which, excuse the pun, really drove everything home.

I desperately need someone to talk to. Unfortunately, Nick's over at Covington Community College making up a test, and my mother is in California on business. I groan and shuffle to the den, where I collapse onto the sofa in an exhausted heap.

The phone rings, and I begrudgingly get up to check the caller ID. It's my Mom's cousin Yvonne, who's aggravatingly talkative, but usually has a good story. Well, I need other people's problems to take up my brain space. For once.

"Yvonne," I say, trying to sound enthusiastic. "How's life?"

"Roxie? Is that you? God, you sound just like your mother. No offense, of course." Yvonne cannot stand my mother yet refuses to call her any less than four times a week.

"Oh, none taken," I reply. "What's up?"

"Thornton," Yvonne snaps. "That's what's up."

Whether or not she realizes it, Thornton is always what's up. Yvonne cannot shut up about him. After eighteen years of this, most of my mother's extended family are about to snap, but I come from a nice family that doesn't verbalize their frustrations. Cousin Thorn gets straight As, doesn't take a course unless it's AP, and was once called the next Michael Jordan by the local paper. For some reason, Alyssa, his younger sister, takes up far less of Yvonne's focus and energy despite being the gymnastics team captain, smart in her own way, and, in my opinion, a lot more interesting.

"He has a girlfriend!" Yvonne gasps.

"...and?"

"And? My baby is dating some girl!"

"Would you rather he dated some boy?"

Yvonne huffs. "All I'm saying is she's going to screw with his mind and his grades and mess up his chances of playing for UCLA. He texts her all the time now. How will he discover the cure for cerebral palsy?"

I clear my throat. I'm regretting taking this call more each passing second. "Have you met her yet?"

"No," Yvonne says. "I don't want to. If I bring her to the house, she'll feel she's gotten in good with us. I don't want her to have that idea."

"Yeah, but if you haven't met her, you can't really judge, can you?" I say. "Maybe she's really cool. How's Alyssa doing?"

"She's fine," Yvonne says hurriedly. "Where's your mother? She'll want to hear about this."

"On a business trip," I say. "She'll be home Friday."

"Okay, I got to go," Yvonne says disinterestedly. "Later, kiddo."

I lay the phone on its cradle and flop down to watch some TV. Scrolling through the daytime programming, I keep thinking to earlier today and ponder why Chaz seems able to get away with everything. Today wasn't his first strike, and without a doubt, other girls have complained. Sure, his mom's a teacher, but Hanna's mom sits on the board, and that should outrank Mrs. Humbert by at least a few degrees. Plus, Kelsey and Brooke, Hanna's twin older sisters, were insanely popular back when they went to the school, so where's

Hanna's special treatment in all of this? Perplexed, I stand up and jog to the kitchen to grab the landline.

"Jerome," Hanna sighs when she answers the phone. "I told you—I need some space."

Jerome Greene is Hanna's boyfriend. I try to forget this relationship exists, but they've been a couple for two years and are still going strong. Back in seventh grade, Hanna made a rare, impulsive decision and asked Jerome out to the movies after Jenna Carmichael dumped him for Cameron, a popular eighth grader who was rebounding with her. Unloading Jerome was the one thing Jenna ever did that made sense to me, while Hanna, who'd been wanting Cameron to ask her out for months, snatched up Jerome to spite Jenna. The rest, as they say, is history.

"It's me," I say quickly. "We need to talk."

Hanna exhales. "Thank God. He's been texting and calling me nonstop, wanting to know what I want to do for our anniversary."

I laugh. "Dinner and a breakup?"

Hanna sighs. "Sounds nice."

"Do it!" I say. "It's been way too long."

"Which is exactly my point," Hanna says. "I've put two years into this. I can't just walk away from it."

"Look," I begin. "If you aren't feeling it now, you aren't going to be feeling it *ever*. Last year, it was a non-issue. Boys in our grade were whelps. Now, we're surrounded by hunks of man meat at every turn! Look around!"

"Roxie," she sighs.

"You're the one who mentioned the two years," I point out. "Is Jerome stepping up? Is he becoming the man he needs to be for you?"

"No," Hanna admits. "But I care about him. I don't want it to end on bad terms. It should be mutual, and we should stay friends."

"No, no, no!" I object. "Stay friends? Girl, please. 'Stay friends' and Jerome will be getting down on one knee before graduation. Or you'll be popping out Jerome Junior after prom. Trust me, it won't end without a clean break."

Hanna groans. "Easy for you to say."

"It *is* easy for me to say," I reply. "I'm single. I don't catch feelings, and it helps me see clearer. Guys are like buses. Another one comes by every ten minutes. Yeah, some are hot, but seriously, what do most of them offer us emotionally? Nothing!"

"Jerome cares," Hanna says, but she's quiet. Both of us know thoughtfulness isn't something he's capable of. It's not that he's a bad person. This is just a terrible match.

"Where do you get this stuff anyway?"

"I layer it as I go along," I laugh. "It's my own brand of psychology. I call it schlong-ology. The study of the male mind. A graphed inquiry into the *driving* force behind their actions. It's not complicated."

Hanna gasps. "You're sick."

"Don't say that. You're lucky to have a friend like me. And it's not like I'm saying anything that isn't true. If you knew what Jerome was thinking about 99 percent of the time, you'd probably have a heart attack."

"So, what were you calling about...before?" Hanna asks after a moment's silence.

"Chaz."

"What, today?" Hanna exhales. "That was rough."

"He's stepping it up," I say. "He's smarter. Sunglasses? A wig? He was thinking ahead. That can only mean he's got more tricks up his sleeve. God only knows what's coming."

Hanna exhales. "Lord help us."

"Okay," I begin, remembering the entire reason I called. "What's the deal with him never getting punished? Like, we might be his favorite victims, but we're not the only girls he does shit to. I heard he stuffed a pair of his briefs in Kat Santiago's purse during the pep rally last week, and like five other kids saw him do it. Why did nothing happen to him?"

"Well," Hanna begins, "I've actually done some asking around, and my mom, who's still on the school board even though she does nothing, told me Mrs. Humbert got hit by a school bus several years ago. The driver was under the influence, and the collision shattered her leg and hip bone."

"A school bus."

"Yeah. I think it was a short bus, even. Shattered her bones completely."

Though I'm the last person to find auto accidents funny, the thought of Mrs. Humbert getting railed by a bus sends me into hysterics.

"Come on," Hanna scolds, trying not to laugh herself. "Be a little understanding. She could've been killed."

I cackle. "Understanding of what? Starring in *Jackass*? Why didn't they give her a face transplant? And a new body?"

"You know what," Hanna says, exasperated. "Never mind. My point in all this was she probably sued the school district or that there was a settlement."

I can hear the muted clicking of a mouse on the other line before Hanna continues. "Yeah, there had to have been. There's no record of anything going to trial. They would've paid her medical bills since she works there and because she got hit on school property by a school employee. And, I mean, after something like that, who wants to deal with him? Deal with Chaz? He's her kid, so…"

I groan. If Hanna's even partially correct, everything makes sense. If Mrs. Humbert played nice and decided to settle while continuing to work for the district, they owe her big time. Settling would save them a fortune in legal fees, as well as avoid tons of bad publicity. Letting Chaz run amok for a few years is a small concession for them to make. Chaz isn't stupid either; he probably figured this out ages ago and hasn't looked back since.

"Hit by a bus." I shake my head in disbelief. "The poor heifer. No, the bus. The poor bus."

"Poor *us*," Hanna moans. "It'll probably never stop."

"What about your mom?" I ask. "She's on the board. Can she do anything?"

Hanna snorts. "Cynthia? Doubt it. When you drink through the fundraiser and show up to board meetings stoned, your credibility is toast." She laughs. "The last one was a real doozy."

"Did your mom tell you about the bus incident and Mrs. Humbert?"

"Yeah."

Obvious issues aside, Cynthia Gilbert is the only cool mom I've ever met. She got into school politics solely to pick up the dirt on everyone but is serially absent from meetings or events she's expected to help run. She gets away with a lot, mostly because she's gorgeous. Even though Hanna looks a lot like her, the two of them couldn't be more dissimilar in terms of personality and temperament. Besides my own mom of course, Cynthia's the only adult I've ever trusted wholeheartedly. Whenever I spend the night, she always orders Chinese takeout, sits Hanna and me down, and rips into any of the mean girls we go to school with. When she called Michelle Carmichael, Jenna's mother, a "try-hard bitch," I knew she was solid.

"Your mom never gets her facts wrong," I point out. "She's the gossip goddess. I'm sure she got it right this time."

"She gets everything else wrong," Hanna says. "But this? Yeah, she's probably right. But look, I got to get started on pre-calc, okay?"

"Yeah, yeah," I say. "When can we hang out?"

"Friday," Hanna says. "Your house."

***

Friday night, Hanna's sleeping over. We ordered pizza because we thought Eli Barrett, a cute senior who works evenings at Pagliacci's, would bring it, but he ended up being a no-show. Instead, I opened the door to a chubby, irritable, ginger kid with two medium boxes in hand.

Nick joined the party an hour ago, and while most girls would get annoyed with an older brother hanging around, I'm the opposite. While we've had our moments, Nick and I are closer than anyone I know. Eccentric, hilarious, and one of a kind, there's never a dull moment with him around, and whenever the two of us work on something together, we usually end up with tears running down our faces from making each other laugh so hard. We also look alike, with Mom's high cheekbones and bow-shaped lips and our dad's thick, wavy hair, black-brown eyes, and small stature. While Nick feels negatively about it and collects insoles that he swears boost his height, I like being small. It causes people to underestimate my physical strength, and I've got a lot of it.

Hanna and I both have other friends, but I rarely bring them over. School friends are just that, since you never know who'll bounce when the going gets rough. We found this out last year when Jade MacPherson, a one-time friend of ours, got caught with a pack of Marlboros and tried to say we'd sold them to her. No matter what we've done or where we've been, Hanna has never sold me out, and I would die before I'd ever do her wrong.

And of course, no weekend is complete without prank calls. Nick and I pass the phone while Hanna tosses suggestions from the couch, such as placing massive orders at Burger King or setting up fake drug deals with youth group kids we know from school. At least twice a month, we terrorize Jenna and Chaz, but haven't come up with any new material for those two recently.

I'm getting ready to dial Edgar Yarbrough's house when a call comes in.

"Who do you think it is?" Nick asks, staring at the number.

"I don't know." I squint at the caller ID. "I'm picking up." Before he can protest, I answer the call and wait.

"Good evening. Is this Roxanne Nazari?"

"Who's speaking?" I snap, although I know exactly who it is.

"Romeo Montague," Chaz pants into the receiver. "Ready to consummate our love, Juliet?"

"Are you the little shit who keeps harassing my daughter?" Nick thunders from the other phone. The line goes silent. "It's Chaz, right?"

"Mr. Nazari? Is that you?"

"No, it's Richard Nixon. Listen, bud, I think it's time you stopped calling here."

"How old are you, Mr. Nazari?"

"What?"

"Just curious," Chaz says, his voice smooth.

"I don't know how that's any of your business?" Nick says, his voice catching a bit.

Chaz sighs. "Still unemployed, Nicholas? How about a career in adult entertainment? At Humbert Pictures LLC, everyone's encouraged to apply. We're looking for diversity."

"What?" Nick croaks.

"Don't be shy, Nick. You'll be a natural. And don't forget, the less you wear, the more you make." Chaz jangles what sounds like a jar of coins on the other end.

"You know," Nick says, his voice returning to normal. "I'm not interested, but can I pass your offer along?"

"Certainly," Chaz says. "Please do."

Nick hangs up and waits a few minutes before grabbing his cell phone and firing up a new persona. The phone doesn't ring once before Chaz picks up.

"Hello," Nick says, trying out a tone that can best be described as rundown, gravelly, and sexual. "I'm looking for someone named Chaz Humbert. Is he there?"

Chaz's phone voice is calm and collected. "Yes, this is him."

"Hey, I'm Rocco, a former adult film star who has fallen on hard times. I'm ready to get back into acting, and I got a room if you want to talk business. Want to do the first shoot tonight?"

Chaz makes a sound like a hog being gutted. "Oh shit! Are you serious? Give me your work phone and fax. Let's work something out. I'm off at eleven."

Nick doubles over and slaps a hand over his mouth to keep from laughing. I grab the phone and hang it up, horrified at what I've heard.

"Why'd you do that? We were getting somewhere," Nick complains.

"Yeah, but you don't know Chaz. He was getting really turned on hearing that. Our plan was to prank him, not bring him joy," I say, wrinkling my nose. "Now, where were we?" I glance down at the phonebook. "Oh, yeah. Edgar."

Hours later, and Hanna's still going on about Nick's prank. She managed to capture some of the audio from "Rocco's Reply" on her BlackBerry, and every time we listen to it, we laugh harder. After loading up on snacks at Blockbuster, the two of us are now under a blanket in the den watching *Mean Girls*. Well, we were watching it. Nick had to run off to the bathroom after eating an entire Boston cream pie on his own, and guessing by how fast he charged upstairs, he'll be there for a while. Before his hasty departure, Nick insisted we pause the film, even though he knows the entire dialogue by heart, so I honored his request.

"So anyway," Hanna says, passing me the last of the Doritos. "Jerome."

"End it," I say immediately. "Tonight. Over text."

Hanna shoves my arm. "I can't. I've got to talk to him next time I see him, in person. I'll do it. I really will."

I sigh. "What did I tell you yesterday? Firm and final. Just facts. You want him to move on with his life and find someone he's better suited to? Give it to him straight. Don't waste his time, either. I'm telling you; you're doing each of you a big favor."

"You don't know our relationship," Hanna says, but her tone is so unconvincing she doesn't even bother to look at me. "I don't want to hurt him. I can't be mean." She gives me a pointed look. "Unlike some people."

"I'm not mean." I shrug. "Just direct. And honest."

"And what if he can't handle it? What then?" Hanna shakes her head. "If he hurts himself? I'd never forgive—"

I look at her in disbelief. "Jerome's stunted. Emotionally. Physically. Mentally. I don't think he'd get you broke up until you wrote it on loose-leaf."

Having pushed himself to the limit, Nick flops down in his armchair. "Press play."

"Where were you?" Hanna giggles.

"I don't want to talk about it," Nick says, his eyes watery. "It was agony, that's all you need to know."

"Whatever you say," I respond and reach for the remote.

***

"So, class," Mrs. Fullerton begins in the clipped voice she reserves for Monday mornings. "As some of you may notice, I don't really give out homework very often, as I want to keep this class fun for you all. But as of now, I am assigning a group project which will be due one month from today. I've already chosen your partner, and I expect you all to give this assignment one hundred percent." Her gaze lingers on me before she turns her attention to her notebook.

I look over at Hanna. It's not likely we'll get partnered up, as Fullerton thinks I'm a bad influence on her, but hopefully, we'll both get somebody bearable to work with. Tapping one of the front tables with a ruler to get our attention, Mrs. Fullerton turns the page on a pad of paper and clears her throat.

"Meghan and Emma."

Both girls grab each other's hands, squealing with delight. I cover my face, so Mrs. Fullerton won't see my grin. Two people I don't want to work with down in one shot. Excellent.

Mrs. Fullerton squares her shoulders and coughs. "Erik and CeCe."

Hanna and I exchange sly smiles; we know what's coming. CeCe and Erik are one of several "active" couples in our freshman class, and considering they've been going out since seventh grade, no one's surprised. I watch as CeCe's heavily glossed lips curve into a smile. She reaches for Erik, and they begin making out passionately, pawing at each other's clothing.

"Moving on," Fullerton yips. "Hanna and Stephanie."

Hanna lucked out. Stephanie's pretty cool and sometimes hangs out with us at lunch. That just leaves me. I look around the room, hoping I'll land someone who'll do most of the work. Last time I was assigned a group project, I had to do everything. And given that I barely pay attention in class, it didn't go so well.

Mrs. Fullerton reads off a few more pairs until I hear my name. I swallow and look up, hoping for the best.

"...and Jenna."

When I was four years old, I got lost at a train station. My mom found me minutes later, but it was enough time to leave me shaken. I wasn't sure how I was separated from her and my dad, but there I was, standing alone in an ocean of strangers. I feel almost as lost now. The first thing that comes into focus is Hanna's face. Her eyes are wide, and her mouth hangs slightly ajar. She looks over at me and mouths *yikes*. I squeeze my eyes shut, then shake my head like I'm an Etch-a-Sketch, hoping to wipe the slate clean.

I steal a look over at Jenna, who's sitting at Meghan and Emma's table. Their expressions are identical to Hanna's, which makes my blood boil. As if *Jenna* is the unfortunate one in this situation.

I shift my eyes back to Fullerton, whose lips are curled into a sneer. Maybe it's my imagination, but I doubt it. It's no secret Jenna and I loathe each other. At this point, I'm convinced Mrs. Fullerton partnered us to make my life miserable.

The spiteful prune sets her notebook down and clasps her hands together. "Now that you're all partnered, I suggest you get in contact sooner than later. This project will take some time, and I expect you all to give your very best effort." Her eyes flit in my direction, confirming my suspicions.

A boy whose name I can never remember raises his hand.

"Yes, Wendell?"

"Do we have to work on the project outside of school?" Wendell whines.

"I'd recommend it," Fullerton replies. "It's a complex and time-consuming project. The more you work on it, the better."

Great. It was bad enough working with Jenna in school. Now I've got her on the outside too. I'm seriously considering taking a swing at Mrs. Fullerton when someone pokes me impatiently.

Jenna Carmichael was born mean. Spoiled, snide and stuck-up, Jenna will hug you in front of everybody and throttle you when the crowd looks away. According to Hanna, Jerome began to believe in God the day Jenna dumped him, which should tell you everything you need to know. Now, here we are. Jenna and Roxie. And right now, the Jenna half of this infernal duo is tapping her press-on nails on her desk and looking at me hatefully.

"Yeah?"

"We need to get started on our project," she says curtly. "Mrs. Fullerton gave me the guidelines and rubric, and the sooner we start, the better shot we have at getting a good grade."

"Yeah, I know. I'm sitting here, waiting to get started."

Jenna glowers at me. "Well, did you even *bother* to read the paper? It's important we get an A on this project. You might not care, but I actually have plans for my future."

I bristle. "You saying I don't?"

She shrugs. "Not necessarily, but I imagine even *you* have heard the expression 'hard work pays off.' Not that I've ever seen you try hard in your life."

I snort. "Stapling papers and following directions isn't what gets you into Stanford, Jenna. What's your point?"

"Oh, Roxie." She smirks. "I've gone to school with you for the past three years. And I've happened to notice that your grades and efforts in school don't exist. I mean, you might have a hidden talent that we don't know about, but when it comes to academics, maybe you should study woodshop. It's a good class. You know, if you're slow."

"What?" I say, wondering if I'm hearing her correctly.

Jenna grins triumphantly. "My point precisely."

"Let's get this straight," I snarl. My ears are ringing. "I'm smarter, funnier, prettier…*better* than you or anyone in your Wonder Bread family, and you know it. Keep your jealousy and pettiness to yourself. You're worthless. Now, we've got a project to pass. If you say anything that isn't sweet or nice, I'm not lifting a finger. You'll do it alone. Don't, and I'll really tear you up. Got it?"

Jenna stares at me furiously but doesn't say a word.

"Good," I say, wrenching the project guidelines from her hand and slapping them against the table. "Let's get working."

When I get done telling Hanna about Jenna, she's speechless.

"I can't believe she said that to you." Hanna hates it when people are mean to me.

"Right?"

"Well, what are you going to do?"

"I guess I'll have to stick it out," I say. "I mean, Fullerton already told us we can't switch partners, and I'm definitely no exception to *that* rule, so what choice do I have? I gave Jenna the warning, though. She'll play nice."

"And if she doesn't?"

"Let's see." I tap my chin. "I could tell Yale she volunteers for the American Nazi Party. Feed her homework to the shredder. Tell people she peed in the pool at that country club her parents belong to. I don't know. I'll think something up if I need to. I hope it doesn't come to that."

"*Bonjour, mademoiselles.*" Chaz slithers out from behind us, doffing the beret he wore to school today. "*Ménage à trois? Oui!*"

"Piss off," I snap, wheeling around.

"Okay, what about dinner?" he counters. "Two *huevos con chorizo* coming up." He cups his nuts. "*Mi huevos. Y mi chorizo.*"

"The only *fiesta* you're going to go to is a beatdown in my backyard. Now move!"

"Remember to use the back of your hand," Chaz pipes up as I take Hanna by the arm. "A stinging smack always gets *Monsieur Humbert* in the mood."

"I'm pretty sure Edgar got the invite," I yell back. "Try to go easy on him."

Throughout the day, Jenna stares daggers at me, but I'm not backing down. Like Hanna always says, defense fights harder. This is my house. I don't know who's going to blow first, but things are heating up. It's just a matter of time.

Jenna and I became enemies the day I arrived at Parker Middle School, and honestly, the backstory isn't that exciting. The office assistant showed me to my first class and introduced me to the other students. Everyone seemed friendly enough, but Jenna and her minions sat stiffly in the back row whispering to themselves and glancing over at me. When I wound up next to her, purely by chance, she acted super sweet, but every few seconds, her friends would start smiling and giggling. By the end of the month, the rumor was I was dealing amphetamines and stripping during lunch, and though there wasn't evidence, I know exactly who started it.

Obsessed with success, Jenna takes her schoolwork seriously. Truth is she's about as intellectual as a bent protractor, but her ability to memorize, her membership in different student organizations, and her penchant for multiple-choice tests might get her somewhere working in a cubicle selling insurance. Still, she's convinced she's Ivy League-bound and, for some reason, feels compelled to put me down whenever she gets the chance.

I may not be AP material, but no one could call me stupid. I tune out my teachers and pull average grades, but when it comes to innovating,

Jenna's incapable. Considering she named her dog Rufus, it's safe to assume she will never create anything remarkable or revolutionary, and I'm about to launch a spitball into the back of her head when Mr. Tuttle calls on me unexpectedly during history.

I blink. "Sorry?"

"Did you hear the question?"

Disarming the straw, I fake attention. "Say it again?"

Tuttle sniffs. "I asked you where the ruins of the city Antioch lie in modern boundaries."

I chuckle nervously. "Oh, right. Let's see." I look around the room for inspiration. Jenna's staring at me smugly. Hanna smiles encouragingly. Against the far wall, Edgar has acquired an electronic device of unknown origin, which he's activated and holding against his groin. I shudder and turn away, only to stare into Mr. Tuttle's sunken face.

"I don't know," I admit.

"Roxie," Mr. Tuttle begs. "Please pay attention."

As if that's anything new.

"You really should pay more attention," Hanna says, setting her purse down beside me. I stare down at my worn Vans, counting the checkered boxes on the fabric.

"Why?" I say finally. "Everything that matters is already in my head."

"Because we're in high school now. I know you probably hear this a lot, but if you want to get into college, you need to start caring about school."

I stiffen my legs, then stretch them out. "Don't trip. Good grades are the ticket in for boring kids. Don't worry about me. I'll be fine. Once the recruiters meet me and see how awesome I am, I won't have any trouble getting accepted." I take a swig of the cheapo cola the vending machine is stocked with. "Besides, believe it or not, my grades aren't bad. I happen to pull a B average."

Hanna nibbles on her chicken-and-oregano wrap and looks up at me. "Serious?"

"Well, B-minus. Don't sound surprised. The work isn't hard. I could be on the honor roll if I wanted."

That's true, and it isn't. I pull decent grades in history and English, but science and math throw me every time. The material can be dull, the teachers are depressed and boring, and with thirty or more kids per class, individual attention is impossible to get. Finish one assignment, here comes another. Anybody would scream after a while. I screamed after fifteen minutes.

"But you don't try," Hanna insists, taking another mouse-sized bite of her lunch. "What if you applied yourself? That would show Jenna. You could be top of the class."

I shrug. "I got better things to do."

I wasn't always like this. In my earlier years, I was what some might call a prodigy. At six, I read my first novel. At ten, I was entering poetry competitions for high schoolers and winning. Ask anybody about Roxie Nazari, and they'd tell you she was going places. And it came so easily. By the time fifth grade rolled around, my teachers wanted to send me straight to seventh. But once I entered middle school, things changed big time.

I literally couldn't pay attention. Instead of focusing on schoolwork, I let my mind wander into distant lands full of trampolines, baby animals, and cute boys. After school, my books stayed in my locker while I went to the skatepark and ollied and 180-ed away my growing feelings of not belonging. It caught up with me, though. By the end of the year, I was the dumb girl who barely passed, when I bothered to show up at all. Teachers cut me slack, due to my father passing away and my starting over in a new school district, but it started to take its toll. My mom wasn't concerned, though. She told us happiness was more important than perfection, but suggested I keep things in check. So far so good. Kind of.

***

"Is this seat open?"

I extricate my face from my burrito bowl, expecting to see Chaz gyrating in front of me, but am surprised to see two older boys hovering beside our lunch table. I sit back, sliding my feet off the chair opposite me, and look over at Hanna, who appears equally interested. I eyeball the boy closest to me. He's definitely my type: ruddy brown hair, chiseled jaw, eyes like warm honey. He meets my gaze and nods assertively. If I've seen him around, I must've been in a coma because the more I look at him, I find I can't tear my eyes away. The dark-haired boy beside him, who's almost as cute, stares down at his sneakers and crushes an empty soda can in his left hand.

"Well, we saw you two sitting here and were wondering…"

"Hanna, Hanna, hi!" Jerome barrels past the boys and crashes into our table, sending trays and cups rattling across the surface. The boys exchange looks. Hanna cringes. I close my eyes and try to breathe deeply.

"What's up, Jerome?" Hanna asks quietly.

He fidgets with excitement. "You're never going to believe it. Oh my God, you're going to *freak* when I tell you!"

"Tell me!" Hanna says with forced enthusiasm.

"I got us backstage passes at the Wet Banana concert!"

I clamp a hand over my mouth and try not to howl. Wet Banana is a regional screamo band Jerome is obsessed with. The recurring subject material of their songs is slaying their high school foes and losing their virginity, and that's if you can actually understand the lyrics. Some time back, Hanna dragged me to Jerome's to keep her company, which is where I was given the rundown on WB. Jerome nearly had a stroke when I told him I'd never actually heard of the band members—Ned, Ted, Jed, and Maximilian—and audibly gasped when I informed him I'd never listened to any of their songs before. Jerome's room is wallpapered from floor to ceiling with posters, while his shelves are lined with flimsy, plastic memorabilia, purchased from the band website. The entire time I was there, the conversation never strayed far from Wet Banana, mainly because he had one of their albums playing on repeat. After two minutes, I'd had enough, but for Jerome's sake, Hanna pretends to be a fan. Whenever she comes back from his house, the first thing she does is go upstairs and nap to fight off a migraine. How she, or anybody else for that matter, is going to survive an entire concert is a total mystery.

The two boys gape at Jerome. "Wet Banana?" the dark-haired boy snorts. "Really?"

"Liam," Auburn Hair says quietly, shooting his friend a look. "Uh, yeah. So, you three headed to the show or something?"

"Just Jerome," I say quickly. "He's the groupie."

"Ah," Auburn says, nodding. "Well, I'm Blake. That's Liam. And you are?"

"Roxie." He smiles at me, and I'm glad to be seated because I don't think my legs are capable of supporting me right now.

"So, right before Wet Banana was forcibly inserted into our conversation, what were you going to ask us?"

Liam and Blake burst out laughing, and I feel my insides go warm. Blake steps forward, looking suddenly shy.

"There's a party happening at my buddy Tristan's house on Friday. We were asked to get the word out. Do you two want to come?"

"Tristan Sorensen?" I gasp before I can stop myself.

"That's him," Blake replies. "You guys in?"

I'm about ready to jump up on the tabletop, but I manage to keep my composure. Tristan Sorensen's parties are *legendary*. I heard about them back in middle school, and Nick claims they're unlike anything I'll ever see. But actually being invited to one? I feel like a kid on Christmas morning. Nevertheless, I play it cool.

"We'll have to see," I say casually, looking over at a wide-eyed Hanna. "But we should be able to stop by at some point."

Chapter 3

"You *what?*"

"You heard me," I brag, shoving my phone in Nick's face. Blake texted me after lunch today with Tristan's address and a "c u there," followed by a wink face. I immediately showed Hanna, who thinks Blake might be into me, but I'm not telling my brother that detail. Nick shakes his head and turns on the blender. The smell of rum cake floats from the oven, and I swivel my bar stool around, giddy with thoughts of Friday.

Hanna was less enthusiastic about the party, especially when I suggested she call things off with Jerome beforehand.

"This is it," I told her. "This party's going to have hot guys. Lots of them. Guys older than us, who are actually mature." I tried to gauge her reaction. "This means if you're going to break up with Jerome, you should do it now."

"I really don't want to go to that concert," Hanna admitted. "When is it again?"

"Friday night. Same night as the concert. Meaning you have to bail on the concert if you want to go to the party. Plus, think about it. Jerome will be so distracted with his backstage pass to his favorite band, he won't have time to be sad or upset when he gets dumped. It's humane dumping."

"Humane? Jesus, Roxie. You sound like a serial killer."

"Well, I am from Washington," I quipped. "So? Is it Jerome? Or on your own?"

"Stop pressuring me," Hanna whined. "God, you can be so pushy."

I let it go, but forgot I was giving Hanna a break and hummed "Here Comes the Bride" during passing period until she shot me the look of death. We're both going to the party, though, and Hanna knows it. Though I don't hate Jerome, Hanna's miles out of his league and frankly does a lot more for the relationship than he does, which is tough to see sometimes. Hanna's the one who confided in me one night that she wanted to call things off, but, indecisiveness being her worst trait, she is stuck in limbo.

"About this party," Nick begins, peering into the oven at his latest masterpiece. "We need to go over some stuff."

"Okay," I say, still floating from my invitation. "What's up?"

Nick flicks at a bobby pin I left on the counter and turns to me. "So, you're in high school now. You're not a little girl anymore." He suddenly becomes interested in the light fixture above. "So, um, I, well…I just think you need to have a few things in mind before you go to a party with a bunch of older guys."

I stand up abruptly. "I appreciate the concern, but I really don't want to be having this conversation with you."

"Too bad," Nick says firmly, yanking me back down. "We're talking."

"Yo! I can't believe we're having this discussion. You know I'm not going to hook up with some random guy at a party!"

"Of course I know that!" Nick chides. "All I'm saying is there's going to be alcohol at the party, and—"

"You know I hate the taste of beer!" I break in. "Why are you so hung up on this? I'm not going to drink. You can come too!"

His eyes light up. "I can?"

I squeeze my eyes shut and reopen them slowly. "Yes. As long as you promise not to be overprotective and to hang out with *your* friends instead of breathing down my neck. You can make sure I'm safe *from a distance.* Deal?"

"Yeah, totally. Deal." Nick looks considerably more relieved and even a little excited himself. It's better this way. The three of us will look cool walking in together, and if it ends up being a total flop, we'll have each other.

"Good. So that's settled then." I rise from my chair. "Do you want some help with that buttercream frosting? It looks like you were having some trouble." I peer at the flaky substance clumped in the mixing bowl. "Actually, lots of trouble."

"I followed the directions," Nick insists. "It just didn't turn out right."

"You're making these to impress Gabriella? Isn't she going to think it's weird you're bringing baked goods to school every day?"

Nick heaves a sigh. "How else am I supposed to get her attention?"

"I already gave you advice! I said to be an improved version of yourself."

"She talked to me today," he says quietly.

"Really?" I skip over to the couch and throw my feet up. "Tell me about it."

***

"So, how about this one?" I hold up a denim miniskirt for Hanna's approval. She looks over it and shakes her head.

"It's cute," she compliments. "But way too summer. It's October, remember?"

"Yeah, okay." Back to the closet. "Well, I don't have any party clothes, I guess. Looks like a trip to the mall is what we're going to need."

"I don't have money to burn, though," Hanna says, her eyes downcast. "I dropped two hundred on that stupid two-year anniversary gift for Jerome."

I hurl the coat hanger I was holding across the room. "You spent two hundred dollars on *Jerome*?"

"I had to get him something good! He guilt-tripped me by hyping his gift like it was a Coach bag, and it turned out to be an autographed Wet Banana inflatable guitar he got off eBay."

"Well, good thing you're not going to have to buy him a three-year anniversary present," I declare. "So, tell me, Han. When are you going to tell him he's going to experience a wet banana with someone else?"

"Roxie!" Hanna gasps. "And I don't know when to tell him it's over. I mean, he thinks that I'm looking forward to the concert when I'm really bailing to go to the party with you. I feel so guilty. I don't want to hurt his feelings."

"Hanna! For once, do what you want to do. You give enough to that relationship as it is. Too much if you want my two cents. But seriously, would you rather be dry-humped in a mosh pit by like two hundred Jeromes or hang out with cool, attractive upperclassman?"

Hanna opens her mouth to protest.

"I'm done talking about it," I say. "You'll thank me later when you're going on double dates with Liam, Blake, and me instead of sitting in Jerome's basement listening to his scratched Wet Banana CDs for the millionth time."

"Double dates?" Hanna scrunches her face. "You just told me to get out of a relationship. What's changed in the past thirty seconds?"

"A lot," I laugh. "Besides, Blake and Liam are in a whole other league than *Jerome*. Don't even *try* to tell me that you'd rather date Jerome than Liam or Blake. By the way, I call dibs on Blake."

"Have him," Hanna says, balling herself up on my bed. "Never mind the fact we don't actually know them. Seriously, who's that perfect? They probably just want to hook up with us. We should be careful."

"Dear God. Don't shoot it down before it flies. You think every guy besides Jerome has sinister intentions." I fold my arms. "Seriously. Jerome wears a banana pendant around his neck, and, personally, I think that's a lot more forward."

***

"Shit," Hanna whispers, rummaging about in her bag. "I know it's in here somewhere."

Morning break. Hanna's freaking out because she can't find the extra-credit assignment she did for English in her immaculate, color-coded, alphabetized binder. I'm trying to empathize, but let's look over the facts: Hanna's assignment is extra credit. She did the assignment, so she will get credit for it. Her binder is flawlessly organized, so if it isn't here, it's at home on her desk where she can bring it in tomorrow morning instead.

I also had the opportunity to gain some much-needed extra credit points, but the second I got home, I forgot all about it. Nick made hot wings for dinner, and my mom was out of the house, so the two of us rode the quad to his best friend Frankie's house and played *Super Smash Bros. Melee* all night. Like Nick and me, Frankie is often left on his own and lets us crash whenever we want.

"Come on," I say to Hanna. "It's okay. Bet you fifty bucks it's right next to your computer. It's extra credit, remember? Anything you bring in will boost your already-perfect grade."

"You're right," she replies. "I think it's too much caffeine. I gotta stop with the morning frappes." She turns to me. "They're so good, though."

"Damn straight," I reply. "Cynthia's frappes are to die for. How does she make those, anyway?"

"I don't know," Hanna admits. "She won't tell me. It's, like, the one part of her life that she's managed to keep private."

I snort. "Damn, cut the lady a break. She's the only cool mom I've ever known." I give Hanna a quizzical look. "You guys haven't been fighting again, have you?"

Hanna sighs. "It's complicated."

As the two of us drag towards Mrs. Fullerton's class, something stops me dead in my tracks. I blink several times, but I'm seeing what I think I'm seeing.

"What's wrong?" Hanna asks.

I grab her shoulders and wheel her around. "There."

Ahead of us, Chaz and Jerome are walking in synchronization towards the art room. Deep in conversation, one of them occasionally gesticulates, and between the two of them, we hear loud, booming laughter.

"Oh my God."

Hanna behind me, I break from my stupor and jog towards them. Chaz zips through the door, and right before Jerome makes it through, I grab his collar and nearly wrestle him to the floor.

"Really? *Chaz?*"

Jerome brightens. "Oh, him? I was just telling Chaz all about the concert, and he wants to go. We'll probably see him there, Hanna. Do you know him?"

"Are you mentally sound?" I demand. "Are you deaf? Get your head out of Wet Banana's collective anus and look around. Chaz is a predator, Jerome. He snapped your girlfriend's bra and tried to grope under her skirt during the fire drill last week. She definitely knows him. Did you know any of this?"

"Hanna," Jerome gasps, "she's crazy. Roxie's completely lost it."

At this point, I'm about to pile-drive him, but Hanna steps in. "No, Jerome. She's right."

Confusion spreads across his already clueless face. "What do you mean?"

"Do you listen to anything I say?" Hanna asks, suddenly sounding a little hurt. "Do you know what Chaz's done to me? To Roxie?"

Jerome gulps. "Not really." He isn't lying. Looking at his face, this is all news to him. He's truly oblivious.

Hanna takes a breath. "Jerome," she begins. "I've got to be honest about this relationship. About us. I think we should start seeing other people."

Jerome's face sinks, and he suddenly looks very small.

"Are you saying it's over?" His eyes begin to mist. "Does this mean you're not going with me to see Wet Banana?" And on that note, I leave the two alone and walk into Mrs. Fullerton's classroom.

***

"So, class," Mrs. Fullerton announces with a clap of her hands. "Today it's straight to work. From now on, whenever you come to class, find your partner straight away. We have little time as it is." I shuffle towards Jenna and drop my things down by the floor.

"So, did you do any research last night?" Jenna asks finally, looking straight ahead.

"On what?" I ask, too busy looking at a shaken Hanna to pay Jenna any attention.

"On *nutrition*. You know, what our project is on?"

"Yeah, science of food or whatever. And no, I didn't do any research."

Jenna huffs and purses her colorless lips. "So you're saying I'm the only one in the group who took notes last night?"

"Well, unless I did it in a parallel dimension, it's a no." I kick my feet up onto the table.

"So, what, you figured you were too good to do any research?" Jenna snaps, spraying my face with spit.

"No. I'm saying I had better things to do." I try to hide a smile. This is too much fun.

"Like *what?*" Jenna demands, pushing her hair out of her face and staring at me furiously.

"Hey, look who actually cares? I told you. Things. Now, read off your notes, or we might get a bad grade on our project." I gasp. "We all know *that* can't happen."

Jenna groans loudly and reaches into her folder. "Well, I printed off some information regarding the nutrition pyramid."

I snap my gum. "Sounds like hard work."

Jenna adjusts her tortoiseshell headband and ignores my comment. "I also discovered that one in four Americans eats fast food every day, which is a major contributor to childhood obesity."

"Cool," I remark, reaching into my coat pocket for my cell phone. Jenna grinds her teeth but continues reading. "One in three kids and teens in this country are overweight enough to be considered obese."

"Wow," I say, reaching over and poking her midsection. "This really is getting out of hand."

Jenna springs up, knocking her chair to the ground. "You have a really bad attitude, Roxie, you know that?" she says, choking back tears. "What's wrong with you?"

I look directly into her eyes. "I do have a bad attitude, and you know why? Because I don't fucking like you."

Jenna blinks at me. "I have to work with someone who's treated me like shit since I got here," I continue. "Spread rumors about me. Tells me I'm stupid. Don't expect the best."

"You're freaking impossible." Jenna's crying now, but I'm glad. She started this. Snatching up her bag, she gives me one last hateful look and stomps out of the room, slamming the door as hard as it'll go. Of course, five seconds doesn't pass before Mrs. Fullerton descends on my desk with her arms crossed.

"What is it this time?" she demands, enunciating her words and pointing at Jenna's vacant seat.

I shake my head and lower my voice. "I'm at a loss. I was going over the notes, and Jenna had a meltdown. Maybe you should talk to her. I heard she's had a tough week."

***

"Looks like this day blows for both of us," Hanna says glumly as we rush to our respective periods.

"Tell me about it." Throughout the lesson, Fullerton haunted my table, lecturing me about being a team player and whatnot. She must've decided I'd done something, because she handed me a detention slip on the way out. It doesn't matter. Giving it back to Jenna was the highlight of my month.

"One minute until class," Hanna observes, glancing down at her wrist. "I have to go."

Breaking into a sprint, I fly down the hallway towards the science lab and crash through the door seconds after the bell rings.

"I'm here!" I shout in an attempt to prevent another tardy slip.

Mr. Burke looks at me tiredly and wags a rolled-up newspaper at me. "Take a seat, Roxie. Class begins now."

I nod and trudge over to my seat to find Lu Chen, a boy who claims he's related to Genghis Khan and speaks Klingon, sprawled across my desk.

"Move!" I grouch.

He crosses his arms. "No."

"Roxie, I changed the assigned seats yesterday. Look at the board." Mr. Burke points to the overhead projector in the front of the room, and sure enough, Lu is in my old seat.

"Well, where should I sit?"

Burke points to the far corner. "Right there, in the back, next to Edgar."

"Next to *what*?" I splutter before I can stop myself.

"You heard me just fine, young lady. Now, take a seat."

Crossing the room, I slam my binder on the top of my new desk to indicate my rage at this seating arrangement. Mr. Burke points a gnarled finger at me and mouthes "thin ice." Edgar, on the other hand, isn't at all displeased and growls sexually.

I narrow my eyes. "Don't."

Edgar shrugs and instead prods at some dried bubblegum under his desk. I recoil and, for the first time ever, become very interested in what Mr. Burke is saying. He's telling us about the Energy Star and its impact on domestic manufacturing when somebody taps my arm.

I wheel around to see Edgar's slightly off-color finger hovering in front of my face. "Guess where?"

Before I can respond, another freak answers the call. He turns towards it, and I strike up a conversation with CeCe Sanchez, who's seated in front of me.

"How am I going to survive sitting by *Edgar?*"

"I know," CeCe sighs. "I feel so bad for you. Don't worry. If he tries anything weird, I got you." She smiles warmly.

"Thanks," I reply, instantly feeling bad for analyzing her sex life behind her back. "I'll make sure he doesn't try anything on you, either."

"Thanks, but I don't think you need to worry about me. If he tries anything, I'll sic Erik on him. He'll kick his ass." She giggles.

I laugh. "Well, let's hope Edgar decides to harass you too, then. I want to see Erik take him down. Maybe he'll wreck Chaz while he's at it."

CeCe cracks up. "How great would *that* be? A two for one? I'll totally have to ask Erik, and I'd have to repay him, but that's no trouble," she adds, adjusting her bra.

I laugh awkwardly and stare at my shoes. "Sounds like a plan."

***

Another week down. Well, almost. Within twelve hours Nick, Hanna, and I are going to be having the time of our lives, and I'm counting every second. Nick slept in, so I took over breakfast duty and cooked up a storm. Originally, I was planning to eat healthy, so as not to bloat for Blake, but a girl's gotta eat, you know?

I tend to sausage links and bacon while flipping French toast in another pan. Coffee is brewing, and I'm fixing my plate when Nick crashes into the kitchen in his bathrobe. "Coffee?"

"In the pot. Look lively, kid."

"Who are you calling kid, kid?" Nick laughs, grabbing a plate from the pantry. "Just curious. How did you and Hanna get invited to one of Tristan's parties?"

"We're hot," I say. "And available."

Nick snorts. "Yeah. Totally. Ten dollars if you can tell me what a Cowper's gland is."

I wrinkle my nose. "Don't be disgusting, Nick."

"You'll probably be the only freshmen there," Nick says. "Parties mostly start when you're a sophomore." He cuts into his French toast. "Do they know who Hanna's sisters are?"

"Maybe." Though I try not to let it show, I'm really glad Nick's going to come with us. I need someone to guide me through this process. "But they actually seemed kind of nervous asking us."

"Who asked you?" Nick asks. "I might know them."

"Liam Kensington," I say. "Blake Tisdale. Ring any bells?"

"Don't know about the first guy," Nick says, taking a swig of coffee. "But Blake? The pitcher?"

"You know him?" I blurt before I can help myself.

He gives me a pointed look. "Yeah. I know Blake. Or at least of him. Why?"

My stomach flips, and I try and think of what to say. "He's nice. Like, really nice."

Nick smirks. "Nice-looking, you mean."

"No. Well, yeah. Duh. No, I mean nice as in a nice guy."

"Oh, really?" He sets his fork down. "Do tell."

I know he's setting a trap, but I go on. "I can't explain it. We were sitting down, and they both, you know, the boys, came over and asked us to the party. Jerome crashed in, totally ignored them, and told Hanna he got tickets to Wet Banana."

Nick sputters with laughter. "Holy shit. Seriously?"

"Yeah," I chuckle. "And Liam tried to make fun of him, but Blake shut it down."

"How are they still together?" Nick wonders aloud. "I mean, Hanna's so—you know. But Jerome?"

"They're not," I say. "Didn't I tell you?"

Nick looks up from his plate. "They broke up?"

"Uh, yeah." Now it's my turn to set a trap. Call it sisterly intuition, but something changed last summer after eighth grade. Both Hanna and I have grown up a lot, and Nick hasn't, so it's almost like we're just two years apart instead of three. Hanna's irrefutably beautiful, Nick's finally grown out of his lifelong awkward stage, and we all hang out constantly…

"Hanna's always been pretty," I state. "But this year? She's stunning."

"Yeah," Nick agrees, sounding distant. "She'll probably look like her mom."

"She already does," I press. "Can't you see the resemblance?"

"Of course," he says. "I mean, yeah."

"Cynthia's gorgeous," I say. "People think she's Hanna's sister."

"Uh-huh."

I steal a glance at Nick. "She asks about you, you know."

"Who? Cynthia?"

"No, you dork. Hanna."

Nick gags on a mouthful of bacon. "Really?"

I fake surprise. "Nick, do you like her?"

A look of horror crosses his face. "No," he gasps. "No, of course not. That would be weird. Hanna's like my little sister."

I nod. "Mmhmm."

Nick takes an intense interest in the silverware he's using while I try to process the conversation that just happened. We're all high-school age. It wouldn't be unthinkable. But at the same time, the thought of them together just doesn't make sense. They're *too* close for anything other than a deep friendship to take hold. I hope.

"I'd like to meet Blake," Nick says, breaking the silence.

"Well, feel free," I say as nonchalantly as I can. "You'll probably see him tonight."

School drags, and much to my chagrin, Jenna's back in first period. As I expected, her attitude has worsened, and minutes in, she's drilling me mercilessly. I'm planning an extended bathroom break, but the bell rings, and by lunchtime, I can hardly sit still. Slowly but surely, Friday night is approaching. Nervousness is beginning to set in, and I sense the same from Hanna. Throughout the period, I keep my eyes peeled for the boys, but don't see either of them.

"Good afternoon, kittens," Chaz announces, full of verve. "It's Chaz o' cock!" He unsnaps his Casio and holds it in front of his crotch. "Ding dong."

I retch, and he takes a seat across from us. "Any room for the clockmaker?"

"Beat it, sicko!" Hanna swats him away.

"Gladly."

My quesadilla is now unappetizing, and I'm trying to come up with a response when Stephanie Quayle crashes down beside us as Chaz cruises away.

"Did you guys seriously get invited to Tristan Sorensen's party?" she gasps, her mane of bushy brown hair even wilder than usual.

"Yep," Hanna replies, a rarely seen self-satisfied smile on her face. "Two cute juniors, Blake and Liam, asked us to come."

Her eyes go wide. "*Blake Tisdale and Liam Kensington?*"

Hanna wrinkles her brow. "I think so. Do you know them?"

"Do...I *know* them?" Stephanie asks breathily. "Uh, *yeah*. Is it an open invite?"

"I really don't know," I reply, hoping she'll drop it.

"I wish I could date them," Stephanie says wistfully. "God, virginity sucks!"

The table next to us falls silent, though a few football guys guffaw appreciatively. Hanna fiddles with her charm bracelet. I stare at the floor. Stephanie sulks. None of us talk. Eventually, the bell rings, and the three of us are rising to throw away our trash when Hanna nudges my shoulder.

Behind us, Edgar and Chaz are enthusiastically molesting their lunches. While Chaz repeatedly stuffs a corn dog into an éclair, Edgar massages a couple of satsumas. Across from them, a camcorder has been balanced on top of a milk carton, recording the experience.

"Mother of God."

"At least it isn't us," Hanna points out, and Stephanie and I nod. The second bell rings, and Chaz rips the corn dog out of the éclair, licks its circumference, and devours both items in one massive bite. Edgar stiffens and groans, squeezing the oranges until they pulpify, and lets the juice run down his hands onto the table. Catching their breath, they high-five, switch off the camcorder, and slam dunk the remains of their mutilated lunches into the trash.

"I think I'm going to go," Stephanie says finally, her face slightly off-color.

"Yeah," Hanna breathes. "Let's get out of here."

***

After school, Hanna and I took the bus to the mall. Nick's on his way over, and Hanna's upstairs at Nordstrom Rack. I'm in line at the record store waiting to pawn Jerome's anniversary gift, but it's Friday afternoon, and with some record release party going on, the line's taking forever.

Almost an hour later, I'm on foot with cash in hand. Nick and Hanna are upstairs now, so I ride the escalator to the second floor. As I cruise past the perfume counter, I think I spy Nick in the men's section. I swing a fast left and tiptoe over to him. His back is turned, but I can make out his reflection in the mirror.

"Nick."

"Hey," he replies, turning around to face me. His face is partially obscured by a fitted cap, and he's shrouded in an oversized parka, a boxy shirt…everything is too big. Baggy jeans hang from his waist while an unfitted watch dangles from his wrist. "What do you think?"

"You don't have a job."

"Solved," Nick beams, pulling a wad of cash out of a fanny pack that belonged to my mother in the eighties. "I've got the goods. All this stuff is discounted, anyway."

I fold my arms. "No way in hell."

"What's wrong with it?" Nick asks, creasing his forehead. "This stuff is dope. I look like I'm straight hustling.'"

"Where? In the mental ward?"

Nick sighs and toys with the cap. "I don't get it. Why do you have a problem with the way I dress? It's not a reflection on you."

"Nick," I begin, softening my tone. "You're a good-looking guy. Your hair's growing out. Your shoulders got a bit bigger over the summer. Put on a shirt that fits. Put on jeans actually made from *denim*." I run a hand along the jeans' polyester leg. "Be yourself."

He sets his jaw. "This is me."

I snort. "You make fun of people who dress like this. What's changed?"

"It's different," he insists. "We're brown. Or at least Baba was. I've got the right to wear this. You should, too."

"Skin color doesn't mean dressing a certain way." I squint at him. "That's stupid. And kind of racist. Martin Luther King Junior wore a suit everywhere. Why not spiff it up a little?"

"Are they having a suit sale?" Nick asks.

"No," I sigh, exasperated. "My point is just keep it simple. Hang out. Have a beer. Meet some girls. It's a party."

"Seriously? Coming from you?" He laughs. "How many parties have you been to? Besides the one I took you to last year?"

"I don't know, Nick. I'm just saying. You don't always have to stand out so much."

He looks hurt. "What is that supposed to mean?"

I immediately feel horrible. "That was dumb. I mean, it was a bad way to put it. You don't stand out in a bad way at all," I backtrack.

"I'm just saying…I don't know. Tone it down a little bit. Here, like this." I help him out of the parka. "See, it feels lighter. Right?"

"Yeah," Nick says, looking at me quizzically.

"Give me the shirt."

Nick stands in front of me, considerably smaller in just a T-shirt. Before he can react, I whip the cap off his head and replace it with a 49er's beanie lying nearby. Grabbing his wrist, I unsnap the watch and instead slide a couple of Indian-looking woven bracelets onto his left wrist. "What do you think?"

Nick studies his reflection in the mirror and gives a small smile. "I don't want to like it. But I do."

"Buy a black T-shirt," I instruct. "Keep the bracelets. Size down on the jeans and choose a darker color. Not too baggy, but not skinny either. White shoes. Skate hoodie. Done."

"How do you think of this stuff?" Nick laughs.

"I'm a girl, silly." I turn to him. "How do you not?"

"I'm a guy. And straight."

I smile. "I'm going to find Hanna."

Less than an hour to go before the party. Hanna and I are upstairs, mixing and matching up a storm. Nick's in the den watching BET with the sound cranked up to maximum volume. I wish he'd turn it down; the noise is nerve-wracking. No matter what I do, I can't tear my thoughts away from Blake. All I can focus on is his rust-colored hair, pouty lips, and soulful eyes. Nordstrom bags litter my floor. Most of it is Hanna's, but I snagged a few items as well. They looked so much better in the store. I can't seem to figure out if I want to wear my hair up or down, or just wear a hoodie and sweats all night. Hanna looks flawless, per usual. Not a stitch of makeup and she's catwalk ready. Me on the other hand? No such luck.

"Are you overthinking things to death again?" Hanna asks, looking over at me from the vanity.

I laugh. "You know it."

"Let me do your hair," she pleads. "It's so nice and thick. And black. Well, almost black."

I oblige and sit in front of the mirror while Hanna gently combs and parts my hair.

"I'm going to do a French braid," she declares.

"Go for it," I reply, my stomach in knots over seeing Blake in less than an hour.

Fifteen minutes later, the two of us bound downstairs, passing Nick on the way to the kitchen. Hip-hop music blasts from the TV. I open the fridge and scan for any appealing snacks.

"Water?" I ask Hanna.

"Yeah, hit me."

I fill two glasses, and we crash on the couch next to Nick, who's wearing exactly what I told him to. "Can't we just go?"

Nick snorts. "Jesus. Haven't you been to any parties? Rule the first. Never show up on time."

I feel myself blush. "Yeah. I've been to some."

"Hanna? Has Roxie been to any parties?"

"Of course we have," Hanna lies. "We go to parties all the time."

"Jerome's bar mitzvah doesn't count." Nick smirks. "But seriously, parties don't even get good until the midway point. That's when people start freaking out and getting laid and stuff."

"'And stuff,'" Hanna mocks.

Nick frowns. "I'm just saying. Oh, that reminds me. I hope you two are planning on being responsible tonight."

I wrinkle my nose. "What's that supposed to mean? We're not going to make drunken passes at the boys."

"Well, I mean, I'm not," Hanna laughs. Nick slaps her five.

"Screw you guys. I'm not going to fling myself at Blake. I'm not even going to drink. Or smoke pot. I might drop acid, but I'm already crazy enough."

"Yeah, that's the last thing you need," Nick says. "Roxie on acid? End of the world."

"Would you ever try it?" I ask Nick. I like to think I know him well, but every once in a while, he surprises me.

"Acid?" Nick's eyes go wide. "Jesus, wow. I mean, I've eaten a pot brownie once by accident, but that's about it. Frankie gamed for thirty-eight hours once on speed, so he says. But me? Hell no."

Hanna leans back in surprise. "Frankie does drugs?"

"Yeah. He dropped acid a couple nights ago while playing Xbox. I was on the phone with him for some of it. He kept asking if we were real and then screamed because God walked into the room."

"Seriously?" I chuckle. "He's, like, the last person I could imagine tripping out. Remember when he used to wear a pocket protector?"

"Sixth grade," Nick laughs. "Yeah, who would've thought."

"It's usually the ones you least expect," Hanna points out. "Kelsey tried salvia her junior year."

"Your mom probably gave it to her," Nick snorts. He rolls a piece of scratch paper into a makeshift joint and holds it out to Hanna. "Here, Kels."

"My mom's not that bad," Hanna says defensively. "She's just irresponsible most of the time, not all the time."

Nick shrugs. "Hey, I just know what I hear." He unmutes the TV. "But no more talk. *Desperate Housewives* is on."

***

Between the drama onscreen and Nick's hilarious commentary, I lose track of time. Hanna and I both decided on simple but elegant styles, and though I'm not one to brag, we both look really good. Hanna's got on a red tartan skirt over tights and a white sweater, and I'm wearing my new army-green overcoat with black jeans. I've got the directions to Tristan's house committed to memory, but still have some irrational fear that we won't find the house or that Blake is playing a cruel practical joke, and there isn't actually a party.

"What time is it?" I ask, slightly fatigued despite the fact it's early in the evening.

"7:37," Hanna says, stifling a yawn. "Wait, is it actually?"

"It started!" I scream, jostling Nick's shoulders. "Get up. We've got to go."

"Relax," Nick gripes, rolling his eyes. "Did you hear Hanna? It literally started seven minutes ago. Want me to bring your teddy bear, freshie?"

I slug his arm. "Shut up."

"Maybe we should go," Hanna suggests. "We don't know how the traffic is. I mean, it's Friday, and the address he gave you is across town."

"I've been to Tristan's tons of times," Nick says. "We'll take the backroads. Plus, there's no traffic in Chester anyway. It's not like people want to be here."

I fold my arms. "You've been to Tristan's once."

"Twice, actually." Nick glares at me. "He's a nice dude, from what I remember. But he's probably not even there. He rents his house—I'm sorry, I mean his deceased grandpa's rambler—out to high school kids. Tristan's been out of school for years. I don't even know if he graduated."

"But Blake said—" I protest.

"Cat's riding on a name. I bet he hasn't even met Tristan."

"Why are you so anti-Blake?" I ask, slightly miffed. Nick avoids my gaze. "He's nice, he's cute, and I'm seeing him tonight. Don't mess this up for me."

"I'm not," Nick says. "It's just...you're really young, and he's a baseball player, which means he's part of that sports thing."

"Sports thing? What 'sports thing?'"

"Guys!" Hanna yells, positioning herself in between our bickering. "Enough talking. Let's go."

Like killers from the scene of a crime, the three of us tear out the door. Nick unlocks the driver's door, and Hanna and I slide across the bench seat of the El Camino. Located on the outskirts of town,

Tristan's house is out in the woods, which is precisely why his parties are allowed to get crazy. No cops. No neighbors. The butterflies, which have been fluttering in my stomach all week, are fully awake, and, judging by how quiet Hanna is, the same goes for her. Nick fires up the engine and turns off the radio before facing Hanna and me.

"Now I'm going to make this short and sweet," he starts. "No drinking. No drugs. No stripping, no slutty behavior..."

"What is this? *Girls Gone Wild?*" I look at him. "Tell me, when have Hanna and I done any of that?"

Nick says nothing as we turn out of the cul-de-sac and onto the main street. "I don't know," he says finally. "I'm just saying to be cool. People sometimes get a little wild at these things, and there's an energy in there that's just...I don't know."

"Crazy? Good. I need to be entertained." I sneak a look at myself in the rearview. "The best part of parties is watching everybody else. I'm not drinking, and I'm definitely not giving Blake any wrong ideas."

"You and me both," Hanna says. She lowers her voice. "I wonder if Jerome's having fun tonight."

"Where is he?" Nick asks.

Hanna averts her gaze. "Wet Banana."

"Oh. Right."

At last, we turn onto a gravel road and slow to a crawl. Up ahead, the shoulder is lined with the type of beat-up cars teenagers drive. Through the trees, I can see strobe lights pulsing from inside the house. I'm out of the car before Nick so much as touches the parking brake, and Hanna's right on my heels. I recognize at least fifteen people from a distance, most of them a grade or two ahead of us. On the porch, in the windows, and even on the roof of the garage, people I've seen in the halls dot the landscape. This isn't just a high school party. The high school is the party.

"Let's go!" I call over my shoulder. With Nick bringing up the rear, we climb onto the porch and walk through the sliding door.

People, people, everywhere. By the time I make it to the living room, I've spotted at least five kids from my classes. I wave to CeCe and Erik, who are canoodling in an armchair, and wind up in the kitchen, where table upon table has been stacked with every spirit known to man. A giant icebox sits directly adjacent to the drinks table, and I notice, interestingly enough, that there's no food: only booze.

"No food," a fat guy in a Miller Lite trucker hat screams into my face, verbalizing what I've just noticed. "No food. Just booze. Turn it up."

I nod energetically, unable to understand anything else he's saying, and grab a red plastic cup from the stack. I pour in a little Malibu rum, just enough to give my cup some weight, and set off for the front room. By the far wall, a DJ is up on a makeshift stage with two laptops and a turntable. To his left, a scrawny dude with a tattoo sleeve is mixing drinks and serving them to him from a personal minibar. They're definitely not parent volunteers. On the left side of the room is another table with a huge punchbowl and Jell-O shots on top of it. To the far right, a drunken couple is clawing at one another and rolling around on the floor, removing pieces of clothing as they go.

I look around to see if Nick's getting a load of this, but then remember I ditched him as soon as we got through the door. Knowing my brother, he could be having second thoughts about this environment and will drag us back home to watch Cartoon Network or play Monopoly. I see Hanna wander in without a cup, looking unimpressed.

"Having fun?" She musters a smile. I've known her long enough to know she'd rather be anywhere else, and, for some reason, this annoys me. "See anybody we know yet?"

"Give it a chance, Hanna," I say. "Look around. I'm pretty sure I saw Stephanie somewhere after all."

Hanna brightens. "Really?"

"Yeah," I say, scanning the room. "But it's way too hot in here. Grab a cup. Let's find the boys."

At this point, there are easily over fifty people in our section alone, which not only makes the house a fire trap, but impossible to navigate. I don't know if it's the heat, the music, or the smell of weed that's making my head swim, but one more minute and I'm passing out.

"Let's get out of here," I yell over my shoulder. "Outside. Get some air." I exit through the front door and trek around the side of the house to the back porch. Looking back, I realize Hanna has vanished. I slump down in a plastic lawn chair and discard the contents of my cup into a potted plant.

"Tired?" A statement. The motion-sensor light flickers on, and Blake comes into view. My breath catches: he appeared so suddenly.

I lick my lips and fidget with the pendant on my necklace. "A little."

"Long week?" Blake nods towards the other chair parallel to mine. "Do you mind?"

"No." I gesture to the chair clumsily. My senses have heightened dramatically in the last thirty seconds. I can taste the cedarwood notes of his cologne in the air. I place my fist over my heart in the hopes of preventing it from popping out of my chest and lean back in my chair.

Blake smiles slightly and takes a seat. "Have you been inside yet?"

"Yeah," I say. "I was in there a minute ago. You?"

"All afternoon," he laughs. "Liam and I, we set this thing up. I mean, it's Tristan's house and all, but we were in charge of the invites. The drinks alone set us back two weeks." He shows me his hands. "None for me, though."

"Seriously? Why?"

"Baseball," Blake sighs. "I mean, it's what I do. And while you can still play baseball drunk…like, we're not winning this season… I gotta stay up."

"I respect that," I say. "That's cool. I'm not drinking either, see?" I show him my empty cup. "We can be Mormon together."

Blake grins. "Anglican, actually. But I'm Mormon 'til the season's over. And you?"

"Spiritual," I reply after a brief pause. "Looks like we got to the heavy stuff already. Should we talk politics next?"

Blake smiles again. "You're a funny girl, Roxie."

I feel myself blush, even though I know he's right. "You think so?"

He nods. "Is that guy, what's his name, here? The Wet Banana fan?"

"Oh, Jerome? No, he's at the concert." I snicker. "You remember?"

"Of course," Blake says, stifling a laugh. "It was the best opening ever. 'I got backstage passes to Wet Banana.'" The two of us laugh. "Never seen anything like it."

"Jerome is one of a kind," I agree. "I'll give him that."

"You should've brought him tonight," Blake says teasingly. "Might've done him some good to get out there."

I shake my head. "Negative. Hanna just dumped him. He's hanging on by a thread. Ned or Jed better sign his nipple backstage or something. Otherwise, he might do himself in." I snort loudly, then cringe. "Wow, that was mean. Now I look like a total bitch. I'm sorry."

"No, don't be." Blake's face is a carnival. "That was great. A pretty girl who's funny, too…" He trails off mid-sentence and looks down at the ground.

I can feel my heart race and my breathing quicken. Blake is refusing to look at me. It takes everything in me not to jump into his lap and kiss him, but at the same time, I'm unable to move for fear of ruining something so perfect. Neither of us speaks.

"Thanks," I say finally.

Blake looks at me sideways. "For?"

"Nobody's ever said that to me before."

"What?" He looks confused. "No. You probably hear stuff like that all the time. I hope I'm not making you feel weird, or awkward, or anything."

"No, no," I say quickly. "Not at all. It means a lot. Coming from you."

Now it's his turn to blush. Blake looks down at his shoes again. "Why'd you come tonight?"

"Why did I come?" I struggle to think of an appropriate response. "Well, why wouldn't I?"

He shrugs. "We invited a lot of people. I wasn't sure if you'd really show."

"Well, I'm a freshman. It's good to meet people," I laugh. "Plus, you invited me. It would be rude not to come."

A smile tugs at the corners of Blake's mouth, but his eyes never stop sparkling. "Do you dance at all?"

Is he asking me to dance right now? I reach for my phone to text Hanna about this incredible series of events, but then realize that's pathetic and drop my hand in midair.

"Uh, no, actually. Do you?"

Blake laughs. "Depends on who you ask."

"Well, do you or not?" I make a face. "Do or do not. There is no try."

"Okay, my little green friend," Blake chuckles. "Take it easy. I dance."

I tilt my head up in what I hope is a flirty way. "Prove it."

Rising from his chair, Blake takes off his varsity jacket and drapes it over his left shoulder. "You ready?"

A soft breeze whispers through the trees, and I catch a stronger whiff of his heavenly cologne. Willing my legs not to fail me, I stumble from my chair and stand next to him. It's the closest we've ever been. I can see faint stubble along his sharp jawline and darker streaks of brown in his thick tresses. Moving closer, Blake wraps a muscular arm, his pitching arm, around my waist and pulls me to him as we head towards the door.

"Roxie." An unmistakable voice cuts into the stillness of the night and shakes me to my core. "Roxie. *What* is going on?"

Chaz Humbert's eyes are wide and unblinking as he stares into my soul. Only the person staring at me is about as un-Chaz-like as possible. The shapeless Seahawks hoodie he was wearing earlier has been replaced by a black leather jacket. His mop of hair? Gelled and styled off his face. He even looks taller. If I didn't know how utterly revolting he is, I might admit he looks halfway decent. But the person standing ten feet in front of me is undoubtedly Chaz.

Somehow, I manage to downplay my terror and begin talking.

"Hey, Chaz. Looking for Edgar? Probably at the massage parlor waiting for you." I laugh uneasily. "Table for two?"

Chaz shakes his head. "You're unbelievable."

I stare at him, confused. I've said much worse in the past. "What?"

I grab Blake's wrist and turn to go inside, but he doesn't move. Chaz locks eyes with him before turning back to me. "Who's this?"

"Roxie, what's going on?" Blake's voice has a hard edge. "Do you know him?"

"Never wanted to." My thought process is slowing down, and everything's clouding over. I turn to Chaz. "Did you follow me? What are you even doing here?"

"Just trying to enjoy my Friday," Chaz answers, his eyes flitting to the ground. He turns to Blake. "Roxie and I have been exclusive for several months," he says quietly. "I'm sure this is as awkward for you as it is for me. Now I know who the other guy is."

I feel as if the wind has been knocked out of me. Chaz is supposed to be creepy, not *cunning*. He's been obsessed with me for years, but the only consensual physical contact we've had is me kicking or punching him. In ten seconds, he's not only managed to stalk me outside of school but convince the only boy I've ever really liked who wasn't a celebrity or professional athlete that we're together. As if!

"You two are a thing?" Blake asks tonelessly. "Damn, my mistake. I gotta go." I try to form a coherent sentence, but I've completely frozen up. Looking at us like we're insane, Blake turns to go. "See you around, Roxie." Without another word, he slides open the screen door and disappears into the sea of bodies.

Chaz waits until Blake's long gone before blowing me a kiss. "Sorry, hot stuff. Couldn't let you get away that easily." With that, he swings a stumpy leg over the porch railing, thuds into the grass, and disappears into the darkness.

Chapter 4

In a past life, I'm positive I was a guy. I tell off-color jokes and gag at anything romantic. Guns, knives, and weapons of any kind intrigue me, and I'm probably the most competitive person I know. Though I know how to play it down and behave myself in front of company, I've never been known to be demure or ladylike. That's Hanna's area of expertise. Tonight, minus the magical fifteen minutes I just spent with Blake, is no exception.

Standing alone on Tristan's porch, the last thing I'm doing tonight is crying. No talking about my feelings. No pints of ice cream in my pajamas. This is war. I press my fingernails into my palm as hard as they'll go without breaking and dig my phone out of my pocket. I hit the speed dial and wait for Nick's reply.

"Hey, what's going on?" Based on his voice alone, I can tell he was speaking with an attractive girl just moments ago. Normally, I'd be excited for him, but right now, I couldn't care less.

"We're going home. Call Hanna and meet me outside on the back deck, right now."

"Is something wrong?"

"I don't want to talk about it," I say tersely. "I'll fill you in. Later."

Seconds later, the two of them appear. "Roxie," Hanna begins, rushing toward me.

"What happened?" Nick demands, his hair shiny under the light. "Did that boy take advantage of you? I'll destroy him."

"No," I grunt. "Not Blake. But another boy, or should I say a *thing,* is headed for the mortuary. Get some bleach. We're going to have some tracks to cover."

"Let's go," Hanna says, grabbing my hand. Nick nods in agreement. They both know me well enough to see I'm about to blow.

Miraculously, I hold it together until we're home. I kick off my shoes, close the door behind us, and scream at the top of my lungs. Far from satisfied, I hurl my purse across the foyer, headbutt the grandfather clock, and begin cussing like a sailor gone mad.

"I swear!" I roar. "That leather jacket, the pomade, the platform shoes he wore, they're all going straight up his flabby ass!" I grab my shoes off the floor and throw those as well.

I notice my mother at the top of the landing, watching me with amazing calm. Between my antics and Nick's, she's not at all phased by these sorts of things.

"Hi, Mom," I say quietly. "How was work?"

"Never mind that," she breathes. "Start talking."

Nobody knows anything that happened yet, and I didn't say a word the whole ride home. I begin with Blake and Liam inviting Hanna and me to the party and move chronologically from there. I describe meeting Blake, and the connection we seemed to have, before delving into the arrival of Chaz and his masterful deception. I conclude this evening's tale with more foul language and fouler gesticulations towards the Humbert home.

Nobody utters a word. Then Nick, whose reactions are never appropriate, begins cackling. Hanna starts next, and then Mom, who's usually composed, joins in. The three of them seem to find the entire thing hilarious. I give them a look to kill, but that just makes them laugh harder.

"I'm sorry," Nick gasps. "It's not funny. But come on. You got owned. You've got to hand it to him. Well played."

"I hate Chaz," Hanna agrees. "He's disgusting. But that was brilliant."

"There's nothing funny about it," I seethe, running my hands through my sweat-soaked hair. "Nothing. Chaz ruined everything. Everything he touches turns to shit." I stare down at the carpet. "The best night of my life got destroyed by the worst thing in my life."

"Relax," Mom says. "Just explain the whole thing to Blake when you get to school on Monday. It'll be fine. I promise."

Monday morning, I charge off the bus and almost faceplant into the asphalt looking for Blake. No sign of him. He probably parks with the other upperclassmen by the senior lot or rides to school with other guys on the baseball team. First bell; I'm out of time. Irritated, I picture a shirtless Blake slaying Chaz with a pitchfork and head to class. By the time home economics rolls around, I'm so far gone I don't realize Jenna's making fun of me until the last fifteen minutes of class. I don't care. I've got way bigger things going on. I don't know if Blake and I share a lunch period on Mondays, but I'll get Hanna and maybe Stephanie to help me find him and explain.

As usual, the only person who can cheer me up is Hanna. Unable to track down Blake, she buys me a warm, gooey chocolate chip cookie from the snack cart and a couple of milks. It's the only thing the cafeteria serves that doesn't look doubly digested, and I rarely treat myself. I nibble along the crispy circumference and savor the chocolate dissolving on my tongue. At first, Hanna found Chaz's shenanigans amusing, but after failing to find Blake, she realized how upsetting the whole thing was. Nick, distrustful of Blake from the beginning, still hasn't reversed his stance and now views Chaz as some type of divine savior.

Final bell and I can't get out here fast enough. On the way out, I beg Hanna to ditch soccer practice and come over, but unlike me, Hanna has discipline and ambitions in life and refuses. We walk to the soccer field, and I stay and chat a bit with the girls' team before splitting off. As I walk, I figure I'll make a trip to the corner store a few blocks away to grab a sandwich. All I've had to eat today was that cookie Hanna bought me at lunch, so I'm starving.

While cruising past the portables, I hear a mechanical clicking coming from the surrounding bushes. I pause, trying to identify the origin of the sound amidst the silence, then whirl around and charge full tilt into the brush. Petrified screams pierce the air, and somebody tosses a ratty ski cap at me as I plow ahead in time to see Edgar fall backward with a pair of military-grade binoculars around his neck. Beside him, Chaz fumbles a disposable camera and freezes as I approach. I get to Chaz first and throw my entire weight on top of him, slamming him to the ground. Edgar, the faithful friend, regains his legs and gallops into the forest to return for further harassment.

Chaz flops on the ground like a mackerel, thrashing underneath me. A couple of hard punches to the gut and he stops moving.

"Let go," he wheezes, his hands clutching at the dirt. I hold him down and plant my knees on his chest, dominating him.

"What the hell were you doing?" I demand, struggling to control my anger. "Were you stalking me? Answer me, dammit!"

"I like this position." He smiles coyly. "I wonder what Blake would say if he saw us now."

"Listen to me," I snarl, driving my fist into his throat. "You tell Blake you lied. If you don't, I'll kill you myself."

Chaz's breathing is ragged, but he laughs, nonetheless. "Forget it." He looks me in the eye and puckers his lips. "One day, when you and I are riding in a convertible buck-naked down the Pacific Coast Highway, you'll understand why I did it." I drive my knees into his ribs, throwing my weight on top of him. Wiggling underneath me, he bucks his hips. I scream and get up, only to realize at once it was a mistake. Chaz scrambles to his feet, flips me two birds, and flees into the woods, leaving me standing alone.

***

I beg Nick to pick me up, and he relents, though not without admonishing me for not catching the bus. Though Chaz escaped, he did manage to leave behind what may be a damning piece of evidence. On the ride home, I fill Nick in on the latest, and as we pass by the pharmacy, he turns into the parking lot.

"Let's see what he's got on here," Nick says, locking his door. "I mean, we have an idea, but this could get him in a lot of trouble."

"Doubt it," I say glumly. "He could have a dead hooker in his locker, and the teachers wouldn't care. Kid's immune."

"True that," Nick agrees. "Any other time, I'd say turn it into the principal, but the district's corrupt."

"I'll probably have to handle this on my own," I sigh, cracking my knuckles for effect.

Nick raises a brow. "What do you mean?"

"I don't know," I admit, dropping my hands to my sides. "Let's see what's on the roll."

We drop the camera off and meander through the aisles. Nick grabs a bag of chips, and I take a soda. Posted in the back of the store, I ramble about the latest gossip, and Nick soaks it all in. Periodically, I circle the photo center, where the clerk stares back at me with a horrified expression. Once the photos are developed, I thank the man and hightail it out of there. After climbing into the car, I tear open the envelope, remove the photos, and understand everything.

About thirty low-quality photographs of random girls from school, Hanna, and I are in almost every shot. I shudder through a couple of closeups of the boys giving the thumbs-up and vow to burn those when I get home while continuing to rifle through the images. As I go through them, I find the girls pictured are wearing less and less clothing. Near the end, I find one of me getting changed for gym, turned around in nothing more than my bra and underwear. I wordlessly pass it to Nick, whose face is the picture of rage.

This is it. I know what needs to be done.

The battered chariot Nick calls his car rattles to a stop, and I bolt inside the house. The second the door's unlocked, I hurtle up the stairs towards the computer and launch myself into the office chair. A few months back, Mom purchased photo editing software she thought she needed for work but didn't end up using it. It's already downloaded onto the computer and ready to go. I'll admit I'm hardly tech-savvy, but when I put my mind to something, it gets done a hundred percent. Though "hard work pays off" is a cheesy slogan Jenna probably has taped to her bathroom mirror, it isn't untrue. Invest an hour and you might just get somewhere. A couple clicks here, a couple drags there, and *voila*: revenge.

It took a little browsing on the seedier side of the internet before I discovered the photo that changed everything. Right when I was about to throw in the towel, I came across a high-quality image of two young men, completely nude, with body types strikingly similar to Edgar and Chaz. Should you desire further description, the men are connected…and they're not holding hands.

I downloaded it, then opened a new window. Next stop? Chaz's social media. I ripped several pictures of the boys, downloaded those, and edited their faces onto the porn. But I wasn't near done. A third window was opened, this time from the school district webpage. I found a picture of the inside of the locker room at the high school, downloaded that, and used it as a backdrop. A little touch-up here, some gentle pixelating here, and the final product is flawless.

I print off a handful of copies, delete the files, and shut down the computer. Laying the images face up, I place them on a blank poster board and carry them down the hall to my room to dry.

***

Whenever I need to think, I hide out in the bathroom. It's usually quiet. Unfortunately, somebody else is in the stall next to me, and by the sound of things, it isn't going well. Without warning, the reek of decaying colon hits me until my eyes water. Unlocking the door, I wash my hands and slink away into the hallway, wondering who's trying to flush a corpse down the john.

Like that, the universe sends me a gift as Hanna rounds the corner.

"You won't believe it," I squeal.

"What?" Hanna says. "What's not to believe?"

"Check it." I grab her by the arm and pull her into an empty classroom.

"Jeez," Hanna complains, rubbing her forearm. "What now? Do I really want to know?"

I lock eyes with her. "You need to." I unzip my backpack and retrieve a photo. "Ta-da."

Hanna gasps and slowly raises a hand to her mouth. "This isn't real, is it?"

I snicker. "You tell me."

Her tone is flat. "You're not really going to, are you?"

I gape at her. "I'm sorry, what? After everything he's done?"

"I know, but Roxie, this is really…"

"What? It's what, Hanna? You wanna know what happened yesterday? Want to know what I was dealing with?" I stuff a hand into my backpack and rummage around for the photos Nick and I developed. "Sit down," I say, gesturing to the floor. "Crisscross applesauce, however you want, I don't give a shit, and see for yourself who Chaz is."

Hanna's jaw tightens as she flips through the photographs until she comes upon the shot of me changing. "Where did you get these?"

"I didn't 'get them,'" I sigh, squatting down beside her. "I took them. Nobody ever gave me anything in life. You were at practice, and I was walking, and Chaz and Edgar were taking pictures of me in the bushes, so I went after them. Beat up Chaz. Edgar got away but left the camera. Nick and I took it to the drug store and got the photos and here we are." I stare at her and narrow my eyes. "Still want to forget about it?"

"Let's just take these pictures to the office," Hanna reasons. "See, there they are. Chaz and Edgar together. There's rock-solid evidence."

"They'll bury it," I say, the anger starting to bubble up inside me. "They'll make it go away. Chaz never gets punished, and something's wrong with Edgar. It'll keep happening."

"You don't know that." Hanna's voice is small.

"We *do*," I insist. "Come on, you know it's true."

"It's true," Hanna agrees. "I know. But there's got to be a better way. I mean when life gives you lemons, make lemonade, right?"

"Oh my God! No! When life gives you lemons, throw them at people you hate. Turn lemons into Photoshop porn. Make lemons into fucking hand grenades." I stare at her. "Seriously?"

A smile plays at the corner of her mouth. "Those were good. I've never heard of those before. Who came up with those?"

"I did. Now listen. I gotta get even. Nothing else has worked. We need to stand up to him and if you don't want to, I'll do this alone." I wipe my sweaty palms on my shirt. "Think about us. Think about the girls whose privacy was violated in these photos. Now it's this, or I'm setting fire to the Humberts' lawn. You choose."

"I'm not choosing anything," Hanna says sharply. "You don't know how this could end. You could be expelled."

I rise to my feet and shove the photos into my backpack. "Yeah. You're right. But who said anything about getting caught?"

***

Second period science. I'm counting every breath. Some years back, the district finally figured out Americans don't read and added a fifteen-minute silent reading period to the curriculum. The bell rings, and Mr. Burke instructs us to take out our books. All of us groan. I pull out a random book I swiped from the library during the passing period and pretend to read it. I glance around to see Edgar's absorbed in what looks like pornographic manga, while in front of me, CeCe's leafing through our history textbook.

I risk a quick glance about the room before reaching into my backpack and silently pulling out one printout. Uncapping my gel pen, I scrawl, "*Chaz and Edgar are really into each other—literally! Pass it on!*" on the backside of the photo using my left hand, so they won't trace it back to me. Holding my breath, I lower the photograph to the ground and slide it with my foot along the floor until it rests face down next to CeCe's chair.

Peeking over the top of my book, I see CeCe has noticed the paper beside her and is reaching for it. Her reaction is instant. Gasping dramatically, she claps a manicured hand over her mouth, shaking with suppressed giggles. She glances around the room before sliding the paper along the floor to an emo girl with various piercings. The girl cracks a rare smile, and her eyes glint maliciously. She then passes the picture to a redheaded boy sitting beside her, who laughs so hard he almost falls out of his chair.

"Keep it down." Mr. Burke's voice is stern.

"Sorry," Ginger croaks. "I just, uh, read a funny part." He waits until Mr. Burke resumes typing before nudging the kid sitting next to him and handing him the printout.

Miraculously, the photo makes the rounds without Mr. Burke's knowledge, and by the time he announces the end of silent reading, Loren Faye and her group are laughing hysterically in the back of the class. One of the girls Loren hangs out with, whose name I can never remember, snaps a photo with her cell phone and begins texting while Loren places the photo in her binder, presumably to take to her next class. Throughout the lesson, people start laughing randomly, and while Mr. Burke can't seem to figure it out, I can. Whatever bits of conversation I overhear during the lab don't get very far before the words "Chaz," "Edgar," "homo," or "up the ass" surface, and while I feel a rush of ecstasy I can't quite describe, it gradually gives way to a feeling of acknowledgment that I've started something big, and I don't know how it's going to end.

Guilt is a useless emotion. It cannot help anyone or anything. When I first ran across that little bit of philosophy, I didn't understand it. It didn't make any sense. If somebody does something wrong, shouldn't they feel something? I mean, it's better than not feeling, right? In theory, it should kind of distribute the burden amongst the wrongdoer and the victim, but it doesn't. It doesn't.

Three days in, Chaz Humbert is officially gay and sexually active with his best friend, and the whole school's in on it. Somewhere down the line, the picture went viral, and the boys have had lotion, lube, and abuse hurled at them wherever they go ever since. Last I heard, the two of them were living together in Canada, where gay marriage is apparently legal, with an adopted infant from China before they both die of AIDS. I thought I'd be reveling in my victory; instead, I feel disgusted with myself. In the beginning, I was thrilled those two were finally getting a taste of what they'd put on us girls for so many years. Somebody copied the original photo hundreds of times, and I'm guessing several students tacked it up all over campus. The terror on Chaz's face when he bumbled into the commons Tuesday morning was hilarious and, at the time, very satisfying, though I'm ashamed to admit it now. At lunch, I saw him disappear into the boys' bathroom with his lunch tray and didn't see him come out, and he was absent from most of our shared periods.

In an attempt to shut down the bullying, the school has now made it illegal to put up flyers without permission, utilize the printer for anything unrelated to school, or use homophobic language, but it's clearly not helping. The students are out of control. On the bright side, bullying overall has decreased, and, in some cases, the bullied are joining up with their former tormentors to cover more ground in the Chaz hunt. Two students got caught putting up pictures early Wednesday, but by the time those were taken down, dozens were put up in their place an hour later.

I rush into home ec, late as usual, and fall into my assigned seat next to Jenna. Usually, she shows her distaste the second she lays eyes on me, but there's something noticeably different about her body language. I can't figure it out.

"What?" I snap, unable to help myself. She waits before turning to me, smiling thinly as though to hint at some unspoken knowledge between the two of us. I shrug and turn away.

"Roxie," she says in a near whisper. "Enjoying your reception?"

I nearly faint. How could she know? How did she find out? Is this really happening?

"What are you talking about?"

Jenna just smiles.

***

Leave it to Jenna Carmichael. Girl's had it in for me since the first day, and now, she's about to cross the finish line. How did she find out? More importantly, what's she going to do now that she knows? She could out me to the principal. She could report me to Mrs. Humbert. She could hold this over my head for the rest of my time here, and I'll have to capitulate to her demands, whatever they may be. Given that my actions have effectively turned the school upside down this week, and considering what's on the picture I passed around, I could easily be expelled. Even Hanna didn't know what to say when I told her about Jenna. Of course, she could easily be bluffing. Chaz harasses a lot of girls. Pretty much everybody hates him. In theory, anybody could have done it, but somehow Jenna, being obsessed with me almost as much as Chaz is, knows I'd be the only one to take this type of drastic action. Plus, if she got wind of what went on at Tristan's party or was somehow there, she'd know I had a motive. And that's all she needs to start building her case.

As usual, I'm probably overthinking things. Unless she's attached a tracking device to my backpack, Jenna doesn't have a shred of evidence. If I get accused, all I have to do is plead the fifth and stay calm. And given this is the first time anybody's ever tacked up naked pictures of Chaz Humbert penetrating a ginger forest creature, I can't say I've officially broken any school rules.

Friday morning, I'm sitting on the bus alone, trying to think of ways to protect myself should things get out of hand. So far, I've come up with nothing. Threatening Jenna won't work anymore, especially if she's got something on me. I've just got to play it cool and wait out the storm.

"Roxie," a timid voice says quietly. "Roxie, can we talk?"

I look up to see Jerome sitting on the bench seat across from me, his eyes wide and imploring. We haven't spoken since his split with Hanna, but for some reason, my heart goes out to him. I nod and meet his eyes.

"What's up, Jerome?"

"Well, how do I put this? I mean, I know you're Hanna's best friend, and…" He falls silent. "I blew it. I royally screwed up. I should've listened to her more, and I had no idea about Chaz. I mean, I did, but somehow, I didn't put two and two together. Some teachers call him Charles, so I got confused." He bites his lip and stares at me with misty eyes. "I'll fight him. I'll do whatever she needs me to do. Plus, he lied about going to the concert. He's not a real fan."

"Jerome," I start.

"Please," he begs. "I want to win her back. She's the love of my life. Tell me what to do. I'll do it."

A while passes before I speak. "Okay," I begin. "Listen. I can't make Hanna do anything. I can't make her get back together with you. I can't make her fall in love. It's her choice and her choice only." I decline to mention the fact I've been pressuring Hanna to dump him since they met. "If you want her back, you need to grow up. Be nice. Be attentive. Not too nice, or too interested. Us girls, we find that stupid."

Jerome nods. "Got it. Good advice, yo."

I hold up a hand. "I'm not done. If it's not working, leave it be. Find another girl and remember what I told you."

He leans back in his seat and winds a piece of curly brown hair around his finger. "Thanks, Roxie." He sighs. "And I'm really sorry about Chaz. If he bothers Hanna or you again, just ask me to step in."

I snort. "Chaz ain't bothering anybody now."

Jerome laughs. "Goddamn. Who knew he was gay? I mean, he and Edgar are always together, but seriously? I wouldn't have guessed."

"Well, we don't know. I mean, I'm pretty sure those pictures were fake," I say quickly. "But yeah. World's a complicated place."

"Thanks again, Roxie," Jerome says. "And if Hanna ever asks about me, let her know I'm doing okay."

I smile and nod. Jerome might be oblivious and more than a little immature, but he's a decent spud. He's not Liam, and he's definitely not Blake, but still. Even just a little time away from Hanna has made him grow up, and it's good for him. The bus pulls into the parking lot, and I rise to leave. Jerome looks decidedly more upbeat as he slings his Wet Banana swag bag over his shoulder and stands up to go. Whatever happens, it's completely up to those two.

***

By the second week, things haven't improved. In the freshman hall, the girls' bathroom mirror was defaced with anti-Chaz graffiti, while the entire boys' bathroom had to be repainted. During morning announcements, Stephanie abused her intercom privileges to make a crude announcement about celebrating gay sex and encouraged questioning males to "use their fists" for solutions. Before getting dragged away from the loudspeaker, she went on to advertise a pride march that she's organizing to kick start her new charity, "Quayle for Queers."

Naturally, the class couldn't stop laughing. Ordinarily, I would've found it hysterical, but I couldn't crack a smile. Even two people as repugnant as Edgar and Chaz don't deserve this level of brutality.

Hanna's been giving me scathing looks every time someone utters the words *gay*, *Edgar*, and *Chaz* in the same sentence, and I can't say I blame her. She never approved of my plan. I'll be the first to admit I regret it, but it'd still be nice for her to stand by me through one of the worst decisions of my life.

Unable to take any more, I quietly excuse myself from class and walk home. The whole way, I contemplate what this means for all of us. Chaz, Edgar, me. Jenna might have something on me, or she might not. What I'm more concerned about is my own conscience. Climbing the front steps, I ring the doorbell and break from my thoughts. Through the stained glass, I can see Nick's smiling face as he comes to open the door. I wait until we're both in the foyer before turning to him.

"Can we talk?"

"Yeah, always." Nick's eyes meet mine. "What's the matter?"

"There's something I've gotta tell you."

"Let's sit."

Nick strides over to the living room and sits cross-legged on the floor. "You're home early."

"Yeah."

"Well, start talking," he says. "I'm listening."

"I need some advice." I take a seat next to him and lie on my back, kicking my legs up onto the couch.

"You're asking me?"

"Well, I value your opinion. But you have to promise you won't judge."

"No judging," Nick agrees. "What's got you wound up?"

"So you know how I was super upset about the whole Chaz thing? The pictures he took of Hanna and me?"

Nick nods. "Of course."

"That, the pictures, everything he's done…it finally got to me," I say. "And something in me snapped. When we developed those photos…I saw red. I couldn't see anything else."

"Same," Nick says. "Should've wrecked his ass."

"Well...I did."

Nick frowns. "*You* wrecked him?"

I bite my lip. "Yes."

"Well, what did you do?" Nick asks, sounding concerned. "He's not dead rotting in the woods, is he?"

I press my hands into my thighs. "You know how whipped up I was about the whole thing. You saw me. Remember when we came home?"

"And you ran out of the car?"

"Yeah. You remember." I rub my eyes. "I went up to the office, in the heat of the moment. Remember how Mom bought that photo-editing software a few years back? Well, I used it. I found some porn on the internet, put Edgar and Chaz on there." I squeeze my eyes shut and force the words out. "And passed the pictures around at school."

I reach deep into my backpack and pull out a crinkled copy of the picture. I smooth it out between my hands before passing it over to Nick, who studies it before his face breaks out into a huge grin. I wish I could feel good about it, but I just feel more confused by his reaction. Of course Nick would find it funny. He's hearing my version and not actually seeing things play out at school the way they have been.

I take a breath. "So?"

Several more seconds pass before Nick bursts into laughter. "Oh my God," he crows. "This is beautiful. I love you so much. I'm so, so proud." The printout falls from his hands as he envelops me in a bear hug and squeezes me tight. "You're my sister, all right. I've got to show this to Frankie. He'll die."

Relief washes over me. "You think I did the right thing?"

Nick steadies himself and folds his arms, his smile fading slightly. "Well, I don't know if I could say that. But... you totally got your revenge."

***

The weekend is solitary. Hanna's skiing with her family while I'm at home with a pile of late work. Rising from my chair, I pick up my hairbrush and drag it through my hair. Staring into the mirror, I lean against my dresser and run everything over in my head for the hundredth time. Did Jenna really see me pass the photo around in science? Or did somebody else see it and tell her, knowing how much she hates me? I try to think if Jenna has any friends in Science, but it doesn't matter. Come to think of it, I don't even know where her seat is after Mr. Burke rearranged everybody.

Let's say I get caught. I'll be suspended and potentially expelled if Mrs. Humbert throws her generous weight around. But the school is slow to discipline, as we've observed over the years with the Chaz situation. If Jenna doesn't have anything beyond a reasonable doubt, I'm a free woman. I hear my phone vibrate, so I set my brush down and go get it. Hopefully, it's Hanna. She hasn't reached out all weekend, and she hits the slopes seriously. I'm thinking of what to text her when I glance down at the screen. It's a multimedia message from an unknown number. I groan, figuring it's something X-rated from Chaz, but remember he's been out of operation since I released the picture. I open the message to see several blurry images taken in what appears to be Mr. Burke's classroom. I can be seen in the right-hand corner of the frame. As I scroll through the pictures again, I can be seen reaching into my binder, writing on the back of the printout, and sliding it along the floor to CeCe. The photos are grainy, but there's no mistaking who's in it. It's concrete proof of where the picture originated, how it got passed, and who passed it.

There are no crystal balls here, but my future is clear: Jenna's got me in her crosshairs. And she's about to pull the trigger.

***

Four in the morning and I'm wide awake, thanks to Jenna and her foul tricks. I keep telling myself not to panic, that there must be a way to deal with this. I just have to stay a step ahead, but that's not going to be easy now that she possesses physical evidence of me committing the crime. In between worrying, I keep wondering why Jenna hates me so much. She's been hell-bent on making me miserable since we met and hasn't stopped. Is she jealous? Racist? Mentally unstable? I'm at a loss and don't know where to go from here, but what I do know is that I've got to do it on my own.

I won't drag Hanna into this. Nick is asleep, and I have no clue how my mother's going to react. I roll over onto my back and scrunch up the blanket into a ball and squeeze it for comfort. Usually, this helps me fall asleep, but tonight, it puts knots in my back. After a while, my throat and mouth become sandpapery, so I rise from my bed and tiptoe towards the staircase. On the way down, my wool sock catches on an unidentified object, and my legs go out from under me, sending me down the stairs like a hockey puck.

The hallway light flips on, and I squint to see my mother at the top of the stairs in her terry cloth robe. She spots me and comes hurrying down the stairs, grabbing the handrail for support.

"What *happened?*"

I look at the object on the stairs, which I'm now able to identify as Nick's Boba Fett action figure he rediscovered from his fourth-grade Star Wars obsession last night. I stomp up the steps, seize the figurine, and snap off his head before throwing his remains into the living room. My frustration tapered, I head into the kitchen to get a drink of water with Mom hot on my heels.

"Roxie," she starts. "What's going on? You've been acting really, really weird."

I clench my teeth. "Weird how?"

"I don't know," she admits. "I guess you just haven't been yourself. Something's weighing on you pretty heavily, isn't it?"

"I guess." I weigh my options. I could go on pretending everything's fine and add another lie to the list. Or I could tell her everything and

win a front-row seat at a lecture titled *what the hell were you thinking?*
Neither sounds very appealing, but I'm officially out of options.

I slide down to the floor and tuck my knees under my chin. "Okay,"
I say slowly. "I'll tell you what went on. But you have to promise me
you won't freak out."

Mom purses her lips but sits down beside me without a word.

I pick at a loose thread on my PJs and begin my confession, making a
point of not omitting a single detail. I talk about everything post-party,
from finding Chaz and Edgar in the woods to developing the photos
on the disposable camera. I take it back to the webcam striptease, the
vile pickup lines, and the everyday struggle of Chaz's sexual harassment.
Mom sits quietly throughout. Much of this is only a review, but I'm
hoping as I lay out the history, she'll understand why I chose to take
such extreme measures. Though I see her eyes widen when I get to
the part about passing around the porn, Mom doesn't interrupt, and
when I bring up Jenna and her threat to narc me out, she doesn't even
flinch. My story comes to an end, and I can feel her confusion through
the space between us. Finally, she looks over at me.

"Wow," she says.

"That's it?"

"I don't know what else to say." Mom laughs tiredly. "You've always
been a fighter. When I was pregnant with you, you'd kick all night.
When I gave birth, you were delivered in under an hour. Chaz scares
off Blake, and you destroy his life." She rubs her eyes. "Don't know
what to tell you."

"You think this is about Blake?" I ask in disbelief. "Did you miss the
part about me being photographed almost naked? That's what set it off.
Really? You honestly think I'd do this over some boy I barely know?"

"I don't know," Mom says, holding up her hands in earnest.
"It's late, and I'm tired. I'm not thinking straight, and neither were
you. Yeah, Chaz's bad news. A terrible person. His mom protects
him and uses her position to do so. But you had the evidence. You

could've turned it in to the principal. And why the hell didn't you tell me about this?"

"You work so much," I reply. "Why would I dump something else on your plate? You didn't need this."

"It's my job to worry," Mom says firmly. "You're my girl. Nick is my son. Do you think this ends when you grow up? Or get closer to growing up? We could've ended it right then and there, the right way. I could've called Cynthia, and we'd both go in there and demand *Chaz's* expulsion." She sighs. "Does Nick know about this?"

"Nick loved it." I smirk. "He developed the pictures with me. He understands. Sometimes you gotta bring a little street justice."

Mom rolls her eyes. "Your brother's a juvenile. Of course he'd think it was great. *Nick* isn't going to get suspended over this. *Nick* isn't going to potentially get expelled. It's your future that's in danger now. Did you even think of the risks?"

"It would've been fine," I huff. "Jenna Bitchmichael was stalking me per usual and got lucky. Nobody else saw, but she just so happened to get the footage." I roll my eyes. "God hates my ass."

Mom cracks her knuckles and looks into my tired eyes. "I'm at a loss, hon."

"What do you think will happen?" I ask quietly.

"I don't know," she admits. "I haven't been in school for decades. Things are different now. I mean, you've got the photos. You've got the disposable camera. He'll get his, too. You're all going down, by the looks of it."

"Do you get why I did it, though?"

"Yeah," she says. "I do. I mean, in some ways, he deserved it. Sexual harassment to the tenth power. Maybe now he gets why it's such a bad thing. Maybe he'll stop. Maybe he won't. I don't know." She looks at me. "But seriously. What will you do if he kills himself? Or tries to? Will you be okay with that on your conscience?"

I gulp and look at the floor. In the days that followed, Chaz's absence and my own guilty conscience floated this possibility more than once. But hearing it from somebody else brings it to life in a way my own brain cannot.

"It'll blow over," Mom says. "Things run their course. Give it another week. But you need to ask yourself what you're going to do from here."

Chapter 5

To my great relief, the harassment seems to have died down by Monday. Chaz might have gotten tased with a vibrator when he entered the school this morning, but CeCe Sanchez is starting to gain weight, and everybody's talking. Her frequent bathroom breaks and four apple turnovers at lunch only fuel the rumor, but, as usual, no one really knows. Chaz appears to be back full-time but keeps to himself. Edgar is nowhere to be found.

As one could imagine, Jenna's in her element and devoted the morning to tormenting me. Whenever we pass each other in the halls, she'll either mime snapping photos or give me a knowing smile.

I'm at the sink washing my hands at lunch when Jenna walks into the bathroom. Not a word, but her usual dopey expression and folded arms are never good. She raises her eyebrows in my direction. I ignore her and scrub harder, hoping I can wash her away along with my billions of other germs.

"Hi, *Roxie*." Nasally, self-satisfied tone? Check. Annoying emphasis on my name? Check. Pinched, awful face? Double-check with a cherry on top.

I curl my toes inside my shoes and run my tongue along my bottom lip. "Yeah?"

Jenna leans up against the wall. "I'm a straight shooter, so this won't take long." She's trying to intimidate me, but just looks stupid. I would mock her if she didn't have the pictures. But she does.

"Cut the shit, Jenna. What do you want?"

Her barracuda grin broadens. "Oh, Roxie. Even *you* aren't that clueless. I'm afraid you know *exactly* why I'm here."

I grit my teeth. "For Christ's sake, this isn't a James Bond flick, and you're really not that interesting. Is this your idea of intimidation?"

Jenna's face turns red, and she sets her jaw. "Yeah, actually. And you should be intimidated. Unless you're as dumb as everyone thinks you are, you must realize you're screwed. I know you made the poster of Edgar and Chaz, and I have the pictures to prove it. You'll get expelled for it."

She pauses in front of me. "So here's the deal. Five hundred dollars. Pay me, in cash, and I'm off your case. I'll delete them right now, and I'll never talk about it again." In one swift motion, she retrieves her cell phone from her bag and shoves it in my face.

Jenna's fast. But I'm faster. Without thinking, I snatch the phone out of her hand and snap it over my knee. Her eyes pop in disbelief, and her mouth opens, but nothing is said.

"Or," I say, striding to the closest toilet and dumping the pieces into the bowl. "You can negotiate with Roto-Rooter. They'll do business with you." I stomp the flusher with my foot. "Just remember to call collect."

With that, I straighten my posture, hold my head high, and exit the restroom. Behind me, I hear choking sobs as once again, Jenna Carmichael is crying because of something I did. But I don't care. She deserves it. Digging into my hip pocket for my own phone, I check to see if Hanna's texted me. Nothing from her, but Stephanie sent me a picture of an unaccompanied Chaz by his locker titled "The Single Life" with several smiley faces. I send a couple of laughing faces back, but don't feel jovial. Between destroying Jenna's phone, ruining Chaz's life, and turning the school upside down, I'm swerving in the fast lane and just passed the point of no return.

***

Tuesday is my least favorite day of the week. It just is. Monday, being the start of the week and all, usually has something exciting waiting for you when you show up to school in the morning. Tuesday doesn't, except for the reality that you have four whole days of torture ahead. I'm sitting in English, bored out of my skull, when the crackle of the intercom cuts into my thoughts.

"Roxanne Nazari, please report to the principal's office. Roxanne Nazari."

Well, I know what that's about. Heads turn across the room, and dozens of eyes bore into me as I look up at the intercom, praying it's a mistake. I begin to rise, then quickly sit back down, hoping nobody will notice if I ignore the announcement.

Everybody continues staring, so I collect my things and head for the gallows. I have to play it cool—not for them, but for myself.

As I step inside the office, I begin to sense what awaits. The behemoth secretaries, who, if you think about it, make up five people in terms of combined mass, are glaring at me with silent anger. Uneasily, I walk past them and knock quietly on the principal's door. Through the warped glass, I can see Edgar, Chaz, and Jenna sitting inside.

"Come in."

Everybody stares as I take a seat. I stuff my hands into the front pouch of my sweatshirt and massage the inside, trying to stop them from shaking. If only someone would hurry up and tell me I'm expelled so this horrible chapter of my life can end. But nobody's talking yet. Finally, Principal Groppe, a heavyset older man around retirement age, breaks the silence. His eyes are sad, and his voice is gentle.

"Miss Nazari, do you know why everybody's here?"

I nod slowly. "I think so."

Mr. Mercer jumps in. "Good. Tell us."

I withdraw my trembling hands from my pocket and clasp them in front of me, thinking of how to begin. "Three years," I say. "Three years I've been inappropriately touched, bothered, and sexually harassed by Chaz Humbert. Yeah. Him. Right there." I chuckle dryly. "Is he seated in the courtroom here today? You bet." I raise my eyes to meet Mercer. "In the beginning, I told people. I told the teachers. I tried to tell Counselor Stein at Parker back when I was a sixth-grader. Nothing got done, so I gave up and just took it."

I look up, trying to ascertain the collective reaction, but nobody's readable. Regardless, I continue. "A few weeks back, Chaz sent me a webchat invite, in which he was almost naked. It was disgusting and, I'm pretty sure, illegal. I told Mr. Mercer, and unsurprisingly, nothing got done."

"No, not quite," Mercer butts in. "There wasn't any proof it was Charles."

"Mr. Mercer threatened to call our parents if I kept complaining," I continue, staring him in the eye. "But let's go on. A little while later, I went to an off-campus party with my brother and a friend. Chaz, after more harassment during lunch, must have overheard my plans, because he followed me to the party and found me among over a hundred other people, where he lied about…"

"Excuse me," Jenna interrupts. "Sorry. How does this relate to anything we're supposed to be talking about?" She crinkles her nose at me. "Principal Groppe?"

"Jenna, enough," Groppe says, cutting her off. "Roxie. Go on."

I exhale slowly and lock eyes with Jenna, who quickly looks at her feet. "Three days after," I continue, "I was walking home. Edgar and Chaz were hiding in the bushes, taking pictures of me. I obtained the camera they were using and developed what was on it." I decline to mention my brutal attack, figuring Chaz or Edgar will bring it up as part of their defense, and keep talking. "Want to know what was on the roll?"

I look over at Chaz, who now quivers like treacle pudding. I smile, savoring his fear. "Different high school girls," I say. "Some of them, almost naked. I'm guessing none of them were taken with permission because none of the girls were posing. I was in some pictures. Hanna Gilbert was in others, and we certainly didn't consent." I stand up and stare at Mercer and Groppe without flinching. "I know almost every girl on the roll. The girls are underage, and those pictures are illegal."

Nobody speaks. The only sound in the room is the hum of the heater. Chaz refuses to look at me. Jenna's stopped smirking, and even Edgar is rocking anxiously. The principal and his underboss share a brief, troubled look between them before reverting their attention to me.

"Where are they now?" Mr. Groppe asks. "The photos? Do you have them here?" How I now wish I would've just talked to him before turning everything on its head. Why couldn't he have been here this entire time? It feels so good to be heard. "If this is true, you boys are in a lot of trouble. A lot."

"Yes, Principal," I say. "I still have them and the camera too."

"Bring it," Mr. Mercer says, his voice cold. "Bring the evidence. You think what you did was any better?" He stares at me maliciously. "Sexual harassment, huh? I think printing and passing around *porn* at school tops that list."

"My picture was fake," I say, shrugging. "I made it. Chaz's were real. And if you want to get technical, I'm underage, too. So no, not equal."

"So you did it, then," Mr. Mercer says triumphantly. "You're admitting you did it."

"Oh, please." I groan, rolling my eyes. "You know damn well I made the picture. Why the hell else is Jenna in here? I know she told you. Maybe I should've just paid her the five hundred dollars she tried to extort from me and walked a free girl, right, Jenna?"

Horrorstruck, Jenna recoils and refuses to look at me. "'Five hundred dollars,'" I mimic. "'Five hundred dollars and I delete the pictures.' That's what you said, didn't you?"

I look Mercer in his beefy face. "You really think Jenna came here because she cares? She only cares about herself." I turn back to face her. "Class act, Jenna. Now we know you sell justice as well as bullshit."

Jenna slumps backward, her credibility smashed. Guess who just took Queen Bitch off this chessboard? I've owned up to my crime. I knew as soon as I walked in I'd be getting sentenced, but it looks like everybody's going to pay up now. Mercer hasn't said another word. Neither has Groppe. The two of them occasionally exchange pained looks and look like they want to speak, but neither does. Having said my piece, I sit quietly.

"Do you feel like you got even?" Chaz asks in a low voice.

"Oh, yeah," I laugh. "I got even. But look at us now. No more distractions. No sideshows. Just Mr. Groppe who actually freaking *listened* to me!" I exhale and lay back in my stiff wooden chair, feeling the tightness in my shoulders gradually ebb away with each passing breath. If I get expelled, I'll take a different path. Find a new school, a new start. Shoot, just a couple of years until I can transfer to a community college like Nick and then maybe actually learn something instead of how to take a standardized test or create chaos to survive.

"Roxie, do you know you could be expelled for this?" Mr. Groppe asks coolly.

Jenna smiles with all fifty of her teeth. Chaz closes his eyes in what looks like a wince. Edgar, completely out of it, pitches himself onto one glute and releases an airy spurt of gas. Mercer is rapt. But Groppe levels with me.

"Give me a reason why I shouldn't."

"Expel me," I say automatically. "Kick me out. Send me out of this hell and I'll love you forever." I rise from my chair. "You know why? This school is a fraud. It's as fake as a three-dollar bill. How many times have we been told about equality? About safety? Acceptance on some banner in the cafeteria? But those are empty words. Nobody and nothing about this place backs any of that up."

I wheel around to face Chaz. "I wish I could feel safe at school. I don't. I'm not. Nobody takes action against him and people like him." I nod contemptuously at the boys. "So you know what? I acted alone. And boy, was I heard. 1400 people heard me." I struggle to control the emotion creeping into my voice. "You think I'm happy about what happened? Do you really think I enjoy wrecking people's lives? I'm not Jenna Carmichael. I hate the way they were treated. But you know what? If it took a fake picture of two students cornholing each other to buy a *week* of no harassment, catcalling, grabbing, and whatever the hell else they feel like doing that day…for myself, for Hanna, and every other girl they've fucked with, I'm not sorry."

Both Mercer and Groppe look astonished. Neither speaks. Jenna's struck dumb. Edgar is now drilling up his nose, but Chaz is transfixed. He's staring at me, not in anger or lust, but instead is radiating a loving, peaceful glow. Ordinarily, I'd be proud my words impacted someone, but the fact Chaz is the beneficiary drives me insane. Exhausted, I sigh and flop down in my seat, unsure of what this latest stretch of uninterrupted silence means for me or for my future.

***

"Two weeks?" Nick is incredulous.

"Believe it," I reply. "It was crazy up in the office today. Never imagined that telling the truth would help me, but you know, life's a surprise."

Nick nods. "Word. What about Chaz? How did he handle it?"

"Well, he'll get put on blast soon," I say, lying horizontally on the loveseat in the den. "I've got the camera. I've got the pictures. He'll probably get it worse than me."

"You know, you could go to the police," Nick points out. "I mean, it's technically child pornography. He could go to juvie. Or at least get registered as a sex offender. I mean, I hate snitching, but snitching on the snitch? The protected little degenerate? That's called karma."

"I've already wrecked his life," I say flatly. "He doesn't need to be registered as a sex offender. If anything, he'll enjoy the title."

"What a freak." Nick turns on the TV and quickly mutes it. "Did you tell Hanna yet?"

"No, not yet." Somehow, I don't want to tell her, mainly because she's right. But Hanna usually is. It's me who's got the hard head. This tends to cause problems in my life, especially with controlling people. Hanna's not at all controlling, but up against her, given everything that's happened, I look bad. I don't need any reminders.

Nick chortles. "Mom's going to be beyond pissed."

"I don't think so, actually. I told her what happened, and she wasn't that mad. I mean, it's my life, and if I wreck it, I'm responsible. She was right. Hanna was right. Was Groppe principal when you were there?"

"Geezer Groppe? He's still alive?"

"Yeah," I say. "What'd you think of him?"

"Dude was all right," Nick affirms. "Nothing ever gets to him, though. Everybody else in that joint is so power-hungry, they never let anything get that far."

"Exactly," I say. "That's what I felt. He was good about everything. Fair."

"Next to Mercer, he's King Solomon," Nick agrees. "Mercer's a total tool."

"Oh God," I grumble. "Don't get me started."

Delivering my Jerry McGuire monologue must've had some effect, because, in case you didn't catch it, I wasn't expelled. My two weeks of in-school suspension begin tomorrow, and according to Mr. Mercer,

I'll be watched closely throughout. Chaz is free for the time being, and Edgar got off scot-free. Judging from his performance earlier, he's either impaired or secretly a Shakespearian actor because he's immune when it comes to disciplinary action. When you grunt and fart your way through your trial, I guess it's unconstitutional to execute you, but after I drop off the photo roll, Edgar could still really get his, and Jenna came out of everything looking really, really bad.

It's still dark when my alarm clock begins blaring from my nightstand, and I rub the sleep out of my eyes. Day one. If I'm late, there's no telling what they'll do, and since I'm skating on thin ice, I can't risk it. I stuff down a couple of English muffins, throw Chaz's camera and photos into my bag, and begin the long trek to school.

The Scandinavian doom metal I chose was an excellent choice. The bleary gray sky, matched by the freezing weather, makes this purgatorial chapter of my short life that much more epic. By the time I enter the building, I've already said the rosary more times than I can count. I ask one of the front desk mastodons if Mr. Groppe is in, but I get only a surly grunt in return as I'm escorted to Ms. Fink's room. I slap my hand against the bulge in my backpack formed by the camera and smile as I walk in.

"Morning."

Chaz is doing his schoolwork in the far-right corner of the room, his backpack unzipped beside him. By the look of things, he's been here a while. Whatever sense of justice or empowerment that carried over from yesterday evaporates in a nanosecond. Once again, Chaz has won.

"What the hell are you doing here?"

"I've been suspended," Chaz responds, not looking up. "I admitted everything. I told them everything I did and that I'm sorry."

"What?" My whole body feels cold.

"Roxie." Chaz looks up from his work. "I'm telling you the truth. Honest."

"You should not be here," I say, my voice beginning to rise the way it does when I'm upset. "You shouldn't be anywhere near me. Where's the supervisor? Where's Mr. Groppe?"

"Ms. Fink's out right now, but she'll be back. What's the difference? I fessed up. You got caught. They didn't have anywhere else to put me. All the other rooms are full. I got a month of in-school suspension."

"Bullshit." I ball my hands into fists. "Don't start with me."

"I want to get past this," Chaz says calmly. "I'm done with my old ways. Seriously. Remote-controlled car with the video camera strapped to it? I confessed. The party? Told them everything. Taking pictures in the woods? I turned myself in. They'll be watching me for the rest of high school, and whatever I get, I deserve." He puts his head down and resumes working. I steal a cursory glance out into the hall to see if Fink's anywhere in the vicinity, but no such luck. Realizing nothing's going to change, I take the seat furthest away from Chaz and throw my backpack to the floor in silent fury.

How can educators be this stupid? How does Chaz always get what he wants? Even now, after everything he's done, he's got everybody wrapped around his finger like a yo-yo. Maybe Nick was right, and I should turn the photos in to the police after all. With that at the forefront of my mind, I take out my history binder and begin working on the latest homework.

***

"Once assignments are completed, students may choose to silently read or begin on homework," Ms. Fink reads aloud from the manual in a monotonous drone, unaware I'm staring at her with raw annoyance. Fink doesn't teach. She doesn't T.A. In fact, she doesn't do much of anything. Nick had her as a sub a few times and warned me she's about as useful as flypaper in a biblical plague. Boy, do I get it now.

"So, yes. Text. Doodle. Listen to your iPod. It's your future. There's a camera right up by the chalkboard, so if anybody does anything they shouldn't be doing, I've got eyes on you." She taps her spectacles for emphasis. "Questions? Comments? Good. I don't want to say more than I have to. If you need me, I'll be in the teacher's lounge. I hope you won't."

Shortly after she leaves, Chaz turns around in his seat. "I just wanted to say I really liked what you said about being safe and accepted at school."

"Eat a dick."

I get up and head to the bookshelf. Bent paperbacks, old atlases, and spiderwebbed teen magazines are mostly laid horizontally on the shelves. I select an old issue of *People* and flop down on a grubby loveseat in the corner to read.

"Why'd you do it?"

"Why do you speak?" I glare at Chaz. "Don't talk to me."

He gets up and walks over to the couch. I reel back as he gets closer, getting ready to throw a one-two combo if he gets too close. But he stops about five feet away and looks me in the eye.

"I just want to know why you made that picture of me and Edgar."

I narrow my eyes. "Seriously?"

"Yeah. Out of all the ways you could've gotten back at us, what gave you that idea?"

I tap my foot. "Let's see. You and your butt buddy were out of control, but your mom owns the staff, so you never got in trouble. Like, ever. From sixth grade 'til now, I've had to deal with you. So did other girls. You didn't understand what it's like to be grabbed at and stalked and have to hear disgusting comments and come-ons, feel dirty…you sure do now." I laugh. "I took it for three years. You got it for a little over a week. Tell me how that's fair?"

Chaz sits quietly, his expression contemplative. "You're right," he says. "I get it. It feels awful. I get what I did now. It makes a lot of sense, and I'm sorry again. It won't happen anymore, I promise."

"It better not." I try to read the magazine, but every few minutes, I look over at him. He's quietly doing his assignments and doesn't look over at me, but I can sense he's thinking deeply, and it unnerves me. Unsettled, I dig down deep into my pocket for my iPod so the music can take me away.

***

Three days in and I'm losing it. From the time I report to the office to the final bell, I am imprisoned with the person I hate the most for no fewer than six hours. And he fills the room. Not because he's fat. Because he's Chaz. The second Ms. Fink leaves, he attempts conversation, which I almost always shoot down. But blame it on solitary confinement, Stockholm Syndrome, or whatever else the DSM has listed, I'm almost tempted to engage.

The most appalling aspect of detention is Ms. Fink. Yesterday, she made two appearances, neither longer than thirty seconds, the entire day. The day before, she didn't even show up at all. I saw her a couple times in the teacher's lounge on the way to the bathroom, sipping a latte and reading a romance novel, and she didn't look up once. It pisses me off to no end my mother's hard-earned tax dollars are paying for this bullshit, but as we've seen time and time again, fairness is a foreign concept in this school.

Figuring she's not going to show, I slip my phone out of my backpack and shoot a quick text to Hanna. She won't reply, since she turns her phone off during class, but it's worth a shot.

"Who are you texting?"

I look up from my phone. "The FBI. I'm locked in a room with a lecherous queer. Code red."

Chaz sighs. "Aren't we past this?"

"Past what?"

"I mean the gay jokes. I think I've suffered enough."

I turn back to my phone. "I'll leave you alone if you put a sock in it. Deal?"

Some time passes before Chaz takes another stab at conversation.

"Maybe we can start fresh," he says. "I've done some thinking, and it's beginning to make sense. I seriously feel bad about everything. It kept me up last night."

"Stop," I say, slamming my phone on the desktop. "Just stop. I don't care. It makes no difference to me. I don't care about you." I flick at a scrap of paper with my left hand. "We're both stuck in here, and I'm bored. I haven't seen my best friend in days, and it's your goddamn fault. So I don't want to talk to you."

"Well, some of it."

"Huh?"

"I mean, some of it's your fault." He purses his lips.

I bristle. "You're saying it's my fault?"

"I wasn't the one who passed around an image of myself boning Edgar, so yeah," Chaz replies calmly. "It is your fault. I mean, I didn't punish you. I didn't turn you in. Jenna did 'cause she's a bitch who hates you. But it's still your fault you're in here."

"I swear to God, Chaz."

"No need," Chaz laughs. "Hate me all you will. I'm just pointing out the facts." With that, he returns to his work and jots away. Taking several deep breaths, I count down from a hundred to help subdue the explosive anger of moments before. Some time passes, and I'm finally about to solve the X variable when...

"Did you really mean everything you said in Mr. Groppe's office?"

"Dude," I begin. "Are you ill? Do you have a learning disability? Do you speak English? Do. Not. Talk. To. Me."

"Please answer me," Chaz says, and I catch something noticeably fragile that wasn't there a moment before. It surprises me a bit, so I turn and look at him to see if he's genuine.

"What do you mean?"

"You know, what you said in Mr. Groppe's office when we were all there. About everybody being safe and accepted for who they are. Do you really believe that?"

"Well, yeah," I say slowly. "Of course. This is America. I'd hope people could be themselves, as long as they're not hurting anyone, and just live." I shrug. "Is that it?"

"Yeah," Chaz says breathily. "That's it."

***

"So, you're telling me he hasn't done or said anything creepy all week?"

"Affirmative," I say, biting into my cheeseburger. Nick took me to the diner after school, which was super nice of him, and Friday always puts me in a good mood. I take a gulp of my milkshake, reflecting on the day. "He's not acting like himself. Totally different. But I'm sure it's another one of his twisted schemes."

Nick swipes an onion ring off my plate. "So, another week with the freak. What'll next week bring?"

"God only knows," I groan. "It's the weekend. Can't we think of happy things?"

"Totally," Nick says. "But you've passed the halfway mark, right?"

"Yeah," I say. "Come to think of it."

"Then let's celebrate," Nick says. "What time's Mom coming home?"

"No idea. But she's got a ton to do, so it'll probably be way later." I lay back in my seat. "We should watch a movie or two. I'm feeling a *South Park* marathon."

"Yeah, or maybe a rom-com or something."

"Really?" I smile. "What's changed? Have you finally hit puberty?"

Nick kicks me under the table. "Piss off."

"Oh, wait." I snap my fingers excitedly. "Gabriella. You talked to her?"

Nick grins. "Maybe."

"What'd she say?"

"A lot," Nick says. "She ended it by saying she wanted to learn more Spanish and if I'd be willing to tutor her."

"That's great," I say. "But you'd better change it up before she finds out you only know, like, three phrases.'

"I think she likes me," Nick says quietly. "The other day, my tag was sticking out from the back of my shirt, and she tucked it back in for me."

"Ooh," I tease. "Maybe she's got the hots for you. You sure dress better now, and your hair isn't shaved like a mental patient…maybe you've got something."

"I even bought hair clay," Nick says, holding up a paper sack and showing me its contents. "Mom said I look good with it gelled off my face."

"Well, Mom knows best." I get up from the booth and start gathering our trash. "You should start listening to her more."

"I need more advice," Nick says. "On girls. You're one, sort of. Help me here."

"What makes you think I'm the person to ask?" I retort. "I don't have a boyfriend. I could have my facts off. Ask Mom or Hanna."

"But I think you're onto something," Nick says. "What you've said so far has worked. It lines up with a lot of the dating tips I've found online…I mean, what I've learned from experience."

I roll my eyes. "It's okay, dude. Everybody looks that stuff up. Don't feel embarrassed or anything."

I decline to mention that I've found some *other* things in his search history that were not related to dating. At all.

Some things are better left unsaid.

***

"The week starts today," Ms. Fink drones, stating the obvious. "Use the remainder of the day to complete your classwork. If you finish early, either read or get started on your homework. If you need me, I'll be in the teacher's lounge."

"Déjà vu!" I say loudly as she exits the room.

"What was that, Roxie?"

"Nothing." I shrug. "It's weird. I feel like I'm in the movie *Groundhog Day*. Every morning, you say the same thing."

"You better watch your tone, young lady," Ms. Fink warns. "One more word from you and there will be reprisals."

I roll my eyes and turn back to my math worksheet, but not before I notice Chaz giving me a disapproving look.

I glare right back. "What's your deal?"

Chaz lifts a shoulder and resumes working. "Nothing," he says. "I just want to know why you always feel the need to antagonize people."

"What?" I look at him in disbelief. "Antagonize? King Perv, is it really you talking?" I shake my head. "Take your meds."

"I just think if you really believe everything you said that day in the office, you wouldn't be such a hard-ass all the time."

"Okay, first of all, forget about what I said in the office," I say, slamming my textbook shut. "I'm a hard-ass because this school sucks. The teachers blow. The work doesn't make any sense. And because I've had to put up with your shit forever." I look at him and shake my head. "You really don't get it, do you?"

"I'm starting to."

"No, you're not." I focus my full attention on the unstable blond lump now just a yard away. "Know what? The more you talk, the more I realize you don't get it. Not that I should be surprised. The only things you do get is a pass to harass and access to Edgar's rump."

"Enough." Chaz's voice is sharp. "Cut it out."

"Or what?" I stand up to my full height, which is only about five feet. "What're you gonna do?"

"You embarrass yourself."

"I *what*?"

"You embarrass yourself," Chaz repeats. "Nobody hears you. You're not going to get any points. Nobody's going to like you more for attacking me. You just look immature."

"Immature?" I gasp. "*You're* calling *me* immature? Your entire existence is harassing girls. You wear the same jizzed-on sweatshirt every day. You made a sex tape with an éclair!" I shake my head. "What does one even say to that?"

Chaz nods. "Touché."

I don't know what to make of this anymore. His complete personality turnaround…it isn't like him. But ever since turning himself in to Groppe, he's been the exact opposite of his former self. While he hasn't done or said anything perverted since our sentencing, this is probably only because he's under intense scrutiny and can't afford to dirty his record any further. Pretending to study the dictionary in case of a random Fink visit, I slide out my phone and text Hanna the latest development.

***

"Do you think he's bipolar?" Cynthia asks me. "Ask me. I'm seeing signs."

Girl time. Hanna and I are sitting with her mother in the master bathroom letting our nails dry while analyzing Chaz's behavioral turnaround. None of us agree on precisely what the cause is, but we all have our theories. Cynthia thinks he's mentally ill. Hanna insists he's playing me. But hate him as I do, I have a strange feeling about what's transpired the past week. Who I'm beginning to see is somebody none of us know—somebody different. I don't tell them this, though. This is a council. And the girls want blood.

"I think he's scared," I offer up. "I mean, the photos he took were pretty bad. I dropped them off with Groppe's secretary. Plus, Chaz owned up to the crime. He could get in serious trouble. Like, legally. And he knows it."

"I know an Army Ranger," Cynthia says offhandedly. "No, really. I used to date him back in my twenties. If Chaz tries anything again, he'll wake up in Anchorage next spring." She peers at her nails. "Just give me the word."

"It's a trap," Hanna says, shaking her head. "Don't you see it, Roxie? Chaz is smart. He knows there's a camera in there, so he's going to play mind games with you. He'll get you to let down your guard, and then he'll try something creepy and claim you wanted it."

"Or maybe I'm right," Cynthia chimes. "After all, I'm rarely wrong."

Hanna mutters something under her breath.

"You could be right," I say quickly. "About him being mentally ill."

"And because of the picture you passed around, he's had a complete mental breakdown," Hanna says. "He'll never be the same again."

"Could be." Don't get it twisted. I still loathe Chaz, but the idea that I may have brought about somebody's mental ruin fills me with shame. I blow on my nails and examine them under the vanity. "You really think he had a breakdown?"

"No, no." Cynthia waves this theory away. "Guys are dense. He probably did ten push-ups, whacked off to *Sports Illustrated,* and got on with his life. I mean, he is alive, right?"

"Do you think he's dangerous?" I ask. "That he's going to blow a fuse or something?"

"I actually did think about it," Cynthia says. "I mean, you did destroy his life. Not that he really had one." She tightens her robe. "You know I'm not one to really care about what other people think. But you need to be careful. Hanna might have a point, that this is just another Humbert scheme. Boy, let me tell you. I have to work with his mother on the school board, and that bitch is *bonkers.* Thumping around like menopausal Frankenstein. I'm guessing the apple didn't fall far from the tree when it comes to mental health." Cynthia shakes her head. "You know, genetics."

Hanna gapes at every politically incorrect thing that just came out of her mother's mouth, but I'm forever a fan. Cynthia gives herself the slow clap before giving me a grin and pulling me close for a hug.

"You got to be careful dealing with crazies," Cynthia laughs. "Keep your eyes open, okay?"

"Roger," I say, nodding solemnly.

"Don't freak her out, Mom," Hanna says, rolling her eyes. "Jesus. Chaz is a sex-crazed freak, not a killer. He's just sketchy. And Roxie can handle creepers, right?"

"Yeah," I say. "No sweat."

"I'm not trying to freak anybody out," Cynthia insists, blowing on her nails for the hundredth time. "I'm just telling her to ride slow. I don't know where she got it, but Roxie got her hood degree. Her street cred, if you will."

"Mom, please," Hanna groans.

"What?" Cynthia says defensively. "I've known rappers. I speak the lingo. One thing they all told me was this: even the best can get got." She cracks her neck. "Chaz isn't going to run up on you and flex a Glock. Will he flex his *jock*? I don't really know. You just gotta stay prepared.

"And remember," Cynthia continues as the three of us begin putting away different bottles of nail polish. "This all comes from my archive of personal experience. I've lived a life. So any time you want to run something by me, feel free to reach out to old Cynthia…and don't ever call me old."

***

"Can I borrow your graphing calculator?" Chaz asks, giving me a hopeful grin.

I wish he would sanitize his hands, but he'll just accuse me of being cruel if I ask. I sigh and hold it out to him.

"Thanks." Chaz punches in a long series of numbers, scribbles something down, and hands it back to me. The two of us have been unattended for hours, but so far, he's staying true to his word and behaving. It's not actually unpleasant, as long as I pretend he's an amoeba floating through the universe rather than a derelict who every day manages to choose a seat closer to me. It would save me a lot of time and anguish if I knew why Chaz is acting so unlike himself, but I'd have to talk to him to find out. And that's not something I'm eager to do.

"Check this out." Chaz's voice sounds from the back of the room. "Have you heard about this?"

"Heard about what?" I ask.

Something flies across the room and lands in front of me. "Page twenty-six."

Curious, I reach down to pick up the magazine at my feet. I flip through it until I come across an article about a well-known television actor who got famous on a buddy sitcom a few years back. He's recently come out of the closet and confessed that he and his old costar, who's apparently also gay, were romantically involved back when they were on the show. I'd actually heard about this but forgotten about it up until now, and the rest of the article is actually pretty interesting.

"What about it?" I look up at Chaz as I finish the final paragraph. "What's the big deal?"

"It's sick," he says, a strange expression on his face. "I mean, it was a show for kids. Boys can be really impressionable." He shakes his head. "Disgusting."

"Why?" I ask. "What's so wrong about it? They weren't hurting anyone and weren't that far apart in age. They didn't do a live taping of them doing the…you know. What's the issue?"

"I just think it's really gross. I mean, I used to love this show as a kid. They were just supposed to be buddies, not butt buddies. Now when I see a rerun, I'll just think about Tommy and Chris hanging out in the nude." Chaz shudders. "Freaking no."

Chaz's rant takes me by surprise. "Uh, did someone say homophobic? What's your deal? People love who they love. It's nobody else's business." I turn around in my seat. "Just curious. Do you have bipolar disorder, Chaz? Because it's okay if you do. My brother Nick thinks I might be afflicted with mild Tourette's. But he might've been joking…"

"I'm not bipolar," Chaz states adamantly. "So be serious for a second." He takes a breath. "If I tell you something, do you swear on your life that it won't leave this room?"

"Wait, what?"

"I'm serious," he says. "You've got to promise me."

I stare into Chaz's angsty face, completely unsure of how to proceed. Seriousness is not something I'm good at. I've laughed at a funeral. I routinely howl at bad news. Throughout the day, I'm known to wear a fool's grin on my face, remembering something funny from the past, and I mock anything I can't understand. I realize this is a defense mechanism and that I bury my feelings. But that can pretty much be expected when you lose a parent unexpectedly at the tender age of eleven.

Nevertheless, I don't want Chaz to think I don't care, but at the same time, I don't really want to know. It's easier to categorize and shelve Chaz as a sexual degenerate to be avoided than to lean in and get a deeper sense of what he's about. Since being detained, I've begun to suspect there's a lot more to him than the image he's put out there and want to know more, but simultaneously, I don't want to know a thing. I've got another week, he's in for three more, and life goes on.

I refocus on Chaz. There's no denying he's serious. I can feel he's about to open the door to something tremendous, so I nod slowly, unsure of what to say.

"You promise?"

"Yeah," I answer hollowly. "I promise."

The door bangs open, startling both of us, and Ms. Fink waltzes in. Given her long absences, I forgot she was a teacher here until this instant. But here she is in front of us, waving her arms like a revivalist preacher. "Up, up," she shouts, flapping uselessly. "Out the door. On to the assembly."

***

"Why does Mrs. Fullerton hate you?" Chaz asks me. We're back from the assembly. I still don't know what he wanted to tell me earlier, but I don't press the issue.

"I don't know," I reply. "I mean, I'm never rude or anything. At least, not *that* rude. Earlier this year, we had to do a skit on table manners, like, a team-building exercise or something, and I wrote ours."

"That sounds like fun."

"Oh hell no. It was like pulling teeth. But I managed to make one up and improvised as I went along."

"So, what happened?" Chaz settles into his chair.

"Well, the plot was, like, these three Southerners go to a diner and are rude to the waitress, who ends up getting pissed off at them, so she dumps coffee on them, and they get covered with third-degree burns," I say. "But the Southerners aren't having it. My character goes back to their pickup, gets her chainsaw, and brutally kills the waitress in broad daylight." I laugh, remembering Mrs. Fullerton's face at that scene. "The class loved it. But teachers hate violence, and Fullerton hates me, so I got an F."

"She hates you because of that?" Chaz asks in disbelief. "That sounds awesome. I would've laughed."

"Yeah, well." I shrug. "Can't please everyone, can you?"

"What was her explanation, you know, for the bad grade?"

"I did ask her about that," I say. "You know what she told me? That my skit was 'offensive to Southerners' and that she'd expect me of all people—you know, one of the only brown kids at this school—to be more 'culturally sensitive' and inclusive."

"She said that?"

"Yeah, no kidding. I mean, we never even explicitly said the people were from Tennessee or something. We just gave them hillbilly accents. They sounded like people from around here. Plus, it was fiction. How many people would kill a waitress for dumping coffee on them? You could just tell the manager and get a free meal."

"Well, the KFC crowd does get pretty crazy around dinner," Chaz chuckles. "But yeah, I get it. That sucks, though. She's always been really nice to me."

"Every teacher is nice to you, Chaz," I say wearily. "At least at this school."

Chaz scrunches his face. "What's that supposed to mean?"

"It doesn't mean anything. It's the truth." I scrawl down a quick answer on my worksheet and lay down my pen.

"What about Hanna? Does Mrs. Fullerton hate her too?"

"Oh, God, no. She just thinks I'm a bad influence on her. I mean, who doesn't love Hanna? She's a saint."

Chaz nods absently. "Yeah."

"So, Fullerton hates me. Mr. Burke, too, probably, since I never show up on time. Who's a teacher you don't like?"

"Mr. Lombardi," Chaz says, making a face. "Can't stand him."

"*What?*" I exclaim. Mr. Lombardi is the godlike PE teacher and girls' volleyball coach. Pretty much every girl at the school is infatuated with him, and Hanna and I are no exception.

"He's not nice to me. You know, always shouting at me to get the ball or run faster or shaking his head when I can't shoot a three-pointer. He's a lot tougher on guys than girls."

"Oh." I nod. "I see."

Neither of us say anything after that. The only sounds are our pencils scraping gently against notebook paper and, occasionally, the whir of the fax machine in the next room. I get up to stretch my legs, crack my back, and walk a few paces to get the blood flowing.

"You ever wish you could go back in time?"

I stare.

"You know, like back to being a little kid. Or just a younger kid."

I nod. "All the time."

"It was so much easier," Chaz says, setting his pencil down. "Being nine, or ten, or even younger than that. Things were so easy, so much simpler back then. You didn't care about what people thought or who your friends were. If you were good-looking or not. Trying to be popular. We didn't care. But once we got to middle school, everything got screwed up."

"Yeah, right?" I'm a little taken, though. Until now, I wasn't sure Chaz was capable of thinking outside the pelvic zone. People are sure to be full of surprises.

"It's part of life, I guess," Chaz says. "Growing pains and all that. But I wish it took longer. Like, really, who among us can find themselves in, what, five, six years? It's not possible. We change so much every day, right? I feel like a different person every hour. What about you?"

"Yeah," I answer, unsure of what to say. "I guess I'm the same way. I think all of us are, in our own way."

"Really? You?"

"What do you mean, me?"

"You seem so well-adjusted," Chaz says finally. "I mean, you're cool. You've got a badass look. Everybody I know respects you whether they like you or not…" He trails off.

"Really?" I feel a surge of happiness and then feel stupid when I remember it's coming from this whelp. "Seriously?"

"Of course," Chaz says. "I mean, word's probably out on the street you made the picture. The whole school bonded over that. You'll get a hero's welcome when you get out of detention."

"So anyway," I say quickly, hoping to change the subject, "why aren't you as supposedly well-adjusted as I am?"

Chaz sighs. "I don't really want to talk about it."

I turn back to conjugating Spanish verbs but keep remembering Chaz wanted to tell me something yesterday. Try as I might, I can't get it out of my head. I don't want to admit it, but I'm curious. I fight the urge a little while longer but can't keep holding out. Turning towards Chaz, I initiate conversation this time.

"Hey, Chaz?"

Chaz looks up, his face pleasantly surprised. "Yes?"

"That stuff we were just talking about."

"Yeah, what about it?"

"What did you want to tell me yesterday?"

Chaz winces. "Oh, that? It's dumb." His eyes flit down to the science textbook he's been reading for the last hour or so.

"You told me it was really important, though."

"It is," Chaz says finally. "But we've got a pretty bad past. I don't expect you to suddenly like me because we've spent time in this classroom, and I don't blame you for continuing to hate me. People have secrets, and this is something I think it's better I keep to myself." He looks at me. "Sorry for wasting your time, okay? It was a bad judgment call."

✳✳✳

Hours later and I still can't figure it out. What is with Chaz's turnaround? True, he admitted everything he's done and truly might want to turn his life around. But tigers don't change their stripes. I turn this over in my mind as I watch Hanna shoot penalties from the bleachers, almost making every shot.

I played soccer when I was younger but got red-carded too many times and gave up. It was my dad who was the fan. Saturday mornings, he'd wake up at four to watch satellite games from Europe or Asia.

He used to try to get Nick to hit the pitch with him, but he couldn't play to save his life. It was something intended to bring them together, but Nick decided he wanted to go out for football instead, and the soccer ball stayed up on the shelf in the garage ever since. Basketball's always been my favorite sport, but being a midget, I couldn't keep up, let alone make passes, so I opt to watch it live or on the big screen.

Hanna's shot makes a perfect arc before swishing into the goal. I clap and yell encouragement from the bleachers. I mean, it's only practice, but I still like watching her play. She's hoping to get a scholarship, and with her athletic ability, charisma, and good grades, she'll probably get a full ride anywhere she wants to go. Me, on the other hand? Unlikely. This year, my grades suck, my teachers can't stand me, and I don't do anything extracurricular except get into fights. Add in an in-school suspension to the résumé, and it's looking like bagging groceries at the supermarket for me. Mom said colleges don't start looking closely at grades until junior and senior year, so I still have time to turn it around.

A pair of grassy cleats clomp up the bleachers, and I turn around to see CeCe Sanchez standing over me. She gives a small smile. "Hey."

"CeCe," I greet. "What's up? Aren't you supposed to be on the field?"

"Yeah," she sighs, tugging at her jersey. "I'm just not feeling it. I'm so tired." She hugs her arms to her chest. "Are you waiting for Hanna?"

"Yeah."

"She's on fire today," CeCe says, sitting down beside me and reaching into her bag. She takes out her L.A. Galaxy hoodie and slips it on, pulling the drawstrings. "If she plays like this, we'll win Saturday for sure."

"How've you been?" I ask. "What's life like on the outside?"

"Same old," she answers, shrugging. "Boring as usual." She chuckles. "Science sure wasn't boring last time you were there, though."

I snort. "Oh yeah. It ain't a science class until Roxie passes the porn."

"Straight up," CeCe agrees. "You're a legend now. Roxie Nazari:

feminist icon." She shakes her head. "That was so great. How did you come up with it?"

"I don't know if it was great," I say, the smile sliding off my face. "I was so angry. Chaz bothered me—bothered us—for years, and nobody did anything. We were so sick of it, or I was, at least." I don't mention finding the camera. Chaz's suffered enough. "But it's over now."

"Where is he?" CeCe asks. "You know, Chaz?"

"Suspended with me."

She gasps. "What? Like, he got suspended, too, or you're both in there…like, together?"

"Option two." I roll my eyes. "This school is a joke."

"That's not okay," CeCe says, her brown eyes wide. "It's messed up. He's a total predator. He shouldn't be in a room alone with you."

"He's actually been fine," I say. "He's pretty tame now. He apologized to me and everything. Said he was done. According to him, he turned himself in to the principal for everything he did, and he's got a month of detention. I only got a couple of weeks." I shake my head. "Weird times. Even weirder people."

"Well, of course he's fine," CeCe giggles. "Turns out he doesn't actually like girls. You're safe."

I laugh. "Yeah, I guess. Maybe they're trying to convert him or something."

Chapter 6

"Hey, Roxie." Chaz cocks an eyebrow at me. "Roxie."

We're back in Fink's room for another round of hell. I look up from my algebra worksheet. "What?"

"If we were to get funky in this classroom, where do you think we'd do it?"

I slam my pencil down, blood pounding in my ears. I knew something was off with him. I knew his sudden nice-guy persona was an act. *This* is the Chaz Humbert I know how to handle.

"Listen. I've got one thing to say to you. Actually, two. First? Don't talk to me. Second? Talk again and I'll chop your knob off, so it'll never see the inside of Edgar again. Got it?"

"Yowch. Well played, Roxie. Good thing you still pack some heat. That sassy lip would serve you well in a cathouse." He stands up and smacks his ample ass. "Roxanne," he yowls. "Roxanne, you don't have to put out the red light. Roxanne!"

I flip him off mid-croon. Chaz grins. "I bet you don't know how tingly I feel when you give me the finger. So good. It's like the next best thing to doing it." Dropping to a crouch, he mounts his desk and swiftly simulates.

"Charles Humbert?" Ms. Fink screams from the doorway. "What on Earth?"

The day goes downhill from there. Instead of being placed in a separate room, Chaz was forced to write "I will not menace school property" a hundred times in chalk while I struggled through my assigned readings on the Roman forum. I scribble down a reference, and the chalk makes a scraping noise as Chaz completes what must be his hundredth line. Stepping a distance away, he rears back and hurls his chalk against the board. It explodes, and a plume of dust rises into the air. The last traces dissipate, though a splatter of white residue still marks the board.

"Money-shot!" Chaz whoops.

I can't help it. I burst out laughing. It's only after I stop that I remember Chaz is back to his old tricks, so I tune him out and turn back to my notes. Earlier, Mrs. Fullerton cruised in to drop a stack of late work on my desk, even though I'm back in class next week. It isn't hard, but there's a lot of it. I'm drained, so I pick up the heaviest book and place it in my bag.

"Roxie." I look up to see Chaz looming over me with a creepy grin on his face. "Baby, you down?"

"Back up," I yell, throwing my book to the floor. "Get the hell up out of my face. I mean it. Step back unless you want your family jewels minced."

Chaz shrugs and steps back. "Since you're down with touching my junk, you should pierce my left one before the last bell. I want a stud. No, a hoop. Whatever you like, kitty cat. I'm with the stud, but nothing screams 'hardcore' like a hoop, know what I mean?" He frowns. "Which does Hanna prefer?"

"God." I bury my face in my hands and squeeze my eyes closed, willing away the hot, salty tears that are threatening to spill over. "Why are you doing this?"

"Aww." Chaz tsks. "Poor Roxie. Is she on her period? Or has she reached her breaking point?" His lip pushes out into a mocking pout. "I'm going with option two. I knew it was a matter of when. Even the strongest of us have to snap sometime."

I can't have a breakdown, or Chaz wins. Whatever sick thing he's got planned, whatever he wants out of this, he's won. I can't fight anymore. I've got nothing left. Turning away, I swipe at my misty eyes with my sweater sleeve and face him full-on, my voice barely audible.

"What do you want from me?"

I hate myself. I really do. What the hell? Why should I care what Chaz wants? After everything he's put me through, the last thing I should be doing is reaching out to him. Way to send a message. Ten out of ten, this isn't ending well. Anticipating the worst, I lean back in my chair and study his face, thinking of ways to insult him. But what's that going to accomplish? It only seems to empower him if anything.

Chaz runs a hand through his unruly hair and exhales, looking everywhere but at me. He's either going to disclose something, or he's playing me like the fool I am.

"You know how I was going to tell you, you know, that thing yesterday but never got to tell you?"

I don't move. "Uh-huh."

"I don't know if I should." Chaz runs his index finger along the spine of his textbook and looks at the floor.

Exasperated and refusing to be lured into another one of Chaz's traps, I jump out of my chair and rip the textbook out of his hand. "What are you reading there? Anthropology?" I sneer at him. "Homo erectus," I exclaim, pretending to flip through the pages. "Well, you're totally homo…and erect, according to the poster everyone saw. You probably wrote the book!"

I smirk and stare into Chaz's face, only to see it crumple and fat tears begin to roll down his cheeks. "Why?" he croaks. "Why do you keep on saying that?" Chaz chokes back a sob. "Do you have any idea what you really did?"

✳✳✳

Looking into his shattered face, everything comes together. How did I not consider this? The Edgar retort was something I came up with back in eighth grade, but I never thought in my wildest dreams Chaz might actually like men. But the more time I spent with him, especially here in detention, there were signs. Asking me constantly about my Groppe address. The overly homophobic reaction to the magazine article. I missed it. I missed it all.

Well, it's too late now. Without trying to, I've successfully deported Chaz from the closet, and he's dying on land. Shaking with sobs, his beefy shoulders bow, and he lowers his head until it thuds against the top of his desk.

"Chaz," I say as gently as I can. "Are you…are you actually gay?"

There. I've said it. There's no going back now. If this is some elaborate hoax, which I know it isn't because you can't fake this type of emotion, I've fallen for it hook, line, and sinker.

"I guess I didn't hide it so well, did I?" Chaz sniffles. "Pretty obvious, huh? I guess up near the end, I was waiting for you to figure it out. Hoping even. It's so hard. I'm so tired of lying to everybody." He slumps out of his chair and curls up in a ball on the worn rug underneath us. "But it's true, Roxie. I'm gay."

Neither of us speaks. The words have been spoken, but my mind somehow is unable to process what he's saying. Almost fifteen years alive and nobody's ever come out to me before. Come to think of it, I don't even know any gay people. I don't even think I've met any. I open my mouth and quickly close it again before I say something stupid or insensitive.

"It's okay," I say finally. "No. What I mean is it'll be okay."

Chaz coughs and wipes his eyes with his shirt sleeve. "Says you."

"Want to talk about it?" I ask, getting out of my own chair and sitting down beside him. "I promise. Anything said will not leave this room. I'm here."

"How did you know?"

"I didn't," I say honestly. "I had no clue. You were so obsessed with girls I figured the only thing that could counter that would be saying you were gay. I didn't know you were, or I wouldn't have said it. And I never would've made that picture." I take a breath. "Really, man, I'm sorry. I'm so, so sorry."

"No," Chaz blubbers. "I am. I am so sorry. For everything. The stalking, grabbing, disgusting conversations. Flashing Hanna. Sneaking into the locker room to take pictures. I feel disgusting. I *am* disgusting. I deserved everything, and I still do. Three years! Three years of that. I was lying to myself, though." He sniffles. "I thought guys did this kind of stuff when they liked girls because I don't know what it's like to like a girl. I don't blame you for what you did. Revenge? I had it coming to me, ten times over. But this is it for me."

I've never felt so ashamed in my life. Even when the school flipped upside down after the porn circulated in science, I didn't grasp the magnitude of my actions until now. Chaz's pain is so intense I can almost feel it covering me like a blanket. How I wish I could go back in time. But at the same time, I feel like this had to happen. There's a reason we're both here in this room at the same time, and there's a reason Chaz has placed his life in my hands.

When in doubt, don't question the universe.

"I can't imagine what you're going through," I say as soothingly as I can. "But when was the last time you ate?"

Chaz shrugs. "Breakfast? I don't remember."

"Here," I say, passing him a Rice Krispie from my lunchbox. "Eat this. It'll raise your blood sugar. I think you need it more than I do."

The wrapper crinkles as Chaz takes a bite. "Thank you."

"When did you find out?"

"That I was gay? I always sort of knew I guess, you know, the more I thought about it. When the, uh, when the feelings started, I wanted them to go away. Even though I was young, I knew what they were. It was that drop in your stomach you'd get, the kind teen romance novels would talk about, except I felt it around boys I would see on the street or even people in my grade. It wasn't sexual or anything, though."

I nod. "Yeah, I kind of figured."

"Then it started to bother me," Chaz says, taking a sip of his water. "I got older. I didn't like those feelings anymore. The older I got, the more I wanted it gone. People began talking. For a time, I really thought I could change. I tried to like girls. But when none of them liked me back, maybe because I was weird or chubby or quiet, I gave up. The harassing freak became my cover." He snorts. "Some story."

"Is there anybody you could talk to?" I ask. "Like a trusted adult or something?"

"You're it." Chaz laughs weakly.

"I don't know, Chaz. I mean, we do have a history, and I did kind of ruin your life."

"Forgiven," he says quickly. "And again, after this, after your detention is over, you don't ever have to talk to me again. You don't have to look at me. You can get back to your life and enjoy a normal high school experience free of trouble. But please, at least for today, just hear me out."

***

After school, Chaz and I hit up downtown. I need a walk, and so does he. Usually, Hanna and I go to Sunbeam Frozen Yogurt in the mini mall to salute the start of the weekend, but today I'm about to treat Chaz Humbert to a bowlful of whatever the hell he wants. Ahead of the crowd, the two of us are the only people in the joint, but I tell Chaz to reserve a spot anyway, somewhere far in the back where we won't be noticed. I text Nick to let him know I'll find my own way home later, and Chaz grabs a paper bowl from the stack.

After weighing and paying, the two of us walk in step to the back of the store. Once seated, I look up out of habit and cringe. Through the glass, I can see Brennan Hodges and Spencer Zimmerman, two massive junior athletes, about to walk inside. The last thing we need is a visit from those two, but the second they enter the store, Brennan spots us. Punching Spencer in the arm, he looks coldly in our direction, and the two of them swagger over.

"Look who it is," Spencer announces at ten times the normal volume. "Chester High's famous fudge packer." He laughs. "It survived."

Brennan hoots and adjusts his ball cap. "True that. Didn't know Humbert was still here. We thought you moved to San Francisco."

"Roxie?" Brennan slides into the booth beside me and ruffles my hair. "Girl, you're literally my freaking idol." He nods at Spencer. "This one's legit."

Spencer meets my gaze and gives me that stupid head nod guys give girls in high school. "Word was you got stuck in detention with Elton here. What's he really like?"

"Ask him," I say, trying to keep my temper under control. "He's right here. Talk to him like a normal person."

"He's not normal, though," Brennan replies, his voice suddenly clipped and refined. "And you don't have to describe how. A picture's worth a thousand words."

The two of them roar and bump fists. Chaz looks like he's just been sentenced to death, and I'd have thrown hands by now, but there's zero point in punching either one of these refrigerators. Some time ago, a couple of other customers must've come in because they're staring at us, but the two ogres don't even notice.

Spencer smirks and helps himself to a spoonful of Chaz's yogurt. "So, Chazster. When did you find the chance to bone in the locker room?"

"Wait!" I break in. "Why do you want to know? Are you trying to get a three-way started, or are you just tired of conventional porn?"

Spencer and I lock eyes. Brennan growls. I just laugh and lean back in my chair; pretty sure I've won this round. Brennan shakes his head and looks at Spencer, who motions towards the exit.

"Let's get out of here," Spencer mutters. "This place blows anyway. Leave the freaks alone."

"Manwich, anyone?" I holler after them as they lumber towards the door. Chaz still hasn't looked up. I don't blame him.

"Are they gone?"

"Oh yeah." I plunge my spoon into my bowl and take in a spoonful of something creamy and delicious. "Don't figure they'll be back for a while."

"Thanks for standing up for me," Chaz says, extracting a gummy bear. "Means a lot. Especially after I was such a dick today, like, earlier."

"Well, you sure paid for it," I laugh. "Here and over there. Consider it over."

"At least they didn't hear us talk about anything," Chaz sighs. "That could've happened if we weren't careful. Imagine how much worse things would be once they figured out the rumor is actually true."

"It's only partially true," I remind him. "The Edgar part, that was straight-up fiction." I pause. "But if it isn't…I really don't need to know about it."

***

After finishing our yogurts, Chaz and I head further into town. I don't want to risk running into anybody else, and most of the high school kids stay within a mile of the school, so we should be good where we are. Chaz kicks at a pinecone and brushes at some dried leaves on one of the benches dotting this part of the park.

"How are you feeling, I mean, about everything?"

"I can't explain it," Chaz says. "I mean, it's not even real. I just came out to a girl I've pretended to be obsessed with for years. Whenever I played this moment—you know, coming out—it was to my mom or dad or maybe to somebody I had feelings for."

"Life doesn't let us plan," I say, sitting down beside him. "It plans for us. So here we are."

"Will my parents hate me?"

"I don't know," I say slowly. In my family, that possibility would be virtually zero, but as I've come to realize growing up, not everybody's as lucky as I've been. "Is something making you think that?"

"No," Chaz says quickly, ducking his head. "My parents love me. My mom said nothing will ever make her stop loving me, and I think my dad's the same. I mean, he loves beer even though it's killing him."

"It's true. Parents love their kids no matter what," I say. "Well, most of the time."

"I'm just worried they'll be disappointed," Chaz says, playing with the drawstrings on his hoodie. "They'll never see this coming. My mom thinks I'm girl crazy and want to get married and have a nice house and kids. Not a boyfriend and a chihuahua and a condo."

"They might take a while to come around," I say. "But just worry about that later. Live in the now."

"How can I? With everything the way it is? Nobody'll even talk to me when I get out of detention." Chaz shrugs. "Not that they liked me anyway."

"I hated you," I say. "Hanna hates you, same with Stephanie and the rest of the girls you bothered. I mean, who wouldn't? Lie low for a while and then just be cool. Be nice and people will move on. They're teenagers. Their brains are like a sieve."

"True." Chaz looks at me sideways. "Do you still hate me, like, even a little bit?"

"No," I say truthfully. "I couldn't. Even if I wanted to. I mean, I hate who you were. But this person I'm talking to isn't even like Chaz. You're actually all right."

"I don't think I can express how awful I feel," he says, looking at the ground. "The longer we sit here, the more I despise myself. You're so cool. More than anything else, going back in…I'm embarrassed. I'm embarrassed to be me, or who I was at least. People will just look at me and remember. If I died today, they'd vote me 'most likely to be arrested for rape' or something." Chaz shakes his head. "I just wish I could do it all over."

I roll my eyes. "Dude! You're not dying in a nursing home. You're a freshman in high school. In two weeks, you'll come back to school, and it'll be yesterday's news. You've got time to get yourself together."

Chaz nods. "Good advice."

"It's the truth," I say, zipping up my jacket. "Just chill out, do your homework, and don't hump any more desks."

***

My house isn't too far from the park, and Nick should be home by now. I text Hanna, who's most likely either done with soccer practice or about to wrap up, and tell her to go to my house immediately. As I walk back home, my thoughts keep circling back to the insanity of the day and how right when you think you've got everything figured out, life throws you a curveball.

Chaz Humbert is gay. Who knew? I mean, ever since the picture hit, people have been repeating it like it's common knowledge, but anybody who took a second look could tell the picture was doctored. But people rarely want the truth. They crave fiction. And in Chester, the fiction's always more interesting.

"Hey, you," Nick calls from the kitchen as I walk through the door. "Hungry?"

"No, I ate." I drop my bag on the floor and kick off my shoes. "How was school?"

"Eh." Nick shrugs. "Gabriella was absent. The day dragged. I hung out with Brandon at lunch. You'll never guess who he's with."

"Who?" I step into the kitchen to see Nick surrounded by bags of sugar and flour. Recipes plaster the countertop. "Who's he dating?"

"Kylee Marshall."

"Never heard of her."

"What? Seriously? You met her last summer."

I rub my eyes. "Sorry, bro. Doesn't ring a bell."

"She's hot, I mean, pretty, anyway…but Brandon? I mean, I like him and stuff, but he's bad news. She's super into him and everything, but he's still gawking at every butt and rack that cruises by right in front of her."

"What a douche." I roll my eyes. "Brandon's such an ass."

"It's the Camaro. The one his dad bought him. He doesn't have to do anything; he just drives around, and the poontang flies at him. I swear he's never even had to ask a girl out. They just land in his lap."

"He is kind of cute," I point out. "I mean, if you like skinny jeans, flat-ironed hair, and abs. Plus he's always been nice to me."

Nick glares at me. "Don't even think about it."

"Hey guys," Hanna calls from the foyer.

Nick flips on the oven light and peers in. "Where were you today?"

"Soccer practice," Hanna answers, grabbing a glass and filling it at the sink.

"No, Roxie."

I take a breath, thinking of how to answer this. "I was hanging out with Chaz."

The two of them laugh.

"I'm serious," I say. "I swear. We hung out, and we're going to chill again."

Nick and Hanna exchange looks. "What's going on?" Nick asks finally. "Are you on drugs?"

"No, it's not like that."

"Why are you going to bat for him?" Hanna demands. "He's probably got a high-definition picture of your birth canal on his monitor, and you're actually willingly spending time with him?"

"Think about it," I say, folding my arms. "Nick wanted to beat him up and report him to the cops. You wanted to turn him in to the principal. I'm the one who wanted to fire a gun into his head. Why a complete turnaround if I didn't have a good reason?"

"Because you went nuts," Nick says. "That's it. Locked in the funny farm with Humbert…you finally cracked. But seriously, who wouldn't? I read *The Count of Monte Cristo*. People can only take so much."

"You know what?" I get up and walk towards my bag. "I'm going to call him. Right now. He's coming over tomorrow too."

"*You're* going to bring *Chaz* into the *house*?" Hanna shrieks. "Make sure you've got your rape whistle."

"Nope," Nick says, trying to play dad. "Not happening."

I tune them both out and pull out my phone. Scrolling through my contacts, I see Chaz's name and laugh at the irony. The phone rings a couple of times before Chaz picks up.

"Hello?"

"Hey, Chaz," I say. "How are you holding up?"

"I'm good," he says quietly. "Everything okay?"

"Can I put you on speaker?"

"Go ahead."

I switch to speakerphone and turn up the volume. "Talk. Anything."

"Who's around?"

Hanna and Nick look at each other in shock. "It's him."

"Just so you know, my brother Nick and Hanna are here," I say. "They're in on the conversation."

"Hey, guys," Chaz says, suddenly sounding shy. Neither of them replies.

"Can I tell them?" I ask. "About you know. I trust them more than anybody else in the world, and I promise they'll help you out."

"I'm gay," Chaz says nonchalantly. "And don't worry, Nick…Humbert Pictures LLC never existed. I'm not trying to recruit you for any future projects. But, yeah, I'm sorry about everything, Hanna."

"How do we know you're telling the truth?" Hanna says after a short time passes. "And thanks for the apology. I still don't like you."

Chaz chuckles. "I get it. Trust me. And again, I'm sorry. You don't have to like me, and I don't blame you. But pranking? Come on. Who bullshits the bullshitter?"

All of us laugh at that one. "Okay," I say after a short pause. "We've got a long conversation ahead of us. But I'll see you tomorrow, okay?"

"Wouldn't miss it for the world."

I end the call. Hanna and Nick are sitting down on the couch trying to process this. Nick sighs and massages his face with his hands like he does when he's extremely unsure of what to do in life. Hanna looks at me as if to say, "What now?"

"Told you," I say smugly. "Now, we've got to talk."

***

"First rule. Don't overthink things."

Nick, Hanna, Chaz, and I are sitting around the kitchen table over a plate of homemade nachos, trying to determine a strategy to help Chaz navigate reentering society as a redeemed sexual predator. At first, Chaz was nervous, probably because Nick carried a baseball bat around for the first half hour, but after explaining himself and giving Hanna a sincere, thoughtful apology, he's managed to transition from hated to neutral.

"Totally agree," Chaz says, leaning forward and scooping up some cheese with a tortilla chip. "It's pretty easy. I just don't want to be the oversexed fat kid anymore. Beyond that, I don't really care."

"Easy," I say. "Join a gym, go for a run, and be nice to girls. Done and done." I reach for a particularly loaded tortilla chip. "That we can accomplish."

"Mostly, just relax," Nick instructs. "Do what you want, but be reasonable. But you are original, Chaz." He laughs. "Humbert Pictures LLC. Goddamn genius."

"Nick!"

"Sorry, sorry," Nick says. "What I meant was don't care what people think. Be calm. Be cool. And if people hate you for it, do it anyway."

"Well, how?" Chaz furrows his brow. "What steps do I need to take?"

"Get some good clothes," Hanna coaches. "Present a clean appearance. Simple, classic haircut and style. And try new things."

"Okay, what about sports?" Chaz asks. "I mean, I suck at football. Soccer is boring. Baseball, maybe, but I did want to try out for tennis."

"Do you even like sports?" I load a little ground beef onto my chip before crashing it into a mound of guacamole.

He sighs. "Not really."

"Then forget it," Hanna says. "Do things you like or have an interest in, or they won't get done. Period."

"Here's what I would do if I were a freshman again." Nick leans back in his chair, looking thoughtful. "First off, I'd exercise. You sit around, mooch, hit the bong, and your mind goes to weird places. Seen it and been there. Don't like organized sports? Go for a run. Swim. Hell, play some kickball with some kids from your neighborhood. Just get active. Second? Don't put yourself in a box or let other people judge you. Emo, jock, hip-hopper…just forget it. You don't need to be a billboard for what you like, and you don't need to be categorized."

"Excellent point." I dab at my face with a napkin. "You're trying to break out of a category. Don't dive into a new one."

"Agreed," Hanna says. "And when you get out of detention, come find us. We'll help set you up."

Chaz nibbles his lip. "I don't know if you know this, but I'm really into music."

I tilt my head. "What kind of music?" The Village People's "YMCA" plays in my mind, and I immediately hate myself. Thank God he doesn't have ESP.

"Who isn't?" Nick asks. "Rock? Metal? House?"

"Anything, really," Chaz replies. "I love house music. Techno's cool. Sometimes swing and big band music."

"Don't be a band kid," I moan. "Please, just no."

"Roxie," Hanna says quickly. "Let him decide."

"Well, not that kind of 'band kid,'" Chaz says, laughing. "But… this kid did always want to be in a band."

***

"Their debut album was released three years ago on Maximilian's twenty-second birthday," Jerome explains, running his finger along the CD's pristine case dotingly. "It was supposed to be called *Love Glove,* but at the last minute, they switched it to *Cat in the Bag.* An excellent name for an excellent album."

One phone call to Jerome and here he is, standing in my living room and giving us the complete history of Wet Banana. It was Hanna's idea to bring Jerome into the project, and I didn't want to be a killjoy, so I went with it. Clearly, a huge mistake.

"Seventeen weeks later, *Squelch* was released." Jerome grins. "Since the previous album was a big hit, the band probably figured waiting was a waste of time. Me personally? I think it was a great decision because *Squelch* is my favorite album, hands down." He points to the cover art. "Look here. See the banana shooting milk into the guava? Jed drew it when he was in jail. I think it's pretty deep and artistic."

I groan and glance at the clock. Hanna sends me an apologetic look, but Chaz and Nick are on the edge of their chairs.

"Here's a fun fact. The milk was supposed to be full-fat, but Jed deliberately made it watery because he had epididymitis when he was drawing it."

"Okay, cool," I cut in. "The reason we brought you here is that Chaz wants to be in a band. Do you know anybody looking for a singer or something? Do you play anything? Can you teach him a few drum patterns?" I wave my hands around, unable to think of anything more to say.

"Totally." Jerome smiles. "I'm looking to start one. Chaz, want to join my band?"

"Sure," Chaz says enthusiastically. "Nick, you in?"

"Oh my god!" Jerome crows. "Nick? Say yes! The three of us can form a band right here."

"What'll we call it?" Chaz asks.

"What about Dry Cucumber?" Jerome suggests hopefully.

"I mean, it'll work until we get some groupies," Nick says, laughing.

"It's settled then." Jerome reaches forward to fist-bump Nick and Chaz.

It's bad enough Chaz and Jerome are about to be musical collaborators, but I can't believe Nick is on board with this. Someone please shoot me dead. I look over at Hanna, who appears equally horrified.

"We have incredible synergy already," Jerome states. "I'm on the guitar. Chaz will get going on the drums. And Nick." He pauses for effect. "Nick will be our multitalented wild card. Some days he'll be on the keys, other times vocals. Don't you even play the accordion?"

"Hell to the yeah!" Nick bellows, jumping onto the couch and wind-milling his arms. "This is going to be dope. Let's start practicing tonight."

***

"Why'd you turn left?" I yell over my shoulder. "I thought we were going to the mall."

Behind me, Chaz is puffing on his mountain bike, and Hanna's cruising on my left. As it turned out, school got canceled Friday for conferences, and the three of us met up at Hanna's. It was wild introducing Chaz to Cynthia, but after a while, Chaz kind of fell in step with us girls, and by the time we left, he might as well have always been there. I mean, he has, in a sense, if you really think about it, and he's taken care to point out the fact that had he not been in the picture from day one, Hanna and I may never have been friends.

"See, *I* was your first mutual friend. *I introduced* you," Chaz said as the three of us exchanged looks in Cynthia's living room. "Say thank you, girls."

The night before, Chaz trashed his wardrobe and managed to scrape together seventy-odd bucks, and Hanna and I promised to take him shopping.

"The mall's too much," Chaz says. "Everything's expensive, even the discounted stuff. I want to shop about two blocks from here."

"What store?" Hanna asks. "We're in the middle of nowhere."

I look around and it hits. "Dude," I say. "I'm not taking you to Bargain World. The whole point of this trip is to get you good clothes, decent stuff, you know, like the ones you wore when you *wrecked my chances with Blake.*"

"I said sorry," Chaz says, cringing. "And by the way, those clothes weren't mine. I borrowed them from my step-uncle Alfonso."

"Why didn't you just ask Alfonso if he wanted to sell?" Hanna asks. "They were nice enough to convince Blake you were dating Roxie, and she's a straight ten. They must've worked for you."

"No, I'm just hot."

"Chaz, shut up."

We ride for a while longer and hit the intersection. "Well, whatever," I say, spotting Bargain World up ahead. "If you want to be a rock god, you've got to dress the part, I suppose. Have you ever seen Van Halen rocking sweats?"

The light goes green. I can see the Bargain World sign, which is supposed to be lit up, but nobody ever turns it on. We cut through a battered flowerbed and roll into the parking lot, Chaz in the lead.

"And here we be," Chaz says, rolling up to the bike rack by the front door. He dismounts and takes a lock out of his coat pocket. "You two bring locks, you know, for your bikes and stuff?"

"No need."

With two forceful pedals, I fly through the automatic door, picking up speed as I go. An unshaven man in a shabby overcoat stares in wonder as I zip past, gliding around piles of household appliances and used furniture.

"What are you doing?" Chaz screams from somewhere behind me. "Get off the bike!"

"Did you not hear me?" I shout. "I said this would be a fast shopping trip."

Zooming past shelves lined with battered toys and ragged stuffed animals, I nearly level an antique dollhouse with my right axle peg while Chaz chugs behind me. I can hear Hanna saying something, but my mind is elsewhere. By now, I've heard two announcements over the loudspeaker that I'm guessing have to do with me, so I duck my head down and wheel my BMX over to the bike section, where I plan on hiding it among dozens of other, worse-for-wear bicycles.

"That was sick," I laugh, dusting myself off for effect. "Got my kicks for the day."

Chaz gapes at me in shock and shakes his head. Hanna appears moments later, laughing like crazy.

"Your best yet," she says. "Too bad we didn't get it on camera."

I look at Chaz. "If you want to hang, this is what goes down on any given day. Get with it or get off. Where's the men's section?"

"Try right behind you."

I whip around. Towering over me, a middle-aged man with pockmarked skin and a full handlebar mustache stares me down, his eyes like black holes. Cold sweat begins to gather at the edges of my hair, and reflux creeps into my throat.

"Think causing a ruckus is funny, do you?" Porn Stache's bulldog-ish face hovers in front of my eyes as he levels with me. Realizing I'm holding my breath, I inhale, only to have my nostrils violated by a putrid combination of cigarette smoke and beef stroganoff. Fear grips me. If this man takes me anywhere, I won't return alive. He reeks of rape. Even on his worst day, Chaz didn't come close to this level of sketchiness. We gotta get out, and fast.

"Oh my," Hanna sighs, shaking her blond curls and wringing her hands. "She's done it again. I'm so sorry, sir."

"Excuse me?" Porn Stache raises a furry eyebrow.

"Please, understand something," Hanna says, her voice full of anguish. "Gretchen suffers from CID."

Gretchen? Seriously?

"CI what now?"

"Compulsive Impulse Disorder," Hanna says, letting the lie roll off her tongue. She isn't exactly lying. I make stupid choices without thinking all the time. If CID exists, I probably have it.

"She can't control herself," Hanna continues, cradling her face in her hands. "Not even the strongest medication or exposure therapy can change her behavior."

"Let's dip," I whisper to Chaz. Fully focused on nonsense, Porn Stache has either forgotten I exist or decided he'll settle for dismembering Hanna. Slinking away, the two of us duck down amidst the shelves and scuttle into the men's clothing department.

"Are you nuts!?" Chaz demands. "What the hell was that? Why didn't you just lock up at the front? I had an extra lock I could've given you."

"It's not about the bike," I scoff. "Duh. Chester's boring. I need excitement. In just a few years, I can move to L.A. or Vegas or somewhere cool." I look at him. "Until then, this is how it goes. Don't like it? Hang out with Jenna or something."

"Okay," Chaz says, holding up a hand. "I get it. Next time, I'll invite a lawyer."

"Please do."

"You know, I've never actually heard of that," Porn Stache rumbles from afar. "CID or whatever."

"It's incredibly uncommon," Hanna replies. "You should see her at school. The staff doesn't know what to do with her anymore. After today, we'll probably send her to a facility."

"What did you say your name was, again?"

"Ramona. I'm Gretchen's mentor. Taking care of her, it's a school project. It's part of my elective for the Helping Hands program at Chester High."

Chaz turns to me. "Is that true?"

"No!" I grouch. "Go find yourself a two-dollar shirt and be done with it. We need to get out of here."

As fast as we can, Chaz and I comb through racks overflowing with used clothing. Most of them are atrocious. I wouldn't wear the nicest thing in this place to go mud wrestling in, but Chaz seems to have liked quite a few things so far.

"What about this?" He holds up a gigantic graphic hoodie adorned with rhinestones and beaded illustrations. Sweat stains visibly discolor the armpits. It reeks of marijuana and hangs defeatedly on a bent coat hanger.

"You said you wanted clothes. That's a boat cover," I say. "Get something that fits. You want to look your best, not like you've walked away from the shelter."

"True," Chaz says, tossing it aside. "It was stained too. I did kind of like it, though, even just for wearing around the house."

Shirts, shirts, shirts. Everything's hideous. By now, we've been at it for at least fifteen minutes and still haven't found anything wearable. I've lost Hanna and can only hope she hasn't been gagged and bound, if not already butchered.

"We got to leave," I say, the reality setting in. "Hanna could be in danger. Hurry up, pick something out, and let's go. We're going to the mall next, and I don't care if you don't want to. If you like something and it's too much, Hanna and I'll throw a little money your way. But we need to go. Now."

I walk a few paces before spotting a pair of straight leg, True Religion jeans hiding underneath a moth-eaten dinner jacket. They look a little tight, but I figure once Chaz starts exercising, he might be able to rock them.

"Like these?"

"I do. Am I not a little large?"

"You can lose weight. If you jog, it won't take more than a couple of weeks. Plus, these are like a hundred fifty in the store. Get them and let's go."

"Excuse me," an unfamiliar voice calls. "Uh, yo."

I figure whoever it is isn't talking to us, so I keep walking. Folding the jeans, I tuck them under my arm and start towards the register.

"Stop!"

The source of the outburst is a frothing, emaciated punk rocker who looks like he's about to die. Turning around and staring into his bloodshot eyes, I avert my gaze, only to see needle marks up and down his arms, which scares me, so I look back up at his face into a mouthful of rotting teeth. "Give them to me. Don't even think about taking them."

"Go!"

Jeans in hand, Chaz and I backpedal and begin running away from it.

"Stop running!" D.A.R.E screams. "Bitch, no."

I feel his rank breath on my neck, and my skin crawls. Forget Porn Stache. If that thing catches us, we'll be devoured before noon. Charging into the home goods section and winding through the displays, Chaz and I succeed in losing him.

"My God." Chaz shudders. "What a day."

I roll my eyes. "This was supposed to be relaxing."

"It is," Chaz says, balling his hands into fists. "Usually. It's Friday, though. Discount days always bring the crazies."

"Boy, did it."

Slinking back towards the bikes, I do a quick look around to see if Porn Stache is still posted and zero in on my BMX. Further up, near the end of the aisle, Hanna is still talking to Porn Stache while rolling back and forth on a beach cruiser with a wicker basket. Tweak the Freak is gone, at least for now, so we've got a little time to think this through.

"Okay," I whisper to Chaz. "Choose a bike. We're going to ride out and fast."

"My bike's still at the front."

"And it stays there. We'll come back for it tonight."

I can feel my heart beating in my mouth as Chaz and I inch towards the bikes. I reach mine first. Wrapping my fingers around the rubber grips of the handlebars, I climb onto the seat and place my left foot on the pedal. I look behind me and see Chaz perched on a battered ten-speed.

He gives me a nod. "Let's go."

I look up the aisle and cup my hands around my mouth. "Hanna! Ride!"

Wheeling around, Hanna pedals furiously towards Chaz and me. Making sure she's behind us, I give my own pedals a few strong pumps, and the three of us speed out of the aisle.

"Get back here!" Porn Stache yelps. "You punks are really in it now."

At the far end of the store, I can see the exit sign. By the checkout section, a crowd of red-shirted employees is clustered around the door, lying in wait. Hanna speeds up, passing my right, and Chaz flies up ahead of us, pedaling like Lance Armstrong towards the door.

Eighty feet. Seventy feet. "That fatass won't fit in those!"

Our daring doper is back, but I can't pinpoint his location. Granted, in his state, he won't be running much longer, and I'm finally in line for the exit when a blur of red flies out from nowhere. Trying an interception, Porn Stache reappears and hurls himself through the air like a missile at Hanna, who screams and swerves out of the way. With a thud, he hits the concrete floor of Bargain World and shrieks in pain. I try to maneuver around him but don't have enough time and instead run over him with my front tire. Another agonized groan and then the back tire. I can only hope he's got Medicare.

"Out of the way!" I yell at the gaggle of employees blocking the door. With my friends beside me, I rocket through the doors and into the parking lot. Once we reach the highway, I slow to a cruising speed when Chaz pumps his brakes.

"I forgot to pay!" Wheeling around, he faces Bargain World. "I have to go back."

"You want to go back!?" I gawk at him. "We stole jeans, got chased by GG Allin back from the dead, and ran over a possible pedophile. We will *never* go back there."

"I need to," Chaz says firmly. "Chaz Humbert does not steal. I've got to do this."

"There's a donation box at the front," Hanna reasons, her voice quivering slightly. "You can drop money in when we go back for the bikes."

"Yeah," I say quickly. "What she said. But if we don't get out of here, like, right now—we're all spending tonight in lockup."

Chapter 7

Monday goes smoothly. My first day back in actual school and so far, so good. Though I swear teachers are watching me closely in case I decide to release more X-rated imagery, my reception from the students has been nothing but positive. Though I nod and smile, I don't feel good about any of it. If things continue on this trajectory, Chaz is going to get hell when he comes back from suspension. Earlier, he sent me a text to check in on me, and I told him I was fine, though I didn't tell him about some of the comments I'd overheard. Of course, both Stephanie and CeCe wanted the entire thing in detail and wouldn't relent until I spilled.

"He was in the room. Like, the entire time?" Stephanie demands. "That's sick. You should totally sue the school. I know my parents would."

"It was stupid," I agree. "But he was fine. Seriously. Well, mostly."

"Really?" CeCe shakes her head. "You think he's done being a freak? He's still suspended, right?"

"Yup. Two more weeks."

Stephanie smirks. "Maybe Edgar's in there keeping him company. We haven't seen him around since."

I force a laugh. "Yeah, maybe."

"Did you ever get scared?" Stephanie asks. "Like, I know you could KO him, but still. I mean, we're girls."

"He was—is—creepy," I say. "But he's not dangerous or violent. I mean, the staff are dumb as hell for putting us in there together. But when I went to the principal's office, I talked a little bit. I talked about bullying and how we treat each other. Chaz seemed really moved by my speech. I think he finally realized what he was. He apologized to me, guys. He wants to change."

They crack up. "Yeah, I'm not falling for that," Stephanie says.

"Me either," CeCe chimes in. "A month ago, he tried to pay Erik and me two hundred dollars to make a sex tape. He's not any better."

Once school's out, Hanna and I slip to the back door of the office, where Chaz promised to meet us as soon as he got excused. After our disastrous stint at Bargain World, the three of us decided a follow-up trip was not in the cards. If Chaz is going to do this makeover thing right, he needs to be all in, and there's only one place around here to start that process. On the ride over, he keeps asking how the mood is out there, and I tell him it's fine, but somehow, I feel he knows the truth.

The bus shudders to a stop, and the three of us step off in front of Chester Plaza. Shoes caked in gravelly slush, we pass through the main door and wander into the galleria. I can't remember where Hot Topic is, and I'm too lazy to check the map.

"The map's literally right there," Hanna says, pointing ahead of me. "Take some initiative."

I make a face at her. "Chaz, anywhere else you wanted to see?"

He shrugs. "Not really. What's a store cool kids shop at?"

I spin slowly in a circle, trying to see if I can see any "cool" stores from where we're standing, but find something cooler: the churro cart. I fork over what remains of my bus fare for a foot-long, slightly crispy churro dusted with powdered sugar and cayenne pepper. The moment it reaches my hands, I sink my teeth into spicy, sugary goodness and taste the love.

The first bite goes down smoothly, but the second lodges in my throat. Edgar Yarbrough's standing by the south exit with a pair of kids I don't recognize. I walk a little closer to make sure my eyes aren't deceiving me, but there's no mistaking his bulging eyes and flaming red hair. I steal a look over at Hanna and Chaz, who are oblivious.

"Guys," I whisper, beckoning to them. "Come see this."

"What?" Chaz says. "Wait. Oh."

"Edgar?" Hanna says. "He's still around?"

"I guess so."

"What should we do?" Chaz asks. "I can't be seen talking to him."

"Chaz, don't be mean," Hanna scolds. "He's probably hurting, too. Just say hi and we'll go."

I glare at her. "Um, *no*. Do not take advice from Mother Teresa over here. Try to ignore him, but if he sees you, just nod and keep walking."

Chaz jams his hands into his pockets. "Okay."

The three of us try to slink by, but Edgar spots us. Flanked by a boy and a girl who look to be around our age, they are dressed identically in starched shirts and old-fashioned-style shoes with silver buckles. The girl's hair is plaited in two braids, and the boy's pants are held up by leather suspenders.

"Avoiding me?"

Edgar speaks. Who knew? Come to think of it, I've rarely ever heard his voice, other than the grunts and other strange sounds he used to make. Chaz must've understood his lingo, but now, something about him is different. Way different.

Chaz coughs. "I was suspended, remember? That's where I've been. And you?"

"I don't go to that school anymore," Edgar says frostily, his eyes drifting over us. "Life had other plans for me."

He nods to his companions. "After everything that happened, I had a vision. I saw the truth." Edgar looks Chaz in the eye. "What about you, Charles? Have you heard the good news?"

Chaz begins to say something, but Edgar cuts him off. "Our lust blinded us, Charles," he says, getting into his sermon. "We were punished with mockery and indignity. But it isn't too late. Come to Jesus, Chaz. Come to us."

"Praise him!" The boy bows his head while the girl turns to us.

"I'm Ruth," she says with a smile. "That's my brother, Nathaniel. Edgar has been called by God the Father to lead us and show us the way."

"We've got to go," I say, suddenly finding my voice. I take Chaz by the wrist to pull him away, but Edgar blocks our path.

"You made that photograph," he says, glaring at me. "But I care not. You are forgiven. But you know who is not? The *actual* men on that poster."

"Sodomites will burn!" Nathaniel shouts unexpectedly. Ruth nods, her braids bouncing.

"It isn't too late," Edgar continues. "But forsake temptation before God forsakes you." He glowers at Hanna and me. "Temptations."

"Temptations?" Hanna bursts out laughing. "I'm sorry, do you mean us? The girls you took pictures of in the locker room? Who you tried to grope while walking by? Did you take mushrooms before coming to the mall, Edgar, or are you that much of a dick?"

"Past life," Edgar says calmly. "I've been reborn."

"Guys," I say, turning to Ruth and Nathaniel. "Edgar's not a prophet. He's a predator. Back in school, he used to follow Hanna and me around, take pictures of random girls naked, and get sexually excited by his lunch. I'm pretty sure there's a video out there because he recorded it to get off to later." I snort. "It's been fun, Pastor Ed. Don't forget to rinse the apple pie crumbs off your junk."

"It's not too late," Edgar repeats, reddening in the face. He steps back and turns to his disciples. "Let's leave." Under his breath, he begins muttering something and speedily walks away from us, followed closely by Ruth and Nathaniel. We watch them turn the corner and disappear into the afternoon crowd.

"What an asshole," Chaz says, rolling his eyes. "Seriously?"

"Religion," Hanna sighs. "A great idea for awful people. My dad's now a licensed marriage counselor, in case you wondered."

"Hosanna," I mock, waving my hands in a crude impersonation of Edgar. "Hallelujah. Rosh Hashanah." I fall to the floor and fake a seizure. "Holy, holy. Save my soul. Deliver me into a vagina." Hanna and Chaz scream with laughter. "I wanted the Ten Commandments, not the *men* commandments."

"Roxie?" Nick looks down at me. "Everything okay?"

"What are you doing here?" I ask, rising to my feet and brushing mall dirt off my knees. "Shopping for your hot date?"

"Just passing through." He takes a sip of a fruit smoothie and stares down at his shoes.

"Nick," I say quietly. "Did Gabriella accept?"

"I don't know."

"What do you mean you don't know?"

He winces. "I didn't ask her out."

I look at him. "What?"

"I know, right? Pathetic! I totally froze. We were finished with class, and I was helping her carry books to her car, and I forgot what to do."

I put my arm around Nick, who sags a little bit and takes in a long pull of his drink. "It's okay, Nick," I say. "These things do happen. Try again next week."

"But wait a couple of days," Hanna puts in. "Don't be too available. No more favors or nice things unless she asks. Just be cool. Not cold. But a little detached."

"We're just here shopping for Chaz," I say. "Want to come along? You'll never guess who we ran into."

***

"Behold, Lot, Sodom is among us. But where's Gomorrah?"
Building on yesterday's biblical theme, Brennan hoots and points

at Chaz. Time might crawl when you're stuck in a room alone for hours, but outside of suspension, the weeks come and go at a rapid rate. Today is Chaz's first day back in the general population. And so far, it really isn't going great.

Everybody nearby laughs at Brennan's roast. A couple boys make fisting motions in Chaz's direction. Somebody swears at him.

"Probably getting lubed for lunch," Spencer replies, slapping Brennan on the back. "Penis butter and KY jelly sandwiches for the Chazster."

The two of them barge through the crowd and stand in front of us, cruel grins splayed across their blocky faces. Chaz stands like a statue and avoids eye contact, hands stuffed in the front pocket of his parka.

"Don't listen to them," I retort. "Announcements said wrestling got cancelled today. No nudity, singlets or skin-to-skin contact for Brenna and Sarah." I smirk and fold my arms. "Sexual frustration is real."

"Yo, fruit fly, why are you always around?" Spencer asks, raising an eyebrow. "You like him more than Edgar does. Too scared to hang with us real guys?"

I roll my eyes and flip him off. "Jump on a jock."

"Oh, man," Brennan grunts, fanning himself. "She's hot. Give me that dirty talk, honey. I'm pitching a big tent down here."

"*Ahem?*" Ms. Fink stops in front of us and clears her throat. "*What did I just hear?*"

Brennan stares at his sneakers. "Nothing."

"I better not hear anything of the sort again," Fink says sniffily. "I don't appreciate that kind of talk."

Out of ideas, all of us turn away and split off in separate directions. Chaz is silent.

"You okay?"

He sighs. "Yeah."

"I'm sorry, man."

"Thanks for standing up for me," Chaz says, the light gradually returning to his eyes. "It's not that I like being bullied, but sometimes I'm willing to take it just to hear your comebacks."

I laugh. "Yeah, that last one was pretty good, wasn't it?"

"Where did you learn to do that?"

"Do what?" I say. "Comebacks? School of hard knocks. Doctorate."

"It's so easy for you," Chaz says. "Seriously. Respect."

"I wasn't always good at it," I say. "People used to say stuff to me, and I'd take it. Or go home and cry later. One day, I just got sick of it, and the rest is history."

"Did you get nervous?" Chaz asks. "Like, about what they might say about you?"

"Used to," I reply. "Really, I don't care anymore. People can say whatever they want. If I hear them, it's go time, but hey, freedom of speech. But yeah, when I was younger."

"I'm still nervous." Chaz runs a hand through his hair. "This is only day one. What the hell is day two going to look like? And why do those guys have beef with me? I literally had never met them before all this."

"Because they're losers," I snort. "I mean, they're not good-looking. They're not smart. They're definitely not nice. They play a few sports and spend the rest of their time using steroids. The only power they're ever going to have, you know, in life, is here. At this high school. After this, it's all downhill for them."

"How do you know so much?" Chaz shakes his head. "You're a freaking encyclopedia. Why don't you just skip third period and go to Harvard?"

"I'm the second child," I say calmly. "Nick was life's crash test dummy for me. I don't know how he survived, but he did. And everything he told me I filed away. He's right about so much." I turn to Chaz. "Some things don't change. Year to year. Generation to generation. I've got you, though."

"You know, you say stuff like that, and I hate myself even more," Chaz says, staring down at his clasped hands. "For how I was. We could've been friends years ago, and I blew it." He shakes his head. "Does Hanna know?"

"Know what?"

"How desperate I am to make this right." Chaz rummages in his backpack. "Shit, I left my protractor in my locker. The bell's about to ring."

"Hanna's a saint," I say. "That girl is one hundred percent love. I'm pretty sure she knows how you feel. But the Gilberts are also Catholic. In that religion, you pay for your sins. And right now, buddy, you're smack dab in the middle of purgatory."

***

"So," Hanna says, licking the frosting off an Oreo. "What are we going to do about the cavemen?"

"The cavemen." I laugh. "Fred and Flintstone?"

Chaz smiles. "I see the resemblance."

For the first time ever, Hanna and I have invited Chaz to lunch. Back in the day, he used to show up unannounced and uninvited, usually to say something perverted, but other times he'd just skulk around. We got some looks walking in, but since Hanna and I know a lot of people, nobody says anything to us directly. Chaz dunks a carrot stick in a packet of ranch and crunches it with his teeth.

"Next steps," I say. "Ideas?"

"Toughen up," Chaz says immediately. "I look like a fat bitch. It's time to start boxing. Muay Thai style. Start kicking ass." He tenses his jaw and throws a combo into the air.

"No," I groan. "Don't go thug. Nick started that up when he was your age and—I don't know, it brings a certain type. And hint: they don't like gays." I shrug. "If you really do like boxing, do it for the sport. Do it for self-defense. But don't do it to be gangster."

"I didn't say gangster."

"You know what I mean."

"Why don't you just work on your comebacks?" Hanna asks.

"Because I'm a dude," Chaz says. "You and Roxie…you two can get away with a lot because you're pretty girls who are sort of popular. The worst any guy can do is say something back, but if a guy says that stuff to a dude bigger than him? That's disrespect. You can get punched. You can get beat down." He shakes his head. "And those two are huge."

"They're not going to hit you," I say, cracking open the seal on my SoBe. "You're a teacher's kid. They're not going to risk getting into that kind of trouble."

"Maybe." Chaz doesn't look convinced.

"What do you mean, maybe?" I say, studying his face.

"Well," Chaz begins. "Some people left me notes. Like, in my locker."

"When?" Hanna asks, sitting up straight. "What notes?"

"After the picture went around," Chaz replies. "They were pretty hateful. I ripped them up, but I read them all. Someone threatened to hurt me."

"Who would do that?" Hanna says, her voice rising. "What kind of coward leaves a note? At least threaten you face to face."

"I don't know," I say, my pulse quickening. "And I hope they never meet me in person. Get up, you two. There's someone Chaz needs to meet."

The three of us power walk out of the lunchroom and into the parking lot. I quickly scan the rows of cars, most of them beaters, before my eyes fall upon a waxed, shimmering 1964 Chevrolet Impala SS convertible.

"Is that—?"

"Yeah, he's here," I say, nodding at Hanna. "I don't have service out here, though. You?"

"Nope."

"Where are we going?" Chaz asks. "Did you guys buy me a car? Is Chad Michael Murray driving me?"

Hanna laughs. "Not quite. And if he's driving anybody, it'll be me."

"Okay, enough," I say, waving my hands impatiently. "He's usually here around this time."

"Who's not here? Who are we even looking for?" Chaz asks.

"The Swindler."

Birthname Emilio Sanchez, "The Swindler" is the go-to guy for us kids to get just about anything you *can't* find in stores. Want something on the fly? The Swindler's got it. Need something taken care of? He's on the job. Of course, nobody calls him The Swindler to his face, but Emilio's errands come at a pretty big markup, and this rubs a lot of people the wrong way. He's also unpredictable, angers easily, and even robs students who he thinks are snitches or aren't of decent repute. He's always been kind to me, though, and gives me significant discounts on food or drinks. Last year, when I tried to take up smoking, he refunded me after I couldn't get through a single Pall Mall, and he's been on my speed dial ever since.

Besides that, I really don't know much about him. From what I've heard, he's some kind of bookie and "picks winners," whatever that means. Anything coming and going out of the middle or high school has to be run by him, and he always gets his cut. The last time I saw him, he was complaining about local politics and passing a joint with Larry, the security chief. I'm pretty sure he's related to CeCe because they have the same last name and Chester's a small town, but I'm not certain.

"Why? You want Taco Bell before fifth period starts?" Hanna teases. "But seriously, I could go for a chalupa right now."

"No," I say. "I need to run something by him."

As we pass the bandshell on the way back to the main building, a door crashes open, and a couple of corn-fed boys stumble out. The reek of marijuana smoke and Hot Cheetos clinging to the fatter one makes my head spin, and I have to take a step back. The other one bends down to tie his shoe, takes it off, and begins walking semi-barefoot towards the baseball diamond.

"*Hola,* Roxie."

"Hey, Emilio," I greet as The Swindler steps out of the darkness. "Smoke break?"

"For them," The Swindler says. "Not me. They wanted to get stoned in a 'controlled environment.' They needed a guide, and I know the way."

I laugh. "You know it the best."

He nods. "Who's the new guy?"

"This is Chaz," I say. "A friend of ours."

Chaz extends a hand, and The Swindler takes it. He stares into Chaz's face for a second before the recognition hits. "Hold up. Are you that guy on the poster?"

"Yup." Chaz produces a pained smile. "Well, one of the guys."

The Swindler laughs out loud. "Hey man, I don't judge. Love is love. I've got a couple *Playgirls* on me right now. Take both for fifteen?"

"That's not what we came for," I say quickly. "Can we walk?"

"What are you doing hanging out with *him*?" Emilio whispers the second we're out of earshot. "Of course I know who that is. He's the chubby kid who bothers girls. He's some kind of sex freak. Why's he around you?"

"It's a long story," I say. "I kind of owe him." I blow out a breath. "I'm the one who made the poster."

"Holy shit! That was you?" Emilio cackles. "Damn, *mija,* that was dank. I couldn't stop laughing. I still have a couple copies I was going to retro before graduation."

"I wrecked his life," I say flatly. "I figured you'd get it, though. We kind of became friends while suspended, and, well, he's not going to be doing that anymore. Being creepy, I mean. Problem is, because of the, you know, poster and stuff, people think he's gay. Like, really gay."

The Swindler looks at me sideways. "Is he?"

"Not that I know of." I swallow hard. "He's been getting threats. He gets bullied badly. Do you have anything in case he gets jumped? Like, pepper spray or a stun gun, maybe?"

The Swindler rubs his chin. "Hm. Let me think. I don't know what's legal on campus. He could get busted for that."

"His mom's a teacher," I offer. "Part of the reason why he got away with so much for so long. Those days are over, though. So don't worry about that."

"Is he decent?"

"What do you mean?" I ask. "Like a good person?"

"Solid," The Swindler says. "Okay. Is he a stand-up guy? If he gets caught with whatever I outfit him with, is he going to snitch and get me run off campus?"

"Oh, hell no," I say. "Chaz isn't a rat. I'll put my name on it, *Don* Emilio."

"*Don* Emilio?" The Swindler laughs. "Are you buttering me up, *Señorita*?"

I smile. "Maybe."

"I'll see what I can do," he says finally. "I'll find you before the week's out. Give me some time. I'll make sure I've got something for him."

***

"Welcome to your very first lesson in baking with your esteemed instructor, Chef Nicholas Nazari. I hope you're as hungry to delve into this exciting class as I am."

"Get to the point," I call from my stool. "Just get to it, bro."

Nick folds his arms. "Do you want me to teach him or not?"

An obvious fan of food, Chaz wanted to try his hand at cooking, so naturally, Nick took the reins. The kitchen counter is lined with ingredients to make pound cake, and the oven's currently preheating.

"I do," I say. "And sorry to cramp your style, but we're running a tight ship here. Jerome wants to do a couple street performances over the weekend, and then he said something about the Cobra Cove."

Nick's wooden spoon falls from his hand. "No."

Last year, Nick's manager, who would later end up on the FBI's Ten Most Wanted list, booked him a slot at the Cobra Cove one Saturday night. A local punk hangout, the Cove is treated as a sort of a milestone for local artists. If you want to be anyone in the music scene around here, you must play it at least once. For his set, Nick was to play several rock arrangements, with a freestyle over some popular beats serving as the grand finale. From what he later told me, his accordion arrangement was only mildly hated, but the second he started rapping, the audience began throwing things. No later than the second verse, Nick had been dragged offstage, roughed up, and hung from the rafters by his sagging khakis while being pelted with garbage and cigarette butts. On the way out, somebody in a leather mask stabbed him with a frozen turd, and after that night, Nick hasn't performed anywhere since.

"Why are you doing this to me?" Nick chokes, his voice strangled by fear. "Why?"

"What's the big deal?" Chaz asks. "Did you get stage fright?"

Nick flails his arms. "Don't talk about it." He tears off his oven mitt and cracks an egg forcefully over the edge of the bowl.

"Nick's still traumatized from last year," I explain. "He had a really rough time at the Cobra Cove."

"Don't say the name!" Nick shrieks, whipping the ingredients as though possessed by demons. "Please, don't say the name."

"Exposure therapy," Chaz says. "Might help you." He walks over and stands next to Nick, who's now sifting flour over a bowl.

"No," Nick says, shaking his head. "Absolutely not. I'm not going there, and neither should you, given you've only been playing for a week."

"It's been a couple weeks actually," Chaz replies. "And I'm not afraid of whatever's in there. We need a keyboard player. The first person they'll lynch will be the stool pusher who sucks at the drums. You'll be safe."

Nick chuckles. "So you think I'll be able to escape?"

"That's not the point," I break in. "Chaz is offering to take a bullet for you. Or a pitchfork. That's a fair deal, don't you think?"

Nick shrugs. "I guess."

"Plus, you won't even get a slot until months from now," I say. "By that time, everybody will have forgotten about your performance last year. They probably forgot it on the way out."

"I don't know," Nick says. "We'll check it out closer to the time. But if I'm going, I'm wearing a disguise and using a fake name. If anybody in that crowd recognizes me…I'm a dead man."

An hour later, we have a full house. Jerome and Hanna have joined us, and the anxious mood of earlier has been replaced by one of laughter and ease. Since Dry Cucumber was formed, those two have been spending way more time together. Any day now, I figure Hanna will waltz in with a cubic zirconia engagement ring, but truthfully, I find myself becoming fond of Jerome. Yeah, he might be a little offbeat and more than a tad obsessed with Wet Banana, but he's grown up a lot and become a better friend to Hanna since their split. Still, there's no talk of them officially getting back together.

"What's good, homies?" Jerome whoops. After meeting Nick, he switched his punk-rocker style to more of a hip-hop look. Today, he's sporting a backwards cap, oversized jersey, and tennis chain from the mall jewelry kiosk.

"Nice bling," I laugh. "Did Nick give it to you or something?"

Jerome shakes his head. "Nah, this is mine. Straight pimpin'." He throws up the dub. "West Coast is the best coast."

"Hey, Jerome, pass me the baker's sugar, would you?"

Jerome slides a pink carton across the countertop towards Nick and leans close to Chaz.

"We need to rehearse more, you guys," he says. "The Cobra Cove is filling up for next summer, and I want in."

"About practicing," Nick says. "We need at least two hours a night."

"All the legends started out playing 'Da Cove,'" Jerome continues, addressing the group but looking at Hanna. "Wet Banana, Dying Mammoth, Hot Carl. Steamer to Cleveland."

For the next several moments, Jerome mentions scores of bands none of us, not even Nick, have ever heard of before reaching the pinnacle of his speech.

"It's ours, boys," he declares, standing on his chair and holding his hands to the ceiling. "The age of Dry Cucumber has begun!"

"Dude," Nick says wearily, pushing his hair out of his eyes. "Freaking stop. You think we're talented? You think we've had a single good rehearsal?"

Jerome tenses. "Yeah. I would say so."

"Well, we haven't. At least you haven't. You just scream into the mic." Nick sighs. "I've tried to be supportive, but I can't lie anymore. You don't have what it takes, dawg."

Hanna and I exchange shocked glances. Nick has never acted like this, toward us or anybody else. Concerned, I open my mouth to say something, but Jerome beats me to it.

"*I* don't have what it takes? *You* don't even leave the house. I put this whole shebang together. It was my idea, so I call the shots. Got it?"

Nick snorts. "Seriously? You think I'm going to take this from you? Tell me one thing about music theory and I'll shut up."

Several seconds pass in silence. "Yeah. That's what I thought." Nick laughs scornfully. "You're obsessed with music, yet you don't know the first thing about it. And 'Da Cove?' You couldn't find it on a map, bud. Stop frontin'."

"You know what?" Jerome says, his face purple. "I might've put this together, but really, you would have been in charge. Chaz and I would listen to you because you're older and would mentor and lead us. But now I know the truth. You don't have a job. You aren't a musician, either. You're single and probably still a virgin."

Nick bristles, and Jerome smiles smugly. "You know what you are, Nick? What you really are? You're a big, unemployed man-douche who will never get laid or move out of his mom's basement."

"Okay," I cut in, holding up my hands. "Enough is enough. Is that it? Is everybody done now? Can we have a civilized conversation?"

"Telling it how it is." Nick chuckles through his pain. "I respect that. I am unemployed. I haven't left the house since yesterday, and some people might describe me as weird. I get it." He pauses. "But let's look at you, sport. Let's look at your life. You recruited me into a band you invented on the spot as a tribute to a phallocentric musical group nobody's heard of. Note: phallocentric. I mean, you're trying to climb onto Wet Banana more than Chaz is, and he's the gay one. Don't leave Hanna hanging, son. Dismount the plantain penis and grow the hell up yourself."

I let out a snort before I can help it, and Jerome glares at me. "Is there a double meaning there, Nick?"

Nick shrugs. "Interpret it however you want."

The two of them stare each other down before Nick turns to go. "I'm out. Later, bitch." He grabs his crotch at Jerome and strides out of the kitchen, muttering under his breath.

"Don't come to rehearsal tonight!" Jerome yells after him. "You're fired."

***

The weekend drags. Without the group intact, the mood has taken a hit big time. Though Nick and Jerome are cool with everybody but each other, it isn't the same. We had something good going, and Chaz was fitting into it perfectly. As Hanna tells it, Jerome was deeply upset by the incident and went off into the woods for a day to find himself after selling his drums at a loss.

Nick didn't fare any better. He tried to paint the conflict like it was no big deal, but I know him better than that, and it's eating at him. He hasn't touched the oven, which is troubling because Nick doesn't go more than a day without baking himself a batch of low-carb cupcakes. Most weekends, he's either binging *South Park* or trying to meet girls at the Roll & Bowl, but today, he's spent all morning reading the *Encyclopedia Britannica* and asking Gabriella out in front of the mirror in the hallway.

Even stranger than that was the text I received from Cynthia late last night after Nick and my mother went to bed. She asked if I could meet later today and, at the end of her text, explicitly asked me not to tell Hanna she reached out. I confirmed immediately, but something told me to save any questions I might have for this afternoon.

Nick's in the shower so I write a note, stick it to the fridge, and walk outside into the afternoon chill. Hanna's house is a few streets over, and I've walked back and forth from it so many times I could almost go there in my sleep. The Gilberts live in a cute, two-story yellow bungalow with a lush green lawn and immaculate flowerbeds. Unlike my house, the inside of Hanna's is spotless, and Cynthia refuses to do any of it. Instead, she enlists the services of gardeners and house cleaners, who are usually around every other day, while Hanna and her sisters manage the cooking. The only thing I've ever seen Cynthia cook was toast, and she burned it after dropping the coffee pot in the sink. The girls are fantastic cooks, though, on top of being great at everything else. Beautiful, capable, and kind, the Gilbert girls are loved across town and known everywhere. Cynthia, on the other hand, is a whole other story.

Walking up the driveway, I look to see if any of the lights are on. Though I knock, nobody comes to the door. I ring the doorbell and, when all else fails, turn the handle and invite myself in.

"I'm here," I announce to the empty house.

"Oh," Cynthia calls from somewhere up above. "I'll be right down, hon. Give me a second, would you?"

I take my shoes off and slide them under the small red bench next to the front door. A couple of new paintings have been put up, and the piano looks shinier than it did last week, but everything's more or less the same. I stop and smile at the picture of first-grade Hanna in her soccer uniform before wandering into the sitting room. I hear the rubber slap of bedroom slippers coming down the stairs and look to see Cynthia descending in a velour tracksuit and holding a fluted glass.

"Hey, girl. Go ahead and take a seat at the bar." She nods towards the mini bar in the corner. "Just got out of the bath. Rose hips and lavender." She sighs. "Not that my life is hard or anything, but it is."

"You wouldn't know by looking at you," I say. "How're things?"

"Oh, you're such a dear." Cynthia smiles. "It's fine. It is what it is. Hey, listen, just curious. What've you been up to? I barely see you anymore. And Chaz! How's Chaz fitting into things?"

"Everything's fine," I say, a little taken aback. Cynthia's not acting like herself at all. "We're all okay."

"Cool, cool. I've just been spending Warren's alimony checks and watching that new series. What's it called? The one with the transvestite fashion designers?"

"Not sure," I reply. "I haven't been watching much TV. What's up, Cynthia? Why did you decide to reach out? Is Hanna okay?"

"Hanna's fine," Cynthia says brusquely. "Sorry if I worried you. She's great. I mean, as far as I know. She seems really grounded."

"She is," I agree. "I mean, she's always been."

Cynthia reclines in her chair. "Is Jerome still dating my daughter?"

I laugh. "So that's it? That's what you wanted to talk about?"

She finishes the last of her drink. "Yeah. Are they back together?"

"No," I say slowly, trying to gauge her reaction. "Not officially, anyway. They hang out a lot, but it's kind of like ever since Chaz came into the group, Jerome also came back in because we asked him."

"Thank God," Cynthia interrupts. "Oh, thank heaven. Now we're getting somewhere."

I chuckle uneasily. "Uh, where are we getting?"

Cynthia stops. "You want a drink, honey?"

"I'm good," I say.

"No, not that type of drink," Cynthia says hurriedly. "Sprite? Fanta? Dr. Pepper? The fridge is stocked with that shit, and I can't stand any of it."

"I'll have a Coke," I say. "Mexican, if you've got it."

"Done." Rising from her seat, Cynthia flies behind the counter and gets to work procuring us drinks. She pops the top on a small bottle and drops ice into a tall glass before pouring the Coke. Right before she slides it over to me, she takes a detour and whips out a flask, liberally adding some dark liquid to the fizzing soda. She winks at me. "Oops."

I politely accept my spiked cola. "Thanks."

"And a dirty martini for the tramp," she says, reaching for a jar of olives. "Got to start the conversation somehow. I don't know how I'd do it otherwise." She stops. "This is going to sound really bad."

Cynthia empties a tumbler into a martini glass and slides it across the counter before coming around and rejoining me at the bar. "You know how much I love you," she says. "I'm basically a mother to four daughters, and I hope we'll always be that way. But what I'm going to talk to you about today—it can't leave this table."

"Cynthia," I say slowly. "Is. Everything. Okay?"

"Everything's great!" she says shrilly. "Hanna's dating life is about to begin. For real this time." She pauses. "There's a new boy in town, and he lives in our neighborhood. A few doors down from us. The green house with the beige trim? You know the one?"

"Yeah," I say quizzically.

"I saw him last Wednesday. Hot damn. Let me tell you, if I were a couple of decades younger, I'd have ditched the ten-speed and ridden him instead! Cross country, no less."

"Uh, wow," I say, uncomfortable with the mental image of Cynthia riding someone.

"I'm telling you the kid's a *hunk*. I introduced myself to his mother, and eventually, we got to talking like old friends. Nice family. The boy's name is Owen. He's, like, I don't know, six foot one." She sighs dreamily. "Looks like he's straight off the Disney Channel. They moved up from Santa Barbara over break, and he's transferring in as a junior at the high school."

"What does all this have to do with Jerome and Hanna?" I ask dumbly, even though I already know the answer.

Cynthia grins. "Just hold on. What I'm saying is Brooke and Kelsey are both thriving in college, dating amazing guys. We had them both over for dinner last weekend, and Hanna loved them. Both are on the debate team. All-American wrestlers. The taller one's pre-med; I think he's with Kelsey. It's a perfect match. But Hanna? Dating Jerome. *Jerome!* Eek!"

"They're technically not dating," I remind her.

"You're Hanna's bestie," she says, disregarding me. "I'm her mom. We both know her and know what she needs. Between the two of us working our magic, getting Hanna and Owen to be Chester's new 'it' couple should be a cinch."

"I think we should stay out of it," I say firmly. "If Hanna's happy with Jerome, I think we should leave it alone."

"Whoa, girly, you said they weren't together."

I gnaw on my lip. "Yeah, they aren't."

"Then why did you just say she was happy with Jerome?" Cynthia stares at me intently.

I heave a sigh. "I don't know." I take a tiny sip of my rum and Coke. "My generation is complicated. Some people date. Others don't and hook up with their friends. Some are on again and off again. It depends. I'm almost positive they aren't together, but I don't actually know for sure."

Cynthia sits quietly for a moment, digesting this.

"You want to know why I'm so emphatic about this?" she asks finally, leaning closer to me. "It doesn't come from a superficial place. It's deeper than that, love. Growing up, I had *very* low self-esteem. My father didn't really know me, and my mother couldn't have cared less." She steals a glance at me, as though to make sure I'm expressing adequate sympathy. "So when I started dating, I never went out with the guys I actually liked. I jumped for the first boy who would pay attention to me. And with Hanna missing a father in her life…" She trails off and takes a messy sip of her drink. I stare at my hands, unsure of what to say.

"I'm just scared Hanna's headed down my path," Cynthia continues, wiping her mouth with her wrist. "That's all. What does she really have in common with Jerome? Does he even try to meet her halfway? Does he listen to her? How are they at all alike?"

She's got a point there. From the day they made it official in seventh grade, I'd find myself wondering constantly what Jerome and Hanna had in common. After a while, I just figured they were happy the way things were and left it at that. I never considered the possibility Hanna would have any self-esteem issues, but the more I listen to Cynthia, the more I realize there could easily be a side to her I don't know.

"I guess I'm trying to say that when I was her age, I would kill to date a guy like Owen, but wouldn't pursue him out of fear. Instead, I'd settle for a dependable doofus with a slew of other issues—a Jerome—and drunkenly hook up with an Owen at a party or on vacay. But you're right, Roxie. If Hanna's happy, I should be too. We all should be."

Cynthia tips back the remainder of her martini and stands up. "You might not get it for some time. Maybe not even until you have a girl of your own. You probably think I'm one of those parents who try to live vicariously through their kids."

"I don't think that," I say. "You're one of the coolest moms ever.

Hanna is the best person I know. Sometimes, I wonder what I did to deserve a best friend like her. And you raised her, Cynthia. You did."

"At least I did one thing right," Cynthia says, giving me a small smile. "And I know Hanna's got a good head on those shoulders. I just want her to be fulfilled. I just want to see her happy."

"She is happy," I say. "I mean, as happy as a ninth grader can be. School sucks, but we have each other."

"I worry how her childhood shaped her," Cynthia admits quietly. "When Warren left, she took it the hardest. She was so young! I tried my best to be a mother, as well as fill the gaps he left us with, but you can't have a united front when there's nobody to make a front with."

Hanna's dad has been out of the picture since she was nine, and she rarely talks about him. A few months after we became friends, Hanna confided in me that her parents separated after he'd gotten another woman pregnant. Though Cynthia jokes that his departure was the only thing he did right, she admits she was a wreck for years afterward. I get where she's coming from. At least, in a way.

"I know you're her mother," I say. "And moms worry. My mom worries about me when I'm asleep down the hall. But I talk to Hanna every day. She and I? We talk about things she probably wouldn't feel comfortable sharing with you. But she's a straight-A student, and she'll probably be varsity team captain by the time junior year comes around.

"Trust me," I say, looking Cynthia in the eye. "Hanna's okay."

***

It's been weeks since anyone's seen CeCe, and gossip is rampant. Some think she's pregnant. Others claim she got deported. In science, a kid asked Mr. Burke if she was dead. Having heard enough, I voice my fears to Hanna, who's equally concerned.

"Where could she go?" I ask. "Maybe she transferred. Moved? Is she sick?"

"I don't know," Hanna says, looking stricken. "She didn't say anything to any of us on the team. I mean, she's one of our better players. Coach Kristen is furious, but she doesn't know either."

"I haven't seen her in ages," I say. "But she did say something to me the Friday before my last week in detention. She mentioned she was really tired or couldn't play the game or something."

"Yeah." Hanna nods her head. "She kept having to take breaks during practice. She was slowing down and drinking tons of water. It was really weird, you know?"

"Is she sick?" I wonder aloud. "Like, really sick?" I look at Hanna anxiously. "I sure hope not. She's so nice."

"There could have been a family emergency," Hanna points out. "Here or back in Mexico. We really don't know."

The handful of other people I've asked have zero idea either, and the teachers wouldn't say anything even if they knew. In between periods, I find myself scanning the halls, looking for a cute girl with long black hair wearing colorful apparel, but there's no trace of her.

"Erik's missing too," Chaz observes, unwrapping his burrito. "I actually asked Jerome about him since they kind of know each other. He hasn't been seen around and doesn't answer texts or IMs."

"Something's not right," I say, popping a grape into my mouth. "I mean, both of them gone? It's just too weird."

Chaz nods in agreement and is reaching for a fork when something beans him in the back of the head.

"Ow!" he squeals. His exclamation is followed by an eruption of laughter from a nearby table where Brennan and Spencer are seated. Chaz rubs his head and bends down to retrieve what hit him. Grimacing, he drops a used tampon with an AA battery taped to it onto the floor.

"Put it up your poop chute, *puto*!" Victor Ruiz, another wrestling goon, shouts. The table cracks up, exchanging high fives and fist bumps. Enraged, I get up from my seat, and Hanna does the same, but Chaz pulls us down by our shirtsleeves.

"Don't bother," he whispers hoarsely. "I'm going to take this to the trash. Just let it slide."

"Bullshit." I pull up my right sleeve, pick up the battery, and hurl it hard as I can at the boys. It makes an arc before crashing down in the middle of their table, smack dab in Spencer's Caesar salad. Shrieking in disgust, the guys jump backward and scramble to get away from it. My friends look at me in admiration, and I stare down at the boys.

"Whose was it?" I demand. "Which mangina is on the rag this week? Brenna? Is it yours? You look like you'd have a heavy flow."

Brennan shakes his head. "Nope. Not mine. It said, 'return to sender.' If Trans Humbert keeps cramping, feed it Midol."

"God, those guys are dicks," I mutter, sitting back down. "That should hold them off. For a while, at least."

The three of us laugh together, but Chaz looks awestruck. He waits until I sit down before wrapping his arms around me. "I love you so much."

I feel a swell of emotion rise, but like every other emotion I've ever had, I bury it as quickly as it comes. I hug him back awkwardly. "Love you too, Chaz," I say. "But scoot over. I need to wash my hands. Badly."

***

"We need to take care of those douchebags," Hanna says as the three of us squeeze into a bus seat after school. "I'm serious. It's getting out of control. That tampon today? Revolting."

"It was," I agree. "I used the entire soap dispenser up to my elbows and still don't feel clean. I hope it wasn't Jenna's."

"Chaz," Hanna says, looking out the window as the bus starts to roll. "Don't get any ideas, and don't take this the wrong way, but what happened to the original Chaz? You know, the way you used to be?"

"He became a porn star and died." Chaz shrugs. "I mean, schoolwide humiliation and a month of suspension will do that to a person."

Hanna frowns. "So, it's over?"

"Um, yeah." Chaz looks at her in bewilderment. "Are you saying you want him back? You had him, nonstop, for years and hated every second of it. Now that he's gone, you want his return?"

"No!" Hanna says, shaking her head frantically. "No, bad idea. What I meant was you were awful but fearless. You said and did things most people couldn't dream of doing sober."

"You mean like webcam strip shows and offering Erik Samuels money to make a sex tape?" Chaz inquires. "It wasn't hard. Erik was willing. It was CeCe who vetoed it in the end."

"Yeah, I didn't need that bit of info," I say quickly. "Hanna, where are you going with this?"

"That Chaz was a disgusting predator, and I don't want him back around us ever," Hanna clarifies. "But sexual harassment? Awkwardness? Discomfort? There are some people I think who'd deserve that treatment."

I think for a moment. "Are you saying that should be his reply to Brennan and Spencer? Like a reboot of classic Chaz?"

"*Please* don't say 'Classic Chaz.'" Chaz cringes. "I'm trying very hard to erase that chapter."

"Well, we might need to open that chapter again," Hanna laughs. "At least for them. It's the only way I see you fighting back and getting them off you for good."

"So, you want me to resurrect the one-man show?" Chaz asks. "Back from retirement. Is this for one night only, or a residency?"

"It's just for Brennan and Spencer," I say. "Nobody else. Especially not any girls."

Chaz nods. "Okay. When do I start?"

"Tomorrow morning," I say. "The next time they say or do anything, out comes Classic Chaz. And we'll call it that, so you know to turn it off when the confrontation is over. Capisce?"

"It's risky," Chaz says. "What if I can't turn it off? What if I revert to that and can't stop? Oh, I hate to think."

"You'll know when to stop," I say. "What you had going…that shtick or whatever. It was a mask, right? If everything is as you told me, you were doing that because you were scared and afraid of being outed. It's not natural. Therefore, you only put it on when you have to. Right?"

A smile begins to tug at the corners of Chaz's mouth, and he nods slowly. "Yeah," he says. "I get it. I get where you two are going with this. What it is, is if Spencer or Brennan starts bothering me, I basically own it. I absorb the homophobia and go full homo…on them."

Hanna nods. "Exactly. What'll scare them worse than a flamer fighting back?"

Chaz cracks up. "Absolutely nothing."

"There it is," I say. "Hanna Gilbert, you really are a genius."

Hanna smiles. "Just did some thinking. You know, while everything was going down at lunch today."

"Well, if you want to give it a formula, a negative plus a negative equals a positive," Chaz says, his eyes glowing. "Let me see what I can do."

Chapter 8

By Wednesday, there's still no trace of CeCe, and all of us are worried. I swore I caught a glimpse of her walking out of French after third period, but I could be imagining things. Hanna and I are asking around, but as expected, nobody knows. Even Stephanie, who's got the skinny on everyone, hasn't seen her in weeks.

"I just don't get it," I say as Hanna and I get up to throw out our trash at lunch. "It's so weird."

"Doesn't make sense," Hanna agrees. "It wasn't like CeCe didn't have friends. Everyone on our team likes her well enough. Plus, she would hang out with her friend group or Erik's friends when she wasn't with us. None of them know where she is either. She didn't tell anybody where she went. She just disappeared."

"What about Erik?" I say. "That's what makes this whole thing whack. I mean, he plays tight end for the JV team. They're both gone. I really, really hope nothing happened to them."

The CeCe thing eats me up for more reasons than one. True, she and I weren't close, and we only know each other on a friendly basis, but she's always been really nice and just cute and cuddly in a way. Maybe it's because we kind of look alike, or because she also has a multicolor gel pen collection in her binder, but the longer she's gone, the more I want to keep her close by. Just to make sure she's okay.

"We should've talked to her more," Hanna says, reading my mind the way only she's able to do.

"I know," I agree, sighing. "We should've taken more of an interest in her instead of what we thought she did after school. I feel so guilty."

But then again, maybe everything's fine. If both of them are gone, and no announcements have been made at school regarding a disappearance or foul play, there's a good chance they got up and eloped like many star-crossed lovers before them. A happier image, this time of the two of them running through a marigold field holding hands, comes into my mind. I smile, hoping it's the truth.

"I have to use the bathroom," Hanna says. "You?"

"I gotta freshen up too," I say, suddenly feeling gross and unkempt. "I'll tag along."

While I'm washing my hands, I hear a faint wailing coming from somewhere further down. I turn off the water and nudge Hanna, who looks at me worriedly.

"Hanna. Listen! Jenna's auditioning for *American Idol!*"

"You're so insensitive." Hanna shakes her head. "High school's a really hard time for some girls. She's probably going through something."

I roll my eyes. "Yeah. Welcome to the club."

Losing a parent does something to you. Even now, I can't really describe it; I just know it as a feeling. It means coming home to a house that's never full, where there's always a vacant seat at the table. An empty parking space in the garage. Boxes full of his belongings in storage that nobody has the emotional bandwidth to sort through. There's a constant emptiness that can't be filled, no matter how hard you try and move on. Since his death, I've had a tough time relating to other people's pain or even recognizing it. Hanna understands, though. She lost her father too, but in a different way. Even if she's cut all contact with him, he's still out there somewhere, whereas I will never see mine again. In this life, anyway.

"I'm going to check it out," Hanna says, peering down the vacant corridor. "What if someone's injured?"

"Okay, let's do it," I relent. "But if it's Jenna, I call finishing her off."

The two of us trot down the hallway, picking up speed as the cries grow louder. As we pass different classrooms, I peek in, but all of them are dark and empty. The only door we haven't checked is the last one on the left. The weeping, now barely audible, has to be coming from there.

"Hello," Hanna calls out. "Can you hear me?"

"Are you okay?" I depress the handle and step carefully into the room.

"Do you need help?" Hanna asks loudly to the dark room.

"Keep it down," I hiss. "It could be a trap. Nick told me about this nutjob in Spokane who called out for help and stabbed the people who tried helping him. What if he's in there?"

"I doubt it," Hanna says, rolling her eyes. "That's messed up. But nobody's going to do that here."

"Still," I say. "I'm not taking any chances. Danger lurks in unexpected places. Remember our stint at Bargain World?"

"Go away."

Hanna and I stumble back and flatten ourselves against the wall. Neither of us moves. Finally, I venture forward a couple of inches and look for the source of the voice.

"Who's there?"

A shuffling noise grabs my attention, and I spin around to see a figure huddled underneath a shelf wearing gray sweats and Reeboks with candy-colored laces.

"CeCe?" I whisper. "Is that you?"

The sniffling ceases. "Please leave me alone. Just go." She pauses. "Who is it?"

"It's us," Hanna leaps in. "Hanna and Roxie. Where were you? A lot of people are really worried about you right now."

CeCe snorts. "Right. What jokes were they making this week?"

"Well." I shrug. "Nothing really. Except for one asshole who said—"

"Nothing," Hanna interrupts, elbowing me. "Nobody's saying anything. They're just wondering where you are. We've missed you at practice. Coach asked around, but nobody knew."

CeCe doesn't reply and curls into an even smaller ball than before.

"Please," I plead. "Come on. Just get out from under there so we can see you. I was scared. Hanna was too. This is a small town; people don't just disappear. You don't have to tell us anything you don't want to. Just let me see your face."

CeCe obliges and slides out from under the shelf. Her eyes have heavy bags underneath, and she's a little rounder in the face, but she still looks pretty. I make a point to tell her this at some point.

"Look," I say quietly. "I'm not going to lie to you, okay? People are talking. Some rumors are going around. But they aren't nasty rumors, really. People are just concerned. But let me say this. Hanna and me? We don't tell secrets. To anyone. We don't stand to gain anything from knowing where you've been, or where you've gone, or anything like that. I hate drama. God knows we have enough of it these days. But whatever's going on, it's eating you up in front of me, girl."

CeCe plays absently with her shoelace. "I don't want to talk about it here," she says finally. "Not at school."

"Okay then. Time to ditch." I rummage in my backpack and pull out a roll of hall passes I cribbed from Ms. Fink's desk drawer. "We're covered. Let's get a smoothie."

Hanna opens her mouth to protest, but I hold up a hand. "No objections. You're coming."

***

"Few situations can't be improved by a tropical blend of fruit and ice," I say to CeCe, doling out our drinks. "My favorite? Magic Mango or the Berry Burst. Sometimes, I even order both. Isn't that right?"

"Yup," Hanna says flatly, unwrapping her straw. I know she's pissed that I made her skip fifth, but what choice did we have? CeCe clearly is in the throes of crisis. I pop my straw into my smoothie and pull a long sip.

"So," I say, glancing around the shop to make sure nobody's around. "Now that we're here, what did you want to tell us?"

Drawing a swirl absently on the cup's condensation, CeCe knits her brow. "You absolutely promise to keep it a secret?"

I hold out my pinkie, and she locks hers with mine. "On my life."

CeCe exhales and meets my gaze. "I'm pregnant."

I gasp. Looking at Hanna, she's equally surprised. I don't know why either of us is shocked, though. The rumors had to begin somewhere, and the longer time went on, I suspected she was in a bit of trouble. Around here, it isn't totally unheard of for girls to get pregnant in high school, but usually, they're at least juniors or seniors. I can't even conceive of someone my age getting pregnant or giving birth. And given the physical appearance of most boys at the high school, the thought of being intimate with them is horrific.

"Of course, it won't be a secret for long," CeCe says. Her lower lip wobbles. "I already look five hundred pounds. It's expected of Mexican girls. I'm basically a walking stereotype."

"That's not true," Hanna cuts in. "You don't look five hundred pounds. Not even close. I mean, yes, stereotypes exist. But most people will respect you for being brave, regardless of what decision you make."

What Hanna's saying is a load, but I'm not going to contradict her. In the jungle that is high school, CeCe will be shunned, judged, and maybe even bullied. Most kids aren't mature enough to realize she's more grown up than they'll ever be. Instead, it'll just be harder for her than it already is for the rest of us, and all of us know it.

"Where's Erik in all this?" I ask, the shock beginning to wear off.

The color drains from CeCe's face. "Gone."

I reel back. "*Gone?*"

"Well, where is he?" Hanna demands, a hard edge creeping into her voice.

"After I told him," CeCe begins, "he took it really well. He told me his parents would support us. They're pretty rich at least." She takes a sip of her smoothie and dabs at the corner of her eyes. "He gave me a kiss on the forehead, like he always did, and said goodbye. I didn't realize he meant forever."

Hanna's nostrils flare. "You're joking."

CeCe shakes her head. "He wouldn't answer my texts. Or phone calls. Finally, I went to his house and rang the bell. Nobody answered. I sat on the porch for five hours." Unable to go on, she breaks into fresh tears. Behind the counter, the wiry doofus who rang us up gawks at us, his mouth slightly ajar. I roll my eyes and shoot him a withering glare while Hanna reaches across the table and takes CeCe's hand.

"He must have blocked my number. But that wasn't it. He also quit football and left school. I haven't seen him again."

"That fucker," Hanna mutters, her eyes blazing. "Do you know where he might've gone? Where he could be now?"

CeCe practically spits on the table. "I know exactly where he is."

Private, Christian, and exclusively male, Elderwood College Preparatory is a school for tools. Open only to the wealthy and gifted, the students are better known for promiscuity and drug abuse than any academic achievements, but you only know that if you're local. Last spring, Nick and I witnessed this firsthand when we cruised by the Gunderson mansion one Friday night and saw a naked basketball game in full swing, as well as what Nick suspected to be a jerk circle on the sidelines. Fascinated, we parked a few hundred yards up the road and crept along the fence, trying to see more of how Chester's upper crust lives. Though we didn't see much, the shaman, sconces, and ten-foot-tall owl carving were enough to send us running back to the car.

Nick applied to Elderwood after almost flunking the tenth grade. Mom thought it might be a fit, given Nick doesn't do well in conventional learning environments. She hoped his musical training might qualify him for a scholarship. Despite this, he didn't get in. According to the admissions office, we made too much money to be eligible for any financial aid, but I think the fact Nick wore a do-rag to his campus visit was the deciding factor. Personally, I was relieved. Elderwood would've ruined him. Plus, being a boarding school and everything, Mom and I would hardly ever see him. Nick is too much of a free spirit for that kind of place, and he's the last person I can see attending black-tie dinners or schmoozing with alumni. I also don't want him playing basketball naked. Ever.

"So, Elderwood," I say, chewing my straw. "That freak show?"

CeCe smirks. "Yeah. Figures, huh?"

"Have you told your parents yet?" Hanna asks gently. "Do they know anything?"

"No," CeCe replies. "I've kept it a secret from everybody. They'll find out soon, though." She sighs. "They'll be so disappointed. I know they had high hopes for me."

"How far along are you?" I ask, changing the subject.

"Four months, I think. Maybe more."

"You need to tell them," Hanna says softly. "You need to let your parents know sooner rather than later. Otherwise, they'll be a lot angrier, especially if the news comes from somewhere else."

"I don't know how they're going to take it," CeCe says, fidgeting in her chair. "What if they disown me? Kick me out of the house?"

My mouth falls open. "Would they seriously do that?"

"They won't throw you out, CeCe," Hanna assures her, grinding the heel of her boot into my foot under the table. "Parents love their kids no matter what. And, yeah, they'll probably be upset and yell and cry when you tell them. But they'll get over it and learn to love the baby too."

"They'll respect you for being mature and owning up to your responsibility," I say. "I know I do. And there are others. There are people who will help you along the way. Like Hanna and me." I nod. "We aren't going anywhere."

"I'm so alone, though," CeCe chokes. "With Erik gone. I'll be a single mom as a sophomore. How will I support us?"

"Erik's a bitch," Hanna snaps. "I mean, he doesn't deserve you. He sucks." She lays her hand on CeCe's. "Once that baby is born, and he sees what could have been…you can tell him whatever you want, okay?"

CeCe nods. "Okay."

I feel suddenly woozy, like the ground's shifting underneath my feet. I flash back to Blake and me on Tristan's porch, having a laugh and getting to know each other. I think about the prank calls that Hanna, Nick, and I've done over the years. I recall dodging security at Bargain World and riding out triumphantly with Hanna and Chaz on both sides of me. Going to the mall with Hanna and her sisters or egging Jenna's house with Hanna as my spotter. Hundreds of memories, thousands of hours flash in front of my eyes like a slideshow. And then I realize I'm still a kid whose biggest concern right now is handling Brennan and Spencer or passing English Lit. I'll go home tonight, and the most pressing question will be what Nick cooked for dinner, or if I've got enough time to join him and Frankie for a round of *Super Smash Bros* after dessert. Growing up, I'd hear stories of people my age or a little older in pressing situations or see movies and TV shows about teen pregnancy, or drug abuse, or gang violence. But it was so far away it never seemed like a real possibility. Now, something major has happened to somebody I know, which puts a face on it and finally forces it to sink in. I might be tough and be able to take down bullies with a sharp tongue and a sweep of the leg, but when it comes down to it, I'm still just a kid. With just one misstep, CeCe is being forced to enter adulthood.

***

"I feel so lame!" Nick sobs, burying his face in a couch cushion. "I got dissed by a prepubescent fifteen-year-old whose balls probably haven't even dropped! In front of everyone. That's the definition of failure!"

"Well," I begin, approaching him cautiously. "Jerome's not a person whose opinion you should consider. He spends his life tracking down a band no one's heard about. That's what failure really looks like."

Nick sniffles. "I can't believe he said that. 'Big, unemployed man-douche.' That little shit really knew it'd sting."

"Exactly! The delivery was too smooth. It had to have been rehearsed. I bet you anything he practiced that insult in front of the mirror for years and finally got to drop it. Or he read it on the internet. Jerome isn't smart or creative, Nick. I've known him for years."

I lay down beside my despondent brother. "Why don't you bake some brownies?" I suggest. "Or work on that comic you were drawing? It might make you feel a little better."

"No." Nick shakes his head. "I need to man up. Or at least boy up and prove I'm not a giant loser. If I had a job, a girl, and a future, I would get mad respect instead of this—I don't know—this HELL!" He punches the cushion and chucks it across the room. "I hate my life!"

"Whoa, bro," I say gently. "What's gotten into you? Why do you care what people think? Anybody who matters thinks you're great. Everybody I know loves you."

"I don't have friends," Nick moans, shaking his head. "I'm hated."

"Enough," I snap. "People *do* like you. Maybe if you left the house and got involved in stuff, instead of going to community college for, like, two hours a week, you'd make some new friends. You can't do it if you're cooped up in the house all day long. Plus, you know a ton of people. Remember Tristan's party? You couldn't go two feet without somebody shouting your name."

"I guess." Nick sits up. "But think about it. If I'd gotten that deal with the polka label, or if I'd aced my performance at the Cobra

Cove, I'd be on a way different path than I am now. Colleges would be recruiting me, or I'd be on the road. I could've had it all."

"Or the tour bus might've crashed, sending you flying out the window." I shrug. "You might've gotten hooked on heroin. Got an STD from a wild groupie. Sexually abused by the dancing polka bear. No path is the easy path."

Nick nods. "Good point. And I'll never look at dancing bears the same." He laughs. "The only thing I want, though, is for people to take me seriously. I'm sick of being the town fool."

"Who's laughing at you? There's nobody here! It's literally you and me in the house right now."

"You know what I mean," Nick mopes. "I'm just saying, maybe it's time to rein it in a little bit. Grow up. What I wanted last year...I don't want that anymore. I want to study harder and get good grades. Maybe have a girlfriend. Be that guy everybody looks at and says, 'Yeah, that's him. The guy who's going places.' Not some local underachiever everybody thought was destined for greatness who ends up as a greeter at Target."

Nick exhales. "I have to be realistic. Have I got what it takes? Nobody's going to listen to my music anyway, and even if they do, there's probably an Asian preschooler who's ten times better than me. It's a dream, and that's it. It's just a dream."

"I don't know," I say, wrinkling my nose. "It sounds like you're selling out. Big time. Talent isn't the problem. You just need some drive and discipline. Direction is what you need."

"I just want to prove my haters wrong," Nick says, like he's an up-and-coming hip-hop artist. "Show them I can be someone."

"I can't believe this all started because of stupid Jerome." I shake my head. "Please consider the source. He's annoying and over-vaccinated, which is probably why he's a freak. Forget him and get back to the grind. And make brownies tonight. I've got a craving."

Nick waves a hand. "Forget it," he says. "I'm moving on with my life. Growing up begins now."

***

With a closeted gay BFF, a pregnant teenager, and a man-child determined to grow up on my hands, I'm everywhere at once. On top of that, Cynthia's been riding me about Hanna and Jerome nonstop. Though I've ignored most of her calls, I'll have to get back to her eventually, and I'm dreading it. For a while, I predicted Jerome and Hanna would get back together and even supported it. But after his spat with Nick, Jerome got on my nerves in a bad way. No longer the fun-loving older brother, Nick now spends all his time in the library or adding more online classes to his already-packed schedule. If he's not at the gym, he's applying for jobs and, last I checked, wants to be a barista at Covington so he can be around Gabriella more.

I'm not naïve. I mean, I know Nick started the fight, but Jerome swung too hard and knew what he was doing. Neither Chaz nor Jerome can really play an instrument, and without Nick, Dry Cucumber is just a withered gherkin and shouldn't be heard by the deaf. All this is making my head swim, so I try to divert my thoughts. Tired of being the only one juggling everybody else's issues, I pick up the phone and dial Chaz.

"Hello?"

A woman's voice answers, and it's kind of familiar. I'm guessing it's Mrs. Humbert, and a jolt of fear goes through me.

"Hi, is this Chaz's house?" I dialed his cell. Why is she picking up?

"May I ask who's calling?"

"Roxie," I say. "I'm a friend of his."

"Just a moment. He's about to go into the shower. Chaz!" Mrs. Humbert shouts up the stairs, and Chaz comes on moments later.

"Hey, Roxie," Chaz says. "What's up? Happy Saturday."

"You too," I say. "What's going on?"

"Eh, nothing. Just got out of the shower. Jerome and I were supposed to have band practice tonight, but he bailed to go to GameStop. Plus, Dry Cucumber isn't the same without Nick. We suck."

"Yeah, I guess it wasn't meant to be," I say. "Kind of like a breakup. I'm glad it happened, but it doesn't make it any easier."

Chaz laughs. "Jerome keeps saying we don't need him and that Dry Cucumber's going to get a Grammy nod by next year. I don't see it happening, but, hey, you never know."

"Yeah," I say, unsure of where this conversation is going. "I guess."

"Is Hanna with you?"

"No, she's at a soccer tournament. Nick's at Covington, and I'm stuck in my house. It ain't much of a day so far."

"Well, hey," Chaz says. "Let's be bored together. I'm not doing anything either." He pauses. "Come on over."

***

Thinking back, it's strange I know where Chaz lives. I've prank-called the Humberts more times than I care to count, and Stephanie and I put a firecracker in their mailbox last Fourth of July, but that's about as close as we dared to venture. As I turn onto his street, I spot the house and ride up to the garage door. There's nowhere really to rest my bike up against, so I lift it by the frame and dump it off in a parched flowerbed before ringing the bell.

I hope Chaz answers. I don't want to run into Mrs. Humbert, and if Chaz's dad is anything like Chaz pre-suspension, I'm running for the hills. Nobody answers, so I ring again. The door swings open, and a rotund woman with bobbed hair stands in front of me. Nose in the air, her other mitt-like hand is crammed into the front pocket of her housecoat. Heaving a leg forward, she grimaces and meets my gaze.

"Can I help you?"

"Hi," I say as warmly as I can manage. "Is Chaz home?"

"Oh," she says. "Roxie. Come on in. I've heard so much about you. There are some things we need to discuss."

"Uh, great." Well, this is *not* going according to plan. I step into the darkness of the house and look up at a couple of dusty photographs by the front. I really don't want to look anywhere else.

"I know you think because you two are friends now that everything's good," Mrs. Humbert says coldly. "But I happen to be an involved parent. When you walk into the school one morning and see pictures of your son naked on top of another classmate…it isn't something you forget easily. And neither did the students. Weeks on weeks of relentless bullying, and I thank God he's still alive." She glares at me. "Chaz is a lot more forgiving than I am."

"Hey," I say. "Look. I'm not proud of it. Not one bit. But I did my time. So did he. Which reminds me. He was suspended a lot longer than I was, and I'm sure you know why?" I stare at her, but her expression is unreadable. "You should be glad we're friends now. Otherwise, he might be on a registry." I smirk. "Unless you have friends in the police department too, he'd be wearing an ankle monitor."

Mrs. Humbert gasps. "Oh, you watch it, young lady!"

"Or what?" On the ride over, I expected some awkwardness, or maybe a cold shoulder from Chaz's mother, but this is outrageous. Even though Chaz and I have buried the hatchet, there was a lot leading up to that. I'm not backing down, least of all from her. "You got something else you want to say?"

The two of us stare daggers at each other. Finally, I take a breath and think about what I'm going to say next. Somebody's got to be the bigger person here. And even though Mrs. Humbert dwarfs me in mass, it's unlikely it'll be her based on her earlier behavior.

"I'm not proud of what I did," I sigh. "But life has a way of evening the score and righting the wrongs. If none of that happened, I wouldn't be on my way upstairs to meet somebody I consider a good friend. As far as what happened before, that's in the past. We worked our differences out. And I think we both got what we deserved."

Mrs. Humbert gives me a thin smile, but her eyes seem a bit softer than when I first came in.

"I know," she says gruffly. "You're not lying. I can see you mean what you said. I'm glad you two worked it out. Chaz thinks very highly of you. He hasn't stopped talking about you since he was suspended."

I nod stiffly. "The feeling's mutual."

"Well then," she says. "I'm sure he's out of the shower by now. At least somebody's getting him to be social. Otherwise, he'd be holed up in his room the entire weekend." She turns to face upstairs. "Chaz," she bellows up the staircase. "You have a visitor."

"Don't laugh," Chaz mumbles as I step into his room. I wasn't planning on it, but one glance makes it impossible not to. Swimsuit models beckon from every wall, while diecast cars and sports memorabilia line the shelves. A trashcan decorated to look like a keg of Budweiser stands in the corner, while a Tampa Bay Buccaneers laundry basket sits by his desk. Above the bed, a shiny coach gun is mounted next to an autographed picture of Ric Flair, greased up and beaming. Already, I know it's the one thing Chaz won't throw away when he finally comes out.

"Miss Universe, huh?" I glance down at the desk calendar.

"That's her," Chaz snorts. "Too bad it wasn't Mr. Universe!" He pushes his hair out of his face and stretches his legs. "Channing Tatum would've been okay, too."

"Your mom isn't too happy I'm here," I remark, sitting down on the floor and laying my back against the wall. "I got an earful while you were still in the shower."

"Sorry." Chaz rubs his temples. "She knows way more than she lets on. I guess news travels. I didn't tell her anything, but you know, her being a teacher and all…" He trails off.

I'm about to reply when I'm interrupted by heavy footfalls approaching. The door swings open, and Beowulf stands in the doorway, a beer in one hand and a TV remote in the other.

"Chaz, your mom told me to take out the trash, but I'm not missing the game, so it's on you, pal." Beo takes a swig. "You're missing all the action up here. The Giants are kicking ass." He takes another sip and wipes the foam with the back of his hand.

"I'm a little busy, Dad," Chaz mutters, cocking his head in my direction.

The man's face, which is tanned and pleasantly lined, looks at us with confusion. "Whatcha mean, son?"

"Hi," I say, stepping forward. "I'm Roxie. Nice to meet you, Mr. Humbert."

His face changes in a millisecond and breaks out in a huge smile. "Well, hello there yourself," he beams in a rich drawl. He refocuses on Chaz. "You never told me."

Chaz frowns. "Told you what?"

"That you had a *lady*. And a fine one at that." Chaz's dad stands to his full height and gives me another enormous smile.

"Oh, no, we're not dating," I say quickly, stifling a laugh. But Mr. Humbert doesn't seem to hear me.

"I gotta say, Chaz, I never thought you could pull a dime." He raises his hand for a high five. "You're more like your old man than I thought."

Chaz ignores the high five and looks at the floor.

"Roxie," Mr. Humbert says. "Now, forgive me for being bold, but you are a goddamn stunner. I've never seen hair so black in all my life. I mean, Angelina Jolie who?"

"Dad!" Chaz buries his face under a blanket. "Please leave. You're embarrassing everyone."

"Well excuse me if I can't compliment my future in-law," Mr. Humbert chuckles, running a hand through his thinning hair. "Let me introduce myself. Clint Humbert, at your service." He bows, splashing beer onto the carpet.

"Nice to meet you, Mr. Humbert," I say quietly, praying he'll leave us alone.

He holds up a large hand. "Oh no. No ma'am. No titles in this house." He grins like we're in on a big secret. "The name's Blaze."

Blaze? What the hell? Is he a pyromaniac or just a colossal tool? I look over at Chaz to see if he's taking this in, but he's still enveloped in the blanket.

"Uh, okay," I reply, taking his outstretched hand. Blaze crushes it in a firm grip and pumps it enthusiastically. "A firm handshake," he thunders. "The beginning of a lifetime bond. Who said that again? King David?"

I grimace and rub my sore fingers. "Not sure."

Blaze grins, his teeth white and brilliant. "I like this girl," he booms. "This one's a keeper." Chaz, who has finally re-emerged, nods in forced agreement.

Blaze steps forward and grabs his son by the shoulders. "Chaz, my boy. Don't fuck this up."

***

"What the hell is wrong with your dad!?"

"I'm sorry!" Chaz cowers. "What does one say to that? You've finally met Blaze and now know why I try to keep him in the house. Pretty nuts, huh?"

I walk over to the bed and sit on the end of it. "Shit, I had no idea. Looks to me like you've got some pretty masculine roots there."

"I need a beard," Chaz mutters, pacing around the room. "Yeah, that's it. I need a beard."

"No," I say. "Don't even go there. We need to get a grip on this, whatever this is."

"Just in front of him," Chaz says. "Only around him, so he doesn't catch onto the fact that—you know."

I take another gander at the room. After seeing Chaz's dad in action, everything's starting to make sense. Between the posters, the models, and Blaze's ridiculous intro, everything's an extreme. The brand of manhood coming out of the Humbert house is so exaggerated, so over the top, that it's almost staged. Ironically, unless what I just saw was some sort of practical joke, Chaz likely grew up with no idea of what regular manhood is like.

"Fine," I say, looking up at the ceiling. "Okay. Whatever. Three weeks and then we 'break up,' and that's it."

"Thanks," Chaz breathes. "Deal. No more than three weeks."

"Are you even sure this is a good idea?" I ask. "You said you wanted to come out eventually. Why barricade yourself in the closet like this?"

"Because," Chaz sighs, "I want to do it when the time's right. Now is not that time. I need to be comfortable with myself and do things at my own speed. I don't want to be outed."

"Have they heard anything?" I ask. "Rumors and stuff, going around? Both your parents work at the school, don't they?"

"Mom teaches. Dad is the head football coach." Chaz licks his lips. "But you know how it is. None of the kids say stuff around adults."

"True." We sit for a moment, letting the seriousness of the conversation wash over us. Emotions I can't read flit across Chaz's face as he absently draws his fingers across the palm of his hand.

"I just don't want to let my parents down," he says finally. "I can't play football to save my life. Hell, I can barely carry water onto the field. Dad lives and breathes it; he even played college ball. I'm not interested in cars, either. Right now, there's a 1960s Chevy on blocks in the garage he's restoring himself. He loves women. I'm into dudes. Once I tell him, we will have nothing in common. And I mean nothing."

I take a breath. "I get it," I say slowly. "I told you I'd help you, and I will. If you think this fake girlfriend charade will help, then I'll support you one hundred and ten percent." I nod. "I'm in."

"What if they're onto me?" Chaz asks. "I haven't dated girls. I don't have any guy friends, and I'm just not interested in traditional guy things. Guys' things? Yeah. But not regular guy things."

We laugh, letting out some of the tension that has gripped the room since we walked in.

"Just because you aren't macho doesn't make you gay by default," I point out. "Look at Nick. Sometimes, I think he's my sister. Do you know what his favorite movie is?"

Chaz laughs. "What?"

"*Steel Magnolias*," I say. "He bakes. He can do wonders with a pair of knitting needles. The best thing about him is that his interests are his own, and that's why I respect him. He also raps, studies military history, and used to get into street fights when he wasn't crocheting."

"Wow."

"His friends are a lot like he is. And you know what? They're all straight, either in relationships with girls, or playing the field. Every single one of them."

"Good point," Chaz says. "Screw anybody who puts limits on people. But seriously, I just feel like my time's running out. One of these days, I'm gonna be exposed. Everyone's going to know, whether I'm ready for it or not."

"Well." I take a seat on the edge of the bed. "If you don't think your dad's going to understand, why not tell your mom first?"

Chaz gapes at me. "My mom? Missus Religious? You know, back when I was a kid, she used to drag me to this four-step church at a strip mall. Pastor Willard used to talk about how being gay was a sin. Had that in my head before I even knew what it was."

"Jesus, Chaz, I didn't know that."

"Yeah, well."

"I really don't think your parents would kick you out," I say. "But if they do, you can live with us."

Chaz cocks an eyebrow. "You ask your mom?"

"No need. She used to campaign for gay rights in college when she wasn't protesting apartheid. Mom's got a big heart. She'd love an adopted gay son."

"Word." Chaz nods. "Usually, when gay people adopt, they adopt a kid, but with you and Hanna, the kids adopted the gay."

I laugh. "Hey, I see what you did there."

Chaz groans loudly and flops face down onto his bedspread.

"You kiddos using protection?" Blaze trumpets from somewhere beyond. "Don't want to kill the mood, but cover your stump before you hump."

"We're *talking*!" Chaz screams.

"I don't want to know what that's code for," Blaze replies. "But be safe." Seconds later, a chain of condoms slides under the door.

"Dad! *Get. Out.* NOW!" Chaz picks up the condoms, swings open the door, and hurls them into the hallway.

"Okay, okay." Blaze retreats down the hall with his hands in the air.

"Whoa, whoa, *whoa*." I sit up straight. "Do you realize why your dad had condoms in the house? Do you know what this *means*?"

Chaz scrunches his face. "What?"

"Dude. Your parents still smash!"

Chaz shrieks. "Are you serious!?" He gapes at me. "Never mind. I don't want to think about it." He shakes his head like a wet dog. "No wonder I turned out gay."

"Maybe your *dad's* where it all started," I suggest. "He kind of reminds me of old you, except he's a little bit smoother…but not that much."

"He's a freak," Chaz agrees. "But Blaze? Straight as an arrow."

After learning what I've learned about Chaz's parents, I'm curious as to how those two got together. They couldn't be more different. But the longer I think about it, the more I don't want to know.

***

"I think you should go back to school tomorrow," Hanna says, fiddling with the scrunchie around her wrist. "Full time again."

"I don't know if I'm ready yet," CeCe says. "Roxie?"

"You'll have to go back at some point," I point out, sprawled out on the loveseat. "You should probably just do it now. I mean, people don't know you're pregnant. Some people might ask you, but you don't have to answer. Make something up. Me? I lie all the time. It really isn't that hard."

Hanna rolls her eyes. "Our bus driver thinks Roxie's an orphan. Because she lied to her about it."

"I kind of am," I say. "I mean, my dad's dead. Mom works all the time and is never around. I'm a Charles Dickens novel come to life. Olivia Twist, anybody?"

"I didn't know that." CeCe's face falls. "I'm sorry, Roxie."

I look at the floor. "Yeah, it's whatever."

"And about school," CeCe says finally. "I mean, what's the point? I never liked going, and I'm not a great student. As soon as this baby's due, I'll probably have to drop out anyway to work. My parents can barely afford to take care of me and my little brother."

"Bad idea," I say. "Don't quit. At least graduate high school or get your GED. Otherwise, you can kiss off any employment. I guarantee your parents will say the same thing."

"Roxie's right," Hanna says. "You'll have to work part-time, but your high school degree? It's a must. It's the only thing that'll keep employers from tossing a résumé in the trash. Trust me."

CeCe doesn't say anything for a bit before speaking up. "Okay," she says. "I'm going back."

"Do what you have to," I say. "Tomorrow's Tuesday. If anybody asks you where you've been, make something up! You don't owe them anything. Wear a hoodie or a coat, but don't change your look too much or people will know something's up."

"I'm such a bad liar," CeCe says anxiously. "My face will give it away."

"Tune them out," I suggest. "Pretend you don't hear them. Tell them you're pregnant, then laugh like you're being sarcastic."

"Either way, it's none of their business," Hanna reminds her. "Any issues, Roxie and I will feed them something else or distract them."

"You guys rock," CeCe says. "But why all this? I mean, Hanna, you and I both play soccer, and Roxie, we had class together, but we didn't know each other that well before, and people around here can be so closed off." She shrugs. "I guess I'm just a little surprised, that's all."

Hanna smiles. "It was long overdue."

"Damn straight," I agree. "You were always dope."

"Good energy." Hanna nods. "You kind of light up a room whenever you walk in. You're always positive and upbeat and stuff. Everybody noticed your absence."

"You lent me books for silent reading," I say. "Slipped me the answers to pop quizzes. Never asked for any pens back you let me borrow."

"It was time," Hanna says. "And even though this is really tough, and I'm not an expert on teen pregnancy or pregnancy in general, I'm glad I can be here for you."

CeCe doesn't say anything, but she doesn't have to. Hanna and I both have other friends, and people we occasionally hang out with, but for the most part, we don't open the books for just anybody. Chaz unexpectedly crashed into our duo, and CeCe clearly needs us. For a while, I wanted to invite her to hang out with Hanna and me but at the same time was worried she'd change up the dynamic too much or might not be as nice as she seemed. After today, though? I'm thrilled.

"Girls," Nick calls from the landing. "What do you think?"

Gone are the baggy pants and oversized shirts. Dressed to the nines, Nick looks like he's stepped off the Perry Ellis runway. Face shaven to the skin, his hair is greased and parted. A black overcoat hugs his shoulders, while creased trousers barely touch the tops of his brogues.

"Well, hello there," Hanna giggles. "Wow, Nick. What's this all about?"

"New job? A girl?" I cock my head. "What's the deal today, Mr. Nazari?"

"Yeah," he says quietly. "Something like that."

Nick's been distant these past few days, and I can't seem to pinpoint what's changed. He's out a lot and doesn't really talk about where he goes, so anything's possible. Maybe he's going out on dates now, if not seeing somebody already. Whatever he's doing, though, good for him. It's nice to see him finally taking care of his appearance, and growing up a little bit might just do him some good.

"Well," I say as Nick walks into the office and closes the door behind him. "I guess Nick finally grew up."

"Yeah," Hanna says, her expression unreadable. "Looks like it."

***

"Okay," Nick says, as Hanna, CeCe, and I step out of the car. "Remember. If you want a ride home, you'll have to wait until quarter past four. I'm probably going to be late today."

"Got it, Dad," I call behind me as the three of us head toward the commons. Try as I might, I can't seem to figure out what's motivating Nick to go from man-child to man, but in terms of transportation, it's working for me. Last night, we caught up for a bit, and he thinks he landed the barista job at Café Covington. This being his first job prospect in a year, he's on top of the world, and I'm thrilled for him. Through the throngs of students, I look around for Chaz, but he's nowhere in sight.

"Where's Chaz?" CeCe asks, reading my mind. "I mean, I'm supposed to talk with him, right?"

"I know how it sounds," I say. "But trust me. He's okay. You've got something to tell him, and he's got a lot to tell you."

Hanna chuckles. "Oh, does he."

"There." Up ahead, Chaz is feeding coins into the vending machine and wearing the jeans we snatched from Bargain World. They're a little tight still, but the morning jogs he mentioned he was doing seem to be paying off. He turns around and spots us before twisting the cap on his unsweetened tea and waving.

"Hey, girls."

"Hey, Chaz." I say. "Jeans look good."

"Yeah," he laughs shyly. "Thanks. My dad took me to get them hemmed. What's the verdict, Hanna?"

Hanna gives him a thumbs up. "Fashion."

"Okay," I say. "Quick intro. CeCe's going to be hanging out with us after school today, so you guys need to catch up at some point."

Chaz looks confused. "Uh, okay. Glad to see you back, CeCe."

"You'll be close by, though, right?" CeCe asks, her voice slightly panicked.

"Of course," I say. "And don't worry. He's not going to ask you to make another sex tape. Right, Chaz?"

"Of course not," Chaz says, forcing a laugh. "You guys know I wasn't serious…right?"

As it turns out, a few people did ask CeCe where she was. The way she told it, a few words about her sick grandmother in Mexico was enough to answer the question for most people. During the break, CeCe and Chaz managed to get together and share everything between them, and by the time Hanna and I find them at lunch, they're already sitting together waiting for us.

As for Chaz, today was rough. Some moron tried to start up an anti-Chaz chant during the passing period, and Brennan and Spencer are still in the lead with cruel but clever comments. They might be quiet when Hanna and I are around, but the moment we're out of earshot, they start up like no time has passed.

"I think today's the day," CeCe says, crunching on a mini pretzel.

"For?"

"Telling my parents the truth," she says quietly.

"I think it's a good idea," Chaz says. "If I could weigh in a little bit."

"What about you?" CeCe replies, raising her eyebrows. "When are you telling *your* parents the truth?"

"Hey." Chaz shrugs. "I'm not making you do anything. And me?

I've got my own cross to bear. But your situation will never be mine. Courtesy of biology…and more biology."

"Did anybody ask about Erik?" Hanna wonders, sucking on a Go-Gurt. "Anyone?"

"No," CeCe laughs. "I guess he wasn't that popular. I thought football players were always top dogs, but not Erik."

"Poor little Erik," I mock. "Oh well. I guess naked basketball was his true calling."

"Wait, what?"

"Nothing," I say quickly. That's going to be a whole other conversation.

Three o'clock, and CeCe's standing by her decision. The rest of us all had things going on later today, but seeing how serious she is, those commitments will have to wait. I text Nick, who still knows nothing, not to worry about giving us a ride and that Hanna and I will find our own way home.

The entire bus trip over, CeCe is remaining calm, but by the time we pull up at her stop, she's on the verge of a full-on panic attack, and other riders seem to be noticing. Doing what I can to minimize attention, I push her and Hanna out ahead of us and shove Chaz as hard as I can.

"Get away from me!" I shriek, swatting him with my backpack. "You're sick!"

"Ooh, yeah," Chaz retorts. "Anger. I like that in a girl. Chaz likey."

Fooled and distracted, the rest of the passengers focus on our skit while CeCe and Hanna get off the bus. The second Hanna steps off, Chaz and I rush to the front of the bus and dive off onto the street.

"'Chaz likey.'" I gag.

"Hey," Chaz says, slinging his backpack over one shoulder. "Wasn't my idea. Plus, I'm a little rusty with my sexual harassment."

"Which house is it?" Hanna asks gently. "CeCe?"

"That one," CeCe whispers, pointing down the street. "The beige house."

Her house isn't far away, but the fact we're moving down the street at the speed of a sloth with terminal bone cancer means if we're lucky, we'll get there in under an hour. Though it does take a while, we eventually stop in front of a white picket fence, and CeCe unhooks the latch, beckoning for us to come through.

Though located on an otherwise tired-looking street, CeCe's house is small and elegant: perfect for the four people who currently live in it. Creekside, or "Beaner Grove" as some racist prick dubbed it a while back, is a working community in the more industrial part of town. Most, but not all, of Chester's small Latino population lives here, and unless you've got friends in the area, or "got business," as Nick would say, you probably shouldn't walk here alone after dark.

CeCe takes out her key and fumbles it a little bit before sliding it into the lock and pushing on the front door. I want to give her some guidance, anything really, but I've never been pregnant, so I shut up and look straight ahead. The hinges creak, the door swings open, and all four of us step across the threshold.

"Take off your shoes," CeCe says, her voice low. We oblige and place them on a plastic rack adjacent to the door before stepping onto the padding of the carpet. I almost take her hand but, at the last second, pull it back.

"CeCe? Is that you?" a woman's voice calls out.

CeCe's head snaps up. "Hi, Mama."

A petite woman in green hospital scrubs walks out from the living room and smiles at us, her face tired but warm. "Friends of yours?"

"Yeah," CeCe says quietly. "Guys, this is my mom."

"Hi, Mrs. Sanchez," the three of us chorus, each one of us finishing the sentence at different times. Without a doubt, all of us can feel the tension in the room, but none of us says a word. I'm terrified just being present. God knows how CeCe's feeling right now.

"It's good to see some new faces around here," Mrs. Sanchez says airily. "We don't get visitors very often. What's the occasion, kids?"

Here we go. If I could be anywhere else, I would. Feeling like a voyeur, I don't want to be anywhere in the room, but CeCe was adamant about us coming, and I'm not about to let her down. Hopefully, she'll remember at least some of the speech we helped her think up on the ride over because I came up with most of it and can't recall a word.

"It's fine," CeCe says, turning back to face us. "Wait in the front yard for me, okay?"

This wasn't supposed to happen, but I'm not about to argue. I merely nod, and the three of us excuse ourselves quietly, retrieving our shoes from the front. Filing out into the driveway, Hanna's the last one to leave and closes the door softly behind her.

"Okay, guys," Chaz whispers urgently. "How do we think Mrs. Sanchez will react? I hope she isn't too hard on her. I hate violence."

I bite my lip. "Hopefully not too badly."

"Please be understanding!" Chaz makes prayer hands in the direction of the house.

I look over at Hanna. "Any thoughts?"

She shakes her head. "I've got no idea."

And it hits. A scream, a shout, and several wails blast out the window, ending the quiet of seconds before. One doesn't need to know Spanish to deduce what Mrs. Sanchez is exclaiming isn't on the good side, and I'm certain she's just warming up. Though I expressed this to no one, I believed for a while CeCe's pregnancy might actually be a cause for joy and positivity. I mean, Mexicans often have big families, right? Baby equals family! But that ain't the case because there's no fiesta in there. Just a pissed-off parent. And that sounds the same in any language.

"Oh my God!" Hanna gasps. "This is bad. I think we should go."

"No!" Chaz peeks out from behind a rosebush. "We can't. We need to help her."

I look at Chaz. "Are you insane? When a mom's pissed, do not, and I repeat, do *not* get in her way, or you're next up. Sit tight, lay low, and wait for her to come out."

"If she ever *does*."

By now, most of the neighborhood has come out to investigate. A small boy on a green trike pedals up the driveway and peeks through the frosted glass in front, while behind him, his obese older brother records on his camera. An older couple stands next to their mailbox in bewilderment, while beside them, an even older dude in a ten-gallon hat stops pushing his barbecue to look toward the commotion. He shakes his head and drops a plastic bag full of marinated meat onto the sidewalk. Any other time, I'd be laughing my ass off at how random things are in CeCe's neighborhood, but if she stays in there any longer, there will be candles on her driveway tonight.

The scene is interrupted by the roar and throttle of classic American muscle mixed with low-quality Spanglish rap filling the air. Moments later, a drop-top Chevy comes screaming down the street. Bouncing on hydraulics, the car sends sparks flying every time the chrome bumper kisses the concrete. Swerving around the cluster of neighbors, the Impala flies up onto CeCe's driveway and idles for a moment before the engine turns off. I crane my neck to get a better look at the driver. As he steps out and adjusts his hat, a beam of light falls across his delicate but masculine features. It's The Swindler.

Chapter 9

"What up, *ese?*" A voice that is unmistakably Nick Nazari floats out from the passenger side. The door opens, and my brother stumbles out, waving at us. His hair has been slicked back with enough pomade to straighten a Clydesdale's mane, but the sides and back of his head are shaved to the skin. His eyebrows, which used to look thick and normal, have been whittled down to sparse peaks that arch over his Locs sunglasses and fly off his face. Enveloped in a woolen Pendleton plaid shirt several sizes too large, Nick swaggers over to us, smiling and confident.

Chaz gapes at him, but Hanna and I are used to this. The Swindler's interesting, and Nick has a history of hanging in the fringe. A prime example of this was when Nick moved "Buddy," a friend he'd made in line at Sharper Image, into his room without telling anyone a couple of years back. I don't know how long he lived in our house, but a week later, Mom found out and lost it. After that, Buddy had to go, but he and Nick are still friends on MySpace, and while the worst thing Buddy may have done was spill Cheeto dust on the upholstery, The Swindler deals with stuff both legal and illegal.

I grab Nick by the shirtsleeve and whisper into his ear. "Why are you hanging out with *The Swindler?*"

He scrunches his face. "Why not? He's in my computer class at Covington. We hang out now."

"No, he isn't!" I hiss. "He just hangs around and sells stuff. How could you not know that?"

Nick holds up a hand. "Save the questions. I've got a few of my own. First off, why the hell are you three all the way out here? You were supposed to check in with me."

"We're with CeCe Sanchez," I say. "She plays soccer with Hanna. This is where she lives."

He raises a brow. "Really? Then where is she?"

I chew my lip. "It's a long story."

Before Nick can answer, the door crashes open and CeCe comes running out, tears streaming down her face. We us rush towards her, but The Swindler flies past us and embraces her. Conversing rapidly in Spanish, the two of them must be going over what led to today because the longer she goes on, the more irate The Swindler looks. By now, I'm convinced the two are related because they're not only comfortable around each other but share many of the same mannerisms and expressions. Nick, translating what he can, manages to deduce that Erik is a piece of shit, but we already knew that. The neighbors are still milling around, but most of the noise is now coming out of the lowrider's subwoofer.

"You hear that?" Nick says, bopping his head to the latest frightful track. "Two hours of Emilio and me flowing. We're going to drive our demo across town once we get it mixed."

I fold my arms. "You and The Swindler, huh? Who would have thought?"

"And not just anywhere," Nick continues. "Our first gig? *The Nick Nazari and Friends Cobra Cove Reunion Tour*! The audience will be the scared ones now." He laughs. "Just you wait."

"Right," I say. "So, now you're going back? What happens if anybody in the audience recognizes you?"

"Already thought of," he says smugly. "Emilio's bringing a crew. You know, in case things pop off."

"And what crew is this?"

"So many questions," Nick trills, batting his hands at me. "I don't know. I'm not going to badger the man. I have faith. Emilio's got this thing on lock."

"Whatever you say, big bro." I take another look at his makeover. "What happened to the Transylvanian getup you had going on? Too much starch in the collar?"

Nick scoffs. "Why restrict oneself? Variety is the spice of life, Roxie. Some days, I'll stand as Chancellor Nazari in my overcoat and pocket watch. The next day, it's Nico Loco turned loose on the hood. No one will know what hit them."

"What's so bad about sticking with one?"

"How boring! Why not have multiple personas? That way, no one really knows what you're about. And if yesterday's Nick fails to achieve his objective, the Nick of tomorrow succeeds!" He narrows his eyes. "Suck it, Jerome."

Before I can answer that, Hanna turns to me. "Any ideas?"

"None whatsoever."

This day sure has been surprising. Even I don't know what to do now. The longer I go on, less and less makes sense. I hope at least one of us knows what they're doing. I glance over at The Swindler, who is holding an inconsolable CeCe in a tight embrace.

We lock eyes, and he points at Hanna, Chaz, and me. "Going somewhere after this?"

I answer for the group. "No."

"Good. Nico, you three, hop in the back and double buckle. We're going to find Erik Samuels."

***

The first and last time I saw Elderwood College Prep up close, I decided it was a sprawling, affluent playhouse and nothing more. Even today, I hold it in great contempt. Whenever there's a rape, riot, or a drunk-driving incident in Chester involving minors, the perps are almost always Elderwood boys. Somehow, they never get charged. When my family visited the campus, Mom and I took a tour after dropping Nick off with the dean, and within five minutes, I decided I didn't want him anywhere near the place. We still have the handbook in the living room, and Nick and I pull it out whenever we need a laugh. The front page is glossed with pictures of uniformed, smiling white boys standing beside even whiter teachers. Post-grad, most of the Elderwood crowd wind up in local politics, embezzlement suits, or prison, but with excellent marketing, dedicated alumni, and massive endowments, none of this ever gets out.

The Impala zooms up to the school's wrought-iron gates. An older man in a maroon vest with a pockmarked face leans out of the security booth window and eyes us warily.

"Can I help you?"

The guard investigates the car and coughs. Underneath his cap, I can see he's wearing a monocle, probably to look up students' butts for drugs. His name tag reads *Oliver.*

"Good afternoon, sir," The Swindler says. "Rogelio Castro. Groundskeeping and maintenance. Four-thirty."

"Identification?"

Reaching into his work jacket, The Swindler takes out an ID card and hands it to Oliver. Screwing up his left eye, Oliver squints at the card and flicks at it with a liver-spotted finger. "Very well. Proceed."

He buzzes us in, and the gate creaks open. Emilio pumps the gas, and we cruise at a leisurely pace, gravel crunching underneath the tires.

Chaz looks around at the sprawling campus. "Anyone else feel out of place?"

"Tell me about it," Nick says. "Roxie, remember when we came here?"

I laugh. "Memories."

The Swindler still hasn't told us the plan, and, to be honest, I'm a bit skeptical. Besides making a couple of phone calls, he's remained silent the entire drive. Before we got in the car, he had us change into ill-fitting groundskeeper uniforms already caked with mud but wouldn't tell us why. During the journey, CeCe explained to us what had happened in the house. In between screams, Mrs. Sanchez told her she'd not only have to stay in school but get a part-time job before the end of the month. Having never held a job in her life, being fifteen and all, and unsure what to do, CeCe told Cousin Emilio everything.

We pull to a stop near the front of the school, and The Swindler kills the switch. Behind us, the hills roll on for miles and evergreen trees tower in the distance. A Victorian clock tells us the time, while the main building rises in front of us. Since the beginning, the school has remained shrouded in secrecy, and the students aren't known to mix with outsiders very much. There's one open house, once a year on the anniversary of the school's founding, and a few buildings on campus stay completely off-limits to visitors.

"Everybody out."

All of us step out of the car and cluster around. About fifty paces away is a shed with a dark red door, which The Swindler begins walking toward. Once we get there, he produces a ring of keys from his coat pocket and jams the biggest one into the lock, twisting the knob. The door creaks open, he flips a switch, and a dim glow illuminates the shed. Inside, different tools and types of lawn equipment lie strewn about, but besides the riding lawn mower, most of the shed is unused, wasted space.

"Okay," he whispers once we're all inside. "Here's the plan. See the card?" He holds up the identification card he showed Oliver earlier. "Fake. Acquired it a few months back. Long story short, this guy? He ain't around and won't be. Now, I don't know if you noticed, but I made a couple of calls while we were driving. If my associates are right, I shouldn't be that long. I'll be back soon as I can."

"Hold on," Chaz says, looking panicked. "What's going on here?"

"Dude." The Swindler pats him on the shoulder. "Relax. I'll explain it all soon. But for now, just dig."

The ground is hard, and the work we're pretending to do is harder. Nevertheless, the five of us pound the earth with purpose. Considering I barely work in my own backyard, I don't know what the hell I'm doing, and by the looks of it, neither does anybody else. Angling my spade, I stomp hard and drive it into the rocky soil.

"Lovely day, isn't it?" a middle-aged woman remarks, smiling as she passes by. "I hope you all are keeping warm out here."

"Don't talk to the help!" a shriveled strumpet in a mink shawl squawks.

I wait until she passes us and flip her off with both hands. "Eat one, you old bitch!"

"Did she really just say that?" Hanna shakes her head.

Chaz sniffs. "She did. The venomous hag!"

Angrily, I slam a shovel into the soil, thinking about The Swindler and his plan. He seems sincere, and CeCe *is* his cousin, but I don't know him that well and really don't know his endgame. The deeper we dig, the lower the sun sets, and I find myself wondering if he's ever coming back. The sky, streaked with pink, grows dimmer, and darkness begins to settle in.

"Hey, look!"

In the distance, I can make out two silhouettes, and I stop to get a better view. The first figure I can identify as The Swindler, but the second one is a stranger. Whoever it is, he's reluctant to come along and drags his feet, almost resisting.

"Who's he got with him?" Nick asks, dropping his rake and squinting.

"Don't know." I toss my shovel down. "Guess we'll find out."

Behind us, CeCe lets out a strangled cry. Throwing her pick to the ground, she tears past us and stomps towards The Swindler, who I can now see is accompanied by Erik Samuels. Holding Erik by the bicep, The Swindler's face is grim and his eyes cold. "Everybody inside that shed."

"Yo, *Jefe*, want me to hold him?"

The Swindler ignores Nick and drags Erik through the door. The rest of us follow close behind, and Hanna shuts the door behind us.

"Lose the coat, *amigo*."

Erik shrugs out of his suede peacoat and holds it out gingerly. Emilio swipes it out of his hands and tosses it to Nick. "Collateral."

CeCe, meanwhile, is staring at Erik with a hatred so intense I'm worried he'll burst into flames. Yesterday, she was telling us even though she didn't want him back, she missed him, and his abandonment was destroying her. What happened earlier has changed her, though. Big time.

Emilio shrugs off his work jacket and removes his thermal, leaving him in just an undershirt. For a second, it looks like he's getting ready to beat up Erik, but instead, he motions for Nick to hand him the peacoat. Slipping it on, it's a little tight at the shoulders, but it suits him. The Swindler seems to think so as well because he buttons it up before speaking.

"I'm not one to start things on bad terms," he begins, creating a tent with his fingertips. "So, let's start from the beginning. My name is Emilio Sanchez. And I play fair. That's all you need to know about me, my friend."

Erik stares at him in terror. His eyes, wide and cornflower-blue, briefly meet my gaze before flitting to CeCe, but she turns away and focuses on her cousin.

"Forgiveness," The Swindler continues. "A most holy undertaking deserved by few but asked for often. Will you ever be forgiven? That part of things isn't up to me. But I'm in charge of something more important than that. And that's responsibility. *Your* responsibility."

He's not talking to me, but I'm taking it all in. After we wrap up here, Father Emilio should maybe reconsider hustling and instead focus on a career in public speaking. But something tells me he's not quite finished, and the speech takes a darker turn.

"Erik," The Swindler says. "In just a few months, do you know what's going to happen?"

Erik gulps. "I think so."

The Swindler smiles. "What's going to happen?"

"Uh, I'm going to, like, be a dad?"

"I don't know. Are you?"

Erik nods. "Yeah."

"Wow." The Swindler shakes his head. "Someone's not very excited. I want to congratulate you, but you aren't even congratulating yourself. Well done, Erik. Your *parte privada* did its job. Go nature!"

Erik opens his mouth to protest, but Emilio cuts him off. "You know what didn't do its job? You! No help, no assistance, and on top of it, you fucking ditch her? You know her family doesn't have much money. You didn't know what she was going to do once she got pregnant, and you didn't care. You. Didn't. Care."

A sharp edge that wasn't there before is present in The Swindler's voice. Erik doesn't look up. Pacing back and forth, Emilio looks over at us before running a hand through his close-cropped hair.

"How much do you actually know, Erik?" he asks. "Anything? Did you try to contact CeCe even once?"

Erik swallows. "No."

"I know that," The Swindler spits. "But here's the news. She's keeping it. Carrying it, giving birth, and looking after it until the day she dies. Whatever she wanted to do with her life, wherever she wanted to go, doesn't matter anymore. Now it's all about what the baby wants, where the baby wants to go, what the baby wants to eat. The baby that is biologically *yours!*"

CeCe wipes at her eyes, and Hanna takes her hand. Chaz looks floored by the entire thing, like he's trying to take it all in, and I am pretty wound up myself. Nick, on the other hand, stands with his arms folded, blocking the door and enjoying every second of this.

"So," The Swindler continues. "You need to step up. Now, this goes one of two ways. You can either tell your parents the truth and ask for their help, or you can continue living your lie. Me? I don't really care. But one thing that's hard and fast after today? You're paying. You will pay your child support. I think that's fair, given you're a young man of wealth, taste, and physical strength."

Erik stares at him, befuddled. "What does that even mean? What are you saying? Am I supposed to change diapers and stuff? Bottle feed it?"

The Swindler laughs. "That's funny. Almost had me for a second there." He walks over until he's face to face with Erik. "But it's going to be a lot more than that."

***

"Five hundred minimum," The Swindler says. "At least for now. That'll take care of some basic expenses, and CeCe will cover her end. See? Told you I was fair."

Erik nods. "Okay."

"Let's do the math," The Swindler says, reaching into his pocket and pulling out a small pad. "In seven days, you need to come up with a hundred twenty-five dollars, which works out to less than eighteen dollars a day." He laughs. "You've probably got that between your couch cushions at home. Peanuts, really."

"Hardly." Erik stares at us dubiously. "Do I look that rich? What makes you think my parents are going to give me money every month?"

"Parents? Who said anything about parents? This is all you, buddy." The Swindler pauses. "But hey, if they give it to you, great. If I were you, though, I'd just get a job."

"A job?" Erik coughs. "I can't get a job. I'm fifteen."

"Bull!" The Swindler bellows, grabbing him by the hair. "I was working corners at *twelve*! At thirteen, I was locked up in county, and the year after that, I formed my own crew. Scoot your *gringo* ass over to the Burger King or Mickie D's and flip a burger, bitch! I know the manager. He'll hire you."

Releasing his hold, Erik stumbles backward and falls flat on his seat. Rubbing his scalp, he gets back up onto his feet, looking determined.

"What you just said," Erik says, looking The Swindler in the eye. "That was real. I respect that. People call me a crazy-ass white boy.

I'm strong, fast, and good with numbers. I can be your number-one dealer, man. Just put me on the game."

Placing both hands on Erik's shoulders, The Swindler punts his steel-toed boot into Erik's taint and once again sends him to the floor. This time, he's down for good. Eyes brimming, Erik's mouth opens and closes in agony as he cups himself and rocks from side to side on the shed's dirty floor. The rest of us look at The Swindler with a mixture of fear and respect. It isn't every day one witnesses assault, let alone one as brutal and unexpected as the one we all just saw.

"Five hundred," The Swindler says crisply. "You understand?"

Erik wills himself to nod. "I can't leave the grounds," he whispers. "Tell me what to do."

The Swindler scoffs. "Elderwood boys are smart. Figure it out. Now, think carefully before you answer. Do we have a deal, young man?"

"Deal," Erik croaks.

The Swindler turns and walks away, but not before throwing a black Nokia at his feet. "That's for you."

"Do I...?"

"I'll contact you. Don't try to reach me. Ever. Use this phone and this phone only. As for me, don't worry. I'm always around. And I know you now. I know your face, where you go to school, and I'm very familiar with Burton Hall. Burton, that's where you stay, right? Room 2A? On the ground floor?"

Erik trembles. "Who told you that?"

The Swindler smiles. "See you in a week."

As soon as we reach the car, we change out of our soggy uniforms and back into dry clothes. We heaved the shovels carelessly into the shed, and the garden looks terrible, but after today it's unlikely any of us will see the place again. The Swindler drives up to the admissions building to collect his check, and after that, we haul ass out of here, flying down the mile-long driveway and through the wrought-iron gates.

CeCe holds it together until we turn onto the highway, then starts crying.

"He didn't say a *word* to me," she sobs. "I at least thought he would *acknowledge* me." She sniffles. "He doesn't care that I'm having his baby. He's not sorry."

"Wait, wait. Hold the phone." Nick sits up straight. "CeCe's *pregnant?*"

All of us look at him in bewilderment, but he doesn't seem to get it.

"Wow," Nick says. "That's crazy. I mean, I know that somebody got pregnant, but nobody explicitly said who. By the way," he says, turning to CeCe. "You inspire me. Strong, brown women are seldom acknowledged, but I see you. May you be blessed with a healthy child and long life."

Hanna and I look at each other and cringe, but The Swindler seems deeply moved.

"That was beautiful," The Swindler says, shaking his head. "Living poetry. Hit me right in the *corazon*."

"How kind of you to say," Nick says, only half joking. "I do love a good stanza." He looks over at The Swindler. "And you?"

"Oh, same," The Swindler says. "If there ever was a way to measure a civilization, poetry would be the yardstick. And me personally? I'm a Jose Marti man. Yeats. Beckett. Any of the Irishmen sit well with me, but John Milton? A legend in his own right."

"Wow," Nick says. "You sure know your stuff."

"As do you," Emilio answers richly. "And if I may say so, it appears you're quite an educated young man. Do you come from money?"

"No," Nick laughs. "Just British grandparents." The two of them laugh warmly and smile at each other. "Cheerio!"

For the next five minutes, nobody else in the car exists. Immersed in their academics, the two boys cover two millennia faster than I'd ever thought possible. As they finish dissecting Goethe and start on other famous literary works, Nick and Emilio are speaking with strong Londoner accents. The rap record blasting before has been changed out for an assortment of baroque classics, and as the capricious notes of Telemann float throughout the car, the cramped lowrider becomes a classroom.

"I do say," Nick remarks as we pull away from the curb outside Chaz's house after dropping him off. "It's not often one meets somebody so erudite around here. Did you go to college?"

"Aha," The Swindler laughs. "Not quite. I was always a hyper kid, and I loved learning, but wasn't good in school. But all that changed a few years back when I was a student at an outstanding school not far from where I grew up."

"Where did you go?" I ask.

"Elderwood Prep."

"No way!" I gape at him. "Seriously?"

"Scout's honor," The Swindler laughs. "Back in the day, when I actually attended school, a recruiter from Elderwood showed up. They needed to fill their liberal arts program. I love history and literature, so I filled out an application. A month later, I was in."

"Wow," Hanna says. "How did you do it?"

"Poetry." The Swindler nods. "'Dante Lives' was the name of my submission. Dark shit about the hood. The recruiters ate it up. I guess they wanted something authentic for a change. Once I got accepted, I had a week to pack. I said goodbye to my family and moved into the dorms."

Hanna, Nick, and I look at each other in amazement. The Swindler is becoming more and more complex, and now I can totally see how he and Nick ended up becoming friends. Rapt, the rest of us call for him to continue.

"At first, it was rough. I was pretty much the only poor kid and one of a handful of nonwhites. There were a few Asians, a couple of Indians, and one or two Hispanic boys. Some of the older boys came at me, but I didn't fold, and in time, I began to earn the respect of my teachers and peers. Not with fighting, but with knowledge and intellect." The Swindler sighs. "The way it should be."

"What's it like?" I ask. "I mean, the school itself."

"Really good," The Swindler says, nodding. "The curriculum is great. They don't just make you memorize stuff without a reason. Everything has a purpose and place. It isn't like the middle school or Chester High which are all standardized tests and overcrowded classrooms. It's like a college, but better because you're still young and hopeful and stuff."

"Did you ever get into it with a prefect?" Nick asks. "Don't ask me how I know, but somebody told me they hit underclassmen with riding crops. Is that true?"

"Oh, shit," The Swindler laughs. "Yeah, that's true. Got a couple turned on me. It took some fast talking and quick thinking, but in the end, they were the ones getting whipped."

"Something must've happened, though," CeCe says quietly. "For you to leave. I remember when you got accepted. We were all so proud."

"Oh, it wasn't just something," The Swindler says. "There's a whole lot of story there to be told. Nobody would believe it, though. Sometimes, I don't even believe it." He flicks his blinker. "That school…those students…the staff. Some of the worst people you'll dig up anywhere."

Nick, Hanna, and I are perched on the end of the rear bench seat, eager to hear more. The more I get to know The Swindler, the more fascinating he becomes, and now I feel like I'm about to see a side of him not even his own cousin knows about. Thrilled, but anxious, I want more than anything else to hear what happened, and looking into my brother and friends' faces, they're thinking the same.

"*Ay, Dios mío!*" The Swindler says. "Can you believe it's seven o'clock already?"

Nick shakes his head. "Time flies when you're extorting Erik."

"It wasn't extortion," Hanna says. "He needed to pay his share like everyone else."

"Agreed," The Swindler says, scratching his chin. "You've got to pay to ride."

"Excuse me?" CeCe glares at her cousin.

The Swindler looks down. "Sorry, *mija*."

"Well, what are we waiting for?" The Swindler asks, breaking the awkward silence he brought on moments before. "You guys must be hungry after all that killer yard work, and I just got the check." He busts up laughing. "Who's down for dinner?"

A few minutes later, we pull into a small hovel near CeCe's house serving fast, greasy food The Swindler swears by. After deciding what we want, he places the order and sends a stack of bills through the drive-through window. Up ahead, there's a small covered eating area, so we park the car and rush out of the downpour, sitting down at a red plastic table. CeCe passes our food around. Ravenous, I tear into my cheeseburger, while Nick, who's trying to be dignified with his panini, ends up doing the same. Hanna, who's usually big on pacing herself, tries to slow down but can't, and with the mountain of fries in front of us, we eat quickly and plentifully.

In CeCe's case, that baby must be growing because she ordered four sliders, two sleeves of onion rings, and an apple-pie milkshake. This doesn't go unnoticed by Emilio, who makes several cracks about larger members of the Sanchez family but stops when she tosses an onion ring at him.

"So, anyway." Nick wipes his hands on his napkin. "Elderwood."

"Oh, yeah." Emilio nods. "Right. There really isn't much to it. I became a problem for them, but not in the way you think."

"A problem?" Hanna asks. "How could you be a problem? They found you, not the other way around."

"Not at first," Emilio says. "Sometimes I play a little rough, but always by the rules. I'm not one of those dumb hoods who thug their way through life, trying to bring the streets into everything. Acting hard and all that. When I get opportunities, I take them, work hard, and try to keep everything respectable and legal. So when I got my acceptance letter to Elderwood, I treated it like a golden ticket to the Willy Wonka chocolate factory."

"You were excited," I say, sipping my soda. "I mean, that much comes through."

"Oh, definitely," Emilio says. "As a young kid, I used to watch BBC dramas with my dad when we were both trying to learn English. I loved it. The uniforms, mornings in the chapel. It was so different from what I knew. I read as much as I could about the school, and when I got there, I read even more. I still remember my first day. I felt like I'd truly arrived in life."

"How did your parents feel about it?" Nick asks, nibbling on a pickle spear. "Were they concerned about you leaving home so young?"

Emilio shakes his head. "Not really. They were so involved in their own shit I don't think they noticed too much. They were both working two jobs. One less mouth to feed."

"The first year was good, though," CeCe says. "You were happy there. Remember when we visited you?"

"Oh yeah." Emilio smiles. "Visiting day. And you got lost in the labyrinth."

"I was so scared," CeCe laughs. "You had to come and find me."

Emilio chuckles. "Never stopped."

"What about racism?" Nick asks. "Was it an issue for you, being a mostly white rich boys' school?"

Emilio blows air through his cheeks. "Oh yeah. Teachers would call on me, but it felt forced, and they'd over-respond to my answers and never talk normally. Students would say stuff, ask ridiculous questions. They wouldn't do it because they were curious, mostly because they could."

Hanna makes a face. "That's terrible."

Emilio shrugs. "What do you expect? Most of those kids…everything belongs to them. They say whatever, do whatever, and somebody comes and cleans up. And in that world? Even more so."

"But that changed," I say. "Right? The way you told it earlier. It sounded like you figured things out, at least for a while."

"I did," Emilio says, squishing the bun on his veggie burger and taking a bite. "Like I said, the first few months were tough. Had to get the lay of the land and roll with the punches. But eventually, teachers began noticing me for me, not just being the token kid they let in to make themselves look good or whatever. Students began nodding at me in the hallways. Even with the most reserved people, the ice breaks. You tell some jokes. Somebody laughs at something, and then you laugh, and you've got a connection. Anywhere I've ever gone, any place I've ever been, there's that night when you're sitting around with a couple of other guys, and you just know. Like, you know you're in."

"Yeah," Nick laughs. "I know the feeling. The bro mode."

"Man bonding." Emilio nods solemnly.

"But what happened?" I press. "When did everything go south? I don't want to be annoying, but I saw your face in the car. Something must have happened. What's the Elderwood secret?"

"Ha!" Emilio laughs. "That's a good one. 'The Elderwood Secret.' Elderwood secrets, actually. The place is like the Tower of London. Skeletons in every closet there. Been to every hood from here to Bakersfield and I still sleep better in Stockton than the dorms."

"So it's dangerous, then," Nick says. "Elderwood."

Emilio nods. "For me, at least."

"But why?" Hanna asks. "Why is it dangerous? Why did you leave? Did somebody force you out? Were you attacked? Threatened? Like, you just keep giving us these vague answers. If it's none of our business, you can tell us, and we'll drop it. But considering we just broke into the place and abducted Erik so you could kick him in the crotch, I think we deserve to know a little."

All of us look at her. Hanna's never pushy, and this is out of character for her. Either she's dying to know, or she, like me, suspects the secret Emilio's alluding to is a lot bigger than we think.

"She's right," CeCe says, slurping down the last of her shake. "I mean, I guess what she's saying, or we're saying, is the same. Everything changed after you went there. Everybody in our family noticed it. We just don't talk about these things. But I need to know. Erik goes to school there. I had to pretend to be a landscaper just to get in, and you couldn't get out fast enough. What do I need to know about that place? What are you not telling us?"

Emilio sighs and crinkles up a wrapper lying on the table. "You wouldn't believe me if I told you."

"Try us," I say as gently as I can. I look across the table into Emilio's dark brown eyes. Dropping his gaze, he kneads his hands and takes a breath.

"Okay," he says finally. "I guess it's time to hear the truth. Let me tell you what really went down at Elderwood Prep."

***

"The first thing you must always remember," Emilio begins, "is that almost everything you've ever learned is a lie if you trace it back far enough. A whopper."

Nick nods. "Amen."

"It's the same growing up," Emilio continues. "Treat people well and they'll treat you well. High school anybody? Another one. Be good and good things will come to you. Like Jesus and his crucifixion."

Emilio taps on the table with his thumb and pauses for a bit. "My point here is that most of the time, when well-meaning people like grandparents or older people tell us things like this, it's because they *want* them to be true, not because they *are* true. They want it to be that way, so they either rewrite pieces of their own life history or don't mention what really happened. Otherwise, they'd jump off a cliff. Education is the same."

CeCe frowns. "Education everywhere?"

Emilio nods. "Yeah. And Elderwood is the best example of that. A classical education typically means you'll be exposed to the foundations of western society. Latin, Greek, Astronomy, the sciences, religion, you name it. Elderwood focuses heavily on those, and they teach the material well. If you remain in those disciplines and take them at face value by engaging with philosophers who've been dead for a thousand years who can't hear you, you'll ride out of there on a golden saddle. But if you read between the lines, really think about things, and apply what you've learned to the modern era? Best-case scenario, you're the horse. And I mean, absolute best case."

Hanna knits her brow. "Did you become a horse?"

"Did I become a horse? I was *the* horse! Fuck that, I was Boxer from fucking *Animal Farm*." Emilio shakes his head. "But I'm getting ahead of myself. My first point is that education is all theory."

"When did you figure that out?" CeCe asks.

"I always had a feeling," Emilio says, folding and unfolding his soiled napkin. "But I didn't have any proof. I mean, try arguing against evolution in a science class. Talk about the earth being billions of years old in Bible school, and you'll be laughed out of the study. To both groups, only they will ever have the truth. And if you don't have their truth? You're not just a liar. You *are* the lie."

"And I thought I was the only one," Nick says, shaking his head. "You know, there was a time I was actually trying to get into Elderwood. Chester High was and is an ideological and literal hell."

"Elderwood is no better," Emilio says curtly. "Stuffier image, same nonsense."

I nod. "Go on."

"I transferred to Elderwood in eighth grade. The transition was rough. First week, typical guy posturing. Call me names, crack some jokes, break into my footlocker. In public school, I could box a little, and people knew who my father was, so I was feared. I wasn't a bully, but people didn't mess with me. Here? I was a nobody. There was a zero-tolerance fighting policy, but that got broken all the time when it came down to it. If I broke that rule? I'd have been expelled. That's just something you know growing up a darker shade in America. Ain't that right, Nico?"

Nick nods. "Indeed."

"I got in a few fights and won most of them. Didn't start any. But even then, I was sort of off-limits until I began to engage with the academics, and then things began opening. At first, I was behind, so the minute school was out, I went straight to the library and hit the books. In a couple months, everything turned around, and the material was making sense. Suddenly, I could identify root words and references to Greek gods and similarities between Athenian law and our federal Constitution. It was amazing."

Emilio smiles. "And the thing was? Everything began to open up. Guys were nodding at me in the hallways. Teachers knew my name. My grades began to go up. And mostly, I began to make my parents proud."

CeCe grins. "Remember *Abuela*'s care packages? How she would give you more stuff if you got a better grade?"

Emilio laughs. "Exactly. People were rooting for me. When I'd go back to the neighborhood for Christmas break, kids would be lining up asking for my help. And I'd give it. Kids my age looked up to me. Feeling like I was succeeding at school and in the hood was like nothing I'd ever felt before." He shakes his head. "Of course, it couldn't last.

"By ninth grade, I was doing okay," Emilio continues. "I made the freshman soccer team. Filled in sometimes as an assistant boxing coach and got paid for it. Walked a straight path. The year before, I still had some street business going, but I stopped all that. Got out of the game. I didn't want that life following me into Elderwood. Plus, if somebody there found out…oh man. No Elderwood man of 'upstanding character' could ever be caught doing those things. Note: caught." He laughs. "Christmas came and went, and winter quarter, I figured I'd try something new. There was this new professor on campus everybody was talking about, a young guy, and he was teaching a civics course. A buddy of mine told me a little bit about it, and it sounded dope. I joined the class a day later."

"Excuse me." All of us turn to see an employee in a green apron waving at us. "The dining area closes in a half hour."

"Got it," Emilio calls back. "We'll be out of here by then."

"And then…" I motion for him to continue.

"By the end of the first class, I was hooked. The professors at Elderwood, they were mostly older, tenured white men who lived for their work and nothing else. Nothing wrong with that, I guess. But this new guy, John? He was the exact opposite. For one, he made us call him by his first name. That was unheard of! I'm pretty sure he was breaking some rule, but he said titles were feudalist. In his classroom, he wanted us all to be equal."

"That's so cool," Hanna says. "Was he young?"

"Early thirties, I'd say," Emilio says. "Harvard graduate. He didn't act like it, though. I mean, as soon as he'd walk into the classroom, he'd switch out his sport coat for a Red Sox hoodie and a ball cap. He wore his hair long, down to his collar, and played bass guitar. His wife, or girlfriend, or whatever, she was from Mozambique, and he could speak a little Bantu, some Portuguese. He was different. Everybody loved him. I came to love him. And in his class, I came alive."

"Debate then," Nick says. "I'm saying debate was a big part of it, right?"

"Debate was ninety percent of it," Emilio says. "We'd get the material the night before. Read up, take notes, et cetera. Once we got to class, the chairs were already waiting for us in a circle. You took a seat. John gave an introduction and sat back and let us do the talking. He'd referee and stuff because sometimes, you know, people would freak out or get into screaming matches, but I never forgot what he said one day. He told us we could learn from each other just as much as we could learn from him, that everybody, no matter where they came from in life, in society, had the answer to at least one of our life questions." Emilio shakes his head. "When he said that, I knew I was exactly where I needed to be."

"He sounds amazing," I say. "Kind of like that guy from *Stand and Deliver*, what was his name, the combover dude?"

"Mr. Escalante," Emilio laughs. "Hell yeah. Or Robin Williams's character in *Dead Poets Society*. The kind of teacher you get once or twice in school if you're lucky. The civics class was dope, though. Plus, the Elderwood students, they weren't all just stuffy, rich conservatives. It was pretty mixed politically, which is why the class discussions were interesting."

"What happened after the class ended?" CeCe asks. "With John? Did you take any more classes with him?"

"I did," Emilio says. "But not until the year after. By that time, he was kind of a campus celebrity. Like, guys would chill in his office after class, and he had like this little group of dudes who just soaked up everything he said."

Nick laughs. "Like a fan club?"

Emilio nods. "Exactly."

"How are we on time?" Hanna asks. "They said this place will close soon. Are we good?"

"Yeah," Emilio says, glancing down at his wrist. "We're good. And that summer, things were different. When I went back to the neighborhood, I saw it with fresh eyes. Not because I'd spent last year living in a fancy bubble, but because I now had context. A year of history, sociology, John's civics course…it changed me. The problems I saw every day, the issues my people faced, I mean, yeah, there's no shortage of dumbasses in the hood. There are plenty of bad people. But what we live under? How we're living? It's a condition. And if you know the history, we didn't bring it on ourselves. It's brought to us, the same way it was 150 years ago."

Emilio rubs his temples. "So much confusion. People do things thinking *they* make the decision, but somewhere, sometime back there, somebody had a plan for them. For the blacks, the Chicano, there's a prison cell and a coffin with your name on it before you're born. By the end of that summer, one of my friends was dead, my uncle was doing five years for a crime I know for a fact somebody else did, and my neighbors I've known almost my entire life had been evicted from their house. I stopped by the day after I got home, and the windows were boarded up. Eviction notice on the front lawn. Some tech couple bought the house a few months later or something. Nothing felt the same. Every time I stepped out my front door, and every time I went back into my parents' house, I'd remember something from one of my classes."

"You'd been enlightened," Nick says. "And you had to be on the outside looking in to diagnose the problems. You couldn't see it when you were in it."

"Oh yeah." Emilio nods. "Well, mostly. I mean, we all know the problems. But being in it, we only see as far as our noses. There's too much emotion. Too much confusion when you're in it. But when you are on the outside, it's a chessboard. Only then do you begin to see who's moving the pieces. In our case, minorities, those people on the outside, immigrants…we're told we're the problem. But if you look at the prisons, lack of opportunities, healthcare discrimination, police brutality, the constant exclusion, it's built for us to fail. And for the Blacks, the Native Americans, and the Mexicans who got conquered in 1848, they didn't come to America. America came to them."

"Wow," Hanna says after some time passes. "I guess I never thought about it that way. Besides what we learn in school, you know, about slavery, and the taking of Indian land and the broken treaties, they don't talk about much of it. Like what you just said about Mexico and 1848…I don't know about that. Most of my family came here from Ireland after getting thrown off their land by the English." She sighs. "There's my family history."

"It's true," Emilio says somberly. "The Irish were the first victims of Anglo aggression. Got some Irish in me myself, somebody named Moran, I think. Guess that's why I love July Fourth."

"Everybody in America's a little bit Irish," I laugh. "But as you were saying."

"I could've started right then and there. Street preaching. Getting my Jesus on," Emilio says. "But prophets are rejected in their hometown. Plus, I didn't fit in anymore. I'd talk, and people would look at me like I was speaking another language. And I was. I mean, there's Spanish, there's English, and then there's Elderwood English. And I was speaking the latter without even knowing it." He shrugs. "I could've pointed out people's errors. I could've told them they were being shortsighted or stupid. Risking everything for a low payout. But who am I to tell other people what to do? It's not like I had the answer. I just saw the problem.

"Instead, I observed," Emilio says. "Every night, after I finished helping my dad drywall or deliver pizzas, I'd go for a bike ride. Take my Schwinn and just pedal. Or I'd go for a walk. And whatever I saw, whatever happened, I wrote it down once I got home. By the end of the summer, I had a notebook full."

"What did you do with it?" CeCe asks. "Your journal?"

"Not a journal, *mija*," Emilio says. "A blueprint. If change was going to come, it had to come at the top. And around here, Elderwood is the top. The local elite send their boys to that school. Anybody who is somebody either goes or knows people there. And now, I was on the inside." He looks at me. "See where I'm going with this?"

"Behind enemy lines," I say. "Right?"

"They weren't my enemies back then," Emilio says. "But yeah. If you're going to tackle a problem, go to the source. Fighting at protests, headbutting cops, punching hate preachers doesn't get you anywhere, except on a registry. But I was politically awakened and inspired by John's class, so the first thing I did was enroll in advanced sociology. And I talked plenty."

"Advanced," Nick says, nodding his head. "Yeah, you were really going all out."

"AP or it ain't for me," Emilio laughs. "But yeah. Thing was, this class was different. Besides being harder, and a lot more legwork, the mood was totally different. The other class was more laidback, more of a talking sort of class. Everybody got along, even if we didn't agree. But this class was cutthroat. Totally different group of guys." He shakes his head. "Sharks looking for blood.

"So one day, we were comparing the idea of multiculturalism to assimilation, you know, weighing the pros and cons, when this pompous asshat started going off on illegal immigrants, talking about how they're stealing jobs and ruining the country. Fitch, his name was. The entire time, he looked at me with this smirk, baiting me, but I didn't bite. Said some nasty other things, too. I let him finish."

"What a chode," Nick interrupts, shaking his head. "Asshat supreme."

"Nick," I snap. "Let him talk."

"Seriously, why?" Nick tenses his jaw. "What's with people? Are they that threatened by someone who isn't like them? Are they scared? Or do they just like dominating people who literally just want what they already have?"

"Both," Emilio says. "Everything you just said. Sometimes all of those put together. I don't understand it, but then again, I'm not like those people. But when John let me answer, I wrecked the kid. Everything he said, I restated, then demolished him in front of twenty-five or so other boys."

"Using the facts?" I ask.

"Just facts," Emilio says. "Stats, historical events, things from the textbook, you name it. I had it in the chamber before I let it fly. By the time I killed his third point, the other boys were hysterical. John had to restore order twice before I was finished."

"That's awesome," Hanna laughs. "Must've felt great."

"Oh, it did," Emilio says. "It was great. I mean, for this brown boy from Creekside, it was epic. I just did it the way he did. I roasted him like a pro. Lawyer style. That's why the students loved it as much as they did. I'd heard Fitch talk, and he was no dummy. Some people probably agreed with him. But after that, nobody listened to him," Emilio says. "They listened to me.

"Thing was, I didn't know who I pissed off," Emilio continues, his mouth drooping a little. "And I didn't realize it until after everything fell apart. But I messed up. Big time. After that, life got crazy."

"How soon after?" CeCe asks. "A week. Two?"

"About a month," Emilio sighs. "Early in November, John got an assistant. That was the first red flag. John was extremely organized and on top of everything in his classroom. He didn't need an assistant for anything. But I walked in one day, and there was this big guy sitting in on our lectures. Macrae, I think his name was. The entire time, I would catch him looking at me. Not, like, normal looking either. He was giving me this weird, thin smile and not blinking. I'd stare back at him, and he'd slowly turn his gaze back to John or whoever was speaking, but he was always there. If I went to pick something up from John's office, Macrae would be there and not John. I got the feeling John didn't like him, but this dude was there for a reason. I just hadn't figured it out yet.

"I just thought it was odd," Emilio says. "This 'Macrae,' if that was even his name, just shows up. Elderwood is a small school. Everybody knows everyone. Sometimes, people know you, and you don't know them, but you know their face. It's like an island, that place. I asked around about him, and anybody not in John's sociology class didn't know him. 'Who's Macrae?' 'Macrae. Mac Ray?' He had no history."

"Nobody else knew him then?" Hanna scrunches her face. "That's really weird. I mean, he'd have to have other classes, and if the school were really tightly knit, other people would know him."

"Right?" Emilio shakes his head. "After that, I'm in the library after class getting started on my report, and some freshman kid comes up to me and shakes my hand. He tells me his name is Rarick. At Elderwood, guys call each other by their last names, so this wasn't too weird. But the next thing was. He asks if he can sit down, and of course I say yeah, so he does. Whole time he's making small talk. Asking me if I caught the latest pay-per-view heavyweight fight or how his synagogue helps undocumented immigrants and how he loves Langston Hughes."

Emilio takes a deep breath. "I thought it was strange, but I figured my mind was playing tricks on me. I tried to avoid him, but 'Rarick' was everywhere. I'd sit down somewhere. So would he. I'd get up, and minutes later, he'd be out of there. He didn't talk normally, either. Everything was a question, overdoing the eye contact. Always staring at me. Shit was creepy."

"Weird," Hanna says. "Sounds sketchy. Did he ever try anything?"

"What'd you mean?"

"Like get you to own up to something illegal or swap stories and stuff?"

Emilio laughs. "As if. But yeah, a couple times he was sniffing around, talking about getting caught with ecstasy or asking me who to buy liquor from. Eventually, he disappeared. Stopped coming around. But by that time, so had almost everybody else I knew.

"Few days later, more weird shit. I'm eating dinner late, and two guys my age come in wearing letterman jackets. Sit down at the end of the table, not too far away from me, but close enough I could hear them talk. The first guy goes, 'Man, this test got me stressed out,' and the other one goes, 'Yeah, I got to relax.' They then started talking about buying weed and how they were willing to pay way above street value for a couple ounces, the whole time looking over at me."

Emilio shakes his head. "At this point, I knew something was up. What I couldn't figure out was why. Thursday that same week, Coach asks me to teach an afternoon class: short notice. I told him sure. I didn't really want to 'cause I had a test and everything, but he was always fair to me, and I felt like I owed him. I took it." He rubs his eyes. "One of the guys, a regular named Pritchard, wanted to spar after class. Pressured me. Kept saying he wanted to catch up, and nobody could meet his level, so I said okay. Bad choice.

"We were boxing, but then he went crazy," Emilio says, his eyes widening ever so slightly. "Started going buck wild. Way too hard for sparring. I kept telling him to calm down, but he just went harder. Had this look in his eye…I can't describe it. It was an animal about to go in for the kill, that's what I thought. So I went full defense, and, you know, defense fights harder. I took two jabs to my ribs before landing an uppercut that almost took his head off. Pritchard woke up a day later."

"My God," I gasp. "What the hell was that about? Why did he do that to you?"

"Somebody was feeding him something," Emilio says. "Bad intel. It's the only answer I've come up with. We'd been cool our entire time there. Sometimes, he even asked me to correct his stances and would offer to hold my bag. But as soon as he went down, a group of guys came charging in out of nowhere, screaming, shoving me out of the way. They hadn't even taken him out of there before Coach dragged me into the office. Firing questions at me nonstop. I answered them. But I had questions, too. Why did Pritchard go berserk? The guys who found us. They showed up way too quickly. Some of them had to have been watching, but none of them got called as witnesses.

"After that, I lost my work-study. Coach let me have it, read me the riot act. Told me I was lucky if Pritchard didn't press charges, even though you have to sign a waiver going in. I was banned indefinitely. Without the money, I had no way to pay for books. I tried to get a job in the cafeteria, but they didn't have any positions. Tried the library. Never got back to me.

"The final incident came a couple weeks after that," Emilio says, blowing at an insect that's landed on our table. "I had just finished a debate on the constitutionality of the 'Stop and Frisk' procedure earlier that day in some political science course I was taking. I walked up onto my floor to see my door wide open and campus security standing around my room with drug-sniffing dogs going through all my shit. Second they saw me, two officers hurried over and took me by each arm. Saw several bags of marijuana, a couple vials of coke. A scale. I kid you not, an actual digital scale. Said they had me on drug charges with intent to distribute and that I was under arrest."

"Bullshit!" I scream, unable to control myself. "How could they do that to you? Fitch? He would do all that over losing a debate?"

"Yeah," Emilio says calmly. "It's okay, Roxie. I'm still here. I'm okay. It wasn't meant to be."

"I didn't know," CeCe whispers, her voice dull and emotionless. "All these years, I just figured you got tired of the place. Dropped out. Got bored. But no." She shakes her head. "They got rid of you. I'm so sorry, *primo*."

"Well, I'm sure you can guess the rest," Emilio says. "Long story short, they forced me out. Stood there while I signed the papers. Forfeiture of scholarship. Transcripts got trashed too." He sighs. "Right before I left, though, I asked to see John."

"Did he come?"

"He did. Second-to-last person I saw on my way out. I asked to be alone with him, just for a few minutes. I told him what happened."

"What did he say?" Hanna demands. "He could've helped you. Did he?"

"There was nothing he could do," Emilio says. "New hires are the first to go. He'd just gotten married and put money down on a house. I mean, this was the dude who taught me about my constitutional rights. Told me things about my people's history I never heard before. He didn't say much. Just shook my hand, told me I was the best student he ever had, and saw me out."

"That's it?" Nick says incredulously. "That's all he said? Why didn't he put that Harvard degree to use and get you some help? Why didn't he stand up to the board? Or do his own investigation?" He shakes his head. "Some people."

"A year later, I got a letter in the mail," Emilio says. "No return address. Inside was enough public record, highlighted newspaper articles, transcripts, city council minutes to choke a humpback whale. Our friend Fitch, as it turns out, was very well-connected and the grandson of one of the most powerful men in the state. That same man would later go on to run for Congress. People like that, connected people, they can do whatever they want to whoever they want. The money, the associations. I mean, it's street politics. Everything that happened to me made sense."

"So Fitch pulled a takedown," Nick says. "He basically used his money and power to ruin your life because of what you said. Like what they did to the Panthers back in the '70s."

"You said it, partner." Emilio shakes his head. "Ain't nothing scarier to this country than an educated brown or black kid. They say they want equality or claim this country is equal. They love their basketball players, their athletes and musicians. But the second you really try to become equal and stand against injustice, they send you back to the auction block."

"But why?" I ask. "You were one person, a kid at school. You yourself said it was an even mix between conservatives and progressives or whatever. Plus, it sounded like most people agreed with you in the end, right?"

"That's the thing," Emilio says, rubbing his chin. "It sounds crazy. Like, why? People did agree with me. But people also like distractions. They like to be entertained. Whatever I said, or didn't say, wouldn't really change anything in the end. But if I'd planted a seed, or maybe lit up somebody's world view the right way, it could help us twenty years down the road. Honestly, I don't think it was Fitch who made the final call. I know somebody higher up was running that op in the end. I mean his grandpa, Rankin, or whatever his name is, took most of the Hispanic vote, ironically enough. I used to see people canvassing for him around my neighborhood back when he was still in state politics."

"I'm so sorry, Emilio," Hanna says finally. Her mouth droops. "It kills me to think you just had to go, for your own safety and protection. They should be the ones leaving. You aren't the threat. They are."

"I know," Emilio replies, beginning to gather up some of our trash and stuff it back in the paper bag it came in. "But when your society is founded on the bones of one group of people, and the enslavement of another…" He trails off. "Let's just say not everybody gets their day in court."

Chapter 10

"Wow," Chaz says. "I don't really know what to say."

"Yeah, you and me both," I reply. Emilio dropped Nick and me off around ten last night. Hanna left her bag over at CeCe's house, so the three of them were driving back to Creekside to go get it last time I checked. Of course, Nick and I were still talking about Emilio's epic life story hours after we left the diner, and I've just given Chaz the abridged version.

"He's so complicated," Chaz breathes. "I always figured he was just this local dude, but he's got this insane backstory. Somebody should give him a book deal."

"I was going to tell him that," I say, adjusting the phone against my ear. "Didn't seem right last night, though."

"No, of course not," Chaz says quickly. "So...what else is new?"

"Nothing. You literally saw me yesterday," I laugh. "You?"

"Jerome called. Wanted me to come over and hang. I mean, I don't want to be rude, but if I have to listen to *Squelch* one more time…"

Speaking of Jerome, I haven't heard a word from him since the kitchen showdown. Hanna told me he's penning lyrics for the demo, but I don't believe it. Jerome, slow as he is, surely knows Dry Cucumber will never exist without Nick, and Chaz spends most of his time at my house now instead of at rehearsals.

"And Blaze," Chaz groans. "He's asking about you nonstop."

"Oop, I gotta go," I say. "Child Protective Services is on the other line."

Chaz snorts. "I'm sure you have a lot to tell them. But seriously, you have to come back at least once. You know, before he figures it out."

"Tell him I died," I interrupt. "You pick the story. Fork in the neck. Abducted by Porn Stache, body-slammed by Biggie Smalls. Whatever, dude, I really can't go back there."

"He's not that bad," Chaz argues. "And by the way, Biggie's dead. Has been for years. How did you not know that?"

"Do not change the subject," I say. "I'm not returning to the Humbert House of Horrors. Invent a reason, or I will."

"Damn, got it."

"I gotta bounce," I say. "My toast is charcoal, and I'm running late. See you at school."

The line goes dead, and my cell vibrates close by. It's Cynthia. I want to ignore it, but, guilted by the number of kind things she's done for me over the years, I answer.

"Finally! Praise the Lord," Cynthia huffs. "Sorry to be a drag, but we gotta get moving. Hanna's at soccer for the next couple of hours. We need to talk."

"Look, Cynthia," I say. "I don't like Jerome. I think he's annoying, and I'm pretty sure he's got some kind of mental problem, but he's not the issue right now. This isn't our business. Have you even met Owen?"

"I sure have," Cynthia replies smugly. "He's nice. And *very* nice-looking, might I add." She giggles. "Come on, girl. Give me something to work with here."

"Okay," I sigh, closing my eyes. "After school today?"

"See you then!" she chirps.

***

The twins' car is out front, which means they're home for the weekend, and Cynthia's favorite gardener is weeding out front in a form-fitting pair of cargo pants. He waves to me, and I wave back, punching the doorbell with my free hand.

"Hey, Roxie!" Kelsey/Brooke greet me at the same time. Even after all these years, I can't tell which one is which. They're both really nice, not to mention stunning, and back when Hanna and I were younger, they used to take us shopping with them. It'd be easier if they wore different colors at least, but part of the fun for them is confusing people.

"Hey, twins," I laugh. "Your mom wanted me to come over so we—"

"There she is!" Cynthia announces from the landing. "Kelsey, Brooke—would you give us a moment?"

"It's fine," I say quickly. "We can just…"

"Living room," Cynthia orders, pointing with a gel-tipped finger. "Have a seat on the couch."

I flop down and throw my feet up onto the cushions while Cynthia settles down in the mauve armchair next to the fireplace. I stare up at the ceiling, noticing a spiderwebbing of slight cracks in the paint. "So, what's up?"

"Not a lot on my end," Cynthia answers, flipping absently through a furniture catalog lying next to her. "I'm doing fine. Kelsey and Brooke are doing wonderfully at college, dating their accomplished, handsome men."

"Are you okay?" I blurt. "I mean, you're kind of obsessed with Jerome's lameness. He's fifteen. It could be worse. How do you know Owen is any better? He might be a huge butt plug, but you haven't considered that because he's so good-looking, so you say. Plus, don't you think it's weird that you're looking more for Hanna's boyfriend than Hanna is?"

I have a few other things I'd like to point out, but even I'm not that cruel. Anyone who knows Cynthia knows she's a terrible judge of character, specifically for the men she's been involved with, which is why I'm so against Owen. Jerome is safe as long as you're not Nick, and while Hanna's not sure how she feels about Jerome, I know he would never hurt her.

Above us, the wall clock is ticking a lot louder than I remember, but I don't regret anything I've said. Love her as I do, Cynthia is not a person you take advice from. Especially when it comes to dating and relationships. She'd understand where I'm coming from because she never takes advice from anyone herself.

Cynthia opens her mouth to say something but doesn't get the chance. The chime of the doorbell reverberates throughout the downstairs, and she rises to get it.

"Hi, Mrs. Gilbert," a deep, unfamiliar voice greets.

"Hi, Owen," Cynthia says warmly. "Come on in. And please, no formalities. Cynthia will do just fine."

Cynthia and Owen stroll into the living room, almost arm in arm.

"Owen," Cynthia begins. "I'd like you to meet Roxie Nazari, my youngest daughter's closest friend."

I smile stiffly, hoping he's decent. Cynthia wasn't exaggerating; he's divine. Tall and muscular with a jawline that could probably cut diamonds, his jet-black hair glistens in the dim hallway lighting. Still, he still can't hold a candle to Blake in my eyes.

"Hey, Roxie," he says in an almost rehearsed tone. He lifts his hand and salutes me.

Cynthia laughs a little too loud and pats his bicep. "At ease."

She smiles and sits down on the sofa, patting the cushion next to her. "Please, sit. Let's all get comfy. Owen, how are you liking Chester so far?"

Owen curls a pillowy lip. "It's fine, I guess."

"I'm sure you've been to the gym by now," Cynthia remarks, eyes glued to his prominent pecs. "You look like you're big into working out."

"Oh yeah," Owen says. "Got back an hour ago. Tris and bis today."

"Your mother mentioned you're quite the surfer," Cynthia says, shooting me a grin.

"Most def." Owen nods. "Every day, back in Santa Barb, me and the dudes used to hit the outdoor gym before riding the waves after school. No beach here, that's for sure. I'm going to suck ass when I go back in June."

"Oh, darn," Cynthia pouts. "Don't worry about the weather, dear. It heats up come summer." She smiles. "You'll have plenty to do by then. I promise."

I sniff the air to see if Cynthia's been hitting the bong again, but all I get is a lungful of Owen's cologne. I recognize the scent from the mall. It's Gucci, or something expensive. Shifting his attention to me, Owen looks me up and down like he's going to rip my clothes off and smiles.

"Looking forward to it," Owen says with fresh enthusiasm in his tone. "I live for the sun. Around here, though? Haven't done much exploring. Roxie, could you maybe show me around?"

"I don't know," I say lamely. "I'd like to, but I'm really busy right now."

I'm not technically lying. Between helping CeCe navigate her unplanned pregnancy, rebuilding Chaz's life, and keeping Nick alive, I'm strapped for time. Cynthia's eyes widen briefly before focusing back on Owen.

"Hanna's free," she says quickly. "I could definitely have her show you around. How does Friday work for you?"

"I'm free on Friday," I blurt out before I can stop myself. "Friday works."

Owen grins, satisfied, and I smile back until I feel my teeth are going to come out of my head. "We'll go to the mall. You like shopping, Owen?"

"Love it," Owen replies. "I need a new watch, something to match my cold-weather gear. You know if they got a North Face at the plaza?"

"West end, south wing," I say. "We can stop there first."

***

"The new kid who lives down the street?"

"I just feel he could use some friends, Hanna," Cynthia replies, dragging the blender out of the cupboard. "He's new, and it's hard transferring mid-year. His mother says he really misses his friends and doesn't know anyone yet. And you two are so friendly. It might boost his self-esteem by having two pretty girls in his friend circle."

"I don't know," I remark. "I think his self-esteem is pretty good as it is."

Cynthia shoots me a shut-up-now look over her shoulder. "Either way, it'll be good for you two to get to know our new neighbor. You know. Grab a little dinner, show him around."

"Why can't Kelsey and Brooke show him around, Mom?" Hanna protests, dropping her soccer bag on the ground. "They'll still be around on break. Roxie and I are supposed to meet Chaz at the arcade on Friday."

"Tell Chaz to reschedule," Cynthia says dismissively. "Go to the arcade Saturday. That place is a middle-school hangout anyway. You'll spend the night being gawked at by horny seventh graders."

"Gross, Mom," Hanna says, making a face. "And like I said before, why can't Brooke and Kelsey show him around? Owen's older than us, anyway. He'll probably want to hang out with girls who can actually drive."

"Yeah," I interject. "Speaking of which. Are we supposed to ride around Chester on the city bus all night with him or what?"

"I don't know," Cynthia replies, tossing several chunks of frozen fruit into the blender and pressing the top down. "I'm just introducing you all. And your sisters are busy Friday. It's their double date night with Ashton and Cliff."

"Fine," Hanna says, clearly out of ammo. "We'll show him around."

"That's my girl," Cynthia says, wrapping her arms around her daughter and slipping her a scrap of paper. "Now put his number in your phone before you forget."

***

I can't believe I'm going along with this. A quarter past four on Friday and Hanna, Cynthia, and I are upstairs in front of the vanity mirror getting Hanna ready for the Academy Awards. Miraculously, Hanna hasn't caught on yet, which is both surprising and infuriating given how much I want Cynthia's plan to fail.

I don't know in what universe your mother greets you at the front door with a designer sweater and high-heeled booties from Nordstrom unless they've got something planned, but Hanna's gone along with everything with no questions asked. On the counter, an array of nail polish, makeup, and hairstyling products covers every square inch of the tile. Cynthia, having seated Hanna in front of the mirror, circles her daughter like a hungry cheetah, surveying her face under the blinding overhead lights.

"Not that I hate the attention or anything," Hanna laughs slowly. "But why are you guys dolling me up like Cinderella before the prince's ball?"

"More like for the prince's *balls*," I mutter under my breath. Cynthia chuckles quietly and gives me a shushing motion behind Hanna's back.

"I didn't say the prince's *balls*," Hanna snaps. "*God*. Anyway, what's with the special treatment?"

Cynthia pauses for a moment, risking glances over at me. She licks her lips. "I just feel like sometimes I pay too much attention to your sisters," she says finally. "I want you to know I'm just as proud of you, sweetheart."

I can't believe Cynthia churned that out without batting an eye, but Hanna doesn't fall for it. "Wait a minute. Are you fixing me up like this because we're going to see Owen?"

"Of course not," Cynthia scolds. "And you better not be getting any ideas. You're too young for an older boy like him."

Man, she's good.

"Okay," Hanna says. "What time is he going to be here again?"

"In an hour," Cynthia says, glancing down at her phone. "Give or take. We've got time. Roxie, plug in the straightener."

"But Hanna's hair looks nice as it is," I argue, staring at Cynthia's state-of-the-art flat iron. "Her curls are pretty."

"Sure, they are," Cynthia says. "But why not switch it up? It'll only take a few minutes. Plug it in."

I do as I'm told while Cynthia brushes powder onto Hanna's porcelain cheeks.

"Roxie? Your opinion, please?" Cynthia holds up two tubes of lip gloss. "Which one better matches Hanna's eyeshadow? Frosted pink or the deep plum?"

This is by far the most boring afternoon I've ever spent at the Gilberts. Makeup has never interested me. The only reason I use it is that I look exponentially better with it than without. And I like to use heavy eyeshadow and liner to look as unapproachable and badass as possible. Besides that, I really couldn't care less.

"The pink one," I say randomly, flicking through an old issue of *Fitness.* "I think the hair straightener is hot enough now."

Cynthia brushes a final coat of lengthening mascara over Hanna's lashes and steps back to admire her work. After another half hour or so, Cynthia has used every trick up her sleeve, and I've read the magazine cover to cover. I don't know how a person can sit that still for that long, but there's a lot Hanna is capable of that I'm not.

"Ta-da," Cynthia announces. "You look amazing, sweetheart."

And she does. With her flawless makeup, new clothes, and sweet innocence, Owen will definitely fall for Hanna after tonight. Cynthia's mission will have been a success, and whatever happens, good or bad, I will share in that outcome. Though I'm by no means a fan of Jerome and wanted that relationship to end almost as badly as I don't want this one to begin, I feel sorry for him. I mean, everybody knew Hanna was lightyears out of his league, and I think he knows it better than anyone. But Owen's on a whole other level, and if he and Hanna do get together, Jerome's chances of winning her back are less than nil.

***

"Hey, hey," Cynthia greets, ushering Owen inside. "You look rather dapper tonight, mister. Are those Doc Martens?"

"Yeah," Owen confirms in a bored monotone.

"Well, they go excellently with that jacket. I do have an eye for style, you know." She does a little twirl in her form-fitting sweater and designer jeans.

Owen brushes past her and plods into the house over to where I'm sitting. I wave, then tune him out completely. Chaz texted, asking if we'd left yet. Earlier, I filled him in on Cynthia's plan. He found the entire thing hilarious and is begging me for the latest details. I'll give him the rest of the scoop first thing tomorrow. For now, all I can do is wait.

"Hanna!" I yell up the stairs. "Come *on*! Let's go!"

"I'm coming, I'm coming," Hanna calls hurriedly, nearly tripping downstairs in her four-inch heeled boots. Owen wanders throughout the downstairs, clunking along like a fool and scuffing the hell out of Cynthia's floor. If he were anybody else, she'd crucify him, but apparently, Immaculate Owen can do no wrong.

"Are we leaving right now?" Hanna asks, finally coming into view. "Sorry about the wait."

"No sweat," Owen replies, perking up considerably after seeing her for the first time. "Where are we headed?"

"You girls tell me," Cynthia says, plucking up her keys. "Anywhere."

"Well, we better get this over with—I mean get going," I say with forced enthusiasm. "I call shotgun."

"Should we go to the mall?" Hanna asks. "It's dark out. Practice was rough today. I don't think I can do the skating rink. Any ideas, Mom?"

"I'm just the driver," Cynthia says breezily. "Roxie?"

"Yeah, let's hit the plaza," I say. "I'm with Hanna on this one. I'm wiped."

"Sounds great," Owen says, his demeanor completely different from earlier. "I mean, that's what we talked about Wednesday, right?"

"Yeah," I say, surprised he remembered. "You wanted to go, right?"

"Well, let's do it," Cynthia says. "Hanna, grab my purse off the kitchen counter, would you?"

Hanna obliges, and the four of us file outside to Cynthia's SUV. Hanna makes a grab for the door handle, but Owen seizes it first and swings it open with gusto.

"After you," he says in a drippy voice. Hanna shoots him a small smile, and the two of them slide into the backseat. Cynthia, in the driver's seat, covertly gives me a thumbs-up. My stomach twists, and I avert my eyes.

"Which entrance?" Cynthia asks, as we cruise past Red Robin. "How about the one by Hollister? Didn't you say you needed a new two-piece, Hanna?"

"It's winter, Mom," Hanna replies flatly.

"Spring break *is* just around the corner," Cynthia reasons. "You'll probably need a new top at least, you know, now that you're older."

Hanna catches my eye in the rearview mirror and mouths, "What the fuck?" I shrug, unsure of what to do. Cynthia's laying this on thick, a lot heavier than I'd originally thought possible. I'm pretty sure even Owen, who seems about as dense as a pound cake, knows something's up. I've got half a mind to tell Cynthia to just wait a couple years and then she can date Owen herself, but somehow, I don't think that would go over well. Remembering our discussion the other day, I sit tight and don't say a word. I can only hope this will work itself out.

"I love Hollister," Owen pipes up. "We can hit up Zumiez, too. I was thinking about getting a longboard now that I'm here. I mean, it's kind of like surfing, I guess."

"It is, isn't it?" Cynthia remarks, even though she's barely left Washington. "Well, Hollister it is. You kids got everything? Wallets? Phones?"

"We're good, Mom," Hanna says testily.

"Well, here we are," Cynthia chirps, putting the car in park outside the west entrance. "And remember. It's Friday night. Have fun. And keep your mind open. Anything can happen."

"What the hell is with her?" Hanna hisses into my ear. Owen's ahead, peering at the mall map and checking himself out in the reflection.

"No clue," I lie, bending down to tie my shoe. I untied it earlier in the car, needing an excuse to hang back. Hanna's not stupid: she knows something's up. Cynthia's really taking this too far. I can't believe I've decided to play a part in it.

"Well, we're free of her, at least for a couple hours," Hanna says. "Let's go in."

"Everything okay back there?" Owen asks over his shoulder.

"Yeah." I nod. "We're fine."

The three of us walk into the mall. It might be Friday, but there aren't a lot of people around. Owen notices this and sighs.

"Is this it?"

"What do you mean?" I ask.

He blinks. "Is this it? Is this the mall?"

"Yeah," I say. "This is it. Chester Plaza. It's pretty quiet, for a Friday at least."

"You could say that again," he mutters. "Back home, we had an outdoor mall. Way bigger than this. Place was full every night."

"You're the first person I've met who actually likes crowds," I observe, matching Owen with barely discernible sarcasm. "Usually, people want to beat rush hour."

Owen shrugs. "Guess I'm just different."

"Are you still up for Hollister?" Hanna asks sweetly. "Owen?"

"Oh, uh, yeah." Owen says. "Definitely. Roxie, you coming?"

"Do I have a choice?" I ask under my breath.

After shuffling into Hollister, I wait for Hanna and Owen to split off before hightailing it out of there. I didn't grab any dinner before I left, and food always cheers me up, so I make a quick jaunt towards the food court. Not far off, I can see the bright neon sign for Orange Julius when something knocks into me so hard, I go flying. Smacking against the side of a lava lamp kiosk, I wheel around with fists raised, ready to lay into whatever idiot just knocked me off my feet.

"Sorry, sorry," a familiar voice apologizes. "Please, excuse me. Are you all right?"

"Emilio?"

"Yes, yes," Emilio laughs, bending down and helping me up onto my feet. "Though 'The Swindler' will also suffice."

"Way to get my attention," I laugh. "How've you been?"

"I've been doing well," he says. "It's pretty dead here for a Friday. Where are all the people?"

"We're all wondering," I laugh, more to myself than Emilio. "I don't know. I'm here with Hanna and a guy from school. I barely know him."

"Ah." Emilio nods. "Yeah. I'm here with CeCe tonight."

"How's she been?" I ask. "Haven't heard from her for the last couple of days. Everything's okay, right?"

"We've been busy," Emilio says, dropping his voice to a whisper. "I had to go pick up some stuff from the maternity store. She went back to the car, though. Didn't want anybody from school to see her."

"Got it."

"She's doing okay, though. Listen, tell Nico Loco to swing by whenever he gets the chance. I had to toss my old phone. I wrote some new raps, and I want to lay them down soon. Okay, kiddo?"

"I'll tell him," I say. "We'll be in touch."

Owen and Hanna find me a moment later, both holding bags. Owen catches sight of Emilio walking toward the exit, and his eyes narrow.

"That guy."

I bristle. "What guy? You mean Emilio?"

Owen grimaces. "You know him?"

"Yeah, I do," I say, fighting to keep the animosity out of my voice. "Why?"

"I see him around," Owen says, sounding decidedly macho. "Don't trust him. I've heard he's bad news. Sells drugs and stuff. Rips people off. Is he bothering you?"

"Emilio's really cool," I say, glaring at Owen. "And he isn't bad news. He's actually a really nice guy. He helps anybody who needs it." I make a fist inside the pocket of my hoodie. "Don't judge people unless you know them."

"Okay, okay." Owen smirks. "Good to know. Where are we going after this?"

"Where do you want to go?"

"Where is there *to* go? It's kind of hick around here," he remarks. "What do people actually do for fun in this cow town?"

"Well," I begin, struggling to sound pleasant, "locally, we have a community center, a zoo, a video arcade, and a skating rink, to name a few. What was in Santa Barbara that we don't have right here?"

Owen snorts. "Uh, try the beach? This place doesn't have one rippin' spot to ride the waves. I used to be a lifeguard back in Santa Barb. I saved lives when I took off my shirt. You should've seen it," he says. "The hottest chicks shrieked like guinea pigs when I ditched the tank top. The ass couldn't handle the abs."

Owen's digital watch beeps, and he looks down and frowns. "Time to feed my six-pack. Where's Benihana?"

My mouth hangs open. "Serious?"

Owen doesn't look up. "About what?"

"Everything you just said," I say. "Do you really think I'm going to sit here and let you shit all over everything I know? You're lucky it's me you're talking to. This attitude? Whatever you've got going on? Leave it at the door, okay?"

"I didn't know a person could be so defensive of such a lame place." Owen shrugs. "My bad."

In disbelief, I turn to see if Hanna's heard a word of this, but she's over at the candy store looking at giant lollipops. This was such a dumb idea. Why the hell did I go along with it? I should just bail before Owen and I get heated.

"Look!" Hanna bounces over to us with a small paper cup of jellybeans. "Free samples! You guys want some?"

Owen paws at the cup, greedily stuffing most of them into his maw. "Pretty good," he mumbles through a mouthful of sugar. "Back in Santa Barb, we had this place that made its taffy in-house. Best candy you'll ever taste."

"I bet," Hanna says. "Want to look at skirts? That's a cute one, huh?" She nods towards a display in one of the windows. "I bet it would look great on you, Roxie."

"Why did your family move here anyway?" I ask Owen as we walk out of the main area into one of the department stores. "You seem to like it a lot better in California."

"My gay-ass dad's stupid job." Owen scowls. "Believe me, it wasn't my choice. I'd take anywhere over here."

By now, I've added Owen to the towering flames over which Brennan, Spencer, Jenna, and Erik sizzle eternally. I don't know why, but I've got a feeling he's not going anywhere anytime soon. Hanna, as usual, is a few paces ahead of us, completely in her own little world.

"Where do you guys want to go next?" she asks. "Ideas?"

"I'm going to grab a pretzel," I say. "You two go on without me."

"No, we'll all go," Hanna says. "Owen, let's grab a table."

"Sounds great," Owen says, smiling. Something's seriously off with this guy. With me, he's all pessimism and attitude, but with Hanna? Nothing less than polite and agreeable. I wonder if she's caught onto any of this, but I doubt it. Hanna might be eons ahead of me in school, but when it comes to the school of life, the girl's dunce cap is taller than the Empire State Building. I realize, as the three of us roam back the way we came, this is probably the worst trip to the mall I've ever taken, and by the time we reach the food court, I'm hardly hungry anymore.

Hanna and Owen grab a table as I head over to the pretzel cart and buy a medium twist, no salt. Over at the table, Owen's cracking jokes, and Hanna's laughing like he's the white version of Eddie Murphy. My pretzel is stale, the mood blows, and my feet are killing me. Tonight has sucked epically. I wait until Hanna's attention is focused on Owen to sneak away from them. As I power-walk away, I overhear Owen telling yet another abysmal joke. Hanna titters and shoves him playfully. If I see any more, I fear my pretzel will be reappearing on the floor of the plaza. I steal a final glance at the two of them before stepping out into the still night air.

***

I don't know how long I've been walking, but my feet are in agony, and my head is throbbing. The pretzel is long gone, but the greasy white paper is still clenched in my fist. I dig out my phone and check the time. It hasn't even been a half hour, but the icy blasts and occasional spray of rainwater make it feel like I've been trekking for days. The sky is pitch black now, and the streets are nearly deserted. In the distance, I can see Walmart looming over me like a fortress. Between the pretzel and the walk, my throat's parched. I need something to drink. Although Frankie works in the electronics section and has no problem slinging me freebies when he gets the chance, I thumb through my wallet to see if I have any singles or spare change.

I jog through the automatic doors and make my way toward the electronics, which are at the back of the store. I don't know whether Frankie's working tonight, but he's usually even here on his off days, playing with the equipment or yelling at employees who rearrange his displays. Francisco Marini, or Frankie, as he's known to the world, is Nick's oldest and dearest friend. Since the sixth grade, those two have spent nearly every day together. When my family moved to Chester, Frankie convinced his parents to follow us here. He and Nick can often be found walking downtown in search of entertainment, wolfing down tacos at Charros, or holed up in Frankie's man cave playing *Halo*.

I can see Frankie up ahead, wearing a blue company shirt and hammering the buttons on a white Xbox controller, a wire headset dangling from his ears.

"Frankie," I greet. "What's happening?"

"Hold on," he says, his eyes glued to the screen. "I'll help you in a second. Just testing the merchandise, ma'am."

"Frankie, it's me."

"Don't go anywhere," Frankie says. "I'm almost finished. This game is butt-raping me big time. Jesus, this was supposed to be fun.

"No!" Frankie howls as his avatar dies in a hail of arrows. "Shit! This game is rigged. Rigged! My advice. Don't buy it. In fact, I'm ordering you. Do. Not. Buy."

"What game is it?" I ask, laughing.

Frankie shakes his head. "Something I won't sell you."

Realizing who it is, he stops. "Oh, hi, Roxie," he mumbles. He shuffles awkwardly in his Crocs and looks at the ground.

"Was it the elves again?" I ask, looking over at the start screen. "Real sons of bitches, those guys."

"Oh, God," Frankie groans. "You've got no idea. What's new with you?"

"Not a ton," I say. "Tonight's been pretty bad." I turn to him and smile. "Besides gaming your way through your shift, what's going on with you?"

Frankie's face turns redder than his hair. "Oh, you know, not much."

This past fall, Nick and I were playing video games over at Frankie's like we've done a million times before. When two of them went upstairs to reload the snack tray, I found myself scrolling through Frankie's avatars, trying to decide which one I wanted to play. Towards the end, I found an avatar that looked a lot like me, albeit with a much more ample chest. Besides being dressed in one of those skimpy outfits the female avatars wear, she had long black hair and huge brown eyes. The fact she was named Roxanne confirmed my suspicions. I'd suspected Frankie had a thing for me, and since I became a high schooler, he's gotten more and more awkward. It bothers me, though, not because he has a crush on me, but because he and I used to be close, and I miss being just friends.

"What happened tonight?" Frankie asks. "You said it sucked."

"Oh, that." I sigh. "How do I even begin?"

"Let me try," Frankie says. "Does it have something to do with Hanna's mom?"

I crack up. "You've known me too long."

"Should I even ask?" Frankie chuckles, playing with the brim of his Bowser baseball cap.

I roll my eyes. "You know I'm going to tell you. Cynthia drafted me into getting Hanna together with some guy. The blind date was today." I shake my head. "I don't know what I was thinking."

"What's he like?" Frankie asks. "I mean, if Cynthia picked him."

"Major douche," I say. "To the tenth. I didn't know they made them like that still."

Frankie laughs. "Does the douche have a name? Or is he off-brand?"

"Owen Smallwood." I snort. "I can't make this shit up."

"*Smallwood?*" Frankie shrieks. "Shut up!"

"I'm serious," I giggle. "I swear that's his name."

He cracks up. "That's anticlimactic."

"You've got to see him," I say. "Good-looking, total tool."

"Is she into him? Hanna?"

I breathe with disdain. "I think so."

"Well, come on," Frankie says finally. "Jerome? That wasn't going to last. Plus, after what he said to Nick, I've sworn revenge." He throws a couple kicks in the air. "This'll hit where it hurts. Go O!"

"Nick's my brother," I say. "I wanted to kill Jerome as much as you did. But Owen's a thousand times worse."

"Oh, damn." Frankie shakes his head. "This is really bad, then."

The two of us stand in silence for a moment, mulling everything over. Frankie motions for me to take a seat on the floor, and the two of us slide down, our backs against a pile of boxed plasmas.

"Hey, Frankie," I say after a few minutes pass. "I hate to be a drag, but can you drive me home?"

"Right now?"

"Hanna and Owen are still at the plaza deciding what they want to name their kids, and I don't have a ride. I really don't want to go back there."

Frankie's face falls. "I mean, I can. It'll be a while though. My shift goes until midnight, but if you want to wait around, it'll only be a few hours."

"It's fine," I say quickly. "Don't worry about it. I'll call Nick. Thanks, though."

"You sure?" Frankie seems sad. "It's no problem. Honestly."

"It's cool," I say. "I appreciate it though. I'll stop by soon."

Remembering the entire reason I'm here, I buy an energy drink from the vending machine on the way out. Back in eighth grade, I would've just bummed one off Frankie, but for some reason, it feels wrong now. I take a large gulp and survey the parking lot, debating whether I should get Nick to take me home. Overall, Chester is a safe town, but nighttime brings out the weirdos, and I probably shouldn't walk alone. Mom's working late, Nick's got homework, and I'm not going back to the mall even if my life depends on it.

You know what? Never mind. I'll go home, download a couple movies, and just kick it. I flip open my phone and text Nick by muscle memory and wait for him to reply. I check it again and realize my phone's dead. Well, damn. Three miles away from the house, nobody's around, and my phone's dead. Right when I thought it couldn't get any worse. I mean, I could use one of the display chargers, or ask Frankie if I could borrow his phone, but I don't want to. In fact, I'm not going home. A molten heat is bubbling up from my core until it reaches every part of my body, and suddenly, I'm alert. Alive.

I jump into the air and charge across the parking lot, my sore feet slapping against the concrete, and spy an abandoned shopping cart on my right. I swivel around and change course. Throwing my purse into the cart basket, I place my drink in the cupholder. I lace up my Vans, firmly grip the handle, plant my foot against the ground, and tee off repeatedly until I'm cruising at a decent speed. I am now rolling freely across the parking lot and gathering momentum by the second.

Faster and faster. I swerve, barely missing the mirror on a brand-new Hummer, and almost lose traction, but balance out and pick up more speed. I'm flying now, faster than I've ever gone in my life, but I've got to turn. If I don't, I'm going to hit the grassy slope that divides the parking lot from the highway, or worse, end up as a hood ornament on someone's 4x4. I put my foot down to slow the cart, but my skate shoes have no tread left on them and do little to slow me down. I could jump off, but that's a sprained wrist at the least, since I can't see much or gauge how far off the ground I actually am.

The cart smashes into a concrete divider and jerks violently, sending me flying up in the air. Somehow, I keep one hand gripping the handle while the rest of me is flung into the heavens. Once I lose that grip, I thump onto the dewy grass of the slope, my breath whooshing out of me. Stunned, I raise my head and realize the cart is rolling towards me for another round. Jittery from the caffeine, I lift my foot and kick at the cart viciously, only to bring it down on top of me. Now trapped in the basket, I push and shove, screaming in a stimulant-induced panic.

A lifted Jeep rolls up beside the curb, country music booming out of the stereo. I panic, figuring some Jethro is going to abduct me. The driver's side door opens, and I spy a pair of red-and-white Air Jordans stepping toward me.

"Help!" I scream. "Stranger danger! Charles Manson's out on parole. Please, help!"

"Relax," a warm, familiar voice laughs. "It's just me."

My insides turn to ice. I'd rather be anywhere else in the world right now—and that includes the back of Porn Stache's perv van. Because that voice that just spoke to me?

It belongs to none other than Blake Tisdale.

***

Blake comes into view and crouches beside me, relaxed and confident. His cologne floods my senses, and I notice his luscious auburn hair is even shinier than usual under the street lamps. I can tell he's trying not to laugh at my predicament. I want nothing more than to vanish.

"Looks like someone needs help," he observes. "Good thing Charles Manson's still in jail. Otherwise, this rescue might've ended up a lot bloodier than it already is. Roxie?"

"I'm fine," I say hurriedly. "I just…"

"Hold still," Blake commands. Bending down, he grips the cart with both hands and heaves it off me. "Are you hurt?"

"Never been better," I say, feeling my face flame. "Wow, didn't you come at a good time?"

Blake chuckles and retrieves my purse from the cart. Handing it to me, he nods at the drink can. "Under the influence? Underage drinking and driving can have serious consequences, young lady."

I smile weakly. "Won't happen again."

"Well," Blake says. "Given I just rescued you from a near-deadly accident, how did you end up at Walmart riding a shopping cart down a hill into Friday traffic?" He looks at me. "I have to hear this."

"That's a cool Jeep you have there," I say, trying to change the subject.

"Thanks. I saved up a bit of money to buy her off my uncle last year. With a bit of elbow grease, got her up and running. But please, I'm a lot more interested in your driving than mine."

"Stupidity," I say. "Excessive caffeine. Stress. Teenage angst and four wheels should never go together." I nod at the cart. "Case in point."

"Rough night, huh?"

"That's an understatement."

"Well," Blake says. "No broken bones or internal bleeding, it looks like. Still, it's late, and you're out here alone. You need a ride?"

"Well, I had the cart, but that's not happening again," I say. "Yeah, actually."

Blake nods towards the Jeep, which is still running. "Hop in."

"Thanks," I mutter. My heart is hammering, and I open the passenger's side door and climb inside. Blake gets in and fastens his seatbelt, turning down the radio before shifting into drive.

"Really, thank you," I say, suddenly able to find my voice again. "You didn't have to do this, you know."

"No worries," Blake replies, signaling out of the shoulder. "It's no problem. I could use the company. Are you warm enough?"

"Yeah," I say. "Damn, it's freezing tonight."

Blake nods. "You could say that again. Where am I going?"

"Make a left," I say, nodding up at the intersection. "Turn on Hillcrest."

"Did you see that traffic?" Blake asks. "Down on the freeway? At this time of night? Never used to see that around here."

I look over at him. "Did you grow up in Chester?"

"Yeah." Blake drums his fingers on the steering wheel. "Born and raised. My mom's from up by Twin Lakes. My dad's from here, though. Even went to the same high school as us."

I nod. "We moved here a few years ago. Used to live about an hour west of here."

"How do you like it?" Blake asks.

"I like it," I say. "It doesn't take much to keep me busy. A few good friends, good food, fresh air…"

"Yeah." Blake smiles. "I'm with you there."

"So, it's busier here now? More than it used to be?"

"Oh yeah," Blake says. "Ever since they put the hospital in, the traffic has gotten insane. Before that, on a night like tonight, you'd be out driving across town and pass two, maybe three cars, tops. Now, you'll never see that. Probably never again."

We're not too far from my house now, which makes me sad since I don't want this ride to end. Should I bring up Tristan's party? I worry it'd seem odd to just bring it up randomly, though I probably should, since I've been waiting for the chance to explain what happened to Blake for ages. At school, Chaz and I spend most of our time together, and, to outside eyes, it might look like we're a couple. Even so, the timing doesn't seem right. Instead, I sit quietly and try to look as cute as I can, stealing glances at Blake the entire time.

"Did you get what you needed?" he asks, breaking the short silence. "At Walmart?"

"I was just visiting a friend," I reply. "And I bought a drink. *The* drink."

Blake smiles. "Does she go to the high school? Your friend, I mean?"

"It's a dude," I say. "A friend of my brother, Nick."

"Oh."

The conversation is beginning to strain. Neither of us have anything to say, which makes me feel worse. I open my mouth to force out an explanation of what went down at Tristan's, but I don't get the chance. Blake's cell phone rings, and he turns down the stereo, fumbling in his pocket.

"Excuse me." He accepts the call and places his phone against his ear. Faintly, I can hear a high-pitched, female voice on the other end. Jealousy slashes through me. As the two of them go back and forth, she laughs at everything he says, no matter if it's actually funny.

"Which house?" Blake asks as the car inches down my street. I point towards it, straining to hear who's on the other line. Whoever it is, she's into him. But again, who wouldn't be? We pull up in front of my driveway, and Blake shifts into park.

"Anybody home?" Blake mouths, pulling his cell away from his head.

"Yeah," I whisper. "My brother's home. Thank you so much."

"No worries," Blake says. "Stay away from shopping carts, okay?"

I smile and hop out of the Jeep. "Promise."

Blake honks once before turning around and driving in the opposite direction. I feel sad for a moment and then try to focus on the positive: Blake gave me a ride home. I should go inside and debrief the evening's events with Nick, but instead, I remain standing in the driveway, breathing in the sharp, cool air.

"Well," a low, rumbling voice says somewhere out in the darkness. "What was *that* all about?"

It takes several seconds before I put a face to it.

"*Blaze?*"

Chaz's father is standing at the far end of our driveway, holding a can of Hefeweizen in one hand and a leash in the other. Bruno, the family bulldog, sniffs at something in the grass before growling at me. If you're like me and believe dogs are people, I've officially been stalked by three male members of one family.

And to think I believed it couldn't get creepier.

"Look," Blaze says, his voice softening. "It's none of my business. But if you're done with Chaz, go on and tell him so. I can't have you breaking my boy's heart. Not on my watch."

"Um, what?"

"You don't need to tell me." Blaze scratches at his stubble. "Chaz takes after his mother's body composition. In the face, he's more of a mix. If there's someone new, just tell him."

Bruno takes advantage of the situation and squats down next to Nick's basketball hoop to take a shit. His back legs strain, trembling with exertion as a pebbly log drops onto my driveway.

"Holy crap," Blaze howls, toeing the poop into the grass. "Sorry, 'bout that. Consider it free fertilizer. Damn dog went twice already. But, as I was saying, I thought you two were a thing?"

I feign confusion. "What are you talking about? Where is this conversation going?"

"Listen, Missy." Blaze shoots me a sharp look. "I never said I was the sharpest tool in the barn. Oh, no. Ask most people, and they'll say I'm just a tool, sharp, dull, or otherwise." He laughs again. "But I ain't dumb. Or blind. That boy who drove you home, there's a spark there nobody could deny. I saw it. Just be honest and I'll stay out of it."

"Whoa, hold up," I say. "Are you talking about *James*? My *cousin*?"

A look of confusion passes across Blaze's face before he doubles over and slaps his thigh. "Damn, you got me good!" he yells. "Sweet Jesus, I done it again!"

I screw up my face in mock confusion. "You didn't think we were, like, going out, did you?"

Blaze suddenly looks embarrassed. "No, no," he lies, staring at his shoes sheepishly. "I do have to say, though, you come from some attractive roots, young lady. Damn good-looking family."

"That's so kind, Mr. Humbert," I say, dredging up every bit of niceness I can. "But I should probably go inside."

"Of course, of course," Blaze calls after me. "And remember. The name's Blaze. Only the Guatemalan lady at the bank and my marriage counselor call me Mr. Humbert." He lets out a booming laugh and polishes off the last of his brew. "Well, I'm off. Swing by the house some time, yeah?" He crushes the can in his fist.

I smile thinly. "Good night, Blaze."

Chapter 11

"What *happened* last night?" Hanna demands. "Where did you go? Owen and I waited for you to come back for over an hour before we realized you just left!"

"Sorry," I grumble, still pissed off from a poor night's rest. I shift the phone against my ear. "But you left waiting for me was the least of my problems. You don't even want to know what I had to go through."

"Well, things would've been fine if you'd just stuck around," Hanna complains. "Owen and I had a lot of fun."

"Owen wasn't having any fun." I sniff. "He ruined my night."

"What do you mean?" Hanna asks. "We went to Brookstone after we got done waiting for you and had a blast. How did he ruin your night?"

"Seriously? All he did was bitch and moan. He was pissed off about everything, trashed the mall, and said some rude shit about Emilio." I roll my eyes. "The dude's a royal dick."

"Wow," Hanna says, sounding taken aback. "He was really nice to me and was super friendly with the people who helped us. Are we talking about the same person here?"

"That conversation can wait," I say flatly. "The bigger issue is I've got a stalker. It's Chaz's dad. I'm not kidding. I got a ride home with Blake and—"

"Wow," Hanna cuts in. "You managed to get a ride with Blake. I'd think you'd be in a better mood."

"Will you let me finish?" I snap. "Listen to me. Blaze appeared out of my bushes and accused me of cheating on Chaz with Blake. I told him Blake was my cousin, and he seemed convinced enough to drop it. It was a close call, though. *Way* too close to happen again."

"Hold up," Hanna says. "Cheating? What do you mean cheating?"

"Remember? I told you about it. Chaz and I pretend to be dating when Blaze is around because he doesn't want his parents knowing he's gay until he's ready to come out."

"Yeah, I remember that now," Hanna says. "But who's Blaze?"

"Do you listen to anything I say? Blaze is Chaz's dad. He refuses to answer to anything besides that. Who knows? Maybe it was his alias when he trafficked underage girls before coaching football."

"You don't know that," Hanna counters. "Maybe he just happened to be on your street. I mean, none of us live that far away from each other."

"Jesus H. Christ, Hanna!" I shake my head. "You think everybody's Siddhartha reincarnated, don't you? I'm telling you, this dude's an adult Chaz pre-suspension. I can't get away!"

"Well, what are you going to do then?" Hanna asks. "Maybe you should tell Chaz to end this arrangement. Fake a breakup in front of Blaze. Chaz isn't stupid, and he's a great actor. I'm sure he'll come up with something."

"Yeah, fair point."

"And we don't know for certain that his parents will even care if he's gay," Hanna points out. "Maybe we've got this entire thing way out of line. They love him, I'm sure. I really don't think this will change how they feel about him."

"I don't know," I say. "The way Chaz tells it, Mrs. Humbert is deeply religious. He thinks she won't be okay with the gay."

Hanna stifles a laugh. "And that she'll pray it away?"

"Exactly."

"What about Blaze?" Hanna asks. "Is he the safer bet?"

"Maybe," I say. "I don't think he's too religious. He's a coin toss." I take a breath. "By the way, I ran into Emilio yesterday. He was buying CeCe maternity clothes. She was in the car, though, so I didn't see her."

"So Erik came through with the money then," Hanna says after a brief pause.

"I guess."

"I need to ask you something," Hanna says, drawing a shaky breath. "And I want your honest opinion."

"Okay," I say, knowing exactly where this is heading.

"What do you think Jerome would do if I started seeing Owen?" Hanna asks. "Exclusively?"

"He'll die," I blurt. "You can't do that to Jerome. At least give it a little time. You just met Owen, and you'll look way too eager. But Jerome? I don't think he'll ever love again."

"Well, well. Somebody's sure changed her tune," Hanna muses. "Two years you've been hounding me to dump him, and all of a sudden, he's the one?"

"It's not like that," I say, racking my brain for bullshit to feed my closest friend. "It's just, from the time you broke up with him, I think he's really grown up since then. I see you two together, and it's like there's this familiarity there. I think you'd miss it, that's all." I finish my lame rambling and squeeze my eyes closed, completely embarrassed by everything I just said.

"Well, familiarity isn't always good," Hanna says. "And you're right. It is too soon. But still. Owen." She sighs dreamily. "Some other force must've brought us together."

"You could say that again," I mutter, thinking of the hours Cynthia spent conspiring.

"Huh?"

"Nothing," I say quickly.

***

"No."

"I'm sorry, man," I say, tossing the hacky sack Chaz brought from home back over to him. "Your dad's a predator."

The two of us met up behind Target and are sitting down outside against the back of the store. Chaz picks at a loose thread and lobs an underhanded toss back to me.

"You can't be serious," Chaz says. "Maybe it's a mistake. Lots of people look like Kid Rock."

I fold my arms. "Where was he this morning?"

"Getting the oil changed," Chaz replies a little uneasily.

"Wrong. He was driving back and forth in front of my house. Nick can confirm there was a 'buff guy in a green truck' circling for about five minutes." I shrug. "Ask him if you want."

"Can't be," Chaz groans. "There's got to be a mix-up."

"Well, maybe. Unless this mix-up also showed up at my front door last night," I say. "Blake dropped me off—you know, after I ditched Hanna and Smallwood at the plaza. Your dad just happened to be at the end of our driveway. He confronted me, too. Told me I should break things off if I was seeing someone else."

Chaz's eyebrows vanish into his hairline. "Seriously?"

I nod. "Oh yeah."

"How does he know where you live?" Chaz mumbles, twisting the hacky sack between his clammy hands.

"Beats me. But he knows. Hell, he probably spends more time on my street than in the man cave."

"My God," Chaz moans. "I'm so sorry. Really, truly am."

"About this morning," I say. "I was taking out the garbage and saw this plaid plant I've never seen in all three years of living there. This plant must be from Lord of the Rings because it was moving around and cracking arthritically and swearing the entire time." I smirk. "Where did Dad say he was going today, Chaz?"

Chaz buries his face in his hands. "Something about getting groceries."

"And what was he wearing?"

"Jeans, boots, and a plaid shirt," Chaz shudders. "Hunter green."

"So, here's what needs to happen," I say. "Before I end up locked in your basement for the next thirty years, you need to break up with me. Act depressed, talk about having your heart broken, say I cheated on you, pretend to cheat on me… I really couldn't care less. But when it comes to stalking, Humbert males Chaz, Blaze, and Bruno, in that particular order, need to cease and desist."

"Agreed," Chaz says. "I never should've asked. It was a stupid idea. I'll figure something out. And again. Sorry about Blaze."

"Well, at least he goes down easier than Owen," I say, making a face. "You don't even want to know what that was all about."

"You were going to tell me," Chaz says. "Do tell. Reveal the mysteries of the Bronze God."

I gag. "Do you think he's hot?"

Chaz fans himself. "Oh, honey. He's third degree."

"Meet him," I say. "Trust me, the effect wears off pretty fast. He was cute until he opened his mouth."

"Well. Is he funny at least?" Chaz asks. "Like, Steve Stifler funny?"

"Oh God, no." I shake my head. "No personality. Super negative. The way he carries on, he was some sort of social butterfly back in Santa Barbara, and his life's over now that he's surrounded by a bunch of hicks who've never been surfing."

"Well, isn't it?" Chaz asks, chuckling. "I mean, Chester is about as sleepy as it gets."

"Beside the point," I grumble. "You don't show up somewhere and disrespect it to the people who live there. You just don't."

"Yeah, I guess," Chaz says. "What other stuff did he do?"

"Oh jeez. I don't know where to begin. First, he doesn't call Santa Barbara 'Santa Barbara.' He calls it 'Santa Barb.'" I roll my eyes. "He has a digital watch that goes off when he needs to stuff his face, he racially profiled Emilio, and he's horrible to me. But with Hanna, he's the exact opposite."

"Shut up."

"No, I'm serious," I say. "The second Hanna's around, he's all smiles and Mr. Charming. Upbeat. Cracking jokes." I sigh. "She's falling for it, Chaz. Hook, line, and sinker."

"Wow," Chaz breathes. "I wish I would've been at the mall Friday."

"Why, so you could see the 'Bronze God' in the flesh?" I mock. "The Burned Turd is more like it. Word up, Owen sucks."

Neither of us speak for a while before Chaz raises his chin and takes a breath.

"I think," he begins, his expression thoughtful. "I think Owen's trying to break you two apart. Before he gets with her."

"Wait," I say. "Break us apart? As in wreck our friendship? He barely knows her!"

"Doesn't matter." Chaz turns to face me. "Think about it. If he showed you that side of himself, and he showed the exact opposite side to Hanna…I mean, you two are girls. Girls talk about everything. Did you tell Hanna how he was when he was with you?"

I groan. "Yeah. I did."

"Well, there you go," Chaz says. "You played right into it. Right into his manicured, SoCal hands."

"And Hanna seemed put out," I recall. "She seemed irritated that I didn't see the fun-loving, cool Owen she did."

Chaz nods. "And there it is. There's a wedge already."

"But why?" I burst out. "What's in it for him? Is he controlling? Does he hate me? What would he get out of ruining our friendship?"

"Two things that I can think of," Chaz says, sitting up straight. "First, he gets Hanna completely. And second, in order to succeed, he needs to reveal his true self to somebody who isn't Hanna. That way, he can divorce himself from the negative ego and fully assume the positive, desirable role."

"Jesus, Chaz. Where do you get this stuff?" I shake my head. "How do you know this? Wait. Was it you who was the Dr. Phil fan?"

"Oh, I do love Dr. Phil," Chaz laughs. "And Oprah. But no. I'm the younger brother of a drug addict who played my family against itself until it was never the same again. A brother who stole thousands of dollars pretending to get clean. And I'm also the boy, in case you forgot, who had an entire middle school and high school staff wrapped around his pinkie finger until the karma hit." He laughs bitterly. "I'm not a good person, Roxie. I'm better, and I'm trying, but it doesn't mean I'm good."

"Damn," I say finally. "I didn't know you had a brother. I'm really sorry. You know, about what you just told me."

"Don't worry about it," Chaz says dismissively. "Didn't know him too well. He's not dead or anything. I mean, my mom still talks to him when she can. But Blaze and him? To those two, the other's as good as gone."

"You are a good person." I scoot closer to him. "I see it. Good people get on a bad path sometimes, too."

"Trying to be," Chaz says. "I'm trying to be a good person."

"Well, thanks for the help," I say. "At least I kind of have an idea of where he's coming from now. Everything makes a lot more sense." I sigh. "And of course, Cynthia chooses him. Surprise, surprise."

"You're a smart cookie," Chaz says, picking a pebble out of the sole of his sneaker. "You know how the game is played. Lay off, cool down. And don't let Owen know anything he says or does gets under your skin. He showed his cards to you. Eventually, Hanna will catch on."

***

"Guess what?" CeCe exclaims. "Guess what Emilio's been up to?"

"What?" Chaz asks, CeCe's glee causing him to smile. "Whatever it is, you sure perked up, didn't you?"

"Erik gave Emilio the money," CeCe says, dropping her voice. "Five hundred in cash."

"Yes!" Chaz and I each hold up a hand, and she high-fives us. "But that's not the best part."

"Does it get any better?" Hanna laughs. "Five hundred; I'd be smiling too."

"I didn't tell you what Erik's job is. He's working a lot harder than a fry cook does, I'll tell you that," CeCe snickers. "He's not allowed to leave the campus, and the only job they had open was at the stables. Collecting horse semen."

Hanna and I scream. "No!"

"Oh yeah," CeCe says. "What did Erik say to the horse?"

"What?" Hanna giggles.

"Pleasure doing business with you. And it must be. Emilio was watching him the whole time to make sure he was doing it right and everything. Apparently, he's really good."

"Employee of the month," I cackle. "Well, from what Emilio told us, Elderwood is a 'stimulating' learning environment. Must've been inspiring."

"Hey." Two tan, muscular arms wind around Hanna's waist and pull her in close. "What's going on, Han?"

"Hey, Owen," Hanna says demurely, laying a small hand on his giant one. "Guys, I want you to meet Owen. Owen, these are my friends."

Owen shoots all of us a cocky grin. "Owen Smallwood," he thunders, extending his hand to each of them. Chaz holds on a little longer than usual for his shake, and I try not to laugh.

"And Roxie of course," Hanna says, gesturing to me.

"Well, of course," Owen says quickly. "Roxie?"

I force a nod. "Owen."

"Anyway," Owen says. "What's the scoop? Everybody looks amped up. Why don't you fill me in on what's going on?"

Wow. On top of being a jerk, he's nosy to boot. He'd be way better matched with Jenna Carmichael, but he brutally shot her down earlier when she tried to talk to him.

"Well, I've got to go," I announce. "Study hall. You two, I need your help with algebra. Come on."

CeCe catches on at once, but Chaz stares at me. "Wait, what?"

"Move," I hiss, grabbing his arm and pulling him along. "Let's bounce."

"What's your deal?" Chaz demands once we reach the library. "Chill, you're freaking me out now."

"We need to be more careful." I drop my voice to a whisper. "CeCe. No more talking about this at school. We're trying to keep your pregnancy on the down low, but extorting Erik? If any of this gets out, we're done for. How long was Owen standing there?"

"Good point," Chaz says. "I don't know. He just showed up out of nowhere."

"You're right." CeCe looks panicked. "It was stupid of me. I should've been way more careful."

"You didn't say anything too obvious," I say. "But still. This is a little too close to the other side of the line to talk about openly. Even if we code it."

The two of them nod their agreement.

Chaz slings his backpack over one shoulder. "Well, I'm off. I'll see you two later. Lunch?"

I nod. "Same time, same spot."

"I don't feel good," CeCe murmurs as the two of us head to science.

"What is it?" I ask. "Did you eat breakfast? Skipping meals always makes me feel sick. Want a Pop-Tart? I've got a couple."

"I'm okay," she says. "Thanks, though."

I stop in my tracks. "You haven't been getting sick recently... have you?"

"No," CeCe replies. "That stopped a while ago. I should be fine."

"Do you want to go to the nurse?" I ask. "I basically live there when I'm not at the principal's. It's comfortable. They've got couches and everything."

"No. She'll just start asking questions."

"She can't press you," I point out. "Plus everything's confidential in the nurse's office."

CeCe shakes her head. "Forget it."

"Okay then," I say slowly. "Let's go to class, I guess."

We step into Mr. Burke's classroom seconds before the bell rings and drop into our seats. The chatter stops, and Burke points to the whiteboard, where 'silent reading' is written in block letters. Opening his laptop, he tunes us out, and thirty or so students reach into their bags for their books.

I pull out whatever book I've got stashed for silent reading, but can't tear my eyes away from CeCe, who looks larger than the week before and is visibly gaining weight in her cheeks. I'm mulling this over when something sharp prods me between my shoulder blades.

"Hey. Roxie."

I turn around. "Yeah?"

"Have you *seen* CeCe lately?" Felicia Walsh demands. A bitchy know-it-all and quintessential mean girl, Felicia is the last person I want noticing CeCe's transformation. I guess the cosmos has decided to send one more unnecessary obstacle our way.

"Yeah, like thirty seconds ago?"

Felicia rolls her eyes skyward. "No, I mean have you noticed how *fat* she's getting?"

I gulp. "She doesn't look any different to me."

Felicia disregards this and leans in closer to me. "Did you hear about Erik?" she asks. "He left. Doesn't play football anymore. He didn't even tell anybody where he went. I heard she's knocked up, which is why he's gone."

"Sounds like a stupid rumor," I say as uninterestedly as I can. "You can never trust stuff like that."

"No talking," Mr. Burke says sternly. "Yeah, you, Roxie." He wags a finger at me threateningly.

I turn away from him and open up *Fun With Dick and Jane*, pretending to read. Aside from a person occasionally coughing or shifting about in their chair, the only noise comes from the people walking past the classroom in the hallway.

Suddenly, CeCe doubles over and retches, vomiting all over the floor of the classroom. Students gasp and pull back as she shudders and pukes again. None of us say a word. As for me? I'm immobilized. I want to go over and comfort her, but there's no way in hell I'm getting near the sixth Great Lake that has formed on the classroom floor. The kids closest to her have either exited their chairs and migrated away, or are sitting on top of their desks, looking in horror at the grayish slop below.

"Okay," Mr. Burke sighs, shaking his head. "No one move."

He pushes a button and picks up the phone, cradling it against his shoulder. "CeCe, why don't you go on and head over to the nurse."

Nodding gratefully, CeCe grabs her backpack and walks quickly out of the room with her head down. A couple students give her sympathetic nods, but stay silent.

"Damn it," Burke mutters, slamming the receiver down. "I'm going to the office. Stay in your chairs."

The second he leaves, the classroom descends into chaos as everybody begins chattering amongst themselves.

"Did you *see* that?" Felicia exclaims. "Freaking disgusting. I called it."

"Did you see her face?" Emma Wilkes sniffs. "I mean, the bathroom's, like, right down the hall. Why couldn't she hold it in?"

"Duh. Do you seriously not get it?" Felicia shakes her head. "She couldn't make it because she's *pregnant*."

"Oh, my God, really?" a third girl gasps. "How do you know?"

"Uh, I don't know." Felicia smirks. "A baggy sweatshirt. Absent from class for like an entire month. Puking all over the place. What more proof do you need, Becca?"

"Maybe she's got the flu," a nice, churchgoing kid named Nolan offers. "I mean, I was sick last week. Something's been going around."

"Oh, my God," Felicia breathes, shaking her head. "You guys are so stupid. Her boyfriend dumped her and left school. She's wearing hoodies big enough to go camping in. She's gone all the time. She's fat. And she just threw up."

"Yeah, it's not that hard to figure out," Emma says, now fully convinced. "And it's morning. She's totally knocked up."

"Lay off, Felicia," someone snaps from further down.

"I'm not judging," Felicia says, holding up her hands in earnest. "I just want to help. I mean, her life is basically over."

"Totally," Emma chimes in. "I mean, I don't know for sure, but I heard Erik transferred to Elderwood."

"Seriously?" Becca purses her lips. "Poor guy."

Mr. Burke returns a minute later with the janitor in tow. Immediately, the class falls silent, and everybody not in the immediate blast radius heads back to their desks.

"Everybody get back to your books," Mr. Burke orders. "Start reading. There's nothing to see here."

****

"This is bad," Nick says, wiping his hands on a flowery summer apron. "And to think, everything was going along so smoothly."

CeCe, Hanna, and I are sitting around the kitchen table while Nick doles out slices of applesauce cake straight from the oven. I just finished filling him in on the latest over a mug of steaming green tea he poured me when I got in. CeCe, feeling a lot better after second period, finished out the day and came straight to my place, where Nick hooked her up with an herbal brew for pregnant women that he and Emilio found on the internet.

"I hate girls," I say finally. "Hate them. She doesn't even leave the room, and Felicia jumps on her. For what? CeCe, you and Felicia never had any problems, did you?"

"None," CeCe replies, shaking her head. "I haven't talked to her once this entire semester."

"Girls are awful," Hanna agrees. "They can be. I'm sorry, CeCe."

"So she got pregnant." I wave my hands. "What's the big deal? I mean, everybody in that room's mother got pregnant at some point. Some start a little earlier."

"Yeah," Nick says with a shrug. "In Baba's village, CeCe would be considered a later-in-life pregnancy."

I snort. "Yeah, she and *Khanum* would have a lot to talk about."

"But that's high school for you," Nick sighs, shaking his head. "Drama, gossip, and living under the microscope. By the way," he says, "if that drink makes you barf again, the bathroom's down the hall. Left side."

"She'll be fine," Hanna says quickly. "Right, CeCe?"

And Hanna. She's been acting way off since this morning. I try not to dwell on it and help myself to another slice of applesauce cake.

"Hey, Nick, where's Emilio?" I ask. "Aren't you two supposed to hang out today? To work on hip-hop or something?"

"He's out," Nick says. "Later, though, yeah. He's collecting his grandpa's social security or something."

"OMG!" Hanna squeals and claps her hands excitedly. "Look!"

I take her phone to get a closer look. Owen is standing outside his house in Hawaiian-print board shorts with several surfboards leaning against the garage door behind him. He's feathered his hair and taken his shirt off. His nipples, which are unusually turgid and pink, shrivel in the late afternoon chill.

"What a douche," Nick gripes. "It's, like, forty degrees out there."

"Nick," I say. "Meet Owen."

"You guys are so judgmental," Hanna pouts, tucking her phone away. "I've finally got someone perfect. He's really sweet and cares." She looks at me. "Once you get to know him."

"Well, good for you," I say. "If he's the way you describe him, maybe he's different with different people. Maybe he just didn't like me or something."

"Owen's stressed," Hanna explains. "Right now. Because of moving and everything. He told me when we sat down that he was super nervous going out with us and was worried we didn't like him."

"We don't," I deadpan.

Hanna looks at me sadly. "Come on, really?"

"What?" I shrug. "If he is who you say he is, I'm happy for you, Han. What more do you want me to say?"

Hanna's phone dings again.

"That fast?"

CeCe shakes her head. "Let it sit, Hanna."

"Wow," Hanna breathes, ignoring CeCe's advice. "This one's really nice. Should I make it my wallpaper?"

"If you want him to dump you," CeCe answers flatly. "Want to lose him? Tell him he means everything to you. Get pregnant. Tell him you think he's the one and it's a done deal."

"You're right," Hanna says, blushing a deep scarlet. "Check it out, though."

Again, the shirt is off, but this time Owen's standing in front of a humongous poster of Bruce Lee. He's squatting in a fighting stance, holding his taped hands in front of him. Wearing the scowl of a man with immobilized bowels, Owen glares rebelliously into the lens, as if to say, "fight me." His legs are covered by loose-fitting black sweatpants with Japanese characters up both legs, and his feet are jammed into wooden clogs likely belonging to his mother. The caption? *Legends Never Die.*

"Well." Hanna looks at us. "What do you think?"

Silence.

"Come on," she says, that defensive tone coming out again. "I think it's cool. And really cute."

That's it. Calmly, I walk out of the kitchen and into the garage where I grab my bike, open the garage door, and make a beeline for Cynthia's.

My legs burn, working at three times their normal speed as I pedal furiously toward Hanna's street. On the way over, I pass Owen's house and see him striking yet another ridiculous pose in his front yard. This time, he's wearing a cowboy hat and leather pants while holding a plastic microphone. I flip him off with both hands and scream a chain of obscenities as I zip past.

I zoom up to Cynthia's front porch and jump off my bike, letting it clatter to the ground under me, before pounding on the front door. Hammering my fists, I pummel until the cold and the force of my knocking make my hands ache.

"Open! Up!"

"Who. The hell. Is that!?" an even louder voice screams from inside the house. "Whoever it is, do not break the goddamn door. I've got an AR-15, and I'm white!" The door swings open. "Roxie?"

"Hi, Cynthia," I say, realizing I've been acting insane. "Just hear me out, okay?"

"Is everything all right?" Cynthia asks, her voice full of concern. "Are you okay? What happened?"

"*Owen* happened."

"What do you mean 'Owen happened?'" Cynthia asks. "Okay, you know what? Come inside. I don't want you catching a chill."

The two of us step into the house, and Cynthia ushers me towards the front room where we both sit down across from each other. "Do you want anything? Water?"

"I'm good," I say quickly. "Cynthia, he's horrible. We've made a mistake, and I don't know what to do."

"How so?" Cynthia's brow knits. "Hanna couldn't stop gushing about how nice he was. Well, now's your time to talk. Hit me."

I rehash our outing to the mall, making a point of highlighting Owen's constant negativity. By the time I'm done, Cynthia looks decidedly more confused than when I was breaking down her front door, though she doesn't question anything I've said.

"I don't know," I finish. "I wasn't on board with this idea, but I wasn't not on board if that makes sense. I want Hanna to be happy. But this guy? He's bad news."

"I'm sure he was nervous," Cynthia reasons. "Maybe going out with you two was too much. It must've been intimidating, you know, meeting two attractive girls who happen to be best friends in one night. Girls can be really hard to please. Especially cute ones like you and Hanna."

"Well, he failed," I say flatly. "When you make fun of the place I live in, talk badly about a friend of my brother's and mine, it doesn't sit well with me."

"Nor should it. But sometimes people get nervous and say stuff. Act a certain way. Like a defensive thing. Try and put yourself in his shoes." Cynthia looks at me. "He's a high schooler. His parents moved in the middle of the year. All his friends are back home, in sunny, warm California, and life is going on without him." She sighs. "I can't imagine how hard that would be. And Chester? Well, it ain't Santa Barbara, that's for sure."

"I don't care," I spit. "He's a dick. Whatever. It's Hanna, Cynthia. She's completely gone, and it hasn't even been a week."

"Who could blame her?" Cynthia asks. "Going from Jerome to Owen? The girl's gone from the toilet in coach to sitting in first class. Maybe they'll listen to actual music now instead of three hours of homoerotic orgasms over death metal. Wet Banana! Ugh!"

I groan. Cynthia's not going to help. I knew she wouldn't be of much use, but I needed somebody outside the group who wasn't Nick to listen to me. But she's made up her mind, Hanna's made up hers, and clearly, Owen's here to stay. It isn't easy being the one who can see trouble coming around the corner, but it's the story of my life. And now, if my predictions are accurate, we're about to get in it deep.

"How's Blake?" Cynthia asks, bringing me out of my thoughts. "Hanna told me he gave you a ride home from the mall the other day."

"He's fine," I say quickly. "Seems like he's doing well."

"You know, Owen came over Saturday afternoon and was talking about trying out for baseball."

I turn around. "Really?"

"And Blake," Cynthia continues. "He's the pitcher, right?"

"Yeah, Blake's the pitcher," I reply. "At least I'm pretty sure."

"Well, if Owen makes the team, he'll probably end up knowing Blake, at least somewhat," Cynthia says lightly. "Maybe you and Hanna can go on double dates. It's the way things go nowadays. Worked great for my other girls."

"Yeah." My stomach clenches. "Maybe we will."

Though the thought of that is more than enticing, I highly doubt it'll ever happen. Tristan's party was months ago, and what we had was a fifteen-minute interaction. Blake, being a varsity athlete, is likely dating somebody and thinks I'm round the twist. Whoever he was talking to in the car the other night was into him, and with his athletic prowess, perfect bone structure, and genuine kindness, he's probably got another ten girls lined up behind her. With that thought, I feel sad. Sad I'm not popular. Not older. People claim that life gets easier when you grow up, but looking at Nick, Cynthia, and my own mother, I really doubt that's the case.

The room feels a lot smaller than when I first sat in it, and the air is getting harder to breathe. I feel like Porn Stache is standing on my chest, shifting his weight to deliberately make me feel uncomfortable. I stay a couple more minutes before thanking Cynthia for lending her ear and step back out into the cold.

***

When you're little, Valentine's Day is awesome. Your parents surprise you with a big basket filled with candies and stuffed animals, and at school all your classmates give you valentines and chocolates. It's one of your favorite holidays, right after Halloween and Christmas, and you look forward to it months in advance. After fourth grade, however, Valentine's Day starts losing its charm. It's no longer required to give your classmates candy or valentines, and those irritating girls who curl their hair and wear ballet flats get paper hearts from admirers in every grade. Still, you don't care that you didn't get one. You convince yourself you didn't want anything, but maybe if you cheered for the cutest boy in school instead of tackling him at recess because he cheated at kickball, you'd have gotten one too.

When you hit middle school, that's when it starts to hurt. Some of your friends have boyfriends, and even though you laugh and make fun of them, something inside you wishes a boy would come decorate your locker and slip you a valentine in between classes. In seventh grade, it didn't look like I had any prospects, so Hanna sent me a bouquet of roses and almost bought out the entire candy aisle for me. When I got to my locker, I acted shocked and flattered that "my man" would do such a thing. Since I never went through an awkward stage, unlike many of my peers, it was totally believable that some phantom boy would go all out like that, and people noticed. The year after that, I pulled a box of chocolates and a hundred-dollar iTunes gift card out in front of Jenna Carmichael. Hanna still laughs about it, remembering the look of spite on her face.

I didn't have to do the same for Hanna because she was dating Jerome by then and got a real card along with a pink inflatable guitar that read *Rock on, Valentine*. It was a thoughtful enough gesture, even though the following year she got the exact same thing.

I step off the bus, and over by the entrance, I spy Emilio's Impala parked over the corner with him outside of it, puffing on a Fuente. He sees me and waves me over. As I get closer to him, I see he's wearing his famous fedora and Carhartt work jacket with blue slacks.

"Want a smoke?" Emilio chuckles, holding out his cigar.

"I'm good," I laugh. "What's new? How've you been?"

"Good," he answers. "I was at your house yesterday. You were asleep, I think." He pauses. "I got to ask you, though. Have you seen CeCe recently? Anywhere? I can't find her."

"No, actually," I say. "Come to think of it, I was going to ask you the same."

Emilio's face grows worried. "Is she okay?"

I grimace. "Well, I don't know. She threw up in second period a few days back."

"Oh shit." Emilio sighs. "In front of everybody?"

"Yep."

"Poor thing." Emilio shakes his head. "That *hijo de puta* Erik. I'll send him some extra horses so he can throw up, too."

"I heard about his new line of work," I laugh. "Sounds like a blast."

Emilio cackles and fist-bumps me. "I like you," he says. "You remind me of your brother in so many ways. You're like the girl version of him. Just a little more normal."

I smile. "Well, I don't know about that. I just hide things a bit better."

"You know how to reach me," Emilio says, patting his jacket pocket. "But enough talk for now. Don't waste any more time with this dropout." He nods towards the building. "Get to class."

Parting ways with Emilio, I walk towards the main building and step inside. The building is adorned with crepe paper and streamers. The normally eggshell hallways are lit up with pink-and-white fairy lights, and everywhere I turn, attraction rages from every side.

In the freshman hall, festivities are alive and well. Girls compare their loot while guys lean up against their lockers, playing it cool. The girls who didn't get anything cluster together by the far door, muttering angrily amongst themselves. Before I reach my locker, I'm nearly flattened, first by a raging fatass holding a bassoon case and then by a gaggle of girls clutching flowers and teddy bears. As I fiddle with my combination, someone taps my shoulder.

"Sorry to be a pain," Chaz says. "But we've got to talk."

"I'm listening."

"You don't have any plans tonight, right?" Chaz asks. "I mean, you aren't going anywhere for Valentine's Day?"

"Nope." I shrug. "After you ran off Blake, the only boy I've been or will be interested in, I've been off to the nunnery. No, I'm not going anywhere."

"Sorry, sorry, sorry," Chaz says, shaking his head. "I swear on my future boo-boo's pecs I'll make that right. Somehow. But listen. You're not sitting at home tonight." He smiles.

I raise my eyebrows. "I'm not? Is Zac Efron taking me out to dinner?"

Chaz's face falls. "Well, not quite. I am. I booked us a reservation at The Three Larks."

"The Three Larks?"

"It's a restaurant," Chaz says. "Fancy place."

"I know what it is," I reply. The Three Larks is an expensive restaurant downtown. It's been there for ages. Though I've never been there, I've been curious about it for years.

"Thanks, but we really don't have to go. You and I could just stay in, rent a DVD or something." Even so, I hope we'll still go. It sounds like it might be fun.

"It's Blaze," Chaz finally says. "He told me you're the best thing that's ever happened to me, and I don't disagree, but he said I needed to 'revitalize our relationship' if I want to keep you."

"I knew it!" Of course Blaze would be behind this. "Great. I'll wear a fancy dress, and let me know an hour in advance. The Three Larks it is."

"Thanks," Chaz breathes, looking grateful. "I promise, I'm trying to get rid of him. But tonight? It's a date."

"You think he'll leave me alone?" I ask. "After tonight? Will this be enough proof we're a thing?"

"I don't know what goes on in that man's head," Chaz sighs. "He should maybe focus more on his failing marriage than on my fake high school relationship. But it's Blaze. And he makes most of his decisions drunk."

"Well, I don't disagree, but I have to go," I say, checking the time. "Fullerton's probably writing my detention slip as we speak."

"Got it." Chaz smiles. "See you at lunch."

I race towards Mrs. Fullerton's room and glance over at the digital hall clock. Three minutes 'til, which means I've got to hoof it if I want to receive my flowers and gift card in front of Jenna. Ducking around students, I'm rounding the corner when I hear a loud gasp.

"Baby," a high-pitched voice coos. "You shouldn't have."

Surrounded by onlookers, Tiffany Verlich is burying her face in a giant plush teddy bear, while in her other hand, she holds a large box of See's Candies. She smiles down at the bear she's motorboating. "He's so cute. Thanks, Blakey."

"No worries, Tiff," Blake Tisdale says, his brown eyes warm underneath his Chester Cavaliers ball cap. "You're welcome."

***

To her credit, Tiffany has never tried to hide the fact she's a ho. With her year-round spray tan, bitchy voice, and legs that are constantly angled one-hundred-eighty degrees, she's earned her title of "Chester Transit." Inspired, Hanna and I drummed up a few of our own, but other nicknames I've heard going around are "Rough Rider," "The Crab Pot," "Red Lobster," "Sushi Cruise," and, my personal favorite, "Please Come Again." Even in the dead of winter, Tiffany will arrive at school scantily dressed, and on any given day, you can find her parading the halls in five-inch heels and miniskirts a Bangkok hooker wouldn't even be wearing. But that's the least of it. Every semester, Tiffany breaks up at least one longterm relationship and carries on countless flings while doing it. Among girls, most of us hate her, but somehow, she's always got a man.

Why is Blake dating her? Is he? There's got to be some explanation for this. Maybe they're friends, and this is just a platonic thing. She certainly needs an image boost. There's no way those two can be together, though. It just doesn't make sense.

"Sweetie," she whispers, pulling him in close and tapping him on the nose. She places the box of chocolates into a brightly colored gift bag and drops the bear to the floor. "You're too good to me."

Blake loops an arm around her waist and brushes a lock of box-dyed blond hair out of her face, pulling her close to him. He whispers something in her ear, and she throws her head back, laughing flirtatiously.

My scalp tightens, and my pulse sounds exponentially louder in my ears. *It's okay,* I try to convince myself. *There still could be an explanation for this.*

I don't want to look anymore, but I have to see this through. The two of them pull closer and closer until Tiffany breaks away.

"I got you something too," Tiffany chirps, reaching into her open locker and handing Blake a gift bag adorned with doilies and lace. She bounces up and down like a toddler on crank. "Open it!"

Blake ruffles the tissue paper and peeks inside. A huge smile spreads across his face. "Thanks, Tiff," he says, opening his backpack and placing it inside. My heart plummets around the same time Blake tilts Tiffany's chin up and pulls her to him. I can't bring myself to look. As cheers and wolf whistles break out all around, I know exactly what just happened.

I can't decide who I'm angrier at—Tiffany or myself. I feel like my heart has been ripped out of my chest, incinerated, and then hurled into a trash compactor. On top of everything else, I feel weak and stupid because I swore I would never allow my heart to get broken. Is it broken? It's not like I have anything else to compare it to, but it is. Even I know that.

What was I thinking? Why would Blake have the slightest interest in me? I'm not girlfriend material. I might look like a girl and stuff, but I certainly don't act like one. I used gay porn to destroy another student's life, pull mediocre grades, and pretty much stick to my small group of equally unpopular friends. I mostly dress in black and adore dirt bikes, heavy metal music, and WWE. I ran over an employee at Bargain World, keep a zip gun in my purse, and helped extort a former Chester student. And all that is just scratching the surface. Dream girl, right?

I'm such an idiot to think Blake liked me. How he made me feel at Tristan's party. The way he spoke to me when he drove me home. He's just a nice guy. A nice, athletic, handsome, popular guy with the world at his fingertips who has no reason to act otherwise. How stupid could I be? I'm not in his league. I'm not even dateable. I don't think a single person's asked me out since I became a teenager, and they probably won't. Even the guy who was "obsessed" with me turned out to be gay. Plus, on top of everything already against me, I look different. I'll never be the all-American girl next door who wears cowgirl boots and doesn't have to use half a pot of wax on her eyebrows and upper lip every week. The girl who's voted homecoming queen every year and lives for Friday night football. It's not like I hate myself or anything, but on days like today, I'd be lying if I said otherwise.

I stumble into the commons, willing myself not to look at the streamers and confetti decorating the walls and try to remember what class I'm currently late for. I look up at a giant Valentine's Day cutout of a beating heart with the silhouette of a boy and girl holding hands glued to it and, in a rage, lunge towards it. Ripping it off the wall, I crumple it into a construction-paper ball and send it flying down the hallway. By the bathroom, more decorations await my destruction, so I tear most of the pink-and-white floral ornaments from the wall and cast them to the ground, where I trample them like a buffalo with anger management issues. Within fifteen seconds, they're thoroughly trashed, and I leave them there in an abused heap.

One piece of particularly long crepe paper gets wrapped around my ankle. I kick at it viciously to dislodge it, but this only reminds me of the time Blake rescued me at Walmart, which goes like a knife through my chest after remembering what Blake was doing earlier. I bite my lip to contain a scream, rip the streamer from my shoe, and charge off to nowhere.

"Roxie," somebody calls. "Roxie. Are you okay?"

"Jerome?" I look at Jerome's worried face, partially obscured by a red hoodie.

"Yeah. You okay?" His eyes widen. "You seem a little out of it."

"Yeah, I'm fine," I say quickly. "And you?"

"Not great. Hanna's got a new boyfriend." Jerome looks down at the ground forlornly. "Why didn't you tell me?"

"Ah." I rack my brain, trying to think of some explanation. "It all happened really fast."

"He just handed her some gold thing, and she kissed him. Kissed him! Just like that. In front of everybody. She never did that with me." Jerome shakes his head. "Please, Roxie. I don't know what to do."

"Jerome," I begin. "Yeah, Hanna's got a new guy. I hate him, and I hate their relationship. True, I never thought you and Hanna were a good fit, but this? It's awful. He's awful." I shake my head. "The day I get my driver's license, I'm starting the car and running over Owen."

Jerome nods and cracks his knuckles. "Keep talking."

"Owen just got here," I say, rolling my eyes. "Just moved here like a month ago. Hanna adores him. She acts like he's the greatest thing to happen to her yet."

The moment I say those words, I want to take them back, but it's too late. Jerome's face drops, and he refuses to look at me.

"Cynthia," I blurt out. "Cynthia's been cheerleading this thing all along. Hanna wouldn't have gone for it if Owen hadn't been dropped in her lap."

"Cynthia," Jerome barks out a laugh. "Yeah. No surprise."

"Eff Owen," I say. "He sucks. You're way cooler."

Jerome tries to hide the smile on his face, but it breaks out in full glory. "Do you think there's a chance?" he asks. "I mean, yeah. I don't look like him. I can't bench much, but I love her, Roxie. I love her."

"I know," I sigh. "I know you do. But I don't know anymore, man."

"Help me," Jerome pleads. "You're her best friend. She listens to everything you say. If anybody can give me a shot in her eyes, it's you. You know what, forget it. Just get her away from him. I saw that guy, and I know he's bad news."

"I don't know." I shake my head. "I really don't. She's in a relationship now. Eventually, they'll split, but we'll have to wait and see. It's not our place to get involved."

"You think I should get another girlfriend?" Jerome asks. "Get her to notice me? Make her jealous?"

"No," I say. "Not to make her jealous. Don't use somebody like that. But girlfriend? Yeah, definitely. Date. You're a single man now."

"Roxie," he begins uncertainly. "I don't want to, like, go too far, but could you, like, pretend to get with me?"

"No!" I charge towards Jerome with fists raised before realizing hitting him will get me in legal trouble. "Why does everybody want me to be their *pretend* girlfriend? Huh? Am I that fucking awful? Answer me, you li'l bitch!"

"No," Jerome squeaks, his eyes wide with fright. "I didn't mean to offend."

"Exes are off-limits," I snap. "In every friendship. Always. You honestly think I'd ruin my friendship with Hanna over something this stupid?"

"No, no," Jerome whimpers. "Totally forgot. I'm a big idiot. My bad."

I turn in disgust to leave, but he stops me again.

"Roxie," Jerome says slowly. "Forget about what I said. It was stupid. I'm stupid. I know you're single right now, but you're one of the prettiest girls in this school. No contest. Anybody would be lucky to date you. I just hope you know what you deserve. Don't settle, okay?"

Strangely touched, I feel myself smiling and give his shoulder a friendly punch. One thing about Jerome, he is sincere. Plus, it's nice to hear something kind once in a while, even when you don't believe a word of it.

I swallow the lump in my throat. "Thanks, Jerome."

Chapter 12

"It was *so* romantic," Hanna gushes to me over the phone. "And absolutely stunning. You have to see this! It's embroidered with tiny diamonds and set in fourteen-carat gold." She giggles. "And that's not all. He's taking me to dinner tonight and then a movie. Whatever I want!"

"Nice," I say with as much enthusiasm as I can muster. "That's great, Han."

"Isn't it?" She giggles again. "But enough about me. How was yours?"

"My what?"

"Valentine's Day?"

"Oh, you know—*horrible*," I reply, struggling to keep the bitterness out of my voice.

"Really?" Hanna's voice drops. "What happened?"

"Never mind," I say, rummaging around in my closet for the only formal thing I own. "It's not important. I don't know what I was expecting today, anyway."

"What do you mean?" Hanna asks, sounding concerned. "What happened?"

I sigh and plop down on my bed. "Blake's dating Tiffany."

She gasps. "No."

"Yup," I say sulkily. "They're a thing. But what's the big deal? I mean, nothing was going to happen between us anyway. I'm too young. She's probably got a 'lot more to offer,' and that's it." I snort. "Plus, it's me we're talking about. Miss Untouchable."

"Come on," Hanna reasons. "I see the way guys look at you. Most of them would probably give their right nut to go out with you. It's just…"

"Yeah," I interrupt. "You're so totally right, Hanna. Why didn't I see it before? That explains the swarm of hunks banging down my door and using up my cell minutes."

"Let me finish," she huffs. "As I was saying, your looks aren't the issue. The problem is you aren't approachable. At all. Yeah, you're friendly and nice to everyone you meet, but you can kind of be intimidating. And a little too spunky if you know what I mean."

"So to get Blake to like me, I have to be part carrot and climb on every man I see? If that's the case, well, we're not happening."

"I doubt Blake goes for homewreckers," Hanna chuckles. "Just doesn't seem like his personality, at least the way you describe him. But maybe we're judging Tiffany too much. Maybe she has something he truly likes about her."

I snort. "Like a gold medal in the oral Olympics?"

"Be serious," Hanna says. "What do we actually know about her? I've only said, like, two or three words to her in my entire life. Maybe she is really sweet and misunderstood. You can't believe everything people say."

"You mean like Chaz pretending to be oversexed and straight?" I laugh. "Yeah, it could be. But I don't care. I'm literally acting as a gay kid's beard—the same kid, might I add, who wrecked any chance I may have had with Blake to begin with. Life isn't charmed right now."

"We don't know what's going on," Hanna says finally. "Could be a platonic thing. A friend thing. An image improvement for her. Just wait and see."

"It's easy for you to say," I huff. "I mean, you've got someone right now. Someone you like falling all over you. Think about if things were different. What if I was going out with Owen tonight, and he was dropping jewelry on me and basically being Mr. Perfect, and you had to go out with Chaz to pretend in front of his insane dad after watching the one guy you've ever liked suck face with some orange skank? The one guy you've ever truly been attracted to? Clicked with in a way that you never thought possible? How would you feel? Because I feel like shit."

Some time goes by before Hanna answers.

"I don't know," she says at last. "I'd feel terrible, I guess. I'm sorry, Roxie. It's not fair. Nothing's fair. I wish you and Blake were dating. Or at least had a chance to know each other. But he's one guy. There are dozens of guys at our school you might be just as compatible with."

"Guys are the least of it." I heave an enormous sigh. "Even Blake, as much as I wish we could be together. There's just something way bigger." I pause. "Do you ever feel like you're living in the last days? Like, everything's slowly coming to an end?"

"No, honestly," Hanna says, her voice concerned. "Can't say I have. Girl, are you good?"

"Yeah," I say quickly. "Yeah, I'm good."

"Are you sure?"

"Yeah, I'm sure," I say. "Anyway, I'd better get ready, and the same goes for you, Ms. Taken."

"Call me after the date," Hanna says. "Don't forget."

***

Taking my dress off the hanger, I lay it gently on top of my bedspread. The last time I wore it, I was twelve and a lot less developed in the chest area. I'm honestly wondering if it'll even fit me now. It's a good thing Chaz is gay and won't get turned on if something pops out this evening 'cause this dress is tight. I hit up my shoe drawer next and dig out the one pair of heels I own to see if I can get a foot in. It's a tight squeeze, but the heels at least fit a bit better than the dress does. Even so, I take a pair of Converse from the closet and toss them in my purse as a backup.

Though I don't want to, I strap on the foot crushers and check the time. Blaze and Chaz will arrive in twenty minutes, and I haven't done anything in terms of makeup. Knowing Blaze, he'll want to take pictures. It'll look weird if I say no, so I apply a little eyeliner and mascara and give my hair a few good brushes before spritzing on some of the Britney Spears perfume I got for Christmas.

Ten to six, I'm barely getting things together when I hear several sharp raps on the front door. Nick's out with Emilio in the lowrider and won't be back until late tonight, so I make sure I've got my keys in hand before closing my bedroom door.

"Hey, girly," Chaz says quietly as I open the door and lock it behind me. "You look nice."

I smile at him. "What's good, lover boy?"

"Ah, the usual," Chaz says. "I mean, I'm excited for tonight and everything, but not as excited as Blaze."

I groan. "Oh, Jesus."

Placing a hand on Chaz's sport coat-clad shoulder, I walk slowly down the front steps, and he pulls me close to him. I can't see us or anything, but I think it looks convincing. Over by the truck, Blaze is standing with a camera around his neck and waves to me.

"Hey, Blaze," I say, waving back.

"Roxie!" he calls. "Looking pretty as a picture, sweetheart."

I stumble towards Blaze's giant, forest-green truck, and Chaz helps me up onto the step bar and into the backseat. Chaz hops into the front, but Blaze shoos him out.

"Don't leave her waiting, boy," Blaze says. "Go on back. Roxie? How's life?"

"It's going," I reply. "Well, I guess."

"Well it is," Blaze chortles. "And you? Looking like you just stepped off the red carpet. No, Cannes. The Cannes Film Festival! Chaz, you've got to start acting classes. Roxie's going to Hollywood!"

Chaz cringes into a fetal position. "Dad. Please shut up."

Blaze clucks his tongue. "Don't listen to him," he says, laughing heartily and pulling a lighter out of his coat pocket. "And son. Pass me a Cohiba, would you?" Blaze turns to look at me. "Chaz knows I'm right. After all, Coach knows best." He lets out another booming laugh and lights the cigar.

"You shouldn't smoke, Dad," Chaz says quietly. "It'll kill you."

"Your mother's killing me faster than the smoke," Blaze cackles. "Sheesh. Old bat makes me want to run to the reaper. But anyway." He trails off. "We'll get to the restaurant, I'll snap a few, and you two go on and have yourselves a time. Have you ever been to The Three Larks, child?"

"No, not yet," I say, choking on the smoke flooding the cabin. Blaze cracks the window and holds the cigar out lazily.

"How's James doing?" he asks. "Cousin, right?"

"James is doing great," I say quickly, remembering Blaze's unannounced visit to my front door not even a week ago. "Doing really well, now that you mention it."

"Glad to hear it! Good-looking fella, that boy is." Blaze nods. "I said it once, and I'll say it again—you come from great genes, darlin'."

"What time's our reservation for, Dad?" Chaz cuts in.

Blaze glances at the clock on the dashboard. "Six-thirty. We're way ahead of schedule." He floors the gas and accelerates through a red light, nearly taking a jogger out at the intersection. "Yeehaw!"

The rest of the ride is relatively quiet. Every now and again, Blaze will make a mean, but hysterical comment about unattractive pedestrians or tell an off-color joke or two, but besides that, nobody speaks. As we drive along Main Street, a plastic Walmart bag skitters across the sidewalk in the breeze and flies up by my window. The sadness of earlier slices into me again. No matter where I turn, there's a reminder of him.

"Here we be," Blaze says cheerily as we pull into the handicapped parking up front. Sandwiching the Dodge between two other cars, he reaches into the glove compartment and retrieves a handicap placard. "God bless your mother's injury," he declares, fastening it on the rearview mirror. "At least she can still do something. Roxie, watch your step going down."

Chaz takes my hand. The two of us step out onto the sidewalk in front of the restaurant, and Blaze grabs his Nikon off the passenger seat.

"Okay you two, gather about," Blaze says, angling the camera. "Chaz, get in a little closer. That's it. There we go." He snaps a few photos. "Okay, turn a bit. There it is. Three more."

I pull Chaz closer to me and whisper in his ear. "Congratulations."

Chaz frowns. "For what?"

"You did it," I snicker. "You were right all along. I finally went out with you."

Chaz laughs throatily. "*Roxie.*"

I drop my arm from his waist. "Do not."

As the two of us watch Blaze drive away, I suddenly realize where we are. A couple of months back, Cynthia met some technology geek in a Maserati at Burger King and agreed to meet him here for a date. The date itself was horribly boring, and, as Cynthia told it, the food was terrible. Around the time the bill arrived, her date had to "use the commode," as he put it, and never returned—leaving her stuck with a three-hundred-dollar check and several empty bottles of rosé.

Fifteen minutes in, I'm realizing Cynthia left out the worst of it. I might've hit some doozies in my life, but The Three Larks takes first place, hands down. First off, it's way too loud to conduct any sort of business here, and most of the patrons are well into their eighties. The owner of this place must be demented as well because every corner of the restaurant has a vastly different theme. The wall furthest from us appears to be Venetian Gothic, while the adjoining wall looks decidedly Jackson Pollack, and the wall beside us is Shangri-La. Onstage, a quartet saws away at untuned instruments while waiters bustle about in dinner jackets taking orders. Directly overhead, a plasma display with terrible picture quality shows advertisements for memory care and funeral homes, all while flickering constantly.

Chaz and I have to be the youngest people in the joint by a good margin because nobody even close to our age is visible. Couples older than Methuselah are clustered all around in groups of threes and fours, shouting to each other across the table. One elderly gentleman dressed like an admiral waves his hands excitedly before opening his mouth and losing his dentures in a glass of chardonnay, but aside from that, nothing interesting happens.

A tall waiter with parted hair hurries towards us, clutching a pad of paper and a pen styled to look like a quill. His shoes click loudly on the tile as he stands before us.

"*Bonjour.* My name is Christophe, and I will be your server this evening. Have you decided on what you'll be having?"

"Good evening," Chaz replies. "Italian wedding soup for me, please. No pine nuts on the salad." Closing his menu, Chaz hands it to Christophe, who nods.

"Ah, the *minestra maritata.* Excellent choice." He turns to me. "And what will you be having, *mademoiselle?*"

I blink. "Okay, just curious. Do you speak French or Italian in this restaurant?"

Christophe sniffs. "We speak *three* languages at this restaurant, aside from English. French, Italian, and German." He takes an audible breath before looking around and continuing. "These three languages symbolize the three larks."

I bite back a laugh and nod. "Cool. Got it. Three larks for three languages."

Christophe smiles and raps his fingers on the pad of paper. "So, you will be having...?"

"Same as him," I say. "Might as well keep it simple."

It's not often I go out to fancy restaurants. Up until tonight, I wasn't aware fine dining could last upwards of an hour. By the time our appetizers and salads arrive, I'm starting to feel lightheaded. Chaz and I talk about a few different things we were planning on discussing tonight, but we're both running out of gas, and my thought process is about as scattered as our initial order.

Still, the elderly pour in. Two couples from the Dark Ages crash down at the table next to us, while an eccentric trio up ahead is analyzing Watergate over and over. Behind us, a crowd of behatted religious folk is debating amongst themselves whether they're bloodline Hebrews, while next to them, two wizened women in frilly outfits are loudly agreeing that the Civil Rights movement was a mistake. I don't know how Blaze found out about this place, and for a moment, I wonder if this is all some sick joke on his part. For now, I try to put on something of a face for Chaz, who seems extremely embarrassed for bringing me here.

"Charles?" A shrill, uppity voice sounds above the hubbub. "Charles Humbert, is that you?"

Both Chaz and I look towards the voice. Across the restaurant, a voluptuous woman looking to be in her seventies is waving a handkerchief at us, trying to get his attention.

"Aunt Edna?" Chaz wonders aloud.

"Charles Milton," Edna barks. "Come!"

Like an abused Labrador, Chaz rises from his seat and shuffles towards her. Unsure of what to do, I get up and follow him. I don't want to be rude and should at least say hello to her, even though I'm getting the feeling Chaz would rather be literally anywhere else.

"Sit, sit, be comfortable." Edna gestures to the table, which is covered with an elaborate spread. "Eat, there's lots to go around." She turns to me. "And this? Who might this be?"

"Roxie," I say, extending a hand. Edna takes it, shaking it with just her fingertips, and gives me a very tight, fake smile.

"The one Clint was talking about," she muses quietly. "'A real beauty, that one.' This is her?"

"Yes," Chaz says cautiously. "That's her. And yeah, she's beautiful. How've you been?"

"Oh, you know," Edna replies. "Been getting on with life the best I can. I never was quite the same after losing Jean Pierre. A house without a man. Well, it's not a house at all. But I'm moving along."

"I understand," Chaz says, shooting her a sympathetic look. "We were all very sad when he passed." He turns to me. "J.P. was a hell of a guy. Used to take me for long drives in the country when I was a kid. Had this Bel Air from the fifties. I loved that thing almost as much as I loved him."

"Hell of a guy he was," Edna agrees, dabbing at her eyes with the tablecloth. "He loved you too, Charles."

"Still got the farm?" Chaz asks, scooping a few roasted vegetables onto a small plate. "Roxie, want anything?" I shake my head.

"Still have the farm indeed," Edna says. "It's working fine. Brandt's coming by with the colts on Wednesday. About damn time. I should've had them last week." She grunts disapprovingly. "But Brandt runs on his own time. As does the rest of this family." She glances over at me, and I look up, expecting her to say something. She doesn't.

"What about Benji?" Chaz asks. "How's Benji?"

"Dead." Edna shrugs, spreading butter on a thick slice of pumpernickel. "Buried. Deceased. You should know that, Charles, considering you mailed your condolences at least twice."

"Oh, of course," Chaz groans, slapping his forehead. "How could I forget?"

"Well," Edna says, "I think there might have been something going on. Something riding you."

"Could've been," Chaz sighs. "High school and all."

"Yeah, high schoolers," Edna agrees. "That age. People can be so *anal*."

"Mm-hm." Chaz nods. "Interesting choice of words there."

Edna chuckles. "Figured you'd pick up on that."

A jolt of panic hits me in the gut. I look over and study Edna's wrinkled face, barely making out a smile at the corner of her bottom lip. There's something about the way she's looking at him. She *knows*.

"Ha," Chaz forces a laugh. "Yeah, you know me. Got to love a little comedy!"

"Ho, ho," Edna lets out a deeper laugh. "Locker-room humor."

Chaz and I lock eyes in terror. This can't be happening. Besides an occasion to talk and catch up, our date tonight was supposed to be the nail in the Chaz Is Not Gay coffin. Well, Edna's about to rip off that lid.

"Is there something you're trying to say here?" I break in, unable to help myself. It feels like this is about to spiral out of control at any moment. "It seems there's something you're not saying here."

Edna looks me in the eye. "Beard, stay out of this."

"*Beard?*" Chaz says, dropping his fork. "Hold on, did you just call my girlfriend 'Beard?'"

"Girlfriend?" Edna snorts. "What girlfriend?"

"Are you implying that I'm gay?" Chaz asks, his voice dangerously soft.

"Implying?" Edna inquires shrilly. "I know! Come on, Charles, it's no secret. Name one straight male, besides yourself, so you claim, who can sing *Annie* in all twelve keys? I've known since you were young. I mean, you didn't know, obviously, but I was certain of it. Don't ask me how, but I knew."

"Okay, I think we're done here," I interrupt, jumping from my chair. "Chaz?"

"Oh, hush, we're not even close," Edna says. "Sit down. We're going to be here a while."

"No, we're not," I shoot back. "Chaz, get up. I don't want to hear another word of this bullshit."

Chaz, however, has become one with his chair and doesn't move an inch. Eyes like saucers, he looks at Edna like a Passover lamb waiting for the knife to come down.

"Remember when you told Grandpa how you wanted to be Barry Manilow when you grew up? Who wanted a Barbie dream house for Christmas?" Edna recounts. "How about when you saw Brett Van Damme lifeguarding at the country club pool the summer you turned twelve? You couldn't get enough of that red speedo."

Chaz gasps for air like a man on the end of a rope, but Edna's just getting started.

"Now, I'm not saying this to be cruel," she continues. "I just want to say I accept you for who you are and will always care for you. Nothing will change that. And nothing will leave this table."

Rummaging in her bag, Edna withdraws a small vial, which she then unscrews.

"Many years ago, back when I was young, I used to work as a typist. Ran into fancy chaps all the time. Real friendly, too. There weren't as many of them around back then, but you knew who was, unlike today. It's a lot more complicated now." Edna stares off into the distance. "And then there was my time working at the department store, at the tie counter. This charming poofter used to walk me out to my Plymouth every night after closing. Arturo, his name was. So handsome. Real smart for a colored, too."

"Uh, Aunt Edna," Chaz says quietly. "That term is really offensive. You can't say things like that."

"Are you suggesting I'm a racist?" Edna demands, her tone loud and indignant. A few couples dining nearby stop to stare in our direction. "Oh, no. Not me. Say, Darkie and Boogie just walked through the door, and I never said a word. Hell, they can even sit up front and drink out of my glass. I don't care! That was back then. This is now. The time has come! Out of the closet, young man!"

Chaz nearly face plants into the dishes. Edna beams, lifts the vial to her nose, and sniffs rapidly in succession. "Better," she says, more to herself than anybody else. "Much better."

"Was that blow?" I ask before I can stop myself.

"Call it what you will." Edna shrugs. "Little bit of Peruvian talcum. But we're not talking about cocaine. We're discussing Charles. Are you still with us?"

"Yes," Chaz squeaks.

"When are you telling your parents? Unless you told them already?"

"What, that you now abuse substances in public?" Chaz laughs. "No, my lips are sealed."

Edna bats a hand. "No, they already know that. The other thing."

"There's nothing to tell," Chaz replies, so nonchalant he's even got me fooled. "Kids go through stages. God knows I went through plenty. Doesn't mean anything. It's way different now. Like, times have changed." He laughs. "And truly, what's the difference between Ken and G.I. Joe?"

"Nothing," Edna confirms. "Both have a smooth slab between their legs, which is why you never took an interest. You'd have to have gotten it from somewhere. I won't say names, but we've had a few funny fellas in our family. Brandt never married, and he's obsessed with studs. Maybe there's something to it." Her eyes flit across our troubled faces. "But right now? It's about Edna's needs."

"Uh," Chaz begins. "Aunt Edna. Maybe you'd better not."

Edna silences him with another wave of her hand.

"Let's go," I whisper, but Chaz doesn't budge. Unscrewing the vial again, Edna raises it to her right nostril and ingests it with a series of forceful inhales.

This time, something's off. Shooting up straight in her chair, Edna stomps both feet to the floor and stands to her full height, raising her martini glass over her head like the Statue of Liberty.

"Tell them!" Edna bellows. "Tell them, tell them."

Greedily taking in a lungful of air, she wheezes and stumbles, her dress whipping about her like a Flamenco dancer. Her chest heaving, she wheels about in a state of disorientation.

"Where am I?" Edna moans in a voice so unlike the one I'd heard before. "Where am I?"

Chaz reaches toward her, but it's too late. Edna falls face-forward, and the table shudders underneath her weight. With a crash, the entire spread, which must've cost upwards of four hundred dollars, joins her down on the floor, and the entire restaurant halts in its tracks.

Chaz and I gape at each other. To date, nothing has rivaled what I've just seen, and I'll be hard-pressed to witness something like this ever again. Unconscious, Edna's dress has ridden up, and I see what I think is a leg holster for a .357 Magnum just above her stockings, along with several loose tablets on the floor next to her.

"Chaz," I say slowly. "We need to go."

"My God," Chaz breathes. "Edna? Edna?" Dropping to a knee, he shakes her.

"Let's go," I say quickly, bending down next to him and placing a hand on his shoulder. "Chaz. Now."

"We can't just leave her here," Chaz protests.

"Gun," I say. "Pills. Aunt high on illegal drugs. Let's bail."

Whiter than Edna's cocaine, Chaz reaches into his wallet and throws a handful of crumpled bills down on our table. With that, the two of us make a dash for the back exit.

***

Ten minutes later, we're standing across the street in the parking lot of a Holiday Inn, watching first responders wheel Edna out on a stretcher. Behind the paramedics, Christophe is frantically waving his arms and saying something in Italian, still holding onto his quill.

"What. The actual. Fuck."

"Took the words right out my mouth," I sigh. Bending down, I begin unstrapping my shoes and pull my sneakers out of my bag. "This sure wasn't what I had in mind for Valentine's Day."

"What happened, though?" Chaz asks, scratching his nose. "Flashback to the beginning. You and I are talking, she calls us over, outs me, and then O.Ds. What the hell else is in store for us tonight? God, I hate to think."

"I don't know about you," I say, lacing up my shoes. "But I've had enough adventure for a while. Oh, and by the way, your family's nuts."

Chaz rolls his eyes. "Like you just figured that out."

"Well, look on the bright side." I point to the ambulance. "The siren's on. There's hope for her yet."

"Oh, Edna," Chaz sighs. "She wasn't always like this. She used to be a lot of fun. Her tenth husband, the guy we were talking about, was the best. All three of us, Edna, J.P., me…we used to sit at our own table at family reunions. And those two? Made for each other. They used to give me whatever I wanted. Sneak me treats and stuff." Chaz shakes his head. "I don't know what tonight was about. I honestly didn't even remember she was still alive. It almost feels like somebody put her there. Put her up to it."

"Now you're freaking me out," I say. "Yeah, it was weird. That whole thing was a freak show. But seriously. You think someone set her on you?"

"Not exactly," Chaz replies. "I mean, I don't think she found out we were going to be here, booked a table, and ordered hundreds of dollars' worth of food just to torture me. Edna loves me."

"'Locker room!'" I shriek, snapping my fingers. "'Locker-room humor.'"

"Oh, Christ," Chaz says, covering his eyes. "That's right."

"She could've caught wind of something from the high school," I point out. "About the poster. Why else would she say that?"

"Students being anal," Chaz groans. "Oh, God."

He jams his hands in his pockets, and the two of us start to walk with no particular destination in mind.

"Edna's a gossip hound. She probably heard everything from somebody else. I mean, everybody did see it. She might even have a copy of the poster somewhere."

"Maybe," I say. "But, dude. Rumors go around. Nick had to put out fires his entire time at Chester High, and Jenna's still telling anyone who will listen that I strip and sell drugs. Remember that? Sixth grade?"

"How could I forget?" Chaz laughs. He pinches his face and widens his eyes the way Jenna does when she's about to stir the pot. "Oh my gosh, Emma. Did you *hear* what Roxie did?"

I laugh. "You're a little too good at that."

Chaz winks at me. "Just a little, huh?"

By now, we're about halfway down Main Street, and I don't have the slightest clue where we're going to end up. It's getting chilly, though, and with my bare shoulders, I'm freezing. Chaz notices and takes off his sport coat, wrapping it around me.

"Better?"

"Yeah, a little," I smile. "Thanks."

"No, thank you," Chaz says. "Thanks for coming. Thanks for going along with this horrible idea. Thank you for trying to help me convince the world I don't like penis." He laughs. "Edna, though. Bitch wasn't biting, was she?"

I chuckle, even though so little of this is funny. Chaz might be joking around, but I saw the fear in his eyes earlier with Edna. The dread. I've noticed that like Nick, Chaz tends to hide his pain behind a smile, and I want nothing more than to take away his sadness, even though I've got plenty of my own. It just doesn't seem fair that somebody that young should be saddled with so much expectation. But, then again, who isn't? I mean, Nick went through hell at our age. Hanna puts way too much pressure on herself. I hate myself at least eighty-five percent of the time, and CeCe's going to be a mom in a few short months. And Emilio? Nobody should have had to endure that.

"I'm hungry," Chaz declares, patting his tummy. "This boy needs to eat. Roxie?"

"Oh yeah," I say. "Count me in."

"What's good to eat around here?" Chaz asks. "Up there? What does the sign say?"

I squint, barely able to make out the lettering, but I know what it is. A few days ago, Emilio took Nick to this hole-in-the-wall Mexican joint, and he hasn't been the same since. Now, every night at our house is Latin night as Nick tries desperately to recreate the food he ate at Salgado's, which looks to be a few blocks ahead of us.

"There," I say, pointing to the sign. "Nick tells me it's heaven on a plate. And cheap."

"Good enough for me," Chaz says. "Salgado's it is."

Outside the door, a hunchbacked man in a raggedy *serape* plays a battered violin, his case open. Before I can drop what little money I have left into his case, Chaz pulls me into the restaurant and closes the door behind us.

We both order massive burritos and Coke in glass bottles before taking a seat outside at a rustic-looking picnic table next to a heat lamp. Brightly colored holiday lights, not unlike the ones hanging up at school today, drape up above us, while kids' drawings and mosaics of old Mexico cover the back wall of the restaurant inside. When the food comes, neither of us speaks until we're nearly done eating. As I dribble a little more habanero sauce on my rice, Chaz takes a sip of his drink and turns to me.

"Here's to us," he says, raising his bottle. I grab mine and lift it too. "Here's to friendship."

"And tight situations," I say. "I can't believe your dad sent us to that whack shack. I don't know about you, but Valentine's Day is never going to be the same."

"I will never, and I mean *never,* take another tidbit of advice from that man," Chaz says. "You can count on that."

"Well, at least he's off your ass for a while," I point out. "And about that. How much longer are we keeping this charade up?"

Chaz shrugs. "I don't know. Why?"

"'Cause it's killing you," I say. "I can see it in your eyes. Every time we do this dog-and-pony show, every time Blaze starts talking me up in front of you…" I trail off. "I just. I don't know. It can't sustain."

"Yeah, so what?" Chaz lifts a shoulder. "What's the big deal? It's not like he really knows me, anyway."

"But you know you, Chaz."

Chaz raises an eyebrow. "Do I?"

"Do any of us?" I sit up straight. "Being gay isn't the only thing that makes a person stick out. Nick claims race or ethnicity is a bigger deal. Me? I think it's not conforming and just being yourself." I shrug. "I think all of us think we stick out, or at least feel we do."

"But look at where we live," Chaz says, taking a gulp of his Coke. "It isn't Seattle. It's not L.A. or another major city. People here live for Costco, football, and church. Kids still go cow-tipping on weekends. Do you know even one other gay person?"

"I'm sure I do," I say. "But nobody's ever come out. Statistically, I'm just saying."

"Exactly my point," Chaz replies. "Think about it. What'll school be like then? What'll Brennan and Spencer do?"

"Stop?" I shrug. "They'll look like cowards, and people will stop laughing eventually. Think about if they were making racist comments toward a black kid or giving someone in a wheelchair a rough time. This is the same principle. People will get sick of it pretty fast, and the bullies will eventually be the ones getting all the negative attention."

"Fair point," Chaz says. "But what about you? You're looking a little lost tonight yourself."

"Well, let me see." I fold my arms. "I show up to school today and find out the boy I like, a boy I've liked more than anybody ever, who might have shown actual interest in me, is dating somebody. I'm begging CeCe to stay in school. Hanna's getting distant with me, and it's all because of Owen. Plus, it's looking like Owen's going to be a part of things now. At least at school."

"You don't know how sorry I am," Chaz says, staring at the tabletop. "About Blake. What I did was so awful. And stalkerish. No, it was one hundred percent stalking. We'll find him tomorrow, and I'll explain everything."

"Too late," I say sharply. "This morning, he was practically on top of Tiffany Verlich. He'll be a busy boy, at least for a month. If the chlamydia doesn't eat his brain first."

"Oh, God," Chaz moans. "Not Tiffany."

I stare straight ahead. "Yup."

We sit in silence. The violinist is playing something somber now, and the music is beginning to affect me. I'm already exhausted from this evening, but more than anything else, the uncertainty of it all immobilizes me. Fiddling with his shirt cuffs, Chaz stretches his legs out in front of him and lets out a long breath.

"You know," he says, sounding unsure. "I don't know if it's my place to say this or anything, but you spend so much time helping other people. You know. Hanna, CeCe, me, Nick. But you never take any time to worry about yourself."

I swallow the lump that has finally forced its way up into my throat and concentrate on anything other than what Chaz just said.

***

"It's good to know you aren't trying to grow up anymore," I remark as Nick slides a pan of blondies into the oven. "You were freaking us out big time."

Nick laughs. "Roger that. Growing up is way overrated. Plus, the other day Gabriella was wearing a fitted cap and grooving to OutKast with her friends. Did you know she drives a Cadillac?"

"Wow," I say, smiling. "Sounds like she's the girl for you."

Nick beams. "Right?"

"Well, there she is," I say. "Right in front of you. Same interests, same styles. Now you just have to locate some balls and ask her out."

Nick nods. "Tomorrow. It's happening after class." Rummaging in the junk drawer, he pulls out a folded piece of paper. "'Ten-step guide to asking out the woman of your dreams.' Emilio printed it off for me at the library."

"Let me see this," I say, reaching for the paper. "Step one. Look, act, and be confident."

"Emilio's been super helpful in all this," Nick tells me. "We help each other out. I helped him chase down a poker cheater. Now, he's helping me chase down my soulmate. Put good things out there, get good things back."

I nod. "Yeah, I guess."

"Speaking of helping out, how was your fake date with Chaz?"

"Oh, my God." I forgot Nick knows nothing about our little night out. "A total disaster."

He frowns. "Seriously? How bad can dinner with your gay guy friend go?"

"Oh, bad it went." I shudder. "Unless you find a creepy dad, a room full of the elderly, lukewarm food, and a coke-snorting great-aunt to be fine company. It was a first-class ticket to hell. It literally couldn't have gone any worse."

"Well, now I got to hear about this," Nick laughs. "What did you say? Great-aunt snorting cocaine?"

"You wouldn't believe me anyway," I sigh. "But it happened. Right in front of us. Anyway, it wasn't all bad. We ended up eating at Salgado's."

"Word!" Nick lights up. "What did you get? Did you try the *mole*?"

"I had a burrito," I say. "And it was really good. Listen, last time you were there did you see some dude playing the violin outside?"

"*Arriba*!" Emilio bursts into the kitchen holding an instrument case in one hand and a duffel bag in the other. "Did you enjoy my playing last night?"

I burst out laughing. "Oh, my God, that was *you*?"

"Sure was." Emilio grins. "*Señor* Ramos and I are tight. He thinks the violin music gives his joint a classic Tijuana feel. I've never been, so I'm going with Ramos on this one." He opens his case and pulls out a wad of cash. "People around here sure love *El Quasimodo*. CeCe won't have to worry this week."

"She told us you got another installment the other day," I say, leaning up against the refrigerator. "I still can't get over Erik's newfound career."

"Aw, yeah," Emilio snickers. "It's really something. You should see him massage that stallion's *cojones* every hour on the hour. They swing like pendulums!" He reaches over and slaps me a high-five.

"Ready to get working on our rap album, Emilio?" Nick asks, untying his apron and hanging it on the back of the pantry door. "I was up late last night throwing down some new rhymes."

"Ditto, my man," Emilio replies, picking up his violin case. "Let's get to work."

With those two occupied, I decide to get started on my homework and head upstairs. Of course, I don't rush. I mean, who likes doing homework besides Jenna Carmichael? Chaz is busy. Otherwise, I'd be hanging out with him. And Hanna? Come to think of it, I haven't seen her outside of school for almost a week.

Goddamn Owen! Ever since they made it official, they've never been away from each other for more than a few minutes, and it's only getting worse. I can't get a second alone with her. Even if I need to run something by her, Owen is never far away. Whenever I see him, I can't help but think of what Chaz hypothesized, and though I don't admit it to anybody, it scares me.

The only person who kind of gets it is CeCe. Though she's always quietly polite the way only she can be, I get the feeling she's onto Owen too. I never told her anything, especially about that first night out at the mall with him. It wouldn't be fair to Hanna, but I can see the look in her eyes whenever she sees him put his arm around Hanna or disarm us with charm or aloofness. I get the feeling she, like me, wants to warn Hanna about not getting too comfortable, but all of us know it'll fall on deaf ears.

Chaz seems to be a fan now, only because Owen acts so unlike he did with me that night and because he engages him without prejudice. There's no way Owen doesn't know what went down with Chaz and the poster, or what some of the rumors going around are, and I could almost respect it if I didn't recognize it as some type of strategic move. Hanna's in love, and Chaz is in like, which only leaves CeCe to be won over. Once that happens, I'm on my own, and whatever I manage to uncover about Owen, or whatever he says to me when Hanna's head is turned, won't be acknowledged, and I'll be the odd one out.

Feeling the anxiety rise, I decide to give CeCe a call since I've been terrible about reaching out and need somebody to talk to. The phone rings a couple of times before CeCe answers.

"Roxie?"

"Hey, CeCe," I say. "What's new?"

"Hm, not much," she answers. "Is Emilio over at your place still?"

"Yeah, got in a few minutes ago," I say. "He and Nick are back on the grind. The music hustle anyway."

She snorts. "Oh, God."

I laugh. "Yeah. They should probably just stick to written poetry, you know?"

"So what's up?" CeCe asks. "Sounds like you've got something on your mind."

Is CeCe a sage? Or is it motherly intuition? Startled, I cradle the phone against my shoulder and lay down on my bed.

"Yeah, actually," I say. "Has Hanna reached out to you recently? Like, at all?"

CeCe breathes quietly on the other end. "No. No, she hasn't. We were supposed to talk to Coach about me coming back next season. I had to quit this year, obviously. I didn't tell her why, but she's not stupid."

"Good idea," I say. "You should definitely go back next year. They'll probably bomb without you."

"I hope not."

"Hey, listen." I suck in a breath. "What's the deal with Owen?"

"What do you mean?" CeCe asks. "Like, what do I think of him?"

"Yeah," I say quietly.

"Honestly, I don't trust him," CeCe says. "Not even a little bit. Everything about him is a show. The way he talks, how he holds his hands. His jokes. None of it feels real. He doesn't seem real. He doesn't even *look* real. I don't know what somebody smart like Hanna sees in him. Other than the fact he's hot."

"Yeah," I breathe. "And I thought I was imagining things. Sorry, I didn't mean to put you on the spot like that. I just..."

"I see the way he looks at you," CeCe says abruptly. "I know because he looks at me the same way."

"He's been here a few weeks now," I observe. "Have you ever seen him out, like, hanging out or talking to other guys at school? Like, friends?"

"Nope," CeCe snorts. "They don't give him what he wants. Why do you think he talks to Chaz so much? He's a narcissist. I think he wears more makeup than Hanna."

I giggle. "Yeah, I can kind of see that. I mean, whose eyes are that green?"

"Besides a Bratz doll? I don't know," CeCe says. "Are you worried or something? Think Owen's going to take her away from us forever?"

"A little," I say, my laughter dissipating like water vapor. "She's falling hard, CeCe. And Owen? He can't stand me. Or at least acts like he can't. I didn't even tell you about the time Hanna and I took him to the mall. I saw Emilio there that night. Owen even said some rude shit about him."

"Like what?" CeCe asks, her voice rising. "Emilio doesn't even know who he is."

"I know," I say. "That's my point. He ruined the night, totally judging everybody and everything. Acted like a huge dick. But the minute Hanna came around, he switched on a different mode. Kind of like the one he puts on around you and Chaz and stuff."

"Wow," CeCe sighs on the other end. "Well, I'm not fooled. Not one bit. The second I met him, I knew he was bad news."

"It's that vibe," I say. "The vibe? You got it too?"

"Oh, yeah."

"Well, what should we do?" I ask. "I mean, we both know something's off. We can't just sit."

"Nothing," CeCe says simply. "There's nothing we can do. Either Hanna figures it out, or she gets hurt. If we step in, we'll look like the bad guys. If we tell her, it'll just push her further away from us than she is already."

"Yeah, you're right," I say. And she is. Trusting, empathetic, and down-to-earth, Hanna's somebody who typically listens to sound advice and aims not to make the same mistakes as others. If things were different, I would call her up and run my findings of Owen by her. She'd at least meditate on it. One of the reasons Hanna and I became such good friends is the fact neither of us is jealous of the other. We're just too different. When Hanna got asked out first or got stopped at the mall last summer because somebody mistook her for a Hallmark actress, I always cheered her on from the sidelines. But despite Cynthia's hopes and well-wishes, Owen is not the missing piece in Hanna's life. Just a jagged edge that's about to cut deep.

Chapter 13

"**G**uess what?" Hanna whispers excitedly to me. "Roxie."

One of the few negative things anybody could point out about Hanna is her timing. Having had an eventful last couple of days, I had to pull an all-nighter last night to make up for it. As a result, my head's throbbing, and my patience level is subzero. Yeah, I could've spent Saturday or Sunday doing my homework, but instead, I devoted my weekend to hanging with Chaz, slamming Red Bulls with Frankie on his break, reading celebrity gossip magazines with CeCe, skateboarding through the botanical garden at dusk, and riding with Nick and Emilio in the drop top. I mean, carpe diem, right?

Minutes before I got on the bus, I got into a heated argument with my mom. I accused her of playing enabler to Nick, and the screaming escalated from there. Between me managing his online dating profile and her driving baked ziti on her lunch break over to Covington, we're both equally guilty. Somehow I only realized this when she stormed her way out of the house.

The icing on the shit cake is Hanna. Not only did she not reach out once this weekend, she also ignored every text message and phone call. When we finally met up earlier this morning, she was more than a little distant with me, staring at her phone the entire time and giggling over what I'm assuming were snaps of the Smallwood.

"What?" I snap, whipping around in my seat. "God, Hanna what is it?"

I was drifting away to a better place, beanie pulled over my eyes, when Hanna finally initiated conversation for the first time in seventy-two hours. Only when I realize the entire class has halted do I shake myself awake and look into Hanna's startled face.

"Everything okay back there?" Mr. Tuttle calls from the front of the room. "Care to move up to the front? We've got plenty of room here."

"Thanks, Mr. T," I say. "But it won't be necessary. The real problem here is a particularly douchey young man. A giant tool with a little…problem."

Hanna's jaw drops, but I'm not done. "Poor guy. I mean, come on. When your last name is Smallwood, it's basically a self-fulfilling prophecy."

Several people gasp. Then, like a dam bursting, the class bursts out laughing. A few guys start clapping and pumping the air with their fists. Tuttle waves his hands for quiet, but it takes several raps on the blackboard before order is restored.

As I resume my slump, the door to the front of the classroom crashes open with such force it smacks against the opposite wall and bangs shut on its own, with Hanna on the other side of it.

"Teenagers," Mr. Tuttle sighs. "Talk about inches, they take it a mile."

***

Rummaging around in my lunch sack, I scan the far reaches of the lunchroom. Hanna wasn't at our usual table, which I expected, but she isn't visible anywhere else either. CeCe and Chaz also have their eyes peeled, but so far, none of us have even caught a glimpse. Knowing Hanna, she either went home to sulk or is off with Owen somewhere making out. Though neither of them has said a word, I'm getting the feeling CeCe and Chaz know I'm slipping, and after my outburst earlier, I'm even starting to get worried.

I rarely lose control to such a degree. Then again, before Chaz came out to me and CeCe got pregnant, I only had my own issues to worry about. But between fooling Blaze, keeping CeCe in school, and guarding Nick against the black dog of depression, I'm completely neglecting my own life. I tend to believe everything that's going wrong is somehow my fault, so I end up taking on other people's problems to get away from mine for a while. This results in ultimately blaming myself when those problems get worse and finally breaking down when everything hits the fan.

"Owen," Chaz whispers, pointing discreetly. "Far wall."

Owen is posted in the corner of the commons, working out his forearms with a pair of handgrips. He's alone, which doesn't surprise me, but scowls and grits his teeth like a diseased canid. Periodically, his eyes flit down to his phone, which makes him smile, but besides that, he continues clenching and releasing.

"Giant shit detected," I mutter. "I can smell it from here."

CeCe laughs. "Why isn't he here with us? I mean, I know how much you love him, Chaz."

Chaz grins. "What can I say? I love 'the wood.' Big, small, or otherwise."

I gag. "Please, just no. He's already about to bone himself. Good thing it's shriveled from aggressive steroid use. Otherwise, he'd invert it and shove it up."

CeCe and Chaz look at me with alarm.

"Sweetie," Chaz begins. "Are you okay?"

I shrug him off. "Hanna and I never fight. I don't know what got into me today, but I just had it. I've had it with her, and I've *definitely* had it with him. This whole thing is just a shitshow, basically."

"Well, she's probably at home then," Chaz says. "I mean, she'd never let Owen sit alone."

"Did you try her cell?" CeCe asks. "Might be worth a shot."

"No," I admit quietly. "Not right now. Trust me, guys. She's pissed."

None of us are very hungry, so the three of us spend the break wandering the halls. Without Hanna, the mood just isn't the same, and with her usual spot next to me vacant, I feel empty. Though a few students are sitting with backs against the wall or milling about, the corridors are more or less unoccupied.

"Hey." Chaz points to the door of the auditorium. "They're doing *Grease* this year."

"Word," I say, nodding. "John Travolta. When he was younger? Can't touch him."

"You should do it," CeCe says. "Didn't you say something about wanting to act?"

"I'm acting right now." Chaz laughs darkly. "Closet on Broadway."

I snort. "Well, there's a place to let out your gayness. Everybody wears makeup and tights onstage. You'll be in heaven."

"I could learn a monologue," Chaz says, more to himself than to any of us. "I mean, it really can't be that hard."

"Brennan!" Spencer's grinning face rounds the corner. "Watch out, bud. It's Crack the Ripper."

"Oh shit, boys," Brennan rumbles. "Hold on to yo' butts."

Behind them, the rest of the lacrosse brutes hoot, holler, and slap each other on the back. Victor narrows his eyes at Chaz and nods at him provokingly.

"Why?" Chaz faces the crew. "So I can pull your hair?"

The laughter ceases. Brennan's expression clouds over.

"What did you say, faggot?"

CeCe and I step in front of Chaz instinctively, but he pushes past us and walks up to the boys.

"Faggot? *I'm* the faggot? Your entire team literally saw me and started fantasizing about gay sex." Chaz shakes his head. "Go to church."

Brennan and Spencer look at each other in shock. Usually, they're quick with the comebacks, but this time, they're silent. Shaking their heads, the rest of the guys fall in line behind them. They shuffle past us, none of them saying a word. Amazed, I think of how to congratulate my friend, but someone else beats me to it.

"Oh, my God," a loud voice rings out. "Okay, I officially love you." A girl, older than us, is staring at Chaz intensely. "I mean it," she says. "That was easily the greatest thing ever."

She's familiar, that's for sure. I don't have her in any classes or electives, but I've seen her around. She's pretty, in an edgy, artistic sort of way, with a nose piercing, heavy eyeliner, and blunt bangs. I'm almost positive we've spoken at some point; I just don't remember when. I do remember her name is Ryan, or Rory, or something. A boy's name. She smiles at CeCe and me, her eyes green and bright. "Wasn't it?"

"Yeah," a burly boy in a cardigan standing beside her says. "Those guys are shitheads. You handled them, though."

"Who are you?" The girl's eyes are glued to Chaz. "I haven't seen you before."

"Chaz," Chaz replies. "Humbert." They shake hands, and a look passes between them. CeCe nudges my foot, and I catch her eye, confirming what we both already know.

"Reece," the girl says. "Junior. Drama student." She laughs lightly. "Not that anybody would have guessed. Were you thinking about auditioning for the play?"

"Maybe," Chaz says, shuffling his feet. "I was a little curious."

"Do it!" Reece encourages. "You totally should. Right, Phil?" She pokes the boy next to her.

"For sure," he agrees. "We need new blood this year."

"I might," Chaz says, chewing his lip. "I've never acted, at least in anything that wasn't a Christmas pageant. This might be something new to try."

"Well, you've got my vote," Reece says airily, her hands on her hips. She turns to the two of us. "I'm sorry. I didn't catch your names."

"Roxie." I give her a nod.

"CeCe," CeCe says, extending her hand. "And I agree. Chaz is just about as A-list as it gets."

***

Three o'clock. School's out. No Hanna.

Now I'm worried. Like I mentioned before, Hanna and I rarely argue, and when we do, we usually make up within a few minutes. What I did was low, and the longer I have to reflect, I regret saying what I said more and more. By now, I've sent Hanna at least half a dozen texts, all of which remain unanswered. If she were me, I wouldn't think anything of her skipping a class or two. But Hanna's the girl who practically had a full-scale nervous breakdown last year when she was asked over the intercom to report to the office.

It turned out to just be Cynthia pulling her out for a spa day.

"Nope," Nurse Kimball says, snapping her gum. "Hanna ain't here. Not that I could tell you if she was, but go on in. Have a look around. Unlike you, Hanna wouldn't try to ditch." She glances down at her pudgy wrist. "Go on, scram. I got a meeting in five."

"You barely even work here," I grumble before I can stop myself.

"What was that?" Kimball squints at me with irritation.

"Nothing, nothing," I say quickly. "Better hit that meeting. I'm sure they won't start without you."

I text CeCe and Chaz again, asking if they've spotted Hanna at all today, but I already know the answer. Nick starts his new job today, so I can't depend on him for a ride, but I've got a while before the buses leave. I figure I'll kill some time and take another walk around the commons in case Hanna's somehow there.

After circling twice, I remember I haven't checked the freshman hallway and head in that direction. I don't know what I'm expecting. Unusually quiet for this time of day, the silence is a little eerie, and I begin to feel uneasy. Normally, there's some student organization holding a meeting, or you can at least hear the rumble of the custodial cart, but today, it's deserted. Undeterred, I hang left and take a faster pace, peeking into different classrooms. Aside from a trio of nerds fighting each other over a prehistoric gaming console, every room is either locked or empty. Taking another turn, this time to the right, I cross into the sophomore hallway to use the bathroom.

As I step inside, muffled groans and rapid panting float out from underneath the stalls to where I can hear them. Something—or someone—is banging against the stall wall so aggressively that I can hear the screws in the door rattling. In between grunts, I can make out a high-pitched giggle, while a deeper voice duets the poundage. Clapping my mouth over my hand to keep from laughing, I tiptoe out of the bathroom and crouch behind a nearby vending machine, curious as to who might be in there. I figure it'll be a funny story to tell Nick and the group to kick off the week with a good laugh.

After the vocal ecstasy inside the bathroom begins to taper down, I detect the wet *splat* of what I'm guessing is a used condom hitting the floor. I feel a sudden pang of sympathy for the poor janitor, unaware of what awaits him in stall three. Scuffling, then more laughter. A few more bangs on the door indicate the couple's either getting dressed or starting in on another round. As the stall door creaks open, I crane my neck out for a better glimpse and scuttle backward when I detect movement.

Like anybody with common sense, the couple doesn't exit together. Tiffany Verlich struts out first, straightening her purple camisole and buttoning her denim skirt. No surprise there. The district probably rents that stall out to her so she can occupy it with a different guy every other day. But then I remember: Tiffany has a *boyfriend*. And not just any boyfriend—she's dating the kindest, best-looking boy in the entire school.

How could she do that to Blake? It's common knowledge Tiffany will get down with anybody, but that was back when she was single. Now that she's supposedly in a relationship, one would think she'd clean up her act. Then again, it was probably Blake in there with her. My heart's about to break again when a red-faced Owen strides out with his chest puffed, grinning. He's doused in sweat and is fanning himself vigorously with an open hand, a pint-sized protrusion at the crotch of his slim-fitting jeans. I'm going out on a limb here and assuming this was his first time, but if he was really that popular back in Santa Barb, maybe not. Well, they sure went out with a bang. Maybe Tiffany and Blake aren't together, and it's just a platonic thing. I suddenly feel hopeful.

It doesn't last for longer than a second, though, as reality hits me like a ton of bricks. Tiffany isn't the only person in this distasteful duo currently involved with someone. As much as I'd like to forget it, Owen Smallwood is in an exclusive relationship, too. With my best friend.

***

"Wait!" I scream, running full speed towards the bus. "Stop!"

Through the windshield, I can see Petra grinning at me evilly. Revving the engine, the bus shoots forward and sends a cloud of black smoke swirling behind it like a plume. Petra's never been big on sympathy, but this is something else. The first day I rode her route, she tossed a stale Danish at me for talking too loudly and never really got better after that. Foolishly, I figured she'd cut me a little slack based on my orphan status, but she's probably figured it out by now. I mean, seriously? What kind of sicko leaves a poor orphaned teenager behind?

Petra, apparently.

I drop my backpack to the ground and kick it angrily. "Shit!" I scream at the top of my lungs. I pick up my backpack, hoist it over my shoulder, and throw it as far as it'll go. "Get back here, you crank-addled peckerwood hick!"

My mother thinks it's unhealthy not to vent. When Nick and I were small, she encouraged us to write down whatever thoughts and feelings we might have in our own personal diaries with the hope we'd find it soothing. Nick and I spent many an afternoon growing up drawing ourselves stabbing or shooting people we despised, and true to her word, my mother never interfered.

While we both still write from time to time, our foray into expressive artwork ended when Nick got in a fight with my dad and drew a cartoon of him dying a brutal death in a car accident. When it really happened, Nick never wrote in that diary again and somehow feels responsible to this day, though we never talk about it.

I sink to my knees, hot tears of frustration stinging my cheeks. If I hadn't been such an idiot and picked a fight over nothing, I could've gone to Hanna immediately and told her everything. If I would've just sat tight and allowed Owen to ruin himself the way Chaz told me to, I wouldn't be here now, collapsed in the parking lot after school alone with a secret this big. But it's way too late. If I can even get Hanna to speak to me ever again, she won't hear another word about Owen and after today, who could blame her? I'm indirectly responsible for whatever pain will result from Owen's infidelity, and I have no one to blame but myself.

I've really been trying not to think about it, but I wonder if Tiffany and Blake have done the deed yet. I'd kind of like to know. I mean, if by some miracle Blake and I do end up together down the line, I want to be sure I won't contract HIV or whatever else that's living in Tiffany's fish tank. But even if my prayers are answered, and somehow Blake and I end up dating, I'm not sure I'll want to have sex at all. I mean, I just don't feel ready right now, and I don't know if anybody I've met so far deserves that much of me. Nick feels similarly, although he's characteristically taken it to an extreme and is waiting for his "one true love." As for me, the only person I want is taken, and not just by some girl, but the worst type of girl there is.

My thoughts float back to Hanna, and my chest feels tight. Regardless of how much I fought Cynthia on it, I played a vital role in bringing Hanna and Owen together. I really hope she's cooled off just a little. I don't know what life would look like without her, and frankly, I don't even want to think about it. She's the one person outside my immediate family I can count on unconditionally, and she came into my life when I needed her the most. If I'm beating myself up over something, Hanna's the first to tell me how great I am and why I should love myself. When I screw up, she'll point out how I'm able to fix it. If I'm in trouble, she'll come to my aid in hell or high water, even if it means putting herself on the line.

But that's changing, and while both of us know it, I can't help but feel I'm the one who's been left behind. Owen seems to be the first priority now, and last weekend and our fight today proved that. If he were anybody else, I would be sad, but at the same time happy that Hanna found somebody else who brought her joy. But for now, I just need to know she's okay. For the billionth time, I hit the speed dial, but predictably, it goes straight to voicemail. I try to think of other reasons as to why she isn't picking up, but I know the truth. She's officially not speaking to me.

***

"I've been thinking," Nick says, drizzling olive oil over the salad he's preparing for tonight's dinner. "Taking care of a baby is expensive. Emilio went easy on Erik big time. I didn't want to say anything, but between you and me? She's got to get a job, man. I mean, that money isn't going to cut it."

"I know," I say. "I thought about it, too. I didn't want to say anything, either."

"Maybe Frankie can help watch the baby," Nick laughs. "You know, he's really good with kids."

A couple years ago, during an entrepreneurial phase, Frankie quit his part-time job at Skippers and opened a daycare in his basement. "Frankie's School for the Gifted" was little more than a video arcade, but a few desperate parents signed up their children for the summer of activities and learning promised in the brochure. Instead of watching the kids, Frankie plugged in several TV screens, loaded up on candy, and bought an arsenal of foam weaponry. Though I never experienced it personally, Nick told me it was out of control, and when one mother showed up unannounced to see her wunderkind riding a Big Wheel down the stairs, Frankie got shut down. After that, he was off to work for the man at Walmart, and according to Nick, he won't be going out on his own anytime soon.

"Speaking of Frankie. What's he been up to?"

"The usual," Nick replies. "Gaming. Work. More gaming. What about your crew? Is Hanna ever going to bring Owen around?"

"I doubt Hanna will ever come here again," I say, looking down at my hands.

"Wait, why?" Nick closes his bag of spices. "Did you two fight?"

"I screwed up today, Nick." I try not to get upset just thinking about it. "I went too far. I embarrassed Hanna in front of everybody by making fun of Owen in class. And that's not even the worst of it."

"What wasn't the worst of it? What happened?" Nick's eyes are full of concern. "I haven't seen you like this in ages. Talk to me."

"Okay." I take in a shuddery breath. "You're right. I need to talk to somebody. But you can't slip up, okay? I mean it."

"On my life."

I press my nails into my palm. "Owen's cheating on Hanna with Blake's girlfriend."

"Okay, hold up. You never told me Blake was dating someone. Who is it?"

"A slut," I reply. "Somebody awful."

"I thought he likes you. Or liked you." Nick squints at me. "Did you guys…"

"No," I interrupt. "We've literally talked, like, three times. That's it. He's just a nice guy. I guess he got together with Tiffany, but she cheated on him with Owen."

"How do you know?" Nick asks. "Who'd you hear it from?"

"I saw it," I say. "Or, at least, I heard it. I went into the bathroom while I was looking for Hanna, and they were banging. I hid by the soda machine, you know, to see who it was, and Tiffany and Owen both walked out."

"Holy shit," Nick gasps. "That's wild. How?"

"How not?" I roll my eyes. "They're both terrible people. It's not hard to see how they wound up together. They're a match made in heaven that should stay in hell."

"That's good," Nick laughs. "I've never heard that one. But I agree. Jesus, man. I don't know what to tell you."

"I mean, do you think we should let Emilio in on this?" I ask. "Like, ask him what to do? He's so wise. He could help get everything out in the open."

"No need," Nick says, returning to his cooking.

"What do you mean?" I ask, puzzled. "No need?"

"Cheaters, liars, cons. People like them. They reveal themselves in due time. Believe me." Nick peeks into the rice cooker and smiles. "Every lid comes off eventually."

"But I don't want to see Hanna hurt," I say. "I mean, if she and Owen stay together for a while, and this comes out, she'll be destroyed by it. And what kind of friend would I be to not pull her out of harm's way, even though telling her is out of the question?" I cradle my head in my hands. "I'm so stuck."

"Then start simple," Nick says. "Call her up. If she's ignoring your calls, use my phone. Apologize to her, tell her you've realized what you did was wrong. But do not, and I repeat, do *not* mention anything you just told me."

I blow out a breath. "Got it."

Nick slides his Sidekick across the counter. I palm it and step into the family room, thinking about how I'm going to approach this. Usually, if I'm feeling low, I'll eat one of my favorite foods, park myself on the couch, and watch a comedy with Nick so I can get away from life for a while. But Hanna? She's the exact opposite. When things go south in her world, she'll barricade herself in her room, close the blinds, and listen to every sad song she knows on repeat to drive herself into further despair.

I wait while the call goes through, focusing intensely on the ringing. Two. Three. Four rings. Nobody's picking up.

Then, somewhere in the background, Kelly Clarkson's "Because of You" fades out, and Hanna's voice breaks through.

"Nick?"

"Hanna, it's me," I blubber. "And before you hang up, hear me out. I'm *so* sorry about what I said about Owen in front of everyone today. I wish I could take it all back. You know I'd never mean to hurt you. I just—" I falter. "I just want you to know that I won't ever say anything bad about Owen again. I'm sorry."

Hanna sniffles. "What do you have against him, Roxie?" She sighs. "I mean, he hasn't done anything but make me happy."

"I know," I lie. "And I'm sorry. I'm so, so sorry."

Silence on her end. This is so unlike her I don't even know what to say. I must've really hit a nerve.

"It's okay," Hanna says at last. "I know you didn't really mean it." She chokes out a tearful laugh. "Maybe the three of us can go to the movies together. Then you can see the side of Owen I've been telling you about. The good side."

"Of course," I say immediately. "That sounds amazing. Tell Owen he can even pick which movie."

"And," Hanna continues, "Owen really wants to be included. I mean, he still doesn't really know anybody here, and he says our group reminds him of some people he used to know back home." She sighs. "He never mentioned anything to me about what you said in Tuttle's class, so he probably doesn't even know it happened."

"Good," I breathe. "Totally. He'll be included from now on."

"Not all the time, but some of the time. You know. Until he tries out for baseball."

"No problem." I shrug. "Bring him to lunch tomorrow."

***

School sucked ass, and I'm in a sour mood when CeCe, Chaz, Hanna, and I climb onto the bus and barrel towards the back. Hanna's phone bleeps for the trillionth time, and all of us groan. I lean over her shoulder to see another picture of Owen, this time seated at a desk with dictionaries stacked around him. Wearing horn-rimmed glasses and parting his lips like a fashion model, he's captioned this foppish display "Professor Heartbreak."

"How sweet," Hanna coos, clutching her phone to her heart. "Is he the cutest boyfriend or what?"

"He left school for *this*?" I choke. "He could have taken it right there. It even *looks* like Mrs. Buford's classroom."

"Come on," Hanna counters. "He's being romantic. It's the way he is. Don't tell me he doesn't look good."

"Whatever," I huff. "I'm glad you've found your man, Hanna. Just help me unseat Tiffany and maybe I'll get to experience married bliss too."

Hanna agrees to help me, and I nearly blab to her about Tiffany's latest romp, but then I remember who the other participant was and clam up. Repeating Nick's words to myself, I flatten myself against the backrest. Owen's misdeed will come to light. I just need to give it time.

Chaz crosses his legs. "Owen's gay."

"What?" Hanna turns to him. "How?"

"Haven't you heard?" Chaz asks, dropping his voice to a whisper. "He's obsessed with a dude."

"Who?" Hanna asks, her eyes wide.

"Himself," Chaz says flatly. The rest of us bust up laughing, and Hanna rolls her eyes. "He's rock hard for Hanna's man."

"Who could blame him?" Hanna giggles. "He's so hot."

CeCe doesn't say anything, but instead looks out the window and kneads her hands every couple of seconds. The further along in the pregnancy she is, the less she's been acting like herself, and we've all noticed. On the bright side, she hasn't experienced the torment or unkindness I worried she'd encounter. Instead, she seems off-limits to students and staff. The way she tells it, teachers barely acknowledge she exists, though she ends up getting high marks for assignments she admits never turning in.

"Why bother showing up?" CeCe asked this morning when I got on her case about skipping class again. "If I die giving birth, I'll pass ninth grade on the dean's list."

Up ahead, I can see my stop, but the bus doesn't slow down. Instead, Petra accelerates and, further down the avenue, picks up speed.

"Hey, excuse me," I yell from the back. "Uh, that was our stop."

"Oh, really?" Petra yells over her shoulder. "Well, someone's going to have to walk."

Swinging the wheel to the right, she slams on the brakes, and I almost break my nose on the seat in front of me.

"Get out!" Petra screams at us. "All of you. Roxie? You stay!"

Fear slashes through my body. Something's off with her for sure. I thought we were on good terms ever since our orphan bond was established. Slowly, my friends and I rise and walk towards the front of the bus, but Petra turns to face me.

"Learned a couple things 'bout you, girl," Petra says icily. "Ran into a real nice lady at the store yesterday. Inez?"

Oh, shit! She met my mom. Time to think up a lie. But my mind is blank this time around.

"How did she find out you were my bus driver?" I wonder, curious despite the circumstances.

Petra stares at me contemptuously. "Who gives a darn? Point is *you lied.* You want to know what Petra does to liars?"

"What?" I ask before I can stop myself.

"You can tell your mother, who's alive and well, to give you a ride, since you are now officially banned from my route."

"You can't ban me," I protest. "My taxes pay your salary."

"Out!" Petra screams. "Get the hell off my bus!"

I don't need a second warning. Petra screeches away, marking the afternoon air with the smell of diesel fumes and burnt rubber.

"If I were you, I'd never ride that bus again," CeCe says, her eyes wide with disbelief. "That bitch's nuts."

"Roger that," Chaz chimes in. "I'd walk. But hey, if you want, I can ask my dad to give you a ride. I'm sure he wouldn't say no."

"I said I wanted a ride, not to be ridden." I snort. "Hell no."

"Yeah. I figured you'd say that," Chaz laughs. "But you're right. He's a creep who needs to come up with new excuses for hiding in your bushes. The 'I'm going to the supermarket' explanation is getting old. Especially when he doesn't come home with groceries."

***

Having Owen as a regular now at lunch has thrown the mood big time, and I think even Hanna agrees, though she'd never admit it. It's a small concession to make, but even so, I find myself looking forward to fifth period. It's not so much what he says or does that's the problem. Like he did at the mall when Hanna was around, Owen keeps it upbeat, positive, and unassuming, though CeCe refuses to be fooled. Whenever he cracks a cheesy joke or calls Chaz "buddy" for the tenth time in a minute, CeCe and I share a look between us, and nothing more needs to be said. Hanna, on the other hand, is falling for it lock, stock, and barrel, which makes Owen's unfaithfulness that much harder for me to stomach.

I'm lounging on the couch Thursday afternoon watching raindrops roll down the window when the sound of heavy footfalls on the front porch breaks me out of my daylight sleep. The doorbell rings moments later, and I try to remember if I have any pending online purchases.

The bell chimes again. I guess I didn't, because the postman only rings once.

"Get the door!" I scream upstairs. "Nick!"

No response. I rub my eyes and rise. It's probably a random visit from one of Nick's weird stoner friends who are obsessed with death metal and refuse to drive. Any given weekday, you can find at least one of them (usually Chet or Kyler) occupying our house or lounging out back in the gazebo if they need space. Loping over to the door, I finger-comb my hair and scratch at a dried ketchup stain on the front of my shirt. I can't see who's out there, but maybe Nick's got a new friend: a Blake lookalike who's going to sweep me off my feet. I unlock the door and pull it open.

"Hello," Owen says quietly. Hair swept a foot in the air, he reeks of pomade and body spray. I recognize the smell of the pomade. It's the same brand Nick buys, except Owen's used the entire container for one afternoon.

"Owen?" I inquire skeptically. "What are you doing here?"

"Uh." Owen looks down at his feet. "I was just in the neighborhood, and I thought I'd stop by, because… well, I don't know how to say this." A look meant to convey vulnerability comes across his face. "I think we have to start from the beginning."

"Wait, hold on," I say, struggling to understand him. "Okay. So, hi. My name is Roxie. You're dating my best friend. And I think you're living scum."

Owen runs a hand along his chin. "Yeah, I get it." He turns slightly to give me his best angle. "Ugh. Forgot to shave again."

Unconvinced, I roll my eyes. "Yeah, okay. You clearly used a stubble creator. Two millimeters today? Cut the shit or get off my porch."

Owen shakes his head. "It's not created, I swear. It's genetics. My grandfather worked on the Gillette razor. You can Google it!"

"Get to the *point*," I growl, fidgeting with the door like I'm about to close it. "I'm serious, dude. I'm really busy right now."

"I just think we got off on the wrong foot," he says finally.

"Could be," I reply. "In fact, I know we did. My wrong foot was this close to going up your ass and still could."

Owen lets out an appreciative hoot and slaps his hands together. "Hanna was right," he chuckles. "Yo, you're a riot."

I blink. "As you were saying?"

Owen turns off the laugh track and continues. "I just want to get along with you. Hanna means the world to me, and you're her best friend. Since we're probably going to be seeing a lot of each other these next few years..." He trails off. "I just want you to know me the way Hanna does."

He looks at me with puppy-dog eyes and throws a muscly arm over the railing. It thunks hollowly, and he winces away his pain.

"But anyway, I know you think you've got me figured out. And you might still feel that way. But me? Haven't really been myself lately." Owen fiddles nervously with the puka shells he's wearing around his neck. "Still adjusting to life away from the beach. Like my buddy Hawk would say, I'm a dude out of the riptide."

This certainly wasn't what I expected. Though I've tried to keep an open mind, Owen is easily the fakest person I've ever met. Jerome, forever offbeat and immature, was at least true to himself and really did love Hanna. Owen only loves himself. Damn it, Cynthia.

"Okay, great," I force out. "Glad we had this talk. We're cool, I guess."

Owen flashes a laser-whitened grin. "Wicked. Nice house, by the way. You got rich parents?"

I smile sweetly. "Thanks. And, no. Just a dead dad with a hefty life insurance policy."

"Ah." He shuffles awkwardly. I relish in his discomfort. "Can I come in?"

"Um, no," I say. "Some other time, maybe. Like I said, I'm really busy right now."

Owen forces a laugh. "I'll hold you to it. See you tomorrow at school, right?"

"Tomorrow," I confirm. "See you at lunch."

"Who was that?" Nick calls from the landing after I close the door.

"Walking HPV," I reply, completely drained from the exchange. I lock the door behind me and walk to the freezer, where I pick up a package of something frozen and hold it against my forehead.

Nick cruises into the kitchen. "That wasn't Owen, was it?"

"Correct," I sigh. "Did you hear any of it?"

"A little," Nick replies. "The window in the office was open. I've never met a dude who talked that much about himself."

"Oh, you must've missed most of it then. He *only* talks about himself." I laugh. "He shows up, tells me we got off on the wrong foot, kisses my ass, and then tries to come in."

"He wanted to come into our house?" Nick laughs in disbelief. "No."

"Oh, yeah," I say. "Don't worry, I put the kibosh on that. Next time, I'll have Emilio waiting in the kitchen with a twelve-gauge. It'll be the last time Owen comes to this house."

"You think he figured out that you know about him cheating?" Nick asks. "Or if Hanna told him about the fight? Might explain the sucking up part."

"I don't know how he would know," I say. "It's not like he saw me creeping. The only thing he did was fan himself after the covert hump. Unless he teleported mid-thrust or can somehow be in different dimensions at once, it's simply impossible."

"True that." Nick shrugs. "Then forget it. Keep your mouth shut and play along with whatever he's doing. Let me guess, Chaz is under his thumb, Hanna thinks he's Saint Stud of Santa Barbara, and you're the odd woman out."

"CeCe hates him too," I say. "Sees right through him."

Nick nods. "Well, there's a plus. At least you got one like mind."

"I know," I say. "And I've got you. I'm not worried anymore. I listened to your advice."

"And to boot," Nick adds, "Owen's a himbo. He isn't smart. He's already bungled this by making an enemy out of you too early. Now, you just wait for his house of cards to collapse."

***

"The popcorn here is delish!" Owen exclaims, plowing his arm into the bucket for a tenth helping. "Back in Santa Barb, my buddies and I used to go to the movies all the time with hot chicks. But none of them were as pretty as you, babe." Mouth full, he turns Hanna's face to his, and they begin making out.

"Blech." I turn away from the spectacle. "Get the damn tickets, Owen, and let's go!"

Hanna extricates herself from him, wiping secondhand popcorn from her lip. "Why can't you be *normal?*"

"I am," I say innocently. "I'm just trying to prevent you from creating a playmate for CeCe's kid."

Owen guffaws and slaps me five, which I begrudgingly accept. "Damn straight! Owen Junior packs a punch!"

"Gross!" Hanna giggles, smacking his arm. "You're such a horndog!"

Owen laughs again. "Roxie's right, babe. You should listen to her," he says. "She knows what I'm made of."

I sip my soda. "Penile enhancements and false bravado?"

Owen stares at me hatefully. "Don't push me."

"No problem," I mutter.

Owen turns to Hanna and places his hand on her forearm. "I'll go get the tickets, babe."

"What's *his* deal?" I ask once Owen's out of earshot.

Hanna sniffs in irritation. "Roxie, you *promised* you'd try to get along with him. Please don't pick a fight for once."

Friday night, and we're at Regal Cinemas for some corny action flick Owen's been dying to see. I'd rather be anywhere else, but I need to smooth things over with Hanna by at least pretending to accept Owen. Groups are great and everything, but one thing I've always hated is the kinks. Before Owen's arrival, our group was perfect. Nobody canceled each other out; we all got along. Hanna, CeCe, Chaz, Nick, and Emilio are the realest people you'll meet. Period.

Now the group's turning into a minefield, and real issues have been shelved in exchange for whatever superficial nonsense Owen can comprehend. Hanna's glued to him, he's not letting go of her, and when those two aren't around, Chaz constantly asks why I can't seem to get on board.

"They're so happy together," he said yesterday as the two of us walked to fourth period. "I mean, they look like a couple from a storybook."

"Well, you're sure singing a different tune," I remarked. "Not long ago, you were the guy warning me about what Owen was up to. What's changed?"

But unless I drop the cheating bomb on everyone, I've got no probable cause, and I just look jealous. To his credit, Owen hasn't been rude. It's no longer surly or insulting. He's basically a plastic ornament who makes pleasant conversation and is nice to look at for thirty minutes a day. Harmless, right?

"Okay, sorry," I relent. "I'm trying. Really. Maybe we're just too different personality-wise. I don't know."

"I know he's not Blake," Hanna says, shooting me a sympathetic look. "But he's good to me and makes me happy. He really is an amazing boyfriend."

"Okay, okay," I say hurriedly. "I get it. I'll hold it together."

"Good." Hanna turns to Owen, who's back with three tickets in hand. "Got the tickets, cutie?"

"Oh yeah," Owen confirms. "Two girls, two tickets. It's on me tonight."

"How sweet are *you*?" Hanna dotes, playfully pinching his nose. Owen basks in the praise and hands me my ticket. I thank him and stuff it in my pocket, wishing it were a plane ticket so I could fly out the door and never come back. Owen's begun attacking the popcorn bucket like a famished refugee, wolfing it down before we've even made it to the line. He fumbles a handful, though, and several buttery kernels roll down the front of his polo. Noticing, he grunts in frustration and paws at the streaks.

"Shit. Hanna, clean me up."

"I sure hope I don't hear that in the theater," I say without thinking. Beside us, a group of middle-school boys overhears and burst out laughing. Owen chortles the loudest and pumps his fist.

"I've got to hit the john, babe," he chuckles. "Ralph Lauren needs a bath." He takes off towards the restroom, and Hanna turns to me.

"Enough."

"Lighten up." Everything I say or do annoys her now, which pisses me off even more. She used to be so much fun. But we're on thin ice as it is, and I don't want to push my luck.

"Okay, sorry," Hanna says. "It was kind of funny. But there's stuff going on right now. I mean, between Owen and me. Things are starting to heat up a little faster than I expected."

"Are you serious? Oh my *God*!" I shriek. "Are you telling me you've been face to face with his Smallwood!?"

"No, that's not what I *meant*," Hanna whispers. "Keep your voice down. I don't want those middle-school twerps hearing another word." She pauses. "All I'm saying is, he doesn't need any more ideas."

Oh, no he doesn't. Owen's sexual wonderings were recently demystified by a spray-tanned cooter licensed to Tiffany, but Hanna doesn't know this. Not yet. And judging by how into him she truly is, I wonder if she'll even allow herself to believe it should anything ever come out.

"I'm back!" Owen announces, throwing his arms around us. "You two ready to catch some action?"

Hanna nods, and we stroll into the theater, she and Owen a couple paces ahead of me. I'm trying not to laugh, but I don't know how much longer I can hold out. Owen's status as a douche cannot be challenged, but he's douched himself into a whole new league this evening.

"Roxie! Over here!" Owen hollers from the back row, waving his arms. "Roxieeeeeeeeee!"

Remaining in motion like a wind turbine, Owen only stops when I fall into my seat, which is to the left of his. I pull out my phone and check the time. It's going to be a long night.

"What movie is this, anyway?" Hanna asks, reaching for the bag of gummy worms Owen strategically placed in his lap. He smiles as she accidentally grazes his junk.

"Wait and see, blondie cakes."

I snort. *"Blondie cakes?"*

Owen chuckles throatily. "I need to slice blondie's cake."

I laugh, unable to help myself. "Keep your knife in its drawers, Owen. Your time is coming."

"Owen!" Hanna's mouth drops open. "Roxie! Wow, can you not?"

As the lights dim, Owen unzips his backpack and withdraws a hard-shell case. Snapping it open, he takes out a pair of aviators and puts them on.

"Yo," I say. "Stevie Wonder. The movie isn't in 3D. Those aren't going to work, dude."

"Shush." Owen smirks. "No talking. Please enjoy the picture."

Owen snaps a photo of himself with his cell phone, and I flop back in my seat. As the first preview begins, Hanna burrows into his chest and sighs.

"I love commitment," Owen announces to no one in particular. He turns to me. "Jealous yet?"

"Eat one," I snap. Immediately, my mind goes to Blake, and Tiffany's face flashes in front of my eyes. I smile, suddenly empowered by what I hold over Owen.

"Who's in this movie?" Hanna asks.

"If you stopped trying to procreate in public, you might actually know," I say under my breath.

"Dude," Owen interjects loudly. "I'm, like, insanely unappreciative of your negative energy right now."

"Deal with it, Yogi."

"Enough!" Hanna hisses, by now completely fed up with the both of us. We fall silent, and Owen refocuses on her. As for the film, it certainly wasn't my choice, and after fifteen minutes of bazookas, breasts, and bravado, I'm certain it won't be winning any awards.

I poke Hanna's arm. "Seen enough?"

"Yup," she admits. "You?"

"God, yes." I roll my eyes. "Let's check out what else is playing. Ten bucks he won't notice we're gone."

"I can't," Hanna says wearily. "He'll take it personally. Let's just sit a little longer and then maybe we'll leave."

As Hanna interlaces her fingers with Owen's and feeds him popcorn, I stare at the movie, hoping it'll pick up. After another ten minutes, I'm ready to walk. I glance down at my phone to see if anybody's sent me anything, but the screen is blank. I sigh, dip my hoodie over my head, and will myself to fall asleep.

***

Halfway through the film, Owen's completely lost interest in Hanna. If you ask me, it's probably due to the fact she can't leave him alone, and guys like the chase. Whether she's kissing him passionately, pulling at his hair, or crawling into his lap, Hanna's gone nympho cubed. It's terrifying, given this is a girl who used to live for baking cookies and making bead jewelry, but dry-humping Owen now seems to be her pastime of choice. As she moans and sighs into his nonexistent neck, I entertain myself by flinging unpopped kernels at different audience members and thinking up insults for Owen. Finally, Owen roughly moves her out of his way before turning to me.

"How did you and Hanna meet?"

"Long story," I say. "Years ago. Been close ever since."

"I get it." Owen nods. "My best buds are still back home. Grew up on the same street, went to the same kindergarten. We might be of different races. But we're all brothers in the surf."

That was about the whitest thing I heard today, but I refrain from saying so. Owen turns to look at me. "What background are you?"

"What do you mean?" I ask. "Like, where's my family from?"

Owen nods intensely. "Yeah."

"I'm kind of a mix," I say. "My mom is first-generation American with British parents. Some of her ancestry comes from the Caribbean back when the islands still belonged to Spain. My other side's Iranian. Why?"

"You don't look like other girls," Owen says quietly. "Not that that's a bad thing. You'd fit right in if we were in California."

I feel my body stiffen. "What makes you think I don't fit in here?"

"I don't think that. I'm just saying, like, most girls out here. Ugh!" Owen makes a face. "Barf-o-rama."

I snort at his crude remark. "Uh, wow. Okay. It's okay to have an opinion, I guess."

"I like black hair," he continues, his gaze drifting over my long braid. "My mom's family is from Napa. She's Greek all the way. My dad's just your average white dude, with a little Italian in him. Mixes really are the best."

"Well, we all have preferences." Where is he planning on taking this?

Owen chews his lip. "What do you think of the movie?"

"Terrible." I laugh. "I still haven't figured out the storyline."

"I know." He winces. "Bad choice. I thought for sure it'd be a blockbuster like *Kill Bill* or *Terminator*."

"Yeah," I say, a little creeped out that he just name-dropped two of my favorite movies of all time. "Guess we can't come with high expectations."

"Look at the girl," Owen says, pointing at the heroine onscreen. "She's got to be like, what, a D cup at least?" He guffaws obnoxiously. "Grab the stool. Someone's got to milk that cow."

I can't believe he said that, but I laugh anyway and move closer to him. "D cups, huh? Damn. Those are, like, the same size as Tiffany's, aren't they?"

Terror darts across Owen's handsome features. "Wait, Tiffany? You mean that slut in my grade?"

"Aw, honey," I say, giving him my most patronizing tone. "I think you know exactly what I'm getting at."

Owen leans in excitedly. "I do."

"Wait, what?" Now I'm confused. Looking at Hanna, I see she's fast asleep, breathing gently while slumped against Owen's shoulder.

"Nothing, nothing," he says quickly. "I just thought we had, uh, a connection."

"A *what?*" I reel back. "Did you say connection? Us? Like a *connection?*"

Owen doesn't say anything but gives me the intense look I've seen dozens of times in the pictures he sends Hanna. "Yeah."

Flustered, I struggle to keep my voice even. "Are you serious right now?"

"Totally. I mean, I know we're a little at odds, so to say, but I saw how you looked at me when we first met. I know I'm tall and really good-looking, but…"

"You're sick." I wrap my arms around myself. "You're really, really off."

Owen studies me. "What do you mean?"

"Split personality, bad attitude." I shrug. "And you're hitting on me. While your girlfriend's asleep."

"Who said I'm hitting on you?" Owen laughs, shaking his head. "Someone's a little full of herself. Connections are complex. Some people, you like them as a friend. Other people, you find yourself really interested in as something more. But I'm in a committed relationship. You know that."

"Enough," I hiss, turning away from him. "We're done here. Don't talk to me."

I try to tune him out, but he's right next to me, so it's impossible. Sighing in her sleep, Hanna snuggles deeper into Owen's side, but he moves her off him and slides her back in her chair. Wishing I was sitting anywhere else, I pick up the almost-empty popcorn bucket and see if I can find anything at the bottom when a strong hand reaches into my shirt and cups my breast.

"Oops," Owen growls in my ear. "Missed the popcorn."

Chapter 14

My mouth reacts first, and I let out a scream that could wake up Helen Keller in the grave. It takes Owen a second to put it together, and he pulls his hand out of my shirt. Rearing back, I try to shove him away from me, but he doesn't move, so I carry on yelling at maximum volume. Calmly, Owen eats the last of the gummies and sips at his root beer. Seconds later, the lights come on.

"Hey!" an idiot in the front row cries. "What happened to the movie?"

The entire audience is looking back at us, but I barely notice. Fully recovered from the shock, I start pummeling Owen. Throwing every combo I've ever learned hard as I can, I expect him to at least wince. But his abs, unlike his character, are rock solid, and instead of feeling pain, my repeated strikes do little but draw out a long, sexual groan.

"You shit!" I shriek. "How could you do that to her? How?"

"Do what?" Owen fakes surprise. "Crazy bitch. What are you talking about?" He turns towards the theatergoers and holds me away with a strong hand. "I didn't do anything. She's nuts."

I palm-strike his face. "Don't fucking touch me!"

"Yeah," Hanna says quietly. "Don't fucking touch her."

Amidst the chaos, I completely forgot Hanna was with us. She's awake now, but somehow maintains her composure. Cool and collected, she turns to us both, looking at Owen with an expression I've never seen before.

"I," Owen begins. "I didn't, uh."

Reaching forward, Hanna grabs his crotch, squeezing it until he emits a high-pitched scream. Writhing in pain, Owen tries to escape, but she grips him tight and doesn't let go.

"You," Hanna whispers, "are a used-up, diseased piece of work."

"Let me go!" Owen wails. "Please let me go."

"People warned me," she continues, twisting his area. "And I should've listened. I don't know what I ever saw in you, Owen."

"Come on," he begs. "They're turning blue. Take your hand away."

"Oh, they'll be blue for a long time." Hanna smirks. "I know people. My sisters were queens when they were your age. You won't go on one date the entire time you're here once I let go of your *small wood*."

Hanna finally releases Owen's appendage, and he gasps, his face redder than it was when he banged Tiffany last week. Wheezing, he lays back in his chair, tears beading at the corners of his eyes.

"Forget the movie," somebody shouts from the middle row. "How about *that*?"

"Tell him, sweetheart!" a middle-aged woman in mom jeans yells from somewhere nearby. "Somebody needed to."

"Roxie?" Hanna says, turning to me. "You ready?"

Smiling, I link arms with Hanna, and the two of us walk out the emergency exit as the alarm starts to sound.

"I'm so sorry about your boob," Hanna cries. "God, Roxie. Why?"

"It's okay," I say quietly. Truthfully, what Owen did to me is far from okay. Right now, though, Hanna's my first priority. This whole time, I've been talking her down, but it's not working because she seems to be getting worse. She managed to hold it together until we made it out of the theater, which was good. With all that drama, someone was bound to call security. Me, though? I haven't even begun to process my situation.

"You think we should call your mom?" I ask. It's dark outside, and there aren't many cars around. We left the cinema a while ago and are now walking along the main drag in the direction of Hanna's place, though it'll take at least an hour. I've been so busy consoling Hanna, I didn't check the time. "I could try Nick. We really shouldn't be out this late."

"Why did I like him?" she sniffles. "I'm so stupid."

"You're not stupid," I say. "He was. Pulling a move like that? In a theater? In front of you? I'm amazed he can open a door."

"Being smart never was his strong point," Hanna weeps, dabbing at her eyes. "And to think I could fix him. Make him interesting. Teach him his times tables." She shakes her head. "Why am I so naïve?"

"You're not naïve," I insist. "Just a good person. Leeches like him find good people like you. It never fails. I've seen this my entire life."

"I changed," Hanna says. "I would've become anything he wanted. And everybody talks about how great I am. Well, I don't feel like anything special now."

"You are special," I say sharply, looking her in the eyes. "The most special person I know. You made a mistake. You're human. There's nothing you or I can do to change Owen. He is who he is. But don't you dare change, either, 'cause you're pretty near perfect."

Hanna breaks into fresh tears, and I pull her close. I'm relieved neither of us owns a scythe, or a heavy blunt object, because if we did, Owen would be ground beef by now. Yet I still can't seem to absorb the fact that a half-hour ago I was assaulted in a movie theater by somebody I knew. I know I need to process this, but I'm not ready. I feel dirty, like the entire thing was my fault and that I'll die if anybody ever discovers this happened.

Hanna's face contorts. "I hate him for what he did to you."

"Yeah, me, too," I say, hugging my arms to my chest. "What's done is done. And yeah, I know it wasn't my fault or anything, but I still feel gross." I shake my head. "Who knew Friday could suck so bad?"

Hanna smiles through her tears. "This one sure did."

"But hey," I say. "It was almost worth everything to watch you wreck his junk and break up with him. In front of a hundred people, no less. I hope somebody got it on film."

"Don't worry. It's all up here," Hanna says, tapping her head. "I don't think we'll ever forget tonight."

I turn to her with a sly smile. "I gotta ask. Was it small?"

Hanna holds back a giggle. "Really?"

"Really," I say. "Bad attitude? Worse personality? Obsessed with the weight room?" I laugh. "And the name. The family name. Who could live that down? Come on, I've got to know."

"Well, I never actually saw it," she admits. "I did feel it, though. Over the pants."

"So? What's the verdict?"

Hanna shrugs. "Micro. A chode, maybe even." She busts up. "I wish I could give you more, but there wasn't much to work with."

"Ding, ding," I force a laugh. "Roxie's right again."

Hanna rolls her eyes. "And to think this was supposed to be the day. The day everything got sorted out and he was going to be a part of things. A part of the group."

"Yeah," I say. "About that. It would've been disastrous. Think about trying to collect Erik's money while Owen did butt lifts in the shed. Trying to protect Chaz's status around Owen's big mouth." I cringe. "It couldn't have worked. But that's not your fault."

"It is my fault," Hanna insists. "If I hadn't invited you along, he never would've done what he did."

"Enough," I interrupt. "Really, dude, you've got to get a grip on this anxiety. It's killing you. You're not responsible for other people's actions, lives, or happiness. You are responsible for you. Yeah, I love your mom and everything, but Cynthia's a wreck. She never got it together after your dad left and dropped everything on you and Kelsey and Brooke." I take a breath, hoping I haven't gone too far. "It was unfair. Nobody should have to deal with those issues, especially not kids. And maybe it's not my place, you know, to say any of this, but somebody's got to. You're fifteen years old. A kid! Stop being so hard on yourself. You don't need the extra weight."

I kick a small rock into the street and watch it bounce underneath the wheels of a passing minivan. "You want to know something? Everything that happened tonight. Want to know whose fault it is? It's mine! Cynthia and I were behind Owen, Hanna. *We* put this thing together, and *we* planned the mall trip. We were the ones who placed Owen in your path because…I don't know all the reasons why, but if anybody besides Owen is guilty of Owen's own personal actions, it's me and your mother. Not you."

Hanna gasps. "You mean…?"

"Yeah," I say. "I met him before you did. You were absolutely right to be skeptical."

Neither of us speaks for some time. I didn't end up calling Nick, so it looks like we're going to have to walk this one. Hopefully, Porn Stache isn't out for a drive in his panel van, 'cause we're sitting ducks this time of night. Hanna doesn't look at me, but wipes her eyes occasionally and fiddles with the clasp on her purse.

"Why am I so unlucky?" she asks. "With guys, I mean."

"What are you talking about?" I squint at her. "Jerome's still in love with you."

"My father," Hanna says, "doesn't know what I look like. What classes I take. Where I want to go to college or even what I want to do with my life at all." She shakes her head. "He's got a new family now, and I don't even know the first thing about them, and they live forty-five minutes west of here. And Jerome? How many years were we together, and he didn't even know who Chaz was? What Chaz did to us before he reformed? And now Owen. Why am I surrounded by them? It's like I'm my mother all over again, and that's the *last* person I want to be."

"You're not your mother, Hanna," I say, remembering the deep fears Cynthia expressed to me during our meeting. "We aren't our parents.

Doesn't matter what genes we get, how we live. We're our own people. And you? You can't help what other people are, what they do. It wasn't your fault Owen cheated on you with Tiffany, and—"

"*What?*"

Oh. Shit. There went another involuntary PSA from yours truly. I frantically try to backpedal, but there's no way out of this one.

"What did you just say?" Hanna demands. "Did I hear what I think I just heard?"

"Hanna," I say slowly. "Uh, well. Yeah." I look down at the sidewalk. "Remember when we had our fight?"

She nods.

"I went looking for you after school," I say. "I called you I don't know how many times, but you never picked up. You were so mad I left you alone, but I just wanted to say sorry about everything that went down, so I tried to find you. I walked in on Owen and Tiffany, you know, having sex, but I didn't say anything because I knew you'd go berserk and not believe me. I just hoped it'd come out later or you'd hear it from somebody else." I shiver from the cold, but also from the relief of finally getting this off my chest. "I told Nick, though. He told me not to tell you, either. That this could really damage our friendship if it came on the heels of our big blowup. I mean, was I right? Was he right? I'm so sorry," I ramble. "If I could've done it differently…"

"You couldn't have," Hanna breaks in. "I wouldn't have heard it. After what you said in Tuttle's class, I would've lost it. Then everybody in the group would either have to pick a side or stay out of it, and with Owen constantly in the picture, yeah, things really would've taken a turn." She rubs her temples. "But after tonight, I could totally see him doing something like that. Doesn't surprise me. At all, in fact."

"He wasn't a good guy," I say finally. "Good-looking, but not good."

"Let's never keep secrets from each other," Hanna says. "Okay?"

I squeeze her hand. "Deal."

We walk in silence, but my mind is going a mile a minute. I think back to the way Owen looked at me when Cynthia first introduced us. How he lingered on my porch the day he came to make amends. How, originally, he'd asked me to show him around and how he couldn't wait to get me alone in the movie theater. It's scary, the more I think about it, and the gravity of what happened or what could've happened is starting to settle in. Nevertheless, I refrain from sharing my thoughts. As much as I love Hanna, and I know she'd listen to me, she's still a girl. And right now, no girl needs to hear that side of it.

***

Monday, I need somebody else to help me celebrate Owen's expulsion from the group, but CeCe has done a bunk. In fact, I'm guessing she doesn't even know of the weekend's events because she hasn't answered a single text I've sent her. Chaz and I planned on swinging by her house on Saturday, but Nick had a panic attack and couldn't find the *Sounds of the Everglades,* so I had to spend two hours calming him down. Hanna needed some time to herself, which I completely understood, and Frankie got promoted. Sunday, I hit the books and did some housekeeping with Nick and my mom, and by the time I got ready for bed, I was asleep as soon as I hit the pillow.

"What if she died?" Chaz wonders aloud as the two of us stand posted by her locker. "I mean, would we know? Would somebody tell us over the loudspeaker or something?"

"Of course," I say, thumping his forehead. "There would be an announcement and everything."

"Okay good," Chaz says. "She was here last week, though. What could've changed?"

"Felicia." I roll my eyes. "Endless drama with that one. I mean, it's basically common knowledge at this point. Everybody knows CeCe's pregnant."

"She barfed in science," Chaz says. "And then got iffy with attendance, which means…"

"There's more room for rumors," I finish. "Erik's AWOL, CeCe's gone, she ralphed in class, and before that…come on. We all knew they went to fourth base, and the rest is history. People aren't stupid."

"They are stupid," Chaz argues. "Look at how they treat her. They treat her differently because she's pregnant. Meanwhile, some of them are off doing the same thing. Having abortions and getting herpes and God knows what else. People here are so hypocritical."

"And the teachers are even worse," I say. "I see how they treat her now. Like she's some ice sculpture." I shake my head. "Know what? You're right. They are stupid."

"I gotta go," Chaz says in disgust. "Any longer I'll punch one of them."

"Yeah," I say tiredly. "You and me both."

The whole day, I can't even pretend to focus. During lunch, Hanna, Chaz, and I walked every inch of the school, but CeCe was nowhere to be found. I called Emilio a bunch of times but only got voicemail, and I didn't see his car here today or Friday. Even Nick, who's with Emilio any chance he gets, has no clue where either of our Sanchez friends may be.

Chaz nudges me with his foot. "I can't stop thinking about her," he says, nervously nibbling a granola bar.

"She's fine," I say hurriedly. "We'll check on her after school."

Chaz, comforted by my answer, flips through a graphic novel he hasn't put down all day. Me? I just can't convince myself. I've got the feeling something's not quite right with her, but the fear of it being beyond my ability to help has kept me away. And then there's Emilio. To me, Emilio will always be a friendly, dynamic, wise guy who steps up for his family and runs a successful on-campus delivery service. But to others? I don't really know that much about him or what he does when the sun goes down. I try to think the best of people, but as much as I like him and love the way he's befriended Nick, I know there's way more to that story. I just hope he's safe and that, regardless of what he does or doesn't do, it hasn't impacted CeCe or placed her in harm's way.

With that in mind, I rise to my feet. "Okay, let's go," I say. "We're going to find CeCe."

"Word." Chaz slides his comic book back in his bag. "Let's bail."

Ditching school again, Chaz, Hanna and I climb onto the city bus and head towards CeCe's house. None of us talk. Hanna, at this point convinced she's going to fail the ninth grade, is slumped against the window, while Chaz and I spend the ride playing Chaz's Gameboy, switching off every couple of stops. After what seems like forever, I pull the cord, and the bus screeches to a stop at the end of CeCe's street. We step off, and I breathe in the scent of freshly mowed grass, which is strange because it's usually still rainy this time of year.

As the three of us walk towards CeCe's house, I try to think of something to say, but nothing sounds appropriate. I'm just hoping everything's fine and that there's some blanket explanation for CeCe and Emilio's random absence. Somehow, I know there isn't.

Hanna rolls up her sleeves and jabs at the doorbell. The chime echoes dully throughout the quiet house. I listen intently, hoping to make out footsteps, but I hear nothing. Hanna rings it again. I've known her long enough to know this situation is agitating her.

"No one's here," Chaz declares. "Duh. Everyone's at work."

"Relax." I glance at Chaz, who is rocking nervously on his heels. "You're probably right."

"Try the handle," Chaz instructs, nodding at Hanna.

"What are you, crazy?" Hanna wrinkles her nose. "You can't do that."

"Hey," Chaz laughs. "What do you call it when a gay guy breaks into your house? A 'homo' invasion. Get it? Homo? Instead of home?"

Hanna and I chuckle weakly.

"Move, bitches." Chaz snaps his fingers for effect and sidles past us, turning the door handle. To my surprise, it swings open, and he steps forward into the front room.

"Ohmygod! Chaz!" Hanna claps a hand over her mouth. "Get out of there right now."

"Well, he's not going alone," I say, sliding off my shoes and following him. "Come on, girly."

"Hello?" Hanna calls out once all three of us are inside. "CeCe, it's us."

Chaz cups his hands around his mouth. "Cecilia?" he trills. "Baby, you there?"

We trot towards CeCe's room, and I bang on the door. "CeCe?" I ask. "It's us. We're scared to death."

A low murmur answers from the other side of the door. The three of us exchange glances and head inside.

The first time I saw CeCe's house, I noticed how much it stood out from the rest of the neighborhood. The fence was stark white, the shrubs were trimmed, and the lawn was immaculate. CeCe's room was no exception. The walls were tastefully decorated, and the shag carpeting, while a little dated, smelled like apple blossom. It was a room from a magazine. It was a room, being the massive slob that I am, I could never maintain.

The place is unrecognizable now. Looking down at the floor, I realize I'm standing on a pile of dirty laundry, and the windows are sealed shut, trapping in a stale, musty odor. Most of the drawers are hanging open, and the dresser is stacked with what looks like paperwork. Underneath the duvet, CeCe looks at us calmly, like we were invited over opposed to breaking in.

"Hi, guys," she mutters.

"Hey, CeCe," I say. Hanna and Chaz return their own greetings in low tones. I flop down on the bed next to her, while Hanna pulls out a desk chair and Chaz takes a seat cross-legged on the floor.

"Where've you been?" Hanna asks gently. "Hm?"

"My phone plan got cancelled," CeCe replies. "That's why I didn't text anyone. Sorry about that. Not that you'd want to see me like this."

"I just wanted to see you," I say. "I was scared to death. Why didn't you just stop by? We haven't seen Emilio, either."

The second I speak his name, CeCe bursts into tears. A cold pit forms in my stomach and spreads into every inch of my body, confirming my fears.

Hanna's face is paler than ever. "What happened?"

Chaz jumps to his feet. "Is he alive?"

"I don't know," CeCe says finally, her voice choked with emotion. "I don't know what happened. Something went down last week. Something at the grange, and...Emilio got taken away in a raid." She sniffles. "I heard it from somebody who was there, who got away, but I don't know where he is."

She's still talking, but I can't hear. My ears are ringing, almost like tinnitus, and I'm so angry I fear I'll turn what remains of this room upside down if I don't get out right this second. But I can't move. My body has transformed into a thousand pounds of cast iron, and my feet are an extension of the floor. I try to breathe, but the dust and the smell of the room are like mustard gas, and I gasp like I'm drowning before taking a series of shaky breaths.

I look over at my friends to see that Hanna's face is down on the desk with her hood pulled over her head, and Chaz is cradling his head in his hands, refusing to look at us. My brain pivots to Nick. Does he know? Has anyone told him yet? It's going to hit him the hardest after CeCe. With Nick, things like this can throw him. Sometimes for good.

"They'll let him go, though, right?" Hanna says, her voice barely audible. "He's a citizen, isn't he?"

"Emilio wasn't born here," CeCe croaks, wiping her eyes with the back of her hand. "He's Mexican. Well, to them anyway. Brought here when he was four. His parents left their town, looking for work like everybody else. Eventually, they made it to Washington." She coughs. "He loved it here, though. Even with the racism, the unfairness, and what he told us about Elderwood, he still loved America. He says this is his country. This is where he wants to be."

"It is his country!" Hanna yells. Her face is blotchy. "It's where he belongs. Where the hell else is he supposed to go? We've got to help him. Who was there when he got taken?"

"I know a couple people who were there," CeCe says. "At least kind of. Something to do with farm workers. Besides that, I don't know. I don't even know if they're still here."

"We'll figure this out," Chaz says hollowly, though he doesn't sound like he believes a word of it.

Sliding off the chair, Hanna walks over to the window and opens the curtain. Light floods into the room, and, once my eyes adjust, I get my first good look at CeCe. Her face is gaunt, her eyes are drowning in dark circles, and her hair is a greasy mess. I can see hollows now in her cheeks where they weren't before, and her collarbone pops out underneath her nightgown.

"Yeah, not much to look at these days," CeCe remarks, catching my gaze. "I don't look at myself. You shouldn't either."

"You've got to give yourself a break," I say. "Stop being so hard on yourself. You just got thrown a major curveball. I totally get why you stayed home. But seriously, you've got to let us in."

"I can't imagine how upset you are," Hanna says, her voice congested. "I'm upset too. We all are. But we're here for you. Roxie, Chaz, Nick, me. And you know if Emilio was still close by, he'd be here for you too."

"She's right," Chaz says quietly. "Whatever we can change or can't change or help or fix…. I'm here. We're here for you."

CeCe steps into the shower to clean up while the rest of us get to work straightening up the room. The laundry alone will take a couple of days at least, so we pile as much as we can into a hamper so Chaz can take it over to the washer.

"Where did he go?" Hanna asks. "Chaz?"

"Working on a load," Chaz replies, sauntering by with the hamper on his hip. "A big one."

He looks over his shoulder at us. "Get your mind out of the gutter, ladies!"

"What can we actually do for her?" Hanna whispers to me once the two of us are alone. "*Can* we do anything for her? We're her age. None of us have money to throw her way. Emilio was the adult here, and now he's gone."

"I know." I rub my eyes. "She got dealt a shitty hand. No wonder she snapped. Emilio could be anywhere, and Erik's money...well, we can assume that's not coming anymore." I shake my head. "What do I know? I've never been pregnant or faced with anything like this. Who am I, really, to give her any advice?"

"I think it's time," Hanna says quietly.

I squint at her. "For what?"

"I never thought I'd say this...but I think we need to talk to my mom."

***

"Sounds like a nervous breakdown," Cynthia remarks, stirring another spoonful of Splenda into her coffee. "Had a few of those. No sleep. Dark circles. Weight fluctuations. Girl's a hot mess."

Once we got CeCe's room in order, we walked with her down the street to where she usually gets her hair and nails done. We convinced her to use some of Erik's money to get herself in a better place mentally, and by the time she came out of the salon, she looked almost like herself. Still, with Emilio gone, a piece of her seems to have gone with him. That said, I'd be lying if I said a piece of all of us didn't die that day. Despite the heartache, we managed to squeeze in a few laughs, and by the time Hanna, Chaz and I got up to go, I felt CeCe was in a stable place.

"It was awful." Hanna shivers. "Two days later, I can still smell that room. It was a wreck. She was a wreck. She looked so sick. Not like herself at all."

"Yeah," Cynthia says. "Fifteen and all that to deal with. Of course, the guy runs at the first sign of trouble. Nothing has changed since the 80s." She laughs bitterly. "Poor girl's going to have it a lot tougher than she knows."

I glance over at Cynthia. "What would you do if Hanna was the one pregnant?"

"Oh, Jesus," she replies. "There's an icebreaker. I don't know." She stirs her coffee, seemingly deep in thought. "I mean, I never really figured this was a possibility. Even when she was dating, you know, the philandering rake whose name we do not speak, I knew whatever happened she would be responsible.

"When Hanna was eleven," Cynthia continues, "like the rest of my girls, I gave her 'the talk.' That way, she knew what went where, how everything worked, and that, if she ever had any questions, she could always come to me."

"And it worked," I say. "Obviously. But I haven't spent that much time at CeCe's house. I don't know if they're religious or conservative or what. I don't know when CeCe's mother had her. I don't even know how her parents feel right now. Maybe they've accepted it and plan to raise the baby as another sibling or something. Sometimes that works, too. Look at Jack Nicholson!"

"Emilio's gone. Otherwise, we could ask him all these questions." Hanna stares up at the ceiling. "He knew her better than any of us."

"If only." I sigh and slouch in my chair.

"Don't get me wrong," Cynthia begins. "I think what you're doing, or trying to do here, is great. But you need to consider the main player, and you aren't it."

"What do you mean?" Hanna knits her brow.

"Where's CeCe in all of this?" Cynthia shrugs. "It's her future. Have her scope out the course. I mean, how well do you know her?

What does she want out of life? Maybe it was her plan all along to get pregnant. Maybe she wants to start a family early. You said Erik's got money. Maybe she wanted that security, and trapping him didn't work. Or does she just want something of her own to love her back?"

"Mom!" Hanna's mouth is wide open. "I literally can't believe you just said all that."

"Said what?" Cynthia looks equally surprised. "I don't judge. I'm just saying none of us know, and that only she does."

"It wasn't planned," I say firmly, remembering the state Hanna and I found CeCe in. "It was a total accident. I can guarantee that."

"Okay then," Cynthia says. "You're probably right. But I knew some pregnant high-school girls. And unless they got raped or got drunk at a party or were waiting for marriage until they met Brett Michaels backstage, they get pregnant for the reasons I mentioned. You tell me, girls. How hard is it to take a pill? Get an implant? Buy a couple of jimmy hats? It's not!"

Hanna gasps. "Oh my God, Mom. Listen to yourself. You know, not every family is so open about these things."

"I know that." Cynthia folds her arms. "But hey. I mean, maybe she's not legally an American and wants an anchor baby. I mean, Samuels is going to work a lot better than Sanchez when you're trying to get a green card."

"OMG!" Hanna claps a hand over her mouth. "Mom, that's racist. You can't say that."

Cynthia raises an eyebrow. "*I'm* being racist? Sorry, hon. You might want to look at yourself before you point fingers at me."

Hanna pushes her lower lip out. "I'm sorry, what are you talking about?"

"I don't judge," Cynthia says for what seems like the hundredth time. "I have no problems with anybody. Black, Mexican or otherwise. I mean, Alejandro's my favorite gardener, and his ass makes Brad Pitt's look like a Swedish pancake. Bring on los hombres! *Mas, por favor*!"

Hanna's nostrils flare, and I stifle a laugh. "Mom!"

"I'm not judging your friend. I'm saying everybody's got their reasons for what they do, and it's exactly that. *Her* reasons."

"Now I'm confused," I cut in. "What are you saying exactly?"

"CeCe's pregnant," Cynthia states. "Not you, not Hanna. Only she knows what's best for her, and it's her decision to make. It's her life and her baby's life, and she can make the plans. So if you want to get on my case, Hanna, I think maybe you should first ask yourself why a white girl is planning a brown girl's future without said girl even being here in the room."

Hanna opens her mouth to respond, but Cynthia cuts her off.

"It isn't your place to save her," she says. "CeCe's not the child, you aren't the parents, and she's lived a life of her own. Things you probably don't even know about. Situations you've never had to put up with. Is she your friend? Is she equal to you? Or are you adopting her?"

Hanna's face is flushed. "Of course she's equal to us," she says quietly. "All we've been trying to do this entire time is what's best for CeCe. That's it."

Cynthia cracks her neck. "Well, last I checked, you're all fifteen-year-old girls. So no, you don't know what's best for her any more than what you know what's best for you. Support her, love her, but don't control her."

"Well now I feel like a bitch," I say, my cheeks reddening. "I mean, I never thought about it like that. Like, I did the same thing with Chaz a month or so before. It's just what we do."

"I know that," Cynthia says. "You both have good hearts. You're good girls. And I'm not telling you not to help her. Just that if you're going to do it, don't treat her like a project. She's a big girl making adult decisions. Don't be surprised if she ends up becoming the group mom in a couple years. Your job is to be a friend, offer support and advice if she requests it. And love. Lots of love."

"We kind of got swept into it," I say, though Cynthia's points have really impacted me. "Hanna and I found her in an empty classroom, crying and alone. We couldn't not do anything. It's not like we're social workers. We're as lost as she is." I trail off. "Plus we were kind of friends from before. This just cemented it."

"I get that," Cynthia says, sipping her coffee. "And what you did was the right thing. CeCe was Hanna's teammate, and there's no forward without a midfielder, no goalie without defense. It sounds cheesy, but you're all in it together, whether you realize it or not."

She looks off into the distance. "Someday, when you're older, you're going to look back and wish you had the knowledge you have now back then. Wish you could grow young. Wish you weren't so insecure or convinced you were the worst thing in creation. Fix mistakes you made or stop others' mistakes from impacting your own life. But I think all of us parents would be lying to you if we said we never looked back and just thought for a split second what could've been if we'd all just been a little more compassionate. More understanding. Just a little bit nicer."

Cynthia turns to us. "You both make me so proud. I wish I would've been more like either one of you when I was fifteen. Things would've been so different. But the best thing you can do for CeCe? The girl who can't find her cousin or her baby daddy? A girl who's probably feeling about as lost as one can feel? Want to know what'll help her the most? Letting her know she's capable."

***

"Have you ever thought she might want to keep going to school?"

"What do you mean?" I ask Chaz, muting *Terminator 2* and pressing the phone closer to my ear. "She hasn't been in days. I'm pretty sure school's out the door for now."

"We actually talked about it," Chaz says. "The main reason she doesn't want to go is that she says it's pointless. And she's not wrong. The teachers ignore her, and Brennan and Spencer singing 'La Trampa' every time she walks down the hall isn't helping. It's nuts. I even asked my mom to pull some strings. You know, see if we could get her into any special programs, but the district's tapped. 'No money' is the only thing I heard until I dropped it."

"Where the hell does that money go?" I demand. "Every spring, we get an envelope in the mail begging for cash. I mean, it's got to go somewhere."

"Groppe's retirement fund? Mercer's home gym? Hell if I know. That school is the biggest money suck after the Pentagon. We looked into this online program for pregnant teens, and she said she'd think about it. It's the high school she hates."

"CHS can eat a woody," I agree, rolling my eyes. "Four years of our lives we'll never get back."

"And the money situation?"

Without Emilio's muscle, Erik's last payment never came. Though none of us are saying it, it looks like that flow of income is finished. Nick said he and a couple of Emilio's associates, who he met shortly before his disappearance, can resume operations, but I'm not holding my breath. The Impala may be stored in our garage right now, and Emilio's fedora may be hanging on the hat rack in the hall closet, but Nick Nazari is not The Swindler. Any Elderwood connection that Emilio had belonged exclusively to him.

"Broke," I say. "Emilio's God knows where. Nick doesn't know who his connection was. And Erik might be younger than Nick, but he'll break him like a twig. Only Emilio could make it work."

"Shit," Chaz groans. "I mean, now that CeCe's working under the table, at her aunt's store and everything, at least that'll cover some of it."

"It's chump change," I say. "I didn't want to say anything, but that aunt's exploiting her. Paying her way under minimum. She'll be working a thousand years before she can afford that kid."

"I know," Chaz sighs. "But try explaining that to her the way things are. She's down, Roxie. Emilio's gone, maybe for good, and it doesn't sound like things are easy for her at home. Add the teachers and the comments at school and the gravity of everything weighing down on her. She's one of the strongest people I know, but it would be too much for anyone."

"She's going to have to stay in school," I reply. "It's the only way. Even Walmart doesn't hire people without a high-school diploma. I'll talk to her about it. Try and convince her to stay put."

"It makes the most sense for her to finish here," Chaz agrees. "For one, the school offers free daycare. Get this: once the baby arrives, she can take it to school with her. That way, she can visit during lunch and…"

"Great," I cut in. "But think about it: she's working now, and has to keep working to pay for stuff. And yeah, maybe her aunt will pay her more once she learns the ropes, maybe not, but it's money. She needs it."

"I guess." Chaz breathes on the other end and doesn't talk for a moment. "She'll just have to deal with the shit at school. I mean, I do. That's life. And if any of the teachers aren't paying attention to her or have a problem with her personal life, Hanna and I both have parents involved in the school. I mean, I had Prudence Humbert burying my cases for years. She's the one who runs shit around here."

"And boy did she," I mutter. Even now, thinking of Chaz's impunity at school for years makes my mood sour. "But you're right. CeCe's still a student and has a legal right to attend school. Nobody can take that away from her."

"No, they can't," Chaz agrees. "But they're trying to. Three different teachers talked to her about the GED. They're encouraging her to go to vocational school. They'd never do that to the other kids."

"The teachers are garbage," I say. "Always have been. They did the same thing to Nick when he was a sophomore. He had straight B's in every class except geometry, which for some reason was really hard for him. But they only focused on his geometry grades and placed him in special education. They wanted him to learn welding or work as a security guard. They even introduced him to an army recruiter! Well, you can guess how that went. Anybody outside the norm, they literally try to make go away. It's crazy."

"Holy shit, really?" Chaz gasps. "That's terrible."

"Yeah, well." I shrug. "Be glad you've got someone on the inside."

"But Nick is so smart," Chaz says. "He should be teaching the teachers."

"I don't disagree," I say. "But back to CeCe."

"Right." Chaz exhales. "The part that kills me is the fact we won't see her. If she does online school, gets busy with the baby, her job… when will we be able to visit? That can't be good for any of us."

"Especially her," I say. "Cut off from her friends. Her support network. I'd be hella depressed without my peeps around."

"Same," Chaz echoes. "But still, it's up to her."

"Yeah," I say. "She's done her research, I'm sure. We did ours. We'll figure this out."

"On a lighter note," Chaz says. "What've you got going on?"

"Way too much," I grumble. "Piles of homework. Period cramps. The possibility of repeating the ninth grade finally sinking in."

"Don't worry about that," Chaz says quickly. "I'll pull some strings. You'll pass."

"What about you?" I ask. "What's on your agenda? Any downtime?"

"Nope," he replies. "Tomorrow, Blaze and I are driving to Spokane to tape some plays, and I'm on lookout. Apparently, the off-season is the time to do it." Chaz laughs. "He also wants to steal some equipment, but that has to wait until dark. After that, it's Hooters, baseball, and a sippy cup full of Stella for me." Chaz laughs. "At least there's A-Rod to look forward to."

I crack up. "Do you enjoy any of it? Stealing equipment sounds kinda dope. Tons of hot guys play football, and I bet a couple aren't into cheerleaders, if you know what I mean."

"Oh, there are a few," Chaz says. "There's always fruit amongst the vegetables. I'm just not about that right now."

"Copy that." I prop my feet up on the coffee table as Arnold Schwarzenegger swipes Edward Furlong off his dirt bike. "But at least quit being the water boy."

After the poster went around at the beginning of the year, Chaz continued taking heat from the Chester football team, who proceeded to torture him when Blaze wasn't around. As the water boy, Chaz's job is to haul gallons of water back and forth during games and listen to whatever Blaze yells at him to do. He claims to like it, but the one time I went to see Chaz in action, the quarterback dumped an entire cooler of Gatorade on him during halftime and screamed "facial."

Everybody, including Blaze, laughed.

"I can't do that to my dad," Chaz says defeatedly. "The guys can be jerks, and my body hurts like hell afterwards, but at least it's normal. I feel normal. Nobody calls me 'Ass Humper' or 'Cheek Freak' when I'm bringing them water, and I think it makes my dad happy. It's the only time we really hang."

"You know," I say. "You don't have to tell anyone. Like, ever. I know we talk it up and make jokes about you in Glee club or doing the musical this year, but it's nobody's business. Only yours."

"I am coming out," Chaz insists. "And I want to. Oh, I want to. I've just got to get a little bit more together before I make any big switches. Any big jumps. You know?"

"Oh yeah."

"I gotta go," Chaz says as Blaze screams from somewhere in the house. "The Chevelle's overheating. But keep me posted. Oh, and talk to CeCe. She knows what needs to be done. Make sure she knows I've got her six."

"Roger," I reply. "We got this on lock. Keep me in the loop."

***

"What are we going to do about Erik?" I ask Nick as he applies a gentle detergent to his sneakers and begins scrubbing them with a toothbrush. "He's gone. Like, totally out of the picture. CeCe needs that money."

"I know she does," Nick says. "And she's going to need a lot more once that baby's born. If I had a way in…"

"You were the last person from the group to see Emilio, weren't you?" I ask.

"Yeah." The glow slowly fades from Nick's face. "Yeah, I was."

To my surprise, Nick's handling everything well, though with his whole growing up thing, he's hiding his emotions more and more. Not unlike our father did, Nick's internalizing, which concerns me, but I don't bring it up.

Moving the brush in slow circles, Nick wipes at the suds with a damp cloth and shakes his head. "I still can't believe he's gone."

"I know." Even now, I can feel my eyes beginning to sting. I don't know what it was, but something drew me to Emilio. He was so familiar. Almost like I knew him from a past life. Did he remind me of someone? Disturbed, I try to focus on something, anything else, but I can't.

"Emilio taught me a lot," Nick says, sounding far away. "I mean, he's lived a life. Let's be real—I might've helped him repo a couple times or chase down card cheaters, but he was into a whole lot of stuff he kept hidden from all of us. I don't know everything he's done. I don't know who his enemies are. To him, I was just a friend, a buddy who worked on music with him and could discuss the reign of Louis XIV over lunch. I was what you call an outside friend. His inside friends? I don't know who they were. I still don't. The guys I know now, the guys I told you about? They're childhood friends from his old neighborhood. Both of them work at Lowe's. They aren't affiliated."

"Well, good," I say. "You already saw a little bit back in high school. You don't want that life."

"Damn straight I don't," Nick replies. "Wow, look at that white. Ice cream's right here." He holds up his shoe. "Look. Brand new."

"Do mine next," I plead. "Please, they look like hell."

"Bring 'em." Nick nods towards the front door. "*After* I'm done with mine."

"Mom's been pretty good about it," I remark, retrieving my battered DCs and handing them to Nick. "Letting you park a hot car in the garage and everything."

"Mom hates the immigration system," Nick says with a laugh. "She'll stick it to the man any chance she gets. Plus, nobody's parked there since Baba."

"Yeah," I say. "Any idea where he could be?"

"Who? Baba?"

"No, Emilio."

Nick sighs. "I don't know. I mean, he's a smart guy. He's crafty. But wherever they're taking him, or took him to, I don't know. I haven't heard a thing. I mean, Luis and Joaquin and I, we asked around. We were literally driving around Chester every hour asking everybody who knew him. Anybody who was there. No one's talking."

I exhale. "I just hope he's okay."

Nick nods. "Yeah, me too."

"But without him, CeCe's not getting any money," I say. "I can't believe Erik. You know, Chaz took me past his house. Over by the golf course. It's gigantic. All that money, and he can't even come up with a measly five hundred once a month."

"Why do you find it so hard to believe?" Nick asks, looking at me strangely. "Erik's rich and white. He's never had to work for anything in his life. Plus, remember what Emilio told us about the guys at Elderwood? Every mistake those kids ever make, there's somebody behind them cleaning it up. But Erik doesn't have to clean up because CeCe's his dirty secret. I doubt his parents even knew about her."

I shake my head. "That's so messed up."

"What is it with girls?" Nick looks sideways at me. "Brown girls, I mean. Like, they just go running towards white boys who treat them like shit and use them. Guys that all end up growing up and marrying white people like themselves." He rubs his chin. "Not saying I'm a dating expert, but damn. Never made sense to me. I can't wrap my head around it."

"CeCe loved Erik," I argue. My face suddenly feels warm, and there's a sharp pain below my ribs. Nick's comments bother me, though I can't put my finger on why. "You don't know their relationship. Plus, that just sounds like you're judging. Skin color doesn't matter when you love someone."

"Respectfully, I disagree," Nick replies. "Why is it always a Latina or an Asian girl with a white man? How often do you see the inverse? I haven't seen it once, living here."

"Why does it matter?" I say shrilly, unable to keep the irritation out of my tone.

"Because," Nick says, "this is how it ends. Used and alone. Maybe if CeCe was dating somebody from her community, or a person who understands history, *our* history, he'd actually value her instead of just her body."

"What do you mean 'our' history?" I snap. "We're not Mexican. We're not black. We're not even that brown, either."

"We certainly aren't white," Nick shoots back. "Last I checked, we don't look like anyone around here. Baba certainly didn't. And maybe you were too young to really remember, but I sure can. Life right after the towers got hit. The hell we'd face trying to get on a plane or getting pulled over and searched for no reason with Baba in the Buick. The looks we'd get from some people. Managers following us around in stores, watching us. Maybe you don't remember it, but I do."

"What about the people who stood up for us?" I ask. "The kids who defended you when you got bullied? The people who stopped Baba on the street to give him hugs? They were white, weren't they?"

"Yeah, and Frankie was, is, and will always be, my best friend," Nick says. "Him and everybody else who stood by me. And I did the same when they got bullied or people said stuff. I chased one asshole four city blocks to get Frankie's *Team Bowser* hat back. Asthma and everything."

"Well, there you go," I say, crossing my arms. "Good people are good people. It has nothing to do with race. Love wins."

"Sometimes," Nick says. "Sometimes it wins. But did CeCe win? Did Emilio? Those two are love incarnate. And they suffered the most."

I want to argue, but Nick has a point. CeCe and Emilio did suffer the most. Immediately, my thoughts return to that night at the movie theater. Did Owen feel he could do what he did because he's an idiotic douchebag? Or was there another reason he felt entitled to my body? Would he have done it if I looked more like Hanna? Or does he only date girls who look like her and assault and lust after girls who look like me? Disturbed, I mull over Nick's words again and again, and the more I do, the more it starts to make sense.

"I don't know," I say finally. "I'm not you. You're right, I was a kid when all that stuff began. Nobody's really said anything that nasty to me because I'm Middle Eastern or followed me in the store or treated me like I'm dangerous. At least not that I'm aware of. But, really, do you think racism's truly the reason Erik isn't taking care of his kid? Or is he just a spoiled brat who'd do the same to anyone?"

"I don't know," Nick says, his expression cloudy. "I don't know Erik. And I don't really want to. All I'm saying is stuff happens, Roxie. And a lot of people think that way. Not everybody, but a lot." He sighs. "And around these parts? It's a lot more common than you think."

Chapter 15

"Do you think someone tipped the feds about Emilio?" I ask CeCe. The girls and I are outside the auditorium after school waiting for Chaz to wrap up his audition.

"No," CeCe says, shaking her head. "Wrong place at the wrong time. He shouldn't have gone near the grange. People were squatting there. Undocumented people were living in the basement. Gang members were dealing drugs. The feds were probably planning to move in on it for months, and he just got unlucky."

"But will they deport him?" Hanna asks, nibbling her bottom lip. "Back to Mexico?"

"Oh yeah," CeCe says. "Without a doubt. They'll give him hell and interrogate him before they fly him across the border, but he'll come back. If he wants to, he will."

The pit in my stomach is back. "How's work?"

"It's fine," CeCe replies. "Going well. *Tía* Imelda pays peanuts, but I'm lucky to have something going." She pulls a tube of lip gloss out of her purse and applies it. "Beats this place."

"Can't you work after school?" Hanna asks. "And, like, on weekends or something?"

CeCe raises an eyebrow. "Do you know how much kids cost? I should be pulling doubles."

Before Hanna can respond, the auditorium door bursts open, and

Chaz bounds toward us, Reece following close behind. For some reason I can't quite pinpoint, her presence irks me. I stuff down my irritation and hurry toward Chaz, hoping for good news.

"Guess what?" He's beaming. "Guess who's going to be a star?"

"Wait, hold up." Hanna looks at him. "You got a part?"

"Nope." Chaz shakes his head. "Not a part. *The* part."

"What!" CeCe gasps. "You're the lead?"

"Yup." Chaz smiles as I hold up both hands for a high-ten. "I'm going to be a superstar!"

"Yes, you are," Reece laughs, angling her body toward Chaz and grinning in his face. "They're still talking about you. They say you're the best audition they've had in years."

"What monologue did you do?" I ask Chaz. "The one we worked on?"

"No." Chaz shakes his head. "I did the one from *Young Frankenstein.* Still Mel Brooks, though, so I guess I've got a thing for musicals."

"No *Julius Caesar,*" Reece laughs. "*Hamlet,* maybe?"

"No, not this time," Chaz says. "Next year at the Met, though. Did you get your part yet?"

"Yeah," Reece says, rolling her eyes. "They gave me Sandy. *Again.* I was her last year. I was hoping for Rizzo. Our dating histories are… similar." She giggles and turns to Hanna. "You aren't Kelsey and Brooke's sister, are you?"

"Yeah, actually," Hanna replies. She's used to this. Even though they graduated, Kelsey and Brooke are still super popular and sometimes visit the high school. Hanna should've been high school royalty by default, but she's different from her sisters and prefers to avoid attention.

"Cool!" Reece exclaims. "They're, like, gorgeous. And super chill. How are they?"

"They're doing great," Hanna answers, taken aback by Reece's outgoing manner. "They're loving college life. I miss them, though."

"Well, now we all know each other," Reece says, turning away from

Hanna and focusing back on Chaz. "Anyway, I got to go. Nice running into you all." She pushes her bangs out of her eyes and nudges Chaz's shoulder. "Bye, Chaz."

"Bye," Chaz calls after her as she straightens her back and struts away in her skintight ripped jeans. "See you later, I guess."

CeCe, Hanna, and I exchange a look and burst out laughing.

"What?" Chaz says. "What's so funny?"

"Oh, stop." I look at the ceiling. "Do I need to explain?"

"I'm not following," Chaz says, looking between the two of us. "Hanna?"

"She *likes* you," Hanna chuckles. "Roxie?"

I nod. "Yeah, dude. She's definitely into you."

"Oh, stop," Chaz laughs, the tip of his nose turning pink. "That's crazy. She's just nice and excited to have someone new as part of the cast. She also hates Brennan and Spencer. I think she actually dated Brennan at some point or something, but that's really it."

"No, that girl's gone," CeCe says. "She's way into you, Chaz. She is pretty cute, though, so props."

"Get to know her," I say. "Maybe she's got a lookalike brother who rides a motorcycle in assless chaps. It could all work out."

"Wow," Hanna snorts. "Incentivizing, much?"

Chaz and CeCe laugh. "She is a looker," Chaz agrees. "Good-looking, but not for me. Obviously."

Chaz suddenly seems sad, and a look I don't recognize passes across his face. "What are we doing this weekend? I'm free if anybody wants to hang out." I'm about to confirm when a familiar voice reaches my ears.

"I'm not even exaggerating," Owen rumbles. "He started following me in the store. I was there, you know, to pick up some sheaths for the beast, and this random dude who looked like he was 'roided out just showed up out of nowhere. Every aisle I go, boom, he's there too. Stalking me."

None of us say a word. Hanna cranes her neck, eyes wide. I'm barely able to make out the conversation, which is being dominated by Owen's labored breathing.

"And then what happened, babe?" a sickly-sweet voice that can only be Tiffany Verlich asks anxiously.

"I lost him at the checkout and went out into the parking lot," Owen continues. "A couple seconds later, I heard this super-loud engine, and suddenly, my legs went out, and everything flipped. It was freaking unreal."

"Did you trip?" Tiffany chirps, confused.

"No, Tiff, he ran me over," Owen grunts. "I went face-first into the cement. By the time I knew what was up, that guy was long gone."

Tiffany gasps. "That's horrible!"

"It is," Owen agrees defeatedly.

"Well, do you remember anything about the car that hit you?" Tiffany asks. "Make? Model?"

"The ride? It was green." Owen says. "Really, really green. And lifted."

The conversation seems to fade away, and Owen limps into view, supported by crutches. His face is gaunt and bruised, but he's still managed to gel his hair and utilize the infamous stubble creator. He spots the four of us and scowls. Hanna stares him down, and I make some crude gesticulations, but neither party exchanges a word. Tiffany, looking disgusting as usual, simpers at us but stays silent, clinging to Owen like a small child. She turns on her heel, and they disappear out of sight.

"Oh, my God," Chaz breathes. "Did you hear what he just said?"

"What?" I say. "That Blaze almost made roadkill out of Owen?"

Chaz shakes his head. "Holy shit."

"How on Earth did he find out?" I ask. "What does he know?"

Hanna and Chaz share a look. "Hanna told me everything," Chaz admits. "The day after it happened. I didn't go into specifics, but I think my dad figured out it was bad because he started saying I needed to teach Owen a lesson. You know, for messing with 'my girl.' After I showed him Owen's gym pics on MySpace, he figured out that was out of the question and said he'd take care of it."

CeCe's eyes bug. "So he stalked him and ran him over?"

Chaz chuckles wearily. "Gotta love Dad."

"Okay, forget everything I said earlier," I say. "Blaze is redeemed. He's gone from predator to protector. I actually think I love him."

"Don't tell him that," Chaz says, rolling his eyes. "He's already giving me tips about how to get down on one knee. Bragging to anyone who'll listen that the Humbert gene pool is due to improve in the near future."

"Your dad made a critical error, though," Hanna says as we step out into the afternoon sunshine.

"Yeah, obviously," Chaz replies. "I'm pretty sure running over a high schooler gets you some time in the slammer."

"No," Hanna says, batting a hand. "That part was a win. His mistake was not running over him twice."

"So I guess it's official then," CeCe says. "Tiffany and Owen. They're a thing."

"Yeah," I breathe. "They're most definitely a thing."

"Well?" CeCe nudges my shoulder. "Think about it. If they're together, that means Blake's back on the market. You can finally try to get with him."

And just like that, I'm transported back to the passenger's seat of Blake's Jeep. I can picture it. How the night should've gone. We'd exchange easy laughter and banter, and I'd finally feel seen and understood by a boy who isn't Chaz or Nick. It feels wonderful. My body begins to warm as I begin to imagine the two of us slowly becoming friends and the possibility of that blossoming into something more. Maybe every Friday night can be like the one the we shared not too long ago. And we'll talk. Not just about the comings and goings of our classmates or the results of the weekend football game, but about real, pressing issues. What our aspirations are for our futures. The ongoing War on Terror. The direction our nation is headed. The death of my father that I haven't processed after four years. Those kinds of things.

Perhaps then I could finally fall into that escape from mundanity I'm so desperately seeking. Maybe then, I can catch something of a break from life and the never-ending litany of problems my friends and I seem to face.

But then reality kicks in. I'm younger, inexperienced, and kind of weird. I haven't been to a party since Tristan's, and I probably won't get invited to another one. For all intents and purposes, I'm dating Chaz. We're always together, and his appearance on the back porch was more than convincing. And Blake? He's the heartthrob of Chester High, with girls in every grade who'll give him whatever he wants. Us together? Fat chance.

"Yeah," I say to CeCe, trying to sound enthusiastic. "We'll see."

***

Initially, I figured the week would fly by, but it's dragging. I can't tell you a thing about what I learned, what we're supposedly learning, or what I'm supposed to be doing. It's tough staying motivated when each class bleeds into the next and all you did was paperclip different assignments together and write your name at the top before turning it in. I might've been doing this for years, but the thinker in me still can't fathom how this is in any way going to prepare me for the real world.

"School is a prison," Nick reflected one school morning, and his words have never rung truer. I've long suspected public education is little more than tax-funded babysitting for kids that parents no longer know how to handle, but tell people this and they look at you like you're nuts. Not my friends, though. They get it. Come to think of it, maybe CeCe's got the right idea by dropping out. Or had the right idea, rather. She's here today. The one who isn't with us today—or yesterday, for that matter—is Chaz. I was supposed to meet him at the flagpole before school, but he missed me. At lunch, he said he was busy, but I saw him coming out of the library with Reece and a couple of theater kids. I could be wrong, but I'm pretty sure it's unheard of at our school for a junior girl to hang with a freshman guy, which cements my theory Reece is crushing.

"Okay," I say. "What's up with Chaz?"

None of us had plans after school, so Hanna, CeCe and I walked over to the play structure at the elementary school to waste time. CeCe and I are sitting on the swings, absently drawing circles in the dirt with our feet while Hanna stands in front of us.

Hanna shrugs. "No clue."

"Did any of us do something?" CeCe asks. "It feels almost like he's been avoiding us the past couple of days."

"I saw him earlier," I say. "He seemed super mellow. He's usually way chattier."

"It's his new group." CeCe purses her lips. "He's got us, and we're all he had, until he met the theater kids. Maybe he's just trying to make new friends."

"I hope so." I twist, then untwist the chains on my swing. "It's good he's found other people he can relate to. He especially needs a guy friend, you know, besides Nick. Him and Phil seem to really hit it off. There's something else, though."

"Reece," Hanna says at once. "She came out of nowhere, and now she's everywhere. I passed Chaz on the way to French, and the two of them were walking in sync, totally in their own world. Chaz! With a girl!"

"Maybe he's bi," CeCe offers. "A lot of guys actually go both ways. They just don't talk about it." She stops swinging for a moment. "Reece is pretty, and I think she's into him. Maybe he likes her back?"

"That isn't it," I say quickly. "Trust me. I can still see his face when I finally outed him. He's gay. He told every one of us, he and I talk about it constantly, and that's all there is to it. He's definitely gay."

"What if it's a conspiracy?" CeCe asks. "Like, what if somebody put her up to it? To test him. To see if the rumors are true."

"You think?" I frown. "Does anybody really care that much?"

"I doubt it," Hanna says. "For what it's worth, I think Reece really likes him. I think she was impressed with how Chaz handled Spencer and Brennan. Wish I could've seen it."

"It was great," I recall, smiling at the memory. "He owned them. I wonder if they'll be back after that."

"He hasn't texted me once," CeCe says, waving her phone. "Still nothing. What about you guys?"

I shake my head. "Me neither."

"He's probably busy," Hanna reasons. "Being in a play is hard work. And he landed the starring role on his first try. He's probably working on his lines if anything."

"It just isn't like him," I insist, frustrated I'm unable to express myself properly.

"I mean, what if he really *isn't* gay?" CeCe says slowly. "And if before, he was just confused. Then he finally meets Reece, who's into him, and he likes her back…"

"NO!" I scream, stomping my feet. "You know! I know! He knows!"

I grind my feet into the dirt, stopping my swing. My outburst is immature and irrational, but I don't care. "Trust me on this. He and I…we call each other sometimes at night if we can't sleep. Some nights, we would stay up late and go over serious stuff. He'd discuss how he wanted to come out and just be this comfortable, adjusted gay man. We talked about what this might look like, and he said he had to do it not for anybody else but himself." I shake my head. "He's gay. Trust me."

"Does he have anyone to talk to?" CeCe asks quietly. "Someone who knows anything about what he's going through? Somebody with a story like his?"

"What do you mean?" Hanna glances at CeCe. "Like a mentor? A role model?"

"Kind of," CeCe says. "Maybe someone who's stood where he's standing. Who knows what it's like. What I'm saying is, I have this cousin. After I found out I was pregnant, I reached out to her, and we've gotten pretty close since. She's gay, or lesbian I guess, and is a bit older than us. Twenty-four, I think. We talk a lot now, and I tell her about you guys and the crazy stuff we do. Of course, I had to give her the news about Emilio, but she's really interested in Chaz's story. She told us we can come stay with her in Seattle if we want to come check it out."

"Wow." I fold my hands in my lap. "That's really nice of her. Yeah, we should totally go once school gets out. We could take the Greyhound. Or maybe Nick can drive us."

"She's thinking before school lets out," CeCe says. "She's got something going on in June, so it'd have to be before then. We should ask Chaz first, though, to see if it's something he even wants."

"Roxie," Hanna says. "You're the closest to him. You talk to him."

"I would if he'd answer his phone," I say irritably, wondering how to go about doing this. "Next time I see Chaz, I'll run it by him."

***

"Are you sure this is a good idea?" Nick asks, dropping another dollop of batter on waxed paper. "Have you ever been to Seattle? Like, really been?"

I visited Seattle once with my dad to see the SuperSonics play, just a few months before his death. It was in the middle of the fall, and what I remember most is the rain, though the food was good and the surrounding nature was spectacular. The few people we ran into seemed a little offbeat, but Hanna and I have wanted to check it out on our own at least once before she decides whether to apply to the University of Washington.

"Why?" I ask, suddenly curious.

"Take everything you know, flip it on its head," Nick replies. "It was always a little out there, but now it's super weird. Certifiable."

"How so?" I'm genuinely curious now.

"Well for one, it's liberal. Like, *really* liberal. It also rains 24/7. And it's expensive. Almost everybody living there is white, but they're obsessed with being anti-white because it's trendy. It's also full of gay people who ride mountain bikes and listen to NPR and drink organic coffee." Nick shrugs. "That's everything I know about it."

"And whose opinion is this?" I roll my eyes. "Was it from another one of your nutty constitutionalist websites? YouTube?"

"My own assessment, actually," Nick says snippily. "Unlike you, I actually go there. Frankie and I were in Fremont last September for Labor Day. It was out there. Some people wore Lenin shirts and called for worldwide socialism."

"Seriously?"

He nods knowingly. "Yep."

"I think it'll be good for Chaz," I say. "He'll finally be able to meet and interact with other gay people. Ask them questions. Hear their stories. See what the future might look like somewhere away from here."

"What, for dating?" Nick frowns. "Isn't he a little young?"

"No," I say. "I just feel he has questions. I mean, I like to think people around here will accept him and stuff, but I can't claim to know what life is going to be like for him when he finally does come out. People might judge. They might be fine with it. They might hate him."

I pause for a moment. "And let's say Chaz ends up taking real heat for coming out. Don't you think he'd feel better if he knew there are places where being gay isn't just okay but celebrated?"

"I guess it couldn't hurt," Nick says finally.

"Exactly." I'm glad we're now on the same page.

"But in all seriousness," Nick says, "what makes you think Chester is that homophobic? Are you going off the picture reaction? 'Cause let me tell you something. It doesn't matter if a person was straight, gay, bi, whatever. They would take *hell* for something like that." He looks at me. "Like, come on. It was a good try and everything, but take a closer look at that picture, and you know it's a fake. People were sick of Chaz and his bullshit, so they roasted him. That is what happened, isn't it?"

"Oh, yeah," I say. "That they did."

"The real question is, does the high school have a bullying problem?" Nick turns to face me. "I vote yes. But that's gone on for ages, and I don't see it stopping anytime soon. High school is practically synonymous with bullying."

"I see where you're coming from," I say as he drops a dirty ladle into the sink. "But what about you? Do you know any gays?"

"Besides Frankie when Ken from *Street Fighter* comes on?" Nick laughs. "Not really. This one guy I've got calc with at Covington. He doesn't say anything, but I'm pretty sure he's gay. Got one earring in the left ear. Dresses too well, if you know what I mean. People are nice to him, though. He's got a lot of friends and stuff."

"Well, that's good," I say. "That's it?"

"There was a girl too, actually," Nick says. "Kendra. She came out in tenth grade. Really brave if you think about it. I guess she was tired of living a lie. Some people were terrible to her, though, and it used to bother me, stuff I'd hear in passing. But other people supported her and voted her class president. So yeah, I've known people."

"Times have changed when it comes to people our age," I muse. "It's his family he's more concerned about."

"Really?" Nick asks. "His dad seems too cool for that sort of thing. Coach Humbert's an American hero. He'll probably be fine with it."

I roll my eyes. "You just love him now that he ran over Owen. But honestly, I don't think Blaze will care," I say. "It's his mother. A few years back, she dragged him to this whacko church service where they 'cured' a teenager onstage. Big surprise, Chaz was traumatized."

"Jesus," Nick shakes his head. "Some people."

"Oh," I say. "Get this. He's got this aunt, or great-aunt, who figured out he's gay and confronted him about it at our fake Valentine's Day dinner. She was about to tell the whole restaurant, but she OD'd."

"That's right. Aunt Edna. Damn, that family is unhinged," Nick says. "But they'll figure it out eventually. The more comfortable with himself Chaz is, the more you can tell he's a little different in that way. The little things. Like the way he talks or how he sits. You don't know for sure, but you can just tell there's something."

"I'm just happy he's comfortable," I say. "He's made a lot of progress the last few months."

"Agreed." Nick nods. "What about religion? Does he practice?"

"I don't know," I say. "And I don't ask. I don't think he does anymore, but politically, he's pretty conservative. He and I got into it the other day because he told me America's greatest president was Ronald Reagan. *Reagan!*"

"Chaz isn't all that different from most people out here if you think about it," Nick points out. "The only thing setting him apart from everyone else is his preference for penis. And barely anyone even knows about it." He stops for a second and glances into the oven. "What I'm saying is, I totally get why it could be good for him, you know. This trip and everything. But why there? Just bring him to Covington to meet the Gays and Lesbians of America. Go with him to Spokane Pride. Problem solved."

"And if he sees someone he knows?" I raise my eyebrows. "That'll take some explaining. In Seattle, he can be completely anonymous."

"I never thought of that," Nick says. "Fair point."

"Plus, why are you so anti-Seattle?" I scrunch my brow. "It's not like you've lived there. *'Don't be so close-minded, Nick,'*" I say, imitating our mother. Nick laughs and dries his hands. "Maybe it's really cool."

"It is cool. In some ways. Frankie's entire extended family lives in that area," Nick says. "He's there at least a month out of every summer. I've gone with him a bunch of times, especially last year. There's this one dude there that he knows, a guy who rejects every social norm in existence. Sued his workplace. Something about not letting him wear a tail during office hours."

"A tail?" I shake my head. "Shut up, Nick."

"I'm dead serious," Nick says, planting both hands on the counter and staring me down. "His birth name is Guido, but he goes by Topaz and identifies as a man-cat. Meaning a man. And a cat. Anthropomorphized, technically."

I narrow my eyes. "You're lying."

"It gets worse. Frankie and I were having dinner one night over there, and Cat Man wouldn't eat. Something about dietary restrictions or not enough Omega-3s in the food. Nobody answered him, so he put his plate on the floor and began gumming dinner in front of us. Frankie's Aunt Gloria started shouting at him to eat like a normal person. He took it wrong, and next thing I know, Gloria's screaming about a giant shit in the cat litter box. And it wasn't the cat's."

I gape. "And what does this have to do with anything?"

"Nothing," Nick says innocently. "I'm just saying Seattle's weird, and he'll get all sorts of wrong ideas. Maybe just tell him to talk to people over the internet."

"CeCe's cousin offered," I tell him. "She just wants to introduce Chaz to some people and let him hang. It's pretty lowkey. I really don't see the issue."

"Could be cool, I guess," Nick relents. "When do you want to go?"

I pause. "I was thinking at the end of the month. Can you drive us?"

"I actually had something lined up," Nick says. "But never mind. I'll cancel it. This'll be way more fun."

***

"Chaz. Hey, Chaz. Chaz!"

No response. Earbuds blaring, Chaz's deep in the zone. I reach over and poke him in the ribs with my pencil, and he jerks around to face me.

"Ow! What?"

"Wanna meet some gays in Seattle?"

"*What?*"

I smile. "Now you're listening. Get this: CeCe's cousin is gay, too. She lives in Seattle and wants to meet you. And she invited us all to go hang out with her later this month."

"Well, damn." Chaz looks surprised. "They know about me in the 206?"

"Well, they will," I reply. "If you want to go."

"When?"

"I don't know. A few weeks from now, maybe? It's a little up in the air, but sometime around then."

"Oh yeah," Chaz says. "Yeah. Totally. I'll tell my parents I'm checking out colleges." He turns back to his homework.

"Hey, Chaz," I say again.

He doesn't look up. "Hmm?"

"What's the deal with you and Reece?"

Chaz cracks his back in his chair and swivels around to look at me. "What do you mean?"

"She likes you, dude," I say. "Like—*likes* you."

"No, you're way off," he replies. "We're fast friends, but that's it. I mean, with both of us in the play, we kind of have to hang out together, if you know what I mean. I like her, though. Don't get me wrong. She's just cool. Her friends are too."

"We all see it," I persist. "Hanna. CeCe. Me. She's into you." I smirk. "And she might want you in her."

Chaz snorts. "What on earth makes you think that? I'm pretty sure she's just nice."

"You're a guy," I say. "AKA clueless. Guys never know when a girl's into them. Trust us. Since you started jogging and going to the gym, she's noticing you more and more."

"Really?" Chaz visibly perks up. "Wow. Okay then. I mean that's kinda cool, if it's true."

I roll my eyes. "How's the play?"

"Eating me alive." He heaves a sigh. "I never knew so much went into a high-school play. It's killer, though." Chaz sets his book down. "What have I missed?"

"Let's see," I say, drumming my fingers on the desktop. "Hanna's done with dating for the foreseeable future. CeCe's hit and miss with school attendance. Nick got a job, and I heard through the grapevine that Edgar got ticketed for unauthorized baptisms at the wooden boats festival. We're living in strange times."

"Jeez." Chaz shakes his head. "Sounds a hell of a lot more interesting than rehearsal. I miss you guys."

"Yeah," I laugh. "Start coming around again and you won't."

"I'll make it up to you," Chaz says. "Promise. I'm free this weekend. Want to have a *Halo* marathon?"

"Obviously I do, but there's actually something I wanted to ask you about," I say.

"Hit me."

"This Seattle trip. Are you comfortable with it? Is this something you want? Am I forcing it on you?"

"No, no." Chaz shakes his head. "Of course not."

"I just want to make sure," I say quietly. "I just—I thought about our talks, and I feel you've got questions I can't answer, and we've found someone you can talk to, to maybe understand you in a way we can't."

Chaz frowns. "Is CeCe's cousin a shrink?"

"No," I say. "Just someone to know. Who's been in your shoes, kind of."

"Thank you," he says. "I mean it. Really, thank you. Even when I'm not around, you're still thinking of me. You think about me more than I do, which is a lot because I'm male, and we tend to be very me-focused."

I laugh. "It's all of us. This was CeCe's idea."

"I'm in," Chaz says. "One hundred percent."

The bell rings, and we get up to go to our respective periods. Chaz tosses whatever book he was reading into his backpack and waves at me over his shoulder.

"Check your phone," I call to him. "And text me back this time."

"Nope," Chaz hollers over his shoulder. "No need. I'll see you at lunch."

***

After a dreadful first four periods of the day, lunchtime is a welcome escape. I grab a trayful of the slop the cafeteria is serving today—a slab of congealed lasagna and a mushy plum—and make a beeline for our usual table. I'm pleased to see Chaz, as he promised, already seated with Hanna and CeCe.

"How goes it?" I ask, setting my tray down.

"It's going," Chaz confirms, slathering sauce on the pork chops he brought from home. "We have three-hour rehearsals this week, apparently. That's going to be a bitch."

Before any of us can respond, a brutish baritone that can only be Brennan Hodges inserts itself into our conversation.

"Hey! Homo!" he booms from a table away. "How are you enjoying *Grease*?"

"He's loving it," Spencer responds in an equally loud voice, despite the fact he's sitting six inches from Brennan. "Never misses rehearsal. Greased up and ready to go, isn't that right, Chaz-gender?"

You know, lunch was going fine until varsity lacrosse crashed into the room with nothing better to do than unleash some homophobia. Hanna and I jump up to Chaz's defense. Chaz, however, stops us.

"I am," he replies, wiggling his eyebrows at Spencer. "You better shape up, 'cause I need a man."

Hanna, CeCe and I bust up, and to his credit, Spencer laughs too. The rest of the team looks over, stopping whatever conversations they were having to watch this latest round play out.

"Did you guys hear that!?" Victor Ruiz screeches. "He's admitting it. Everything is real!"

"Victor," Chaz calls, rising from his seat. "Join in! Bring lube. Or drugs, if you get nervous."

Now the whole table's laughing. Victor goes scarlet and sits down, but I can tell things are just starting to heat up.

"Shoot, fruit." Spencer lets out a low whistle. "You learned fast. You read the Bible, don't you?"

Chaz furrows his brow. "Indeed, I do."

"John 12:14," Spencer thunders. "'Jesus found an ass and rode it.' You remember that, right?"

"That's not quite the verse, but yeah," Chaz says quietly. Like the rest of us, he's unsure of where this is going.

"Well," Spencer continues, reaching into his backpack and pulling out a gold-lettered New Testament. "Right here, I've got the gospel according to Spencer." Flipping through the pages, he waits until we're all giving him our attention before standing up and clearing his throat. "Spencer 12:14. 'Chaz rode an ass in the locker room. Edgar's ass.'"

Everybody within earshot laughs hysterically, and the lacrosse boys roar and slap each other on the back. The four of us are immobilized, trying to come up with something. But that was brilliant, and all of us know it. Chaz, wallowing in his humiliation, waits for the laughter to die down. Defying all of our expectations, he rises again.

"You do know your Bible," Chaz admits. "A man who walks in the spirit. But allow me now to share a new verse, this time from The Gospel According to Chaz." By now, the entire lunchroom is silent. Chaz walks over to where the boys are seated and steps up onto the table. Arms outstretched, he presides over all like Christ on the mount, feet planted on the tabletop, his voice ringing loud and clear.

"Humbert 5:38," Chaz proclaims. "You've heard how it was said. An eye for an eye, a tooth for a tooth. But I tell you, do not resist a horny person, Spencer. If Brennan slaps you on thine ass cheek, offer to him your other cheek also."

The lunchroom erupts into raucous laughter, but Brennan snaps. Going for the legs, he knocks Chaz off the table and onto the unforgiving linoleum floor. In two strides, I reach Brennan and pounce on him, clawing at his eyes like a koala bear. Screaming, he bucks me off into Victor, who flails his arms wildly, joining the fight. Hanna behind me, the two of us plow full-on into the madness with fists flying, months of pent-up rage unleashed in all directions.

CeCe, visibly pregnant, tries to distance herself from the chaos, but the goaltender barrels into her and knocks her onto her side. Having fallen himself, he tries to get up, but I run over and kick him in the head as hard as I can.

It's like kicking cement. My foot bends backwards, and I shriek, struggling to stay upright. Beside me, Chaz is throwing dozens of punches and taking even more of them while Hanna tries to choke Spencer from behind. As my perception goes into bullet time, I realize the entire cafeteria is in complete disarray, with people either watching, yelling, or contributing to the mayhem. There's food all over the floor. Several students are flipping one of the long tables over, and Phil from drama club just took an uppercut to the chin from somebody in a WSU sweatshirt. My first thought is CeCe, but I can't find her anywhere, and, being in the middle of things as usual, I've got to find a way out before I can focus on the task at hand.

A series of sharp blasts, not unlike a police whistle, reverberate throughout the lunchroom. The pandemonium screeches to a stop, and a pair of strong hands grab my shoulders from behind. On impulse, I wheel around to throw a right hook when a blast of something peppery hits me between the eyes. I'm screaming, louder than I've ever screamed in my life, and thrashing my body in the hope I'll make contact with my assailant. Finally, I slouch down to the floor in agony before everything turns to black.

***

Suspension is a funny thing. Having faced disciplinary action more times than I can count, I've memorized the process. First comes the arrest. Then court at the principal's office. Usually, you're let go after that, but if you've really put your foot in it, your parents get called in. Once tried, you either go to the SHU with Ms. Fink or are released into parental custody. Depending on your parents, the latter is easily worse.

The fight stopped when security got dispatched, and I ended up in the worst shape, as usual. Locked in full berserker mode, I tried to KO the security chief and got pepper-sprayed, which took me out of action. After being dragged to the emergency eye wash station, I was hauled back to the office where Groppe, Mercer, and campus security were waiting for me. As for the actual sentencing, it wasn't that bad. Groppe ended up giving me props for protecting Chaz and "quick thinking," but going Super Saiyan and attacking the goaltender was not the right move. I had to apologize to the security chief and promise not to assault another member of the staff while Mr. Mercer, always on my case, pleaded for my expulsion.

At this point, it doesn't look like I'm going to pass ninth. My grades blow. I'm always late. I don't pay attention, and if you add up the hours, I've spent over a month in detention so far, not to mention all the classes I've skipped. If they end up charging me for attempted battery of a security officer, I'm done for. There's no way in hell the Seattle trip's still happening, and forget any hope of a fun summer when I'll probably be on the first bus to military school. If my prayers are answered, Nick will be at home and take the call, but he's at Covington today. As I sit by the flagpole outside the school, I frantically dial Nick's number, praying he'll get to me first. No such luck; the call goes straight to voicemail. My body aches, both from the physical exertion of the brawl and from the inevitable outcome of our actions today. I'm barely conscious by the time my mother's Honda pulls up to the curb. Summoning whatever strength I have left, I stand and will my feet forward. I toss my backpack into the backseat and climb in the front without saying a word.

"I don't get it," Mom says after we turn out of the parking lot. "I really don't."

"What's not to get?" I mutter, sliding my shoes off and putting my feet up on the dash.

Keeping one hand on the wheel, Mom leans over and shoves my feet off. "Why the hell you're destroying your life."

"Destroying my life? What life? I don't have a life!" I shoot back. "You know what happened today?"

"I don't know, and I don't care!" she yells. "All I know is when your father was alive, I never envisioned in my wildest nightmares you'd wind up like this. Street fights, suspensions, making gay porn and passing it around at school. What's next? A baby? Hard drugs?"

"I can't believe you," I say, digging my finger into the soft spot underneath my seat. "You are so unfair."

"*I'm* unfair? You want to know what's unfair? Working around the clock while my daughter blows off her schoolwork, hangs out with weird kids, and tries to kill lacrosse players." Mom shakes her head. "It's not enough worrying I'm going to find Nick hanging from the chandelier. Now I've got to think about you too."

"Wow," I say, gaping at her for effect. "Thinking about your daughter? There's a first."

"How dare you!" Mom screams, slamming on the brakes at the red light. "Who thinks about me? Who cares about me? Do I ever ask that? No! I'm too busy running around cleaning up your shit on top of working and doing everything else!"

The light turns green, and Mom guns it. "I swear to God I ought to leave you on your own for a week."

I snort. "Please do."

Mom gives me a look to kill. "Shut the hell up."

I have nothing else to say, so I do just that. The ride, which is usually ten minutes, seems to go on for an eternity. When we pull in front of the house, I unbuckle my seatbelt and hurl myself out of the car.

"Wait."

I turn around and give Mom my best "do not talk to me" face, but she ignores it.

"Give me your phone."

"Um, what?"

"Give it. Now." Her palm is up and her expression cold.

I thought we were going to have a heart to heart or share a reconciliatory laugh, but Mom just wants to take away the last thing I like. Rolling my eyes, I surrender my phone and start towards the door.

"Don't even think about going anywhere," she warns. "I mean it. You're grounded. And I'm letting Nick know if he sneaks you out anywhere or lets you use his phone, he's grounded too."

"Do you even know what happened today?" I ask. "Do you even care to ask me? Chaz got attacked. He would've been seriously hurt if Hanna and I hadn't been there. CeCe got hit, almost in the stomach, and wasn't even involved in the fight." I shake my head. "You don't even care."

"I don't care about Chaz," Mom says, shaking her head. "CeCe, I've never met. All I know is those two came into your life, and now everything's falling apart."

"My life was broken," I retort. "Until those two came into my life."

"Chaz was in your life for years," Mom counters. "You despised him. In fact, I recall you and Hanna trying to order a hitman off the internet not too long ago. What's changed?"

"Uh, try being gay in this Bible-thumping hick town?" I narrow my eyes at her. "Being tortured at school? Misunderstood? Confiding in me after I wrecked his life? These things kind of move a person, you know?"

"And where is he now?" Mom demands. "Is Chaz going to talk to Mrs. Humbert? The same woman who made sure he never got in trouble and allowed him to do whatever he wanted to you and Hanna? Or are you out rescuing people who won't lift a finger for you?"

"I know he will," I snap. "He'll move heaven and earth if he has to. And why are you blaming everything on Chaz? He's the victim here. I stepped in to help him after a two-hundred-pound junior threw him off a table."

"Well, what was he doing *on* a table?" Mom asks. "Why wasn't he sitting at it like a normal person? He must've been doing something."

"You know what?" I say. "Forget it. I'm done talking to you. You're trying to make a point, but you're not. You're yelling and pissed off and don't know anything about what happened."

"What? That my only daughter's become a self-destructive hedonist who doesn't care about her future?" My mother shakes her head in disgust. "Why couldn't you be more like Hanna?"

"Oop," I say. "And there it is. Want to know something? Hanna was in that fight too! And did you know Little Miss Perfect suffers from crippling anxiety? That she has to be mom and daughter and confidant and star student all at the same time because Cynthia's such a disaster? Well guess what, Mom? I DO TOO!"

I pick up my backpack, empty its contents, and pitch my lunch box against the garage door.

"I'm so goddamn tired of this shit!" I shout. "You know what? I'm *exactly* like Hanna. My anxiety is so bad sometimes I can't breathe. I have to be mom and sister and friend to Nick because you completely shut off after Baba died. I try to be everything to everybody all the time because my happiness? My security? It's impossible. A completely hopeless case."

I dropkick my backpack into the bushes. "Why did I help Chaz? Why did I help CeCe, who's never asked me for a fucking thing? I help because I can't be. I cannot be helped. I know what it's like to be lost because I am lost and have been for years. Nobody can help me. Not Nick. Not Hanna. And definitely not you. Not that you're even trying."

I turn around. "So I am like Hanna, Mom. I might not get perfect grades and be agreeable all the time and do housework and knit and be somebody off the Lifetime network, but what you don't see with her? She and I are mirrors of each other."

"Roxie," Mom begins. "Roxie, I…"

I ignore her and stomp up the front steps. Fumbling my keys, I drop them on the front stoop, bend down to pick them up, and jam the house key into the lock. Opening the door, I step inside, kick my shoes off carelessly on the front mat, and slam the door behind me so hard the frame shakes. My eyes are still searing, my Pac-Man hoodie is torn in the armpit, and I think my foot is broken, or fractured at least. I take a carton of full-fat milk out of the fridge and flush my eyes out over the sink, waiting for the burn to subside at least a little. Left eye, then the right eye.

When the carton's empty, I punt it into the living room and slump onto the couch to watch TV for a little bit. The daytime programming is horrendous, and I can't concentrate. All I can think about is CeCe miscarrying by herself after trauma to the abdomen, and I can't be there to help her. I switch channels, and a pregnant woman comes on the screen, so I switch channels again, only to land on *Fight Club*. Glancing at the clock, I see Nick should be home in about an hour and shut off the tube, thinking about what exactly I'm going to tell him. Unlike my mother, who I barely have a relationship with, Nick listens and doesn't criticize or cut in. He'll understand the situation and give me viable advice. Not just screaming and an unfair punishment.

The phone rings, and I run towards it, hoping it's news from somebody in the group. Since Mom took my phone away, the only contact I have is through the landline. Knowing me, they've probably figured it out by now. I lift the phone and hold it up to my ear.

"Can you believe it?" Yvonne shrieks into the phone without so much as a hello. "Thornton doesn't want to do pre-med. He said he wants to study kinesiology."

I rip the jack out of the wall, wrap it around the phone, and pitch the entire thing across the room. With a clatter, the phone hits the ground in a tangled mess, but I don't care. Like everything leading up to it, the phone is now a useless disappointment. Examining the wreckage, I zone out for a bit but eventually break my gaze and walk into the dining room, where I remove a small bottle of brandy from the liquor cabinet. Going to the freezer, I pluck the most well-formed cubes I can find and drop them into a small, frosted glass. I pour myself a generous hand, thinking back to the main event of this afternoon and everything else it managed to bring to the surface. I raise the glass to my lips and ask myself inwardly why everybody can't just get along.

Chapter 16

"I'm pretty sure we missed our exit," Nick says as Mom's SUV flies down the highway. The moment we passed through Ellensburg, a deluge of rain came down, making visibility nearly impossible. I'm in the passenger's seat trying to make sense of the map and printed directions, while Chaz and the girls are sitting in the back playing magnetic checkers and talking about Patrick Dempsey's eyes. I wish I could join them, but if I don't chart a course, we'll never make it.

"No, we're fine," I say. "At least from what I can tell. Just drive, bro."

"It's freezing," Hanna complains. "Can't you turn up the heat?"

"It's already roasting," I argue. "You guys want another blanket?"

"We're good," Chaz says. "If that temperature keeps dropping, though, we're going to have to strip and huddle for warmth."

It's Friday afternoon, and we're trying to beat the traffic going into Seattle. Nick claims to have taken this trip many times, but he's lost and has no sense of direction. I hounded my mom to buy a GPS last time we went to Costco, but she told me cartography is a skill everybody needs to master and that global position systems are inaccurate anyway. Well, it'll be years before I'm Amerigo Vespucci, and Nick can barely find the door to our house, so the hand of fate will have to guide us.

CeCe got off the phone with her cousin an hour earlier. We'll be staying with her for two nights and leaving Sunday morning.

Aracely, CeCe's cousin, told us not to worry about food, that she's got the pantry stocked and we'll all go out to dinner tonight. While I've only heard pieces of their conversations, Aracely seems super nice. What she's doing for Chaz, and for all of us, couldn't have come at a better time.

As expected, both Hanna and Chaz got off scot-free because of their family connections to the school district. CeCe got a day of detention, but I got it the worst. Chaz snuck over later that night to check on me and to thank me for coming to his rescue. He told me that Brennan, Spencer, and Victor had each been suspended from school for a week and would be benched for the rest of the lacrosse season.

While the staff might consider me a menace to society, the students certainly don't see it that way. Nick checked my MySpace for me, and I got about ten different messages from kids who were there, including one from Reece and Phil informing me I was the first girl in Chester history to successfully concuss a lacrosse player. Chaz, after thanking me more times than I could count, swore should he ever adopt a daughter that she would be named after me. CeCe ended up being fine, though a little shaken, thank God.

I told Nick everything, and as usual, he was supportive. He managed to clear it up with our mother and explain that had I not intervened, Chaz could've been seriously hurt or worse. Even though I told Mom exactly that on that fateful car ride home, Nick has a way of bringing people around and getting them to see different perspectives. Though she was reluctant to praise my actions, Mom did inform me I was no longer grounded. We kind of made up, but her Hanna comment really pissed me off, and I've barely talked to her since she told me the trip was back on.

As we approach the exit, we run into full-on traffic, and Nick slams on the brakes. I crack my neck and stretch my legs the best I can. Nick, starting to slump, closes his eyes, so I throw him a packet of trail mix to keep his energy up.

He shoos them away. "I'm not hungry."

"Eat," I command. "The last thing we need is for you to pass out at the wheel."

Nick protests but tears the pack open and starts nibbling on hulled almonds, which are the only almonds he'll eat. I unscrew the top of my water bottle and take a sip, hoping the nausea I'm feeling from the car ride will wash away with some liquid.

"She's not too far from downtown," CeCe says. "Once we get off the freeway, she really should be close."

"Thank God," Hanna declares. "I never want to see the back of this thing again."

"You'll see it on Sunday," Chaz points out. "Unless Roxie wants to give up her spot."

"Aracely just texted me the address," CeCe says, tapping Nick's shoulder. "When you get off, swing right, and then drive to the end. Close to a yoga studio and a juice bar, she says. Her place is an apartment, so just park on the street."

The traffic finally breaks up, and we turn onto the exit. The earlier downpour has eased into a soft drizzle, and the sun is beginning to break through the clouds. I fold the map and stick it in the glove compartment. Hanna's drawing stick figures on the window, Chaz is messing around with the Ewok action figure Nick let him take from the house, and CeCe's texting Aracely to tell her we've arrived.

"That's her ahead," CeCe says, pointing. "There."

I look up to see a slender, dark-haired woman in a down vest standing out on the curb. Nick pulls up next to her, and she guides us into a tight parallel parking spot that I'd never be bold enough to try parking in on my own. Killing the engine, Nick opens the door, and the rest of us step out of the car.

CeCe gets to her first, and she and Aracely embrace one another and speak briefly in Spanish before CeCe turns to the rest of us. "Uh. How do we do this?"

"Hi, guys!" Aracely says, smiling at us. "I'm your fairy godmother for the weekend. It's good to finally see you all up close."

"Likewise," Nick says, stepping forward. "Nick. Designated driver."

"Roxie," I say, shaking her outstretched hand.

"Hanna." Hanna smiles and gives her a small wave.

Chaz steps forward to introduce himself, but Aracely stops him. "You must be the man of the hour."

"Indeed!" Chaz smooths the front of his shirt. "Chaz Humbert. Academy Award nominee and lady killer. And never on the guest list."

"Well, this one's not shy," Aracely laughs. "Or lacking confidence. Okay, guys, leave your stuff in the car for now. Come see how I get down."

Chatting all the way, the six of us walk up to the second floor, and Aracely unlocks the door. Inside the small apartment, almost everything is old, but it comes together. On the walls hang timeless watercolor paintings, and while the furniture is older than any of us, it gives the room a certain retro charm. Houseplants of various sizes and shades take up the corners, while a record player sits next to the small heater in the living room.

"Nice place," I say. "You do the decorating?"

"Most of it," Aracely responds. "I mean, the previous tenants left some stuff. People are always throwing stuff out around here. Putting it out on the curb and whatnot. You kind of gather things as you go." She laughs. "I'm glad I like what my richer neighbors like because I can't afford to buy anything else."

"But the watercolors," Nick says. "You must've bought these on your own."

"Yeah, those are mine," Aracely says.

Nick nods. "Chateau?"

Aracely claps her hands. "No way! How did you know that?"

"Emilio took me there once," Nick says quietly. The mood suddenly turns somber, and all of us look at the ground.

"Have you guys heard anything?" Aracely asks. "Like, anything at all? I've been calling every immigrant group in the state. He isn't even on file."

"I went looking for him that weekend," Nick says. "Me and a couple of guys he grew up with. We asked everybody. Nobody knew anything."

"We've got the lowrider, though," I tell Aracely. "His car's safe. Anything in the trunk, too. They won't have anything on him."

Aracely looks down at the ground. "Oh, poor baby."

"Emilio's smart, though," Chaz says. "He'll be back. That guy, he can do anything."

Nick chuckles. "Locating and extorting baby daddies."

"Winning debates," Hanna chimes in. "Bringing Roxie Doritos in third period."

"Breaking balls," CeCe laughs. "With great power comes great responsibility once 'The Swindler' finds you."

"'The Swindler!?'" Aracely shrieks, fanning her face. "That's what they call him? *El Estafador*?"

"*Sí*," CeCe snorts. "That's really his nickname. I mean, who would want that kind of title beside him? He even calls himself that when talking about himself in the third person."

"That third-person shit was creepy," Aracely remarks. "I figured he must've killed someone. Classic disassociation or whatever."

CeCe sighs. "Who knows. 'The Swindler' is fine. At least he didn't try to name himself *Oso* or Li'l Puppet. We already have enough of those in our family."

***

With the ice broken, all of us take turns giving Aracely *A People's History of Chester, Washington* for the next hour. As far as listeners go though, Aracely's gold. She sits rapt through our descriptions of Chaz's various harassments and screams "girl power" when I get to the Photoshopped porn. As we conclude our epic tale, omitting no details, she's spellbound.

"Wow," Aracely says after some time. "Talk about a crazy life. I'm from White Center originally, back when it was rough, so I've seen some shit. But damn. You gave the hood a run for its nonexistent money.

"Seriously," she continues. "Those two? Brennan and Spencer? Jumping you in the lunchroom? That's almost a hate crime if you think about it. Did they ever call you any names before?"

"Yeah, they've called me a faggot a few times," Chaz recalls. "But they're usually more creative. 'Trans Humbert' is my personal favorite, though "Chaz-gender' never fails to amaze."

Aracely shakes her head. "Boys. Boys at that age, especially. Not that girls are any better. Gosh, people suck."

"Not all people," Chaz says. "But most."

"Well, I hope you got some hits in," Aracely says. "I mean, they did start it."

"I got a couple of good ones," Chaz tells her. "I'm in better shape than I used to be. It was Hanna who went in for the kill, though. And Roxie, of course. She knocked one dude out."

"Holy shit!" Aracely exclaims. "Really?"

"Yeah." I sigh. "Not one of my prouder moments. I stomped on his head. I like to think we're past it."

Hanna nods. "I don't think he remembers any of it. Pretty sure he was out cold."

"And Phil." Chaz shakes his head. "Who'd hit Phil? He's the last person to get involved in fights."

"Some sphincter in a WSU sweatshirt," I reply, remembering that particular incident. "Know anybody who fits that bill?"

Hanna rolls her eyes. "Most of the county?"

"Lot of people out here," Aracely says. "Lot of people have been through the same. Just talk to them. They'll tell you what it was like growing up. Getting beat up, pushed around. Being ignored."

"But nobody takes it seriously," Chaz says. "It's just seen as your standard bullying. The kind everyone else gets."

"But it's worse," Aracely says, frowning. "In a way. It's like racism. You can't help what you are or why you're there. It's not like a lame shirt you can just take off or a dorky hairstyle you can fix in five minutes. It's like being hated for…existing."

In a few sentences, Aracely has verbalized something I've tried to understand but couldn't until now. Chaz nods, and the two of them share a long look. Feeling they've been connected by this mutually understood reality, I realize, if for nothing else, Chaz needed to be here for this moment. He needed to hear this from somebody who's stood where he's standing and maybe still stands there from time to time.

It feels inappropriate to speak, so I stay quiet, as do the rest of us. Eventually, conversations resume, and the festive mood from before returns. After resting a bit longer, Nick and I get up to grab our things from the car. The others follow.

"I really wish Emilio could've come with us," Nick says wistfully as we descend the stairs. "He was always down for a trip. The two of us were supposed to come out this summer, maybe bring Frankie along. A guys' trip."

"Yeah, well. It's just you and the girls this time," I say. "And Chaz."

"*And* Chaz?" Chaz's voice floats from behind us. "Uh, isn't this my trip? It's Chaz and the girls. The girls include you, Nick."

Nick stops walking. "Is it a hate crime to punch Chaz?"

"Give me a sign," Chaz sings, pouting his lips. "Hit me baby one more time."

Nick shudders. "I'll pass."

Entertained, I try to keep their banter going while the girls and I take our luggage out of the back. We still haven't figured out where everybody's sleeping, but I'm too worn out to unpack. We're here for two days, and I'm hardly a fashionista. I'll probably spend the weekend in my jeans and sweatshirt. Come to think of it, I've spent most of my fifteen years doing that, so what would another weekend hurt? Even so, I packed a few nice things in case we end up going somewhere upscale. It's always good to be prepared.

For dinner, Aracely takes us to this local spot that serves gelato milkshakes and double burgers. Though we protest when she insists on paying for us all, she refuses to hear a word of it and opens a tab. Our waiter is a ruggedly handsome yet flamboyant man who looks to be in his late twenties, and he tells us about the neighborhood as he sets our plates down.

"Screw Chester. I'm moving out," Chaz says dreamily, dunking a fry in remoulade. "Capitol Hill, here I come."

"Oh my God," CeCe says, rolling her eyes. "You've been here two hours."

"It worked for me," Aracely pipes up. "The world is a big place. Sometimes you aren't born where you're meant to be." She sets down her milkshake. "When I was fifteen, I didn't know where I belonged. Saturn? Maybe Pluto?" She takes a sip. "It wasn't just about being gay. Or Latina. I just always felt I was on the sidelines no matter where I went."

"I get it," Nick says from the other side of the table. "Emilio and I talked a bit about that. I think all of us feel that way at some point. Sometimes our entire lives."

Aracely nods. "People say it's an immigrant thing. A Black thing. A brown thing. A gay thing. I don't think so, though. You're either in or you're out. Even if people see you one way, it doesn't matter. You gotta feel it yourself."

"Kelsey and Brooke," Hanna offers. "My older sisters. They always seem so in sync. With each other, with themselves. Everybody they meet loves them. But me? I've never felt like that. Even if I'm surrounded by people, I always feel like I'm two steps away from everybody else. I can't explain it."

"Does it make you sad?" CeCe asks. "Do you want to be two steps closer? Or do you like the distance sometimes?"

Hanna shrugs. "I don't know the answer to that."

"At least you're not Frankie," Nick laughs. "That dude doesn't have a choice. The only language he speaks is HTML."

I chuckle. "Is Frankie still trying to learn Elvish?"

Nick shakes his head. "I don't ask questions."

"What was it like coming out?" Chaz asks quietly, looking at Aracely.

"Wow," Aracely says, her glass hovering in midair. "Where does one begin? Well, it wasn't easy. By senior year of high school, I'd had enough. I'd been sure of it for years but hid it. I always made excuses when guys asked me out or wanted to get with me. And my parents? I didn't really know what they'd think. I just did it. It sounds kind of weird, but I just walked into the living room one night and was like, 'I'm gay.' Totally in a fit of, like, desperate internalized angst. I didn't yell or scream. I just told my parents and my little sister, who was working on crossword puzzles, and walked out of the room."

Chaz frowns. "That was it?"

"My parents aren't religious," Aracely says. "Or traditional. Mom's a feminist. Dad, well. He's got an interesting concept of everything. I mean, people who didn't know us probably thought we were a simple family, but my parents are kind of out there. Real complex. I didn't think they'd have an issue with it, but I didn't know for certain. I mean, look at Cher when Chastity came out."

"So were they cool with it?" Chaz asks. "You being gay, I mean."

"In the end, yeah," Aracely says. "At first they were a little on edge. Like, they didn't really interact with me much. My dad just said something like, 'Oh, okay. Do you want to talk about it?' Kind of the standard 'what to say when your son or daughter comes out to you' kind of answer. My mom didn't say anything. I think she had a harder time. And my sister didn't say anything either, but later told me not to come out while we were both at the same school together. Which was immature, but she's since apologized for saying it. So yeah, that was about it."

"How did it go at school?" I ask. "That is, if you don't mind me asking."

"Of course," Aracely says. "Please. Ask away. It was okay. Good, bad. Little of both. A few girls started rumors about me, saying they caught me making out with said girl or that I had gonorrhea. Lost a few fake friends. Found some interesting things written about me in the bathroom. You know. The stereotypical high school thing."

"Why are girls like that?" I wonder out loud, thinking about Felicia and Jenna. "Why don't we support each other?"

"The big question," Aracely laughs, throwing up her hands. "You're asking it. I'm asking it. Everybody's asking it. It's the main reason I never had much time for traditional feminism. My friends? All guys. Well, almost. When certain girls come around, it's like drama and bullshit. I'd rather get stoned and play Donkey Kong. Show off the orc sword I made in welding. Build some crappy furniture out of scrap lumber. You just have to find the right tribe. Who wants some entitled white woman with a pixie cut ordering them around, telling us men are oppressive, while she lives in a penthouse on Lake Washington? I certainly don't."

"Girls can be awful," I agree. "When CeCe got sick in class…it was the girls who started in on her. The only one who came to her defense was a guy."

"Well, what about Brennan and Spencer?" Chaz points out. "They're guys. Male versions of Jenna and Felicia. Worse, maybe. We've all had our lives destroyed, or at least people have tried to destroy our lives. I don't think it's because of what gender they are. Erik's a guy. Emilio was deported by men who worked for the government. And Owen? Guys indeed." Chaz shakes his head. "Sorry, I think it's the opposite."

"No, you're right," I say. "We shouldn't generalize. It's just hard for me when girls gossip and talk behind each other's backs and rip into each other for no reason. We're told we're weaker. We go through so much. Obstacles and hurdles and barriers we don't even talk about. But instead, the focus is on 'so-and-so gave somebody's boyfriend a blowjob' or 'look how fat she's gotten.'" I shake my head. "It's just hard. I can't tell you anything beyond that."

"I'm with Roxie on that one," Aracely says. "But Chaz, you're not wrong. Nick, what do you think? Are we overblowing things, or is Chaz onto something?"

"Oh, totally," Nick says, busy playing Jenga with pieces of celery. "Guys aren't any better. Different versions of the same bullshit. We just have pissing contests and dominate each other physically instead of gossiping. And we laugh at each other all the time."

"But there is something to be said about how girls can be," Aracely says. "There's this viciousness I've never seen with guys. I've got nothing to compare it to."

Hanna nods. "What she said."

"We should be in a movie," I say, folding and unfolding my napkin. "We've got so much material right in front of us. A gay teen. A man-child. A very together student. A pregnant freshman. And whatever I am."

"It's like *The Breakfast Club*," Aracely agrees. "You totally should. I'm thinking more reality TV, though."

"I wouldn't mind not getting a job. Someone call MTV," Nick says, and everybody laughs again. We stay for a while and chat, while Aracely closes the tab. Rising to go, we walk towards the door and step outside into the crisp spring air.

***

"You'll have a blast tomorrow, Chaz," Aracely says, revealing her hand to be a four of a kind. "I've known those guys for years. Even though I barely see them now, it's like no time has passed, you know?"

"I'm pumped," Chaz replies, throwing his cards in the discard pile. "Can't wait."

We're back at Aracely's apartment, sitting on the floor playing poker with whatever spare change we could find. Nick's on fire tonight,

Chaz cleared house the round before, and I've lost almost all my coins to the boys. When we got back, I texted my mom to let her know everything was going well. Aracely and Chaz are by now good friends and talk nonstop when they're not with the rest of us, and with the heater on and *Abbey Road* spinning on the record player, it doesn't get much better than this. Everything's set for tomorrow, and while Chaz is going to be learning the ins and outs of gayhood, the rest of us are figuring out how we want to spend our time here.

"What's the other side of the water like?" CeCe asks, looking up from her cards. "Looks amazing. Have you ever been?"

"It is beautiful," Aracely says. "The ferry ride alone is totally worth seeing. Especially if the mountain's out. But check that out if you come back in the summer. There's more than enough to keep you busy on this side."

"What about the UW campus?" Hanna turns to face Aracely. "How far are we from there?"

"Not far," Aracely answers. "Take the bus and you'll get there in fifteen, twenty minutes tops. Depends if there's a game, though."

"'The Underground Tour,'" Nick says, studying a pamphlet he picked up back at the restaurant. "This looks cool. You been?"

Aracely nods. "Yeah. You can see the old Seattle, buried underground. Way back from the 1800s."

"Let's just check out the city," I say. "No plans, just chilling. I don't have money to burn, and, like, why not play it by ear? Get some good food. Catch some views of the port. We can always come back, you know."

"The U District has amazing food," Aracely says. "If you're a foodie, you have to go there. But the best restaurants are within walking distance from here, and they're cheap. Seattle's got great spots no matter where you go, really."

"Why don't we sleep on it?" Hanna yawns, squinting down at her cards. "I'm tired. We can decide in the morning. Oh, and whose turn is it?"

"This city isn't that weird," I remark to Nick as Hanna tosses me the toothpaste. Hanna and I are taking the guest bed, CeCe's on the pullout in Aracely's room, and Nick called dibs on the couch, which leaves Chaz on the floor. He didn't seem to mind and pointed out that waking up with a sore backside was an essential part of the gay experience.

"You've been here a few hours," Nick counters, opening a packet of floss. "That's not enough time. Just wait. I promise freakishness."

"Oh, we know," CeCe says. Hanna giggles.

"Okay, screw you guys," Nick pouts. "Really. I'm serious. Be ready."

"But what are we doing tomorrow?" Hanna glances at us. "I want to plan our Saturday and max out our time. That way, we can see everything we came to see and maybe more if we organize ourselves."

"Oh, come *on*." I wave my hand dismissively. "Don't kill our Seattle bash with a public-school grading rubric. Who cares about organization? We came here to have fun. I want to go to GameWorks and then see Kurt Cobain's house." I hum "Smells Like Teen Spirit" and deep-six my makeup removal wipe into the trash. "And I want teriyaki chicken."

"Don't forget Jimi Hendrix," Hanna says. "We've got to see him, too."

"His statue's down the street from here," Nick says. "Four blocks over. We could see it right now if you want."

I stare at him. "It's the middle of the night."

"So what?" Nick shrugs. "This place doesn't shut down. Let's go."

"We'll go tomorrow," I say, feeling the fatigue wash over me. "Nick, please just be agreeable for once. I promise. First thing."

Nick huffs. "Fine."

"I'll go with you," Hanna says quietly. "If you want."

Nick looks touched. "Really?"

"You two go on then." I rub my eyes. "I'm going to crash."

I glance over my shoulder as Hanna and Nick start towards the door. "Be safe, okay?"

"Yep." They step out of the room. The door creaks as Hanna closes it behind them.

"Are they really going just to see a statue?" CeCe frowns. "It's midnight. They'll barely be able to see anything."

"It's Jimi," I say. "Seeing him in the dark is better than nothing. Plus, Nick gets restless. I've seen him on a trampoline at midnight. This is pretty normal for him."

"Is something going on with those two?" CeCe asks, walking over and standing behind me. "You feel it?"

"I don't know," I say wearily. "I don't ask."

CeCe frowns. "Wouldn't you want to know?"

"It's complicated," I sigh. "Hanna is my best friend in the whole world. Nick is my brother. Those two spend way too much time together as it is, but, like, could there be something more there? I don't really know. I can't think of it, if you know what I mean."

"I hope there is," CeCe says with a small smile. "If you don't mind me saying it. Nick's a really good guy. And Hanna's so sweet. They deserve each other." She pauses. "There are a lot of bad guys out there. Girls can be just as bad, too. And they're so cute together."

"Yeah." I blow out a breath. "Hanna's a dream. Nick's basically a sixth grader mentally. One who happens to be brilliant, but still. He's a little old for her, but I know he won't do anything."

CeCe laughs. "Yeah. And I get why you'd be against it. I mean, your brother and your best friend. It could make things complicated. But complicated is how we grow."

I nod. "It's not that I don't want them to be together, I just think Hanna needs time on her own to get her head straight. I don't want her jumping into something new after the Owen disaster. And especially not with my brother."

"But it's not jumping," CeCe counters. "They've known each other for years. They're comfortable around each other. They're friends."

"I know," I say. "Still."

"Are you afraid she'll hurt Nick?"

"No," I say almost immediately. "Not at all. It's just…"

"Sometimes girls break hearts without trying to," CeCe says. "I know."

"Yeah," I admit. "Or vice versa. Not that either of them would do it on purpose."

"No," CeCe agrees. "But love is like an egg toss. Get too close, you fumble it. Step too far away and it breaks between the two of you. Both of you blame the other, but you both let it pass through your hands."

I stare at her. "Are you and Emilio prophets or something?" I ask. "Did we know each other in a past life? How do you just drop knowledge like that like it's no big deal?" I shake my head. "And you talk about not coming back to school."

"I'm not that smart," CeCe says, folding her hands in her lap. "I've just lived. And I know you have, too. You just haven't had time to process." She pauses. "Or let yourself."

Unnerved, I make up an excuse to get out of there and step out of the room, closing the door behind me. Walking out to the balcony, I leave the sliding door open and look off into the distance. Only two stories up, the view doesn't go very far, but I need to focus on something other than the pull overtaking my body. The walls can't hold forever. Something must be really coming apart because I've spent years building the fortress I am today.

It wasn't easy. I used to be the most sensitive kid I knew. Even more than Nick, who still is, and will likely always be, incredibly emotive. For some reason, people just came at me. Trying circumstances descended on my life and kept coming. It didn't matter what I did or didn't do. Stuff just happened. Friends would come and go. People would respond kindly to me and vanish, usually without explanation. After a while, loneliness emerged. It followed me everywhere until it settled over everything like a fog. I stopped fighting it after a point, figuring it would always be there.

When my father died, whatever security or sanctuary I felt at home went with him. Nothing was the same. Of course, anybody who's experienced loss will tell you that. There's the before and there's the after. Your life will from here on out be split in two, and when the pain gets too great, you'll disassociate and try to live in the memories. For a while, I only lived in the memories. My mother still does and might always stay there, where it's more comfortable. Nick's retreated into his own world, one full of oddities and eccentricities, but his world is open to everyone. Mine? Not so much.

"Sleeping Beauty?" Chaz steps onto the balcony and comes to stand beside me. "Why aren't you sleeping?"

"I'm usually awake at this time of night," I reply. "I make up for it by sleeping through first period. You?"

"I can't sleep in new places," he says. "Never could. I always just want to stay up and look around and find stuff to do."

"You could've gone with Nick and Hanna. See Jimi Hendrix."

"I already did," Chaz laughs. "We passed him on the way to dinner."

I frown. "Serious?"

"Yeah," Chaz says. "I guess you were all so in the zone you missed a legend in the bronze."

"Happens every time." I shake my head. "How are you feeling?"

"What? About tomorrow?" Chaz shrugs. "Ready, I guess. I just texted Blaze to tell him how cool Seattle University looks. Mom's hoping I'll choose WSU, though. She panics when I leave home."

"I think that's just moms in general," I point out. "Dads want us to leave so they can have Mom back to themselves."

Chaz snorts. "I don't think that's the case in my house."

I glance at him. "Trouble in paradise?"

"Oh, it's never been." Chaz lowers his gaze. "I don't know how those two got together. Like, my dad is Blaze, right? He's so independent and on the go. Always doing stuff. Mom? She's the opposite. Goes to work, comes home from work. Done. Doesn't go anywhere. Trips, family reunions. It's always Dad and me. And Darren, back when he was still part of things."

"Your brother," I say quietly.

"Yeah," Chaz breathes. "That's a whole other story. You know he was getting scouted as a freshman to play quarterback for Boise? He never played JV, went straight to varsity at fourteen. Blaze said he'd never seen anything like it."

"Wow," I say. "He was the golden child, huh?"

"Oh yeah," Chaz says. "Like, you and I are both second kids. We never got to have our parents all to ourselves. But Darren was one hundred percent of the Humbert boys as far back as I could remember. I remember showing up to Grandma's house or to family parties, and it was always Darren, Darren, Darren. I wanted to be like him so bad. I tried to play football every year. I sucked. The helmets felt awkward, and I couldn't remember the rules. My dad tried to help me. Even Darren tried, but I couldn't get it. By the time I was in fifth grade, that's when my brother really took off as a player. And everything really became about him."

"So he's four years older than you," I say. "Right?"

"No, five." Chaz scratches his head. "That was the year he got into drugs. I guess he couldn't handle the pressure. Plus, he saw too much too young. I mean, coming out of middle school and basically becoming a king on the football field. Especially in a town like Chester, where high school sports are a huge deal. It goes to your head. There's an endless line of girls, parties, drugs. Anything you want when you want it."

"It's still like that," I say. "Ridiculous. Like, they're kids. And the coaches turn a blind eye to whatever they do as long as they go to state."

Chaz is quiet for a moment. "Darren got five years last week."

I stare at my hands, unsure of what to say.

"None of us went to the sentencing," he continues. "I only know because my mom cried the entire day. Dad just sat in the den and drank. I stayed upstairs in my room until school the next morning. Like, what can you do? What do you say?"

"I'm sorry," I murmur, staring down at my feet. "Wow, man. I didn't know."

"Don't tell the others, okay?" Chaz looks into my eyes. "I don't want this being a topic of discussion."

"Don't worry," I say. "I won't."

Chaz sits down cross-legged on the ground, and I sit beside him. "I think that's the reason why Blaze decided to become a coach."

I nod. "It makes sense."

Chaz studies me. "What makes sense?"

"That he wants to save people," I say. "Stop it from happening again."

Chaz nods. "I think so too. Like, he doesn't like books. I didn't even know he could read. But every night before he goes to bed, he reads *The Catcher in the Rye*. Over and over again."

"There you go," I say. "He wants to be Holden. He wants to be the catcher and save people from going over the edge."

Chaz closes his eyes. "Like Darren did."

We don't talk after that. I can hear frogs outside and, faintly, the hum of Friday night in the city carrying up the hill. Chaz takes off his panda bear slippers and claps the soles together a few times before turning one of them over in his hands.

"You think my parents would be ashamed of me?"

I stare at him. "What gives you that idea?"

"I'm one big lie," Chaz says. "I brought you around like a girlfriend. I pretend to like whatever Blaze likes. I'm lying to them right now about where I am. They think I'm on a college tour to meet acting coaches, not..." He trails off. "Going to meet other gay men like myself."

I think carefully about what to say. "I don't know, Chaz. Did either of them say or tell you something that would make you think that?"

"A long time ago," he begins, "I tested the waters. I guess somebody we knew had a son who came out of the closet. He just told them, boom, 'I'm gay.' My mom knew him since he was like a little kid and stuff, and she was really affected. Couldn't stop talking about it. I finally just asked her what she would've done if I were the one who was gay." Chaz stops. "You know what she said?"

I shake my head. "Go on."

His voice is a whisper. "She looked me right in the face. I can remember exactly where we were. She said, 'I would have failed you as a parent and as someone who loves you, for you to make that choice.'"

Chaz shakes his head. "Even after all these years, I can still hear it."

"It's not a choice!" I exclaim, gritting my teeth. "God! Why is it so fucking hard for people to understand this? Do they ever stop and think for a second that maybe the Bible's got that part wrong? That society has it twisted? Look at this country right now. Any one of these days a terrorist could blow us up. Chester kids are coming back in body bags fighting in a pointless war, the Amazon is getting bulldozed, the US is turning into a police state, but people would rather take sides in the dick-in-butthole dilemma. What the hell?" I shake my head. "I'm sorry, but I can't accept that. We are so close to falling off the edge right now, and most people aren't waking up."

"I agree," Chaz says tiredly. "Completely. It's a mess. Her priorities are so off. I don't get it. What about love? What about acceptance? If it's a sin, how about loving the sinner and letting God do the judging?"

"Critical reasoning," I say. "Some people have it. The rest of the bunch? Don't get me started. Anything uncomfortable gets tossed. Boom. Finished. Don't even bother because they won't hear it. Not now or ever."

"You know what?" Chaz sneers. "Fuck it. I'm glad I'm gay. I can't wait to see the look on her face when I finally break the news. Will she love me? Hate me? Try and send me to conversion therapy? Let's see. Let's see how far Prudence Humbert's love actually goes."

"What about your dad?" I ask.

"Hm." Chaz falls quiet for a second. "Blaze? I don't really know. I mean, he's always making gay jokes. Laughs whenever he hears The Village People. Thinks *Brokeback Mountain* was a deep-state operation funded by the same people who want to take away our guns. But deep down? I don't really know what he thinks."

"Well, you can talk about this tomorrow," I say. "With Aracely's friends. At least one of them has been where you're standing now. Ask them questions. Nobody knows them back home. You won't have to hold back."

"I won't," Chaz says. "I'm done holding back. I'm done with keeping it in."

***

I wake up to the sound of dishes clattering. I'm alone, so Hanna must be in the kitchen with everybody else by now. I walk towards my duffel bag and crack open some Listerine. Swishing it around in my mouth, I open the window and spit it out onto the grass two stories below before deciding on whatever I'm going to wear today.

"Wake up!" Nick shouts from somewhere beyond. "Come on. It's late."

"What time is it?" I mutter to no one in particular. Grabbing my jeans off the desk chair, I pull them on and choose a rumpled T-shirt before heading into the kitchen. Chaz, Hanna, and CeCe are seated at the kitchen table hunched over bowls of Mini-Wheats while Nick and Aracely are trying to outdo each other with the omelets. A pile of scones sits in the center of the table, surrounded by jars of honey and homemade preserves.

"Morning, you," Aracely calls cheerfully, throwing a handful of vegetables into her frying pan. "Hope the bed didn't kill you too much."

"We managed," I laugh, standing behind Nick and staring into his frying pan. "What've you got there?"

"A Man-Let," Nick declares, poking at the edges with a spatula. "Spam, linguica, bacon, chorizo, and the tip of a green onion. Who's down?"

Chaz raises a hand. "I just want the sausage."

CeCe rolls her eyes. "Can someone mute him?"

"Coming right up," Nick says, flipping the pan over and dropping his latest onto Chaz's plate. "Two eggs and a sausage for the man fan. Have fun. Live free."

"That was the gayest infomercial I've ever heard," Aracely remarks, looking at Chaz's plate. "And that's a lot of beef."

"Hot beef!" Chaz exclaims. "Yum."

"Well, someone's excited about his big day," I say. "What time does your crew get here?"

"Pretty soon," Aracely says, joining us at the table. "I just got off the phone with Elaine. She says Theo's being a bitch and tried to back out, but Willie forced him to come. They just left and are on their way."

She turns to Chaz. "You're going to have a wild time with those three."

"Can't wait," Chaz says, dribbling Tabasco on his food. "And where are we going again?"

"Not far," Aracely says. "You're already in the gayborhood. This is it. They're just going to show you around and probably stop for coffee. Maybe Volunteer Park. It's pretty nice out this morning, and it was raining last week."

"What are we going to do?" Nick asks. "While Chaz is off doing his thing?"

"I say GameWorks," I say. "That, and explore Westlake Center."

"Pike Place Market," CeCe adds. "I've been once before. It's cool."

"Yeah, Pike Place sounds good," Nick agrees. "We can watch them throw fish and stuff."

I laugh. "Throwing fish? Does Tiffany work there?"

Hanna groans. "I'm trying to eat here, guys. Can you not?"

"I didn't say anything," Nick says, holding up his hands in earnest. "Roxie made it foul."

"Little wonder how Roxie and I became friends," Chaz observes. "We're both ill. Should we be on medication?"

"You should be," I say. "But me? I'm a lost cause."

"They should be here any minute," Aracely says, looking at us with alarm. "Chaz, do you want to maybe grab a sweatshirt or something? In case it rains?"

"Nah, I'm good." Chaz stares down at his front. "But what about my shirt? Is it hick? Too hetero?"

"No, NASCAR rocks," Aracely says, smiling. "Just be you, my dude. You're cool enough."

"Ditto." Chaz takes a sip of coffee. "This is going to be sweet."

I turn to Aracely. "So where should we go first?"

"Well, it's a beautiful day," she says. "I'd recommend hitting up the waterfront. You'll be able to see the Puget Sound in all its glory. At least see that before you go."

"Sounds like a plan," I reply. "That way, we can see Pike Place too for CeCe and Nick."

"And you guys are still close to Westlake," Aracely says. "Seattle's a small town. Everything big—well, mostly everything—is close in. If you come back in the summer, we can see some stuff further out."

I laugh. "Are you saying you actually want to see us again?"

"Of course." Aracely smiles. "You guys aren't that bad. Trust me, I've had worse."

"I'm in," Nick pipes up. "I like this plan. Hanna?"

"Yeah," Hanna agrees. "Sounds good. I'll do the UW campus tour another time, maybe."

"You have to book that in advance," Chaz says, setting his knife down. "I'm pretty sure."

The doorbell rings, and Aracely jumps up.

"That's them," she says. "Chaz, you got everything you need?"

"Yup." Chaz bobs his head. "I'm all set."

Aracely opens the door, and two guys and a woman stroll in. They're all dressed in woolen outerwear and are talking quietly amongst themselves. Stepping into the living room, they finally break apart long enough to notice us sitting at the kitchen table and shuffle awkwardly before staring at the ground.

Nobody says anything.

"Hi," I offer, hoping to put a pin in the silence. "I'm Roxie."

"Elaine," the woman says hastily. "Sorry about the boys. They're inept."

"Will Burton," the shorter man says. "You can call me Willie."

"Theo," the taller, lanky guy says, smiling shyly at us. "What brings you all to Seattle?"

"Me!" Chaz announces. All of us laugh.

"So *you're* Chaz," Elaine says, peering at him through square frames. She runs a hand through her bobbed hair. "Is that short for Charles or...?"

"Indeed, it is," Chaz says. "The shortened version of a short name."

"It's all good," Will says, his chubby face lighting up impishly. "I used to be Will until I came out of the closet. Then I became Willie."

Nick smirks. "You had to lengthen your name, huh?"

"Oh, fuck yes." Willie laughs musically. "I can sometimes be a lot to... take in."

"Willie, no," Theo sighs. "Can you not scare the children? They've just met you."

"So where are you guys going?" Aracely cuts in. "Did you figure it out on the way over?"

"Broadway for sure," Elaine replies. "It's where everything's at on a Saturday morning. We'll figure it out from there."

"Sounds good." Chaz rises from the table and pushes in his chair. "Let me just clear my plate."

"I've got it." Aracely waves him away. "You go on and get out there. We'll take care of the rest."

"You sure?" Chaz frowns. "It's no biggie."

"Go," Hanna says, giving his shoulder a light shove. "It's your time to shine."

***

"So," Nick says after everything's been put away. "Now that we've delivered Chaz to the gays, what are we all going to do?"

"Waterfront," I say. "Are we driving?"

Aracely shakes her head. "Take the bus or walk. Trust me."

"Bus it is," Nick says, sliding on his penny loafers. "Everybody got change?"

I grab my bag and rummage around for quarters. I manage to scrounge up more than enough to buy me a ride and sling the strap over my shoulder.

CeCe emerges a moment later. "You ready?"

"Yeah," I say, checking myself out in the hallway mirror. "Let's jet."

"If you need anything, don't hesitate to reach out," Aracely calls after us as we barrel towards the door. "I mean it. I've always got my phone on me, so if you get lost, or need directions or get tired…oh, screw it. You guys are almost grown-ups. Sorry to be such a mom."

"No, we appreciate it," Hanna laughs. "And likewise. If you need anything, just let us know."

"Try to be back before six, though," Aracely says. "I usually stop off at the farmer's market on my way home, and I'm cooking pozole tonight. The real stuff, not that sodium-laden shlock you get at restaurants."

"Tight!" Nick exclaims. "We'll definitely be back for that."

"Good," Aracely says. "I'll need an extra set of hands. Let's see if Emilio's taught you well."

Chapter 17

Sticking to our plan, Hanna, Nick, CeCe, and I hop on the bus and ride down to the waterfront to kill some time. It's still gray out, but the sun is beginning to break through the clouds, and I can feel the warmth settling on my face. The call of seagulls sounds overhead, and the occasional hum of a seaplane causes us to all look up. We peruse a few touristy stores that are way too expensive before winding up at a curiosity shop on the waterfront. We sample some fudge, gawk at pickled animals in jars, and snap pictures of some mummified people on display. I take several pictures for Chaz and grab a magnet of the Space Needle to stick on the fridge when we get home, the way my dad used to.

Nick notices this and smiles. "Continuing the tradition?"

"That's what we do," I reply. "For better or worse."

"How are you guys holding up?" Hanna asks as soon as we all step out of the store. "I bought hard candies, in case anybody's still digesting breakfast."

"Those scones, though," Nick remarks, taking a butterscotch disk. "Went down like a rock. Delicious, but very dense."

"I think I ate too much." Hanna massages her abdomen. "I've got to walk. At least for a little while."

"We have time," CeCe says, gazing up at the city skyline. "I wonder what Chaz's up to right now."

Nick chuckles. "What if he's getting a lap dance at a gay bar?"

"Would you grow up?" I roll my eyes. "You're literally an adult. It's time."

"Not really," Nick argues. "What responsibilities do I have?"

"None," I confirm. "I just need you to pretend you're responsible and drive us home in one piece. After that, you can take out the action figures and continue acting out *Revenge of the Sith*. Sound fair?"

Nick makes a face. "You make me sound like a total noob. Am I really that bad?"

We all nod.

"Okay, screw you guys," Nick laughs. "I can always go back to reading encyclopedias and wearing button-down shirts. Did I forget anything?"

I raise my hand innocently. "Practicing asking Gabriella out in front of the hallway mirror?"

Nick gives me the finger. "Have you ever even been asked out, period?"

"Nope," I reply, shrugging. "I liked a boy once, but he preferred mounting a jaundiced Jezebel. I gave up after that."

"Guys are pigs," Hanna sighs. "Even Blake. I'm sorry, Roxie. But what could he have possibly seen in someone like Tiffany besides… you know? I just—I don't get it. Where are all the good ones?"

"Probably right in front of your face," Nick blurts out. "And no, I'm not talking about Jerome. But to answer your question with a question, why do girls only want good guys after they've been badly burned?"

"I really thought Owen was good," Hanna says quietly, her eyes downcast. "I'd only ever dated Jerome, who is a good person. Not a great boyfriend, but he cares about people in the way he knows how. Owen only knows how to pretend. He's built, dresses well, and is confident. And I hate to say it, but he's also super hot. Tell me you wouldn't want to think the best of somebody that perfect who landed right in your lap?"

Nick heaves a sigh. "Well, now that you put it that way…"

"Owen was my fault, too," I remind her. "Cynthia arranged that relationship, and I helped. By the time I figured him out, it was out of our control. We got Owen'd."

"Owen'd." Nick laughs. "Owned by Owen. That's a good one."

Hanna makes a face. "Trust me, it's not."

"I never liked Owen," CeCe offers. "Didn't trust him. I knew he was fake, but I didn't know how to tell you. I saw how into him you were and how he seemed to make you happy, and I guess I hoped maybe I was wrong about him. But sometimes, you just know the truth without any proof."

"The bad vibes." Nick nods. "Emilio always told me to go with my gut. I mean, I do that anyway, but it's good to know I'm not the only one who does this."

"But to answer your question from before, Nick," CeCe says, "girls like unavailable men. Guys who do their own thing and don't let anybody else get in the way. Guys who don't make a big fuss over them and fall all over them at first. I don't know how to put it any other way."

Nick digests this. "Was Erik like that?"

"Erik's a boy," CeCe says disdainfully. "He was never a man. The two of us? We just had a lot of the same classes and played *Oregon Trail* together at lunch. We were both in sports. We spent so much time around each other. It just made sense. We became friends, then boyfriend and girlfriend, and now parents. It just kind of grew out of that."

Nick smiles. "Mom says our dad was like that too. That they were friends first, and then he wouldn't take a hint or leave when she tried to break up with him. I guess after a while, they just couldn't be apart. The longer you spend time together, I guess."

"That's so sweet." Hanna smirks. "Want to know how my parents met?"

I give her a look. "Are you sure you want to share that?"

Hanna wrinkles her nose. "Trust me, you don't want to know."

Nick refocuses his attention on CeCe. "Any news from Erik?"

She nods slowly. "Yeah, actually."

I spin around to face her. "Erik reached out?"

"That's the thing," CeCe says. "I don't know what changed, but he wants to be in the picture. He came clean to his parents about everything—that he got me pregnant, that they were going to be grandparents. He sent me a lot of money last week, all the payments he'd missed since Emilio left. I guess that means he's been working ever since we found him at Elderwood that day. He just didn't know how to get it to me at first."

"Well, that's great," Hanna says, giving CeCe's arm a squeeze. "I mean, congratulations, right?"

"That's the thing. I don't know how I feel," CeCe says, sounding far away. "At first, I was shocked. I didn't see that coming. But I saw his face, and I knew he wasn't lying, that nobody put him up to it. That he was finally doing the right thing because he wanted to. He told me that a little while before Emilio got taken away, the two of them got to know each other. I guess Emilio spent time with him. You know, worked on him a little. He talked to Erik about responsibility, stepping up, and the joy of fatherhood. Finding a purpose. I guess it really spoke to him." She sucks in a breath. "When I told him what happened to Emilio, Erik was really upset. He said Emilio was the one who made him see sense and that he makes things go together in a way nobody else does. I had to stay with him until he calmed down."

"Wow." Nick's eyes are wide. "I had no idea. Emilio never mentioned anything about that to me. To anyone, I'm guessing."

I swallow a lump in my throat. "I don't know what to say. Emilio was amazing. Is amazing."

"Even after all that, he still manages to bring the good out of someone," Hanna says. "Even now, he's still helping us. Helping Erik. Just helping."

CeCe nods. "I avoided Erik for a few days after," she continues. "I ignored his calls, didn't respond to his texts. I guess I wanted him to feel what I felt, at least for a little bit. I wasn't sure I wanted him back in the picture at first, but then I thought about the baby. I mean, he, she, whatever it ends up being, deserves to know who their father is, right? And grandparents? Erik's parents came by the house the day he told them to let me know they'd support us all the way and to just ask whenever I needed something. They're nice people, actually. Older couple. I'd only met them a few times before, but you could just tell."

Nick laughs. "The vibe was good?"

CeCe smiles. "The vibe was good."

"Well, that's really encouraging," I say, feeling uplifted by the news. "Whatever happened, it looks like it's working. It's better this way."

"I'm coming back to school, too," CeCe says. "Full-time. Even after the baby's born, I want to keep going. Chaz said he talked to his mom about my options, and they have a childcare center on campus. I can keep working after school and on weekends, and when I turn sixteen, maybe I can get a better job that actually pays a bit more."

"Good," I say, leaning in close to her. "It wouldn't be the same if you weren't there."

"You guys are the main reason I want to come back," CeCe says. "I mean, if I didn't have you two and Chaz, I'd probably just do online classes. Or finish up at a special school for teen moms. I don't know."

"This is going to sound crazy," I begin. "But I'm glad Erik's back in the picture. I didn't know him that well or anything. It's just better to have a father in the picture than not have one. You know. If you can help it." I straighten my posture. "You're still fifteen. You shouldn't have to make every big decision on your own."

CeCe nods. "I don't know what Emilio said that made him change his mind. And I really don't care. If he was scared of Emilio, or had a come-to-Jesus moment, or felt guilty. Even if his parents forced him to step up. It's between him and his conscience."

"I agree," Hanna says. "You've got enough to worry about."

I nod. "Do you think we'll see him back at school now that he's finally come around?"

CeCe shrugs. "I doubt it. Erik's kind of bought into the whole higher education thing. I guess he thinks Elderwood is going to give him a better shot in life. I mean, I support it. I could never see myself in a place like that, but he was always a crappy student. If he's really turning things around, good on him."

"What about friends?" Hanna asks. "Has he made any by now?"

"Not really." CeCe shakes her head. "He calls me up sometimes on weekends, asks me to hang out, or takes me out to eat. I feel bad for him, honestly. I can tell he's lonely." She stops. "Is that lame?"

"No. It's the right thing to do," Hanna says. She takes a breath. "I was in single digits when my dad left. The first few months, he tried to stay in touch with my sisters and me. He'd leave me cards, mail me money. I even remember him driving to the house a few times when he knew my mom would be away. Looking back, it's not like he didn't try, but I didn't bite." She pauses, her eyes cloudy. "I sometimes regret it. Even though he did abandon us." Hanna stops and faces CeCe. "So no, you're doing the right thing. You're doing the compassionate thing. Don't do it for him. Do it for you."

"Dads are important," Nick interjects. "Especially if you have a son."

"What do you mean?" I ask, staring at him. As close as we are, Nick and I have never discussed this subject. He takes a breath and looks down, jamming his hands in his pockets.

"I don't know what it means to be a man," Nick admits. "I've got no idea what it is, what to be like. When Baba died, I was still a kid. Roxie, you were younger, but me? I was at such a crazy age. The age where you begin to see how you're going to turn out. When right and wrong come into the picture. When you start to make the big decisions." He hesitates. "Once my dad was gone, I had nobody to turn to, nobody to ask for advice. Nobody who could help. Yeah, I had my friends, but they were just as lost as I was. I didn't have a mentor, or a role model, or a coach. I felt so alone. Plus, I was different on top of everything else. Not just brown or nonwhite or whatever, but weird. Still am. I mean, I watched *Dreamgirls* ten times when it came out. I post on forums devoted to Siberian musk deer." Nick laughs. "Freshman year, I tried to change my name to Pookie Loc and said I was a Black Muslim. And I wonder why everything went south from there."

Hanna smiles. "The wave cap?"

"Yes!" Nick shakes his head. "Yes, the wave cap. Like, what was that? Not even the two black kids I went to school with wore those! They thought I was a freak, too. I mean, they weren't completely wrong. I just did this complete turnaround after Baba died, but mostly, I didn't have anybody to guide me on anything." He sighs. "You know, stuff like growing into a man. How to talk to girls. Avoiding bad crowds and influences. Like, Mom had enough on her plate. I didn't need to drag her into it."

"I remember," I say slowly. "I just wondered what was wrong with you. I cared about you so much, but you were so lost. I would've helped you, but you were so out there. I was almost afraid to say anything."

Nick waves a hand. "You were a child. I wasn't much older. You had enough of your own stuff going on."

"Yeah." I force a laugh. "Like almost failing school after being a baby genius?"

Nick sighs. "Exactly."

"But I should've been there," I say firmly. "I should've supported you. I should've at least tried to understand rather than laugh at you for wearing a do-rag or rolling my eyes when you talked about us being different."

"It wasn't your place," Nick argues. "*I* was the older brother. Either I should've known better, or somebody older should've pointed me in the right direction. There just wasn't anybody to do it."

"I know what you mean," Hanna says unexpectedly. All of us turn to look at her.

"Like, I know it's not the same," she continues. "My father's still out there somewhere. I mean, if I really wanted to find him, I could. But I don't. I can't explain it. It's not so much that I'm angry at him for cheating on my mom, although obviously, I am. But the older you get, you realize it really does take two to wreck a marriage. I just feel lost. Kind of like Nick did." She stares at her shoes. "I'm sorry. I've never told anybody that before."

"No," I say quickly. "Please, we're here."

"Go ahead," Nick says. "We're listening."

"Nick, what you said about losing confidence without a dad in the picture... it's spot on. I mean, I'm living proof." Hanna laughs uncomfortably. "Nick didn't have anybody to model being a man for him. I had somebody model what a terrible partner looks like. A bad father. A cheater. A liar. So when I met Jerome, somebody who seemed like he'd stick around no matter what, I ran to him. I know it sounds stupid and immature, but the fact that Jenna brutally dumped him made me feel like I was saving him the way I wish somebody would've saved my mom. Saved me. Saved our family."

"That's not stupid at all," CeCe says, giving Hanna's arm a squeeze. "It makes perfect sense. You're a special person. You care a lot. But special people still need love and care." She smiles at Hanna. "Maybe even more than the rest of us do. They're just so busy running around after the rest of us, they don't stop to ask."

Hanna laughs. "You mean like Roxie?"

"I mean like both of you," CeCe replies. "You're both like that. Any other girls who would've found me that day at school, they might've said nice things. They might have pretended to care and then turned around and told everybody in our grade I was pregnant for their five minutes of fame. Maybe they would've helped after all. I don't know. I just know I'm the lucky one here."

"We're all lucky," I say, slinging my arms around Hanna and CeCe. "We're lucky and unlucky."

"I think that's life," Nick points out. "It's a mixed bag. Yin and yang. Some is good, some is bad, but most of it is just existing. You have to look for the good parts, and even the bad parts have a little good in 'em."

"I think that's why I flipped out over Erik so much," Hanna says thoughtfully. "It was a trigger for me. Never mind that CeCe's the one pregnant. When we were there, in that shed at Elderwood, I swear for a split second, he turned into my dad. I saw my dad's face. Not Erik's."

"How did Brooke and Kelsey take it?" I wonder out loud. "I mean, they were older when that happened. They would've known the ins and outs of your parents' relationship, even more than you did, I'd think."

"They avoided it," Hanna says. "Both of them just pretended it never happened. They continued doing cheer and ballet and Girl Scouts and volleyball like everything was normal. It was, like, the day after my father moved out, and nothing changed with them. It didn't matter that my mom was crying nonstop or had passed out in the tub. Or they had to drive her to the ER after she took too much Xanax. They couldn't even legally drive yet, but they just did what they had to do and went on with their lives. They rotated shifts. One of them stayed with me while the other signed discharge papers or cleared my dad's stuff out of the master bedroom. But they never talked about it and still don't."

"They always seemed so normal," I say, shaking my head in amazement. "Taking us shopping with them or teaching us how to put on makeup or listening to us talk about boys. They always seemed like they had these perfect lives, like a Disney princess or a *Seventeen* cover girl. Nobody would've known."

"That's exactly how they wanted it," Hanna replies. "Appearances are everything to them. I mean, they look good taking out the trash. The guys they date, the people they're friends with. Everything has to be perfect. If I ask them how life is, it's always 'amazing.' It's never just 'good' or 'eh' or 'okay.' Everything's 'super' or 'awesome,' or they can't wait for this event or that trip. It's not like we talk that much anyway, but when we do? It's always the same." Hanna shakes her head. "But you know what? I grew up. I realize that high school, at least a lot of the time, freaking sucks. People suck. Life throws disappointment at you. But when I was younger—like, eleven or twelve—I thought I was the problem. I felt weird and awkward. My sisters would talk about homecoming, or the school letting them go to prom as sophomores, or getting asked out by one popular guy after the next. I just felt I was missing out on so much. I felt invisible, unimportant. Whenever I'd go out and people would know who I was, I was never 'Hanna Gilbert.' I was always 'Kelsey's sister' or 'Brooke's sister' or 'The Twins' sister.' But never 'Hanna.' Because I was nothing on my own."

"So you felt like you were constantly living in their shadow?" CeCe asks, her eyes wide.

"I am a shadow," Hanna responds. "Do you remember when Reece met me? The first thing out of her mouth was, 'Oh, you must be Kelsey and Brooke's sister.' How am I ever going to live up to that? I can't live up to that. I will never live up to that. And I'm okay with that, because I don't want to. I don't care about being the homecoming queen. I don't want to go to WSU like everybody else in my family. I want to travel the world and see Burning Man and ride around in Emilio's lowrider. My favorite shoe is the Air Jordan 3, but I've never even worn them outside of the house because girls don't wear those at our school. Roxie does. Roxie doesn't care. But I do, and I can't help it."

"I'll wear them." Nick shrugs. "I've got little feet."

I look at Nick's face, praying he's joking. CeCe bites her lip and looks down, Hanna starts giggling, and finally, I let loose, and the girls and I laugh hysterically in unison. Nick holds his poker face for a couple of seconds longer before his face splits into a huge grin.

"I got you that time," he chuckles. "You should've seen your faces."

"It's totally something you'd say, though," CeCe snickers. "Right?"

"Yup," I say. "Remember? 'CeCe's pregnant?'"

"Oh, jeez," Hanna slaps her forehead. "I wanted to kill him."

Nick smirks. "You wouldn't be the first."

"Aracely could take you to Burning Man," CeCe offers. "She goes every other year."

"And I take Emilio's low-low out all the time," Nick adds. "Just around the neighborhood, so it doesn't sit. Come ride with me sometime."

I meet her eyes. "And wear your Jordans. Don't take them off."

"But CeCe," Nick says, turning to her, "it's important for a boy to know who he is. Who his father is. Where he comes from. And you and Erik? Well, you'll both grow a lot once that baby is born. It just happens. My dad once told me the scariest day of his life was when I was born. He was happy, but he was scared. And I think most guys are like this, no matter how old they are or how much money they have or how secure their job is."

I nod. "What he said. And remember, Erik's a boy. A scared little boy who did what any stupid kid would do. But he came back. He came clean. Call me crazy, but I've known grown men who still haven't done that."

"Warren Gilbert," Hanna offers up. "He had a high-paying job, went to college and grad school. He was thirty-something when I was born. Founded and sold two businesses. All that, and he still hasn't said the words 'I'm sorry' for completely ruining our lives. I don't know if he gets it, even all these years later. Erik's more of a man than he'll ever be."

"I hope so," CeCe says, rubbing her stomach absently. "We'll still have to see. But if his parents are on board, and he's on board, I'm pretty sure he's not going anywhere this time. Will we get back together? I don't know. Will I be one of those single moms you see at the mall pushing a stroller, calming down their screaming kid while my friends are off at college? It could happen. Will I end up one of those tired-looking women who can't control their kid while he or she gets into all sorts of trouble because I'm busy working three jobs? I swore I wouldn't be, but…"

"Or you stay in school," Hanna breaks in. "Graduate and go on to go to college part-time while working. You and Erik fall in love all over again. Get married. Start a family together. Become partners in life, and everything else."

"You can do all of the above regardless of whether or not Erik's in the picture," I say firmly. "You're one of the most capable people I know."

"Sometimes people have to lose something to realize the value of what they lost," Nick points out. "You and Erik? You were each other's only everything. You've created a life between you. You share a history together. How long have you two known each other?"

"Since the sixth grade," CeCe says quietly. "First day."

"There you go," Nick replies. "Erik knows what it's like to be on his own now. He got manhandled in front of you, which was humiliating. He jerks off horses for money, which is even more humiliating. But few things are more pathetic than leaving somebody pregnant and alone, especially where there was love."

"And he found his way back to you," Hanna says. "Emilio wasn't there to force him. He found you on his own. He didn't stop supporting you. He made sure you got that money. Erik isn't perfect, and he was kind of stupid there for a while, but it seems he might be okay after all."

"Bring him over sometime," Nick adds. "Like, I know we've never been formally introduced, but…"

"Why not?" Hanna agrees. "Not all the time, but once or twice. Let him know there are people backing you. And the baby."

"Yeah, maybe," CeCe says, sounding unsure. "I don't want to rush into things either. Like, we've been out a few times, and we talk, but it's not the same. I don't respond to him the way I did before. I don't know if I can respect him as a man again. My heart might be willing to forgive, but my body and brain remember."

"It takes time," Hanna assures her. "Plus, you're pregnant. All those hormones. We're already emotional creatures as it is, but add a baby to the mix…"

"Just live," Nick advises. "Plan everything and it goes to hell. See where life takes you. Try your best, but depend on yourself where you can."

"Well, my blood pressure just went down," CeCe says with a laugh, leaning down and shaking free her long, wavy hair. She combs her fingers through before pulling it off her face again into a loose pony. "I feel calmer. I feel happy. I'm glad we had this talk. Why are we so hard on ourselves when we have all this wisdom?"

Nick jumps in. "Because we never listen to our own advice?"

Hanna smiles. "I'm starting to think so."

I'm unusually quiet, and while Hanna and Nick are laughing and swapping jokes, CeCe picks up on this.

"Roxie," she says quietly. "Is there something on your mind?"

"Oh, no," I say quickly. "Nothing. Just drifted."

CeCe holds my gaze. "Are you sure?"

I shake my head. "I can't do this. You guys are brave. Putting everything out there in the open like that. It's great. I mean, I feel like everybody's happier now, and we can move on and go see stuff. Problem solved." I smile broadly and point down the pier. "Who's up for the aquarium?"

"Maybe in a bit," Nick cuts in, turning away from Hanna. "But I want to hear it from you."

"Hear what?" I furrow my brow.

"The truth," Nick replies. "I mean, we've all done it. We've all put it all out there. I'm done internalizing. I'm not going to be like Baba and keep it bottled inside until I blow up and scream at my kids over random shit. I'm not going to be held hostage by my fear or regret. I'm done."

"Well, that was a great bar mitzvah speech," I say. "But I'm ready for some action. Let's go see the piranhas."

"But Nick's right," Hanna says. "We all know you better than that. Come on, Roxie. Just talk to us. You don't have to spill everything. Just let us in a little."

"Who said I needed anything?" I challenge. "Uh, last I checked, I was doing well. I mean, I've managed to keep you three going while building Chaz a closet Rock Hudson would be proud of. Trust me, I'm fine."

"Except you're not," Nick insists. "I've watched you this entire year, and with what you've had to put up with, there's no way anybody would come out of that unscathed."

"What was so bad?" I snap. "Suspension? Emilio getting deported? Chaz being bullied to the point where he was almost suicidal because of something I did? Brawling in the cafeteria? Fighting with Mom? What Owen did to me?" I clench my jaw. "That's life. We all have to deal with unpleasant shit. It happens. It could've been much worse."

"What did Owen do to you?" Nick asks, his voice barely audible. His eyes look worried before clouding over with anger. "Why don't I know about this?"

"Owen grabbed my boob under my shirt," I say with forced casualness. "It's the reason why Hanna broke up with him. He was obsessed with me, and he made a move in the worst type of way. I hit him. Hanna neutered him with her bare hands. Blaze literally ran him over. He got his. It's cool."

"Why didn't you tell me?" Nick demands. "You just told me he came onto you. If I'd have known he assaulted you, I would've…"

"That's exactly why," I retort. "You think you need more trouble? Trust me. That would hurt me a lot worse than one boob grab at a movie theater."

"Don't worry about me," Nick says firmly. "I'm tougher than I look."

"I know that," I reply quietly. "I just didn't want anybody to know."

Nick doesn't say anything, but nods. CeCe looks down at her feet. Hanna reaches her arm out and touches my hand but stays silent.

"It wasn't your fault," CeCe says finally. "Things like that, they don't make you dirty. The only person who should feel dirty is Owen himself."

"I know," I say, even though I'm having a harder time believing it. "It's just that I don't even want to think about it. I feel gross, like I made him do it just by sitting there. Maybe I should've worn a hoodie or sat on the other side of him."

"It wasn't your fault," Hanna insists. "Owen's a dickhead. An entitled, terrible person. Good guys don't do that. Normal guys don't do that. Owen's the type of guy, I see now, the type of guy who takes a drunk girl back to his dorm. Who gets married and carries on an old fling on the side because he can. Who takes care of his own needs and burns everybody else."

"Which is why he's with Tiffany," CeCe adds. "Trash brings in the trash."

"It wasn't even a big deal," I say, desperate to change the subject. "It was the day it happened that got me."

"What day was it?" Hanna asks.

"February twenty-third."

"Oh, man," Nick says, looking at his hands. "Okay, yeah, I get it now."

"I didn't even go to the cemetery," I say abruptly. "We always go. Every year. You, me, Mom. Stay for a bit, just stick together. It feels like the one time we're all in one place, you know?"

"I went," Nick replies. "Skipped class. Went there in the morning to pay my respects. I'm just glad it wasn't snowing. I don't think I could've handled that."

"Mom went, too," I say, my voice sounding far away. "I know because she was still crying when she got home. I heard her come in, but she went out again. I didn't see her again that night."

"I did," Nick says, chewing his lip. "She was pretty messed up. We were supposed to all go together, but I'd already gone, and so had she. It's not really something any of us enjoy doing."

"I hate going," I burst out, my throat beginning to feel full. "I hate seeing his name on the headstone. I hate seeing the date. It's like every year, I feel more and more like a visitor. His face is blurry in my mind now, and I can't look at the photo albums because they just make me feel worse."

"I know," Nick says hoarsely. "I get it. I feel it every year, every day. Every hour. When I get in a car. Whenever it snows at night. I can be anywhere, going along just fine, and then suddenly, I'm upside down with the seatbelt cutting into my throat covered in blood. *His* blood."

Hanna claps a hand to her mouth. "You were there?"

"I was in the car with him," Nick chokes out. "I saw it happen. We were driving, and suddenly, we were airborne. Late at night. Black ice all over the roads. And Baba was a good driver—that was the thing. He was experienced. But it got us. I mean, if you think about what he went through before that. The Revolution. Serving in the war. Almost getting shot when he was working at the liquor store back in San Bernardino. But that? On that road? If you asked me what I thought the odds were of that happening, like two months before, I would've said zero to none. Baba drove that road every day coming back from Yakima. He knew that road like the back of his hand."

"The call woke us up," I recall, remembering waking up to the sound of the phone in the middle of the night. "You guys were coming back from a party or something."

"Yeah," Nick says, wiping a rogue tear off his cheek with his sleeve. "It was Baba's friend's birthday. I didn't want to go, but we both said we'd be there, so we went. The whole way over, we didn't talk. I guess we were still pissed off at each other over some stupid shit. I don't even remember what that fight was about. But the party was fun. I enjoyed seeing everybody. I finally got to wear the sport coat I'd bought the year before. Everybody was dancing and talking and just having a good time. And he seemed happy, you know. Like he wasn't so uptight and stressed all the time."

"He loved parties," I say, my voice sounding strangled. "Catching up with people. He lived for that kind of stuff."

"At least he died happy," Nick points out. "In a way. Like, I don't know what was going on in his head in his last moments. But on the way home? He seemed okay. We even got to talking a little bit, about how he could act sometimes and how it affected me." Nick laughs tiredly. "Isn't that typical?"

"What's typical?" I ask.

"Right as we're starting to rekindle things, he dies!" Nick chokes out a sharp laugh. "Right as things are beginning to go well again, they don't."

I sigh. "I can see where you're going with this."

"Think about it," Nick says. "We get in a fight over something stupid. Probably because I didn't do yard work or something around the house exactly the way he asked, when he wanted it. Then he pulls the silent treatment bullshit, and instead focuses on you and Mom because…I don't know. You two are the only people around he isn't pissed at. He probably doesn't even want to go with me to this party, but he will because it'll make *him* look bad if I'm not there. It'll make *his* family look bad in front of people. Maybe if he would have tried to fix things with us instead of keeping up fake appearances, I wouldn't be stuck wrestling with the guilt and confusion and could just focus on missing him."

"I know," I say. "I'm so lost. I feel guilty, like I should miss him more, but I don't. There's just this hollow space. This empty, dead space nothing will ever fill again."

"That we can't run away from," Nick adds. He pulls a napkin out of his pocket and wipes his eyes quickly. "I know."

"And it kills me," I say. "Nothing ever just *happens*. Whenever something bad happens, it's that…and then he's dead. I get a bad grade, and Baba's dead. I get in a fight with Mom, and Baba's fucking dead. It's always this horrible multiplier of whatever misery I've got going on. I thought it would get better with time, but it doesn't! It just gets harder."

"I barely even talk to our family in Iran anymore," Nick says quietly. "I know you don't remember much Farsi, but I call maybe once or twice a year. And I dread it. Because even if we don't talk about him, I'm going to hang up as soon as the call's over. I'm not going to pass Baba the receiver, and he won't pass it to me. I won't hear him laugh about something crude or use bad language and have Mom get on his case. It's pointless now, just like everything else."

"It's not pointless," CeCe says abruptly. "It isn't. Your family, your dad's culture. His family. Are they good people?"

"Most of them," I say. "Some are kind of *eh*, but they're all right."

"They're decent," Nick agrees. "They'd basically do anything for you if you needed help."

"And the language you speak, what was it called?"

"Farsi." Nick nods. "I speak it. Roxie kind of does."

"I understand everything," I say. "But I mostly don't speak because… well, I don't know."

"Talk to them," CeCe insists. "Even if it's just for a few minutes. They're your dad's family. They're your family, and they love you. It might hurt at first because you both know he's gone. But it's important to understand where you come from and to keep that part of you alive. The dad part."

"You're right," I say, wringing my hands. "I should be better about it. Maybe they just want to hear a piece of him in us."

"Yeah," Nick sighs, looking out at the Sound. "People say I sound like him over the phone. It's kind of funny. I mean, he had a super thick accent. Like, we couldn't hear it, but everybody else could."

I smile. "I always thought they were making it up."

"And we look a lot like him," Nick says. "Same hair, same eyes."

"We're hella pasty, though," I laugh. "Especially you. You go in the sun and look like a Hot Tamale."

"I tan," Nick argues. "I just need to build a base first."

CeCe giggles. "I'm tan year-round."

Hanna rolls her eyes. "I gave up."

"Did I change after Baba died?" I ask as the four of us begin walking. I shove my hands in my pockets and look down. "Like, a lot?"

"We both did," Nick says after a brief pause. "Whether or not we wanted to. Mom definitely isn't the same. I'm not. But you? Yeah, you changed a lot. Why?"

"I hate myself," I confess. "Who I became. I don't even recognize myself anymore. It's not like I don't try. I do, but I just don't have patience for people's bullshit. People say or do stuff, and I can't handle it. I can't act or react normally. Who the hell rides a bike through Bargain World and then runs over the manager on the way out? What if Chaz killed himself after I made that poster? What if Edgar did? Kicking that lacrosse dude in the back of the head. That was terrible! I shouldn't have done that. I was so angry after he knocked CeCe down I actually wanted him to die. All I saw was red.

"I've lost it," I conclude. "I'm gone. I try to help people whenever I can, but when it comes down to it, I'm not a good person."

"Well then, I'm a horrible person," Hanna pipes up. "And so are Nick and CeCe and Chaz and everybody else you've ever known. People make mistakes. People screw up. It doesn't mean you're a bad person."

"I wish everybody was as bad as Roxie," CeCe says. "I wish Roxie were as bad as it got. Then, this world could be a paradise. Everybody would stand by each other. Loyalty would be the number-one rule, and it would never get broken. People would actually show love and not just talk about it."

"There'd never be a dull moment," Nick chuckles. "Boredom wouldn't exist. Everything would be funny all the time, and nothing would be politically correct. Everybody would wear black and air guitar to Skid Row and carry out ninjutsu attacks on douchebags."

We all laugh at that one. "That doesn't sound bad to me," I say with a small smile.

"And people would be selfless," Hanna continues. "Their first priority would be other people. They'd give friendship and love unconditionally. They'd listen to you and really care about you, not just say they did. They'd tell the truth even when it hurt."

"But I don't give it unconditionally," I blurt out. "I don't give anything without wanting something in return. In the back of my mind, I'm always afraid I'm too much and that people are going to leave, or can't handle me, or think I'm weird and won't want to come around anymore. Sometimes, I don't know I'm even doing it, but I just want people around because sometimes they leave and don't come back." I sniffle. "Baba would be ashamed of me. And I already know Mom is."

"She's not," Nick says sharply. "Oh God, no. Mom loves you more than you'll ever understand. I don't think any of us can even understand it until we have kids of our own. And she's proud. She's so, so proud of you. She actually laughed about your Brennan attack. I mean, you're like two inches above midget, and you did Shaolin moves on giant athletes to protect a friend. You could've been hurt, but you didn't even think about yourself. Not a lot of people can say the same."

"What would even make you think that, Roxie?" Hanna asks. "Did something happen?"

I stare at my sneakers. "I don't really want to talk about it."

"Baba was proud of you, too," Nick says. "And the things I learned about him after he died? He was a total brat as a kid. Even worse as a teenager. Remember when he used to tell us that story about befriending the black pony?"

"Yeah."

"He stole it!" Nick exclaims. "Well, kind of. He and his friends went on a day trip out to the countryside and found an old stallion there. Tied up and all alone. At that time, Baba had a serious crush on a girl who loved horses. He wanted to impress her, so his friends kept a lookout while he jumped the fence and rode the horse back to her house."

"What!" My mouth falls open. "He always told me he rescued it!"

"Well, that's the thing," Nick laughs. "As it turns out, Baba Suleiman, our grandfather, was going to make Baba give it back. But after asking around, they found out the horse was going to be slaughtered that week. The farmer had no more use for it, and it was too old to work. It had just been left somewhere in the meantime. So Baba kept it and saved its life, and it lived a good couple more years."

"Damn," I say. "I never knew that side of it. Why didn't he tell us that part?"

"Probably because we were young and impressionable," Nick replies. "Especially me. I thought he was the greatest person in the world back then. I would've stolen ten horses if I'd heard that side of it."

"I wish he would've," I say wistfully. "It might've made me see a different side of him. A fun side."

"My point in telling you all that," Nick continues, "is that sometimes you might not start out with the best intentions, but you end up doing the right thing. And if you tell me you help and befriend people because you desperately need people around and want human interaction, well. That's kind of what friends are for."

Hanna laughs. "Yeah, basically. I mean, if friends don't make you happy or cheer you up in return for you helping them or including them, then they're pretty crappy friends."

CeCe shrugs. "I don't believe you, Roxie. But if you can look me in the eye right now and tell me you helped me just because you were hoping I'd join your group and keep you company, then I'm glad you're selfish."

"Be selfish," Hanna says. "But let me say this: the last person on earth I ever imagined you becoming friends with is on this trip with us. He's not here right now, but you managed to find somebody to help him when you couldn't. And tell me, when you took him out for yogurt the day he came out to you, were you thinking of what he could do for you?"

"No," I say automatically. "It didn't even cross my mind."

"I know that," Hanna says, smiling. "And everybody here knows that. That just leaves you. You need to know that."

"Well, thanks." I take a lungful of salty air. "I no longer feel like a giant bitch. I guess I'm okay."

"You're as good as they come," Hanna replies. "Screw anybody who says otherwise."

"Seriously," CeCe agrees. "Don't get so down on yourself. People like you always blame themselves for everything. Most people blame others. It's because you're so good you take responsibility even when you're not responsible, because you want to fix everything."

"What she said." Nick smiles. "You're okay, kid. I mean, there was a time there I wasn't sure how you were going to turn out. Whether or not you'd get through the storm intact. That one day you might just stop keeping it real. But you did."

"Are we always going to be this close?" I wonder aloud as a flock of seagulls flies overhead. "Will we always be like this? Us? This group?"

"I hope so," CeCe says. "And I hope we do. But you're right. Things change. People grow up, move away. Get stuck in life."

"True," Hanna says, winding her arms around CeCe and me. "And nothing stays the same. Not even the good stuff. I hope so, though."

"Well, are we?" Nick looks at us. "Are we going to stay this way?"

I frown. "Well, that's kind of what we're trying to figure out."

"Yeah, but are you or aren't you?" Nick crosses his arms. "Like, if you make a point of staying in each other's lives, checking in and picking up the phone even when you're dead tired, then it'll still be like this. Maybe not the way it was when you all were living blocks away from each other, going to the same school and stuff. But as long as you all check in with each other regularly and make it a priority to keep this going, then I don't see why not."

I nod. "I get what you mean. And it's not like I want to be a teenager forever—God, no. But I'm going to miss this."

"I know," Nick says. "And I get it. Sometimes I want to go back to the bad times because even in those times, there were good times. And I'll never get to experience those good times again. But there'll be other good times, you'll see. Better times, even."

"My mom tells me that," Hanna says. "You know her. High school was her prime. But when I asked her about it, she told me she would never want to go back. For anything."

"It's kind of like Emilio said," CeCe says. "We remember things the way we want to remember them. Meaning, we forget the bad stuff. I guess that's how we move on."

"Otherwise, we'd jump out a window," Nick agrees. He pauses. "Let's just promise ourselves we'll do it."

Hanna raises an eyebrow. "Jump out a window?"

"No," Nick laughs. "I meant stay in each other's lives."

"I promise," I say at once.

Hanna grabs my hand and gives it a squeeze. "I promise."

CeCe nods. "Promise."

"Promise," Nick echoes. "But I am Roxie's brother, so even if I didn't want to…"

I roll my eyes. "This was practically all your idea. One of your better ones, I might add."

"Well," Hanna says cheerily, looking down at her phone. "Chaz just texted. He wants to know where we are."

I scrunch my face. "That wasn't very long."

"It's been over an hour," CeCe points out. "We've been talking for a while."

"I guess." I nudge Hanna. "Tell him to meet us at the aquarium."

***

Milling around aimlessly, we decided to hold off on the aquarium until Chaz shows up. Nick said we should just go in and then text him where we are, but I want to go in as a group. Though I'm feeling refreshed from our conversation, I can't help but wonder why Chaz's morning out on the town was so short. If you do the math, the drive to Seattle was over four times longer than his outing with Willie,

413

Theo, and Elaine, and that was the entire reason we came here. Well, one of the reasons. Aracely is way cool, and Seattle's not too shabby either. I'd like to see more of it, but we're only here for two days. I can always come back in the summer next time Nick and Frankie visit, though I'm not sure how well I'll get along with Topaz the Man Cat.

"Where's Chaz?" Hanna asks, coming up behind me and wrapping me in a hug. She must sense that the conversation we had earlier did an emotional number on me. "Is he on his way yet?"

"I hope so," I reply. "I wish he would've been here with us when we were talking about all that. I just wanted him close."

"Yeah." Hanna smiles. "You and your man. You two should just get married for the benefits."

I laugh. "We actually made a pact to do just that if we're both still spinsters by thirty-five."

Hanna looks up. "There he is."

Jogging towards us, Chaz waves to the group. His sneakers slap the pavement before he stops in front of us. "Hey, guys."

"How'd it go?" I ask eagerly.

"Good, good," he says. "Really good. They're nice people. Good folks to know. Where're CeCe and Nick?"

"They're around," Hanna says, frowning. "You weren't gone that long, though."

"Ah." Chaz scratches his head absently. "There wasn't that much to go over. I had some questions, they answered them, and we all got coffee together. I've got a thing for macchiatos now, I guess." He laughs. "What have you guys been up to?"

"Hanging out," I say. "We talked a lot. Saw some wild stuff in a curiosity shop. You want to go?"

"Let's catch it on the way back from the aquarium," Chaz says. "I did see that mummy from the picture you sent. Looked pretty good for being, what, a hundred years old?"

Hanna shoots him a look. "Are you crushing on Sylvester?"

"He's dead," I say. "Plus, I really don't think Chaz would need to go down that road."

Chaz rolls his eyes. "I mean, older men can be hot and everything, but keep it under a century please. I do have standards."

"Let's go," I say, laughing. "Nick's desperate to see the otter pups. Let's not keep him waiting."

"Totally," Chaz says breathlessly. "I'm down."

Hanna starts off towards the entrance, but I don't move. "Hang back a second, Chaz."

He raises an eyebrow. "Are we good?"

"Yeah, yeah." I lower my voice. "I just…I don't know. Did it go okay today? Everything was good?"

"Yeah, of course." He smiles. "It was great. Really."

"Okay." I pause. "I just wanted to make sure."

"This city's amazing," Chaz says, grinning. "Aracely called it a small town, but to me? We might as well be in Manhattan." He twirls around. "Are you sleepless in Seattle, Roxanne?"

"I slept like the dead," I laugh. "That car ride wiped me out."

"I could stay here another few days and just soak it all in," Chaz says, his eyes full of wonder. "The buildings. The views of the Sound. Everything's so green. Have you guys tried the food yet?"

"No," I say. "We were waiting for you. Aracely's cooking tonight, but we'll eat lunch in the city."

"Sick." Chaz nods. "Can't wait."

CeCe calls to us from up ahead. "We'd better go," I say. "We wanted to save the aquarium for you, too."

"Appreciate it." Chaz gives my wrist a squeeze as we both start towards the aquarium's entrance. "And thanks for waiting up."

They say time flies when you're having fun, and today has proven that to be true. Much to Nick's delight, we managed to witness feeding time for the otters and harbor seals at the aquarium, and after that, we hit up the downtown area and grabbed lunch at an authentic Japanese spot. As it turns out, Jimi Hendrix is buried a twenty-minute drive away from downtown, and Kurt Cobain's house is somewhere off by Lake Washington. We didn't end up crossing paths with any of the Microsoft founders, but still, the day was a blast. After lunch, we decided to abandon any attempt at planning and opted instead to meander around, seeing the city in action. We ended up at Pike Place Market, where Nick bought an assortment of handmade soaps and soy candles for Mom, and Chaz picked up a pair of crocheted mittens.

"Could you see yourself here?" I ask Hanna as we zigzag throughout the various stalls and displays. "There's a lot more to do here than back home, that's for sure."

"You could say that again," Hanna says, craning her neck to see a fishmonger send a salmon airborne. "I don't think I'd be bored once."

"There's definitely a different energy here," I observe, treading carefully on the wet sidewalk. "I don't know if it's good or bad, but you can feel it. It's alive. People are doing things."

"Yeah, I get that," Hanna says. "Back home, it seems that once people grow up, they don't do anything. They just stay close to home, get stuck in their boring jobs, and hang out with the same people. Like, we kind of do that now, you know?"

"Yeah." I nod. "That seems to be the norm in a small town."

"True," Hanna says. "But I don't know if I'd come here."

I stare at her. "Why not?"

"It's so...huge. I feel like it would swallow me up."

"You've never lived anywhere else, have you?" I ask. "Before Chester?"

"No," Hanna replies. "We moved there when I was just a baby. Before that, we lived in Montana, but my mom went to Chester High, so she wanted to come back. God knows why."

"Well, supposedly most people don't end up living further than twenty miles away from where they grew up," I say. "My mom couldn't wait to get out of California, though. She never wants to live there again."

"I get that," Hanna says. "I want to leave Chester more than anything. But I don't think this is the place."

"You should at least see the UDub before you decide," I point out. "It's not downtown, either. It's located in a whole other area we haven't seen yet."

Hanna nods. "I will."

"I want to come back this summer," I say. "I think we all should. We've got a friend here now, and once CeCe's baby is born, she won't be able to travel much. At least for the first year or so. It's so cool here and only like a four-hour drive away."

"I want to see Boise, too," Hanna says. "I've never been. Kelsey and Brooke go all the time with their boyfriends, and they love it. Good skiing. Cute town."

"We can visit there next," I suggest. "Nick can drive. Or by next year, maybe just you and I can go."

"Yo!" Chaz bounds over, dressed in a fake lion's-fur cape from a nearby stand. "Check it out."

"See," Nick chuckles, appearing moments later in a bejeweled plush crown. "Dress up can still be fun once you're grown."

I smirk. "You two seem to enjoy role-playing."

"Ugh." Nick makes a face. "Did you have to take it there?"

Chaz shrugs off the cape and balls it up. "He's not my type. Sorry, Nicky."

"I think I better take these back," Nick says as the cashier eyes them warily. "Chaz, hand over the cape."

Chaz pouts. "Can't I cuddle it for, like, two more seconds?"

Nick rolls his eyes. "Just buy it if you love it so much."

Without needing further encouragement, Chaz buys the cape and proceeds to wear it around. A couple of old timers stare, but the reactions are positive. We linger around Pike Place a little longer before heading back toward the main drag, where rush hour is in full swing and cars are backed up in every direction. We take a group shot by an enormous hammering man sculpture outside of the art museum and, without anywhere to be, enjoy each other's company.

I've noticed the past few hours that something about Chaz is decidedly different. I don't know if it was meeting with Aracely's friends this morning, the vibrancy of the city at this time of day, or just getting out of Chester for the weekend, but he's *alive*. Whether he's trying to put Nick in a headlock, running around like a superhero in his fur cape, or cracking self-deprecating jokes, I feel like a weight has been lifted off him. He seems comfortable, almost like he's starting to come into his own, and while people are always more fun on vacation, I feel like something's shifted in him for the better. Since he became a part of the group, Chaz and Nick have gotten close. It's nice to see those two, different as they are, trying to spar with each other or laughing about stupid stuff the way guys do. Besides Nick, Chaz doesn't have any male friends, and while us girls love him to death, there's something important about having at least one bro that he can count on.

"I need a pick-me-up," Chaz announces, reaching into his wallet. He points across the street. "Who wants gelato?"

The rest of us chorus our agreement.

"Let's each get a scoop," he says. "My treat."

The five of us snag a large table outside the shop, soaking in the warmth of the late afternoon. Chaz, seated across from me, shoots me a huge grin.

"This has been a perfect afternoon," he states. "I love you guys. And I love you for bringing me here."

Hanna picks up her gelato cup and holds it in the center of the table for a toast. "To our friendship," she says.

My heart feels full. "To our friendship," I echo. I spoon some gelato into my mouth and take a mental snapshot of this moment to ensure that I never forget it.

Chapter 18

"I can't keep doing this," Chaz says, his voice cracking. "I just can't."

Back in seventh grade, I went through an interesting phase. I acted so unlike myself that I would wake up in the morning and forget who I was by breakfast. Despite this, many people at school responded positively to the new me, and a few even started copying my style, attitude, and opinions. Some might label this transformation a success or even say I was moving up in the world. Yet even though I'd achieved my goal of sitting at the popular table at lunch and being affiliated with the "it" girls, I was still falling every step of the way.

The only person who dared to address this was Nick. One day, when I was on my way out the door to hang with some older kids I didn't really know, he stopped me. At first, I was defensive and became angry when he questioned my sudden turnaround, but eventually, I let it all out and told him the truth about how I felt. Not just about school, or boys or friends, but everything I'd ever felt about myself. From that point forward, I gradually slipped back into my old self—a lot less popular, but a whole lot wiser and adjusted.

Though Chaz just called himself a "pathetic homo" mere minutes ago, I don't think anybody would buy it. A regular now in the weight room, Chaz is unrecognizable from the oversexed fat kid he was at the beginning of the year or even from the quietly funny, reliable confidant he became to me after suspension. In fact, I don't know much about him now, as he's cut ties with all of us. He still gives me a nod every now and then or a brief hello in passing, but otherwise, Chaz can only be heard from by telephone at odd hours of the night. Despite the sting of his unexplained abandonment, I'm devoted to him and haven't let a single call go to voicemail, though Hanna and CeCe tell me I should back off and let him go.

The strangest part about all of it? Chaz left us all on great terms. After we finished our excursion downtown, we spent our last night in Seattle eating bowls of the delicious pozole Aracely and Nick cooked and watched *Dude, Where's My Car?* before bed. In the morning, Aracely gave us each a hug, told us we were the coolest teenagers she'd ever met, and to promise to write to her every now and again. We thanked her about ten times on the way out and the whole way home had a blast. When we finally dropped Chaz off, he didn't want to leave and begged Nick and me to adopt him so the party could go on.

"You guys are so effing cool," Chaz said as he grabbed his duffel bag out of the Honda. "Please, just talk to Inez. I need to get out of that nuthouse."

"You could probably just move in," Nick suggested. "I mean, Mom's barely home. I don't think she'd even notice."

"We'll think of a plan," I said. "There's central heating. You could stay in the garage until we get the guest room ready."

"No, not the guest room," Chaz laughed. "The 'Chaz Chamber.' Has a good ring to it."

"Chaz chamber" must have been code for "I'm leaving your life forever" because the following Monday, Chaz was nowhere to be found. He didn't appear until lunch, and when he did, he was smack in the middle of the drama table. Hanna, CeCe, and I each texted him countless times, but all our texts went unanswered. I couldn't figure it out to save my life. Neither could the other two. By the end of the week, aside from a few chance sightings, Chaz completely vanished from our lives. Well, almost.

"But I like myself," Chaz continues. "I like the way I am now. I'm stronger, I'm better looking, and people don't talk shit to me. New and improved, right?"

"I suppose," I say evenly. "And?"

"Reece and I are talking now," Chaz continues. "We're, like, comfortable around each other, and the rest of her friends are pretty cool, too. Phil and the other guys, we talk about all sorts of stuff. Girls, movies. Going camping this summer in Idaho. I finally feel life is working out for me. I always wanted to be part of something like this."

"Well, that's great," I say, hoping the bitterness I feel isn't evident in my tone. "Then what's the issue?"

"Other days, I hate myself," Chaz says. "I feel fake. I'm not them. Everything I do takes so much planning. Making sure I don't say the wrong thing. Not to make them dislike me for any reason whatsoever or out myself by accident. If I have to think this hard, whatever 'this' is isn't me, is it?"

"I think you're way overthinking it, dude," I say tiredly. "You're happy. They like you. The end. Life isn't a coloring book. I mean, jeez, look at where you were earlier this year. Be glad people aren't squirting lube on you or finding you on a flyer. Enjoy the peaks."

"You're right." Chaz coughs. "Sorry to keep you up." The line goes dead.

Under normal circumstances, I'd tell him to take his midnight pontificating and shove it, but since he seems to hate being gay now, that could just complicate things. Instead, I listen to whatever he throws at me during our late-night talks. Being the enabler I am, I will continue to allow him to live his double life and ignore the people who love him most.

***

"I mean it," Nick says, shaking his head in disappointment. "Taking him to Seattle was a huge mistake."

Seven in the morning, I've barely slept. I'm slouched at the kitchen table, and Nick is begging me to try his silver-dollar pancakes with boysenberry jam. Ordinarily, they'd smell delicious, but today, I want to hurl.

"Can you not."

Nick holds up his hands. "I'm just saying. Technically, I'm just as guilty." He shrugs, fixing his own plate and plunking down across from me. "I drove you there. Don't tell me how, but I had a feeling it wasn't going to go well. I just knew it was going to do more harm than good. Call it a gut feeling."

"*What* harm?" I say, sitting up straight. "*What* didn't go well? It wasn't like they took him to a motel and ran a train on him. They took him out for coffee!"

Nick saws at a sausage link with his dull knife. "Maybe he'd have preferred the train. I mean, that's certainly immersive."

I exhale. "You're not helping."

"But really," Nick says. "How could it have been bad? Willie, or Will, whatever his name was, seemed hilarious. I wanted to go just to hear his inappropriate commentary on everything."

"That's what I thought too," I say. "They seemed nice enough. A little odd, but so are we."

"They're Aracely's friends," Nick assures. "She wouldn't send him with them if they were bad news. Maybe it's something else bothering him."

"Come *on*," I persist. "We both know something happened there. The meeting with Aracely's friends was the sole variable. We sent him one way and got him back another."

"I know," Nick admits. "But I haven't heard anything from him since, and I'm guessing neither has anybody else. If anybody's going to find out, it's you. You're his best friend."

***

"I don't know what I was so worried about," Chaz says later that night. Sounding way more upbeat than before, he's describing his day to me, and while I want to share in the positivity, everything he's saying sounds phony and contrived.

"I mean, a lot of people at school are actually super nice," Chaz continues. "The ones who matter, anyway. Yeah, I know what some of them did to me and how they treated me when all that went down, but still."

I say nothing, even though I want to scream.

Chaz pauses. "What I'm saying is, it isn't like this place totally blows. Nobody bothers me in the gym. Well, not really." He takes a breath. "Brennan and Spencer are a no-show now. I sometimes see Victor, but he doesn't say anything without his honchos around. Maybe we were worried for nothing this whole time."

"I wasn't worried," I say, sharper than I mean to. "I mean, yeah, people can be cruel, but most of us are just trying to live our lives and get by. Also, the older we get, the more the drama, and the 'he said, she said' all die away. Pretty soon it'll be SATs. College plans. Graduation. Nothing else will matter."

"How've you been?" Chaz asks after a long pause.

"Come see me sometime and find out," I say coolly. "It's been a while since we played catch up."

"I will," he says. "I want to see you guys so bad. I've just been super busy."

"With the play?"

"Yeah, and the gym. And with Reece."

"Reece?" I sputter. "As in *girl* Reece?"

I hear Chaz swallow sharply on the other end. "Yeah. Her."

I take a deep breath. "You guys aren't...dating...are you?"

"Well, no. I mean, not exactly." Chaz coughs. "How do I explain this?"

"Chaz?" I say, dumbfounded. "I think you need to try."

"I—well."

My heart sinks. "Are you gay?" I whisper.
"Roxie, I—I don't know."

***

"There she is," Hanna mutters. "Over by the soda machine."

CeCe, Hanna, and I crane our necks to see Reece strutting by, hoop earrings glistening in the fluorescent lights of the cafeteria. I used to like seeing her walk, but now she just irks me. She purchases a can of something orange and skips over to her table, swinging her long legs over the seat and snuggling up against Chaz.

CeCe's mouth is hanging open. "Are they *together*?"

"Looks like it," I reply. I take a violent bite out of my peanut-butter sandwich and curl my toes inside my shoes. Though I haven't said a word to anyone, my last conversation with Chaz has left me unnerved. Three tables over, Reece is giggling at everything Chaz says while constantly finding excuses to touch him or lay her body against his.

I shake my head in disgust. "Get a load of that."

"I'm sorry, but he just pisses me off," Hanna says, snapping a grape off the cluster. "I mean, who was there for him after three years of what he did to us? We were. We forgave him. Nobody else on God's green earth would do that shit." She shakes her head, her blond curls bouncing. "Were any of those theater kids there for him back then? Was Reece there? What about that other guy he's always with? I didn't see any of them sticking up for him back when dirty tampons were being chucked at his face."

"You said it, sister." I feel drained, and it's not even noon. "I don't know. I really don't get it anymore."

"It's like he was never here," CeCe muses. "Last month, we were watching videos at my house, he was braiding my hair, and we were talking about life. What we hoped our futures would look like. Places we wanted to see. But it's been a while. What does he know about my life now? About the pregnancy? Or Hanna's life? Or yours, Roxie? Especially yours?"

"Nothing," I reply flatly.

"Does he care?"

"I don't know," I say, crumpling up my lunch sack and throwing it in Reece's direction. "I can't watch any more of this crap. Let's take a walk."

***

"Do the girls ask about me?"

"Yup."

Chaz lowers his voice. "Do you tell them anything that I've told you?"

"No."

"Why not? I mean, I don't care if you do."

"Because you should be telling them, not me." I struggle to keep the irritation out of my tone. "It's not my place or responsibility to."

Chaz sighs. "I know. I should be better about all this."

"About all what!?" I demand. "Better about what? What the hell happened, Chaz?"

"I don't know," he says, his voice cracking slightly. "I don't know what you mean."

I suck in a breath and will myself not to unload on him. "What happened in Seattle?"

"Nothing happened."

"Yes, it did!"

He feigns confusion. "No, it really didn't."

I sigh in exasperation. "Yes, it did! I'm tired of dancing around this, Chaz. Something clearly happened, and I don't have all night to try and dig it out of you."

"What gave you that idea?" Chaz says. "Like, it was a good trip. I had a blast. You had fun. Right?"

"I sure did," I reply. "But don't think you did. In fact, I know you didn't because as soon as you went home, you ditched us. All of us. Without explanation. Now you're about to enter a civil union with Reece, and we're not even invited to the ceremony. You used to be a part of things. A big part. You were the glue that held our group together. But you couldn't get away fast enough once we got home from Seattle. A trip that we took because of *you*!"

"Well, now I feel like a huge dick," Chaz says. I can hear him shifting uncomfortably on the other line. "But, you see… damn, how do I put this?"

"Just tell me the truth," I plead. "Please."

"I'll tell you some other time," Chaz says quietly. "It wasn't a big deal. Really."

"Well, I hope it was, honestly," I snap. "Because something small shouldn't have triggered this kind of reaction."

"Okay, hold on." He sounds like he's rummaging around in his desk drawer. "Let me make sure no one's listening."

I walk over to my bed and flop down, propping my feet up against the headboard. I don't know what I'm expecting to get out of this, but I've lost a week of sleep so far, so I better get something. I press the phone closer to my ear and listen as Chaz settles down.

"It blew. The meeting was a huge letdown. I mean, that first night, that was nice. Aracely and I still text each other now and again. And it was sweet that you and the girls and Nick would put something together like that for me. But what actually happened…" He pauses. "Let me think about how to say this."

Some time passes before Chaz speaks. "Remember how Aracely said sometimes you aren't born in the right place or the place you're meant to be?"

"Yeah, I remember."

"Well, I'm not meant to be there. In that city. That scene. With those people. Especially with those types of people. I didn't fit in there and never will. So yeah, that's kind of it."

I don't know the first thing about what happened that morning. I am one hundred percent sure there's more to that story. But I've got something to work with now, and at 11:35 on a Thursday, I'm not pressing the issue. Instead, we chat a little longer about the mundane before calling it a night.

***

"No," Hanna murmurs. "This cannot be happening."

Smack dab in the middle of the lunchroom, Reece's arms are wrapped around Chaz's torso, and she's pulling him close. Chaz slides his hands to her waist and folds her into him. The pair, lost in their blissful romance, appear completely unaware of their surroundings, and probably like it that way. It makes sense. The more I see them together, it dawns on me how narcissistic, ego-driven, and selfish both of them actually are. They've become the very center of the drama club and always manage to position themselves in the middle of everything: elevated like royals holding court. The rest of the group goes along with it, either smiling during moments such as these or deliberately directing attention towards them, as if they needed any more encouragement.

Back in the early days of our friendship, Chaz and I used to go scouting for hot guys whenever we got bored. It became our thing. Sometimes, we wouldn't go anywhere in particular and just ride the city bus, since it gave us a good vantage point to see what we could find. We'd point said guy out, ask the other if he was hot or not, and proceed to rate them. I was usually selective, but Chaz typically liked them all.

"I'm a guy," he laughed when I told him he had no standards. "Beggars can't be choosers." It seems like a lifetime ago now. Reece's wrists, obscured by cheap bangles, catch the light as she massages Chaz's hair and continues tonguing him, running her hands along his fresh undercut and tracing his jaw.

"Never thought I'd see the day," Hanna remarks, turning away from the spectacle.

"He's a good kisser," CeCe observes. "Erik was a disaster. Went all the way with him, and he still didn't know what to do with his tongue." She snorts. "Kissing or otherwise."

I laugh. "How is he, by the way?"

"Erik? I mean, it seems like he's doing well. Getting good grades, staying out of trouble. He plays golf for Elderwood now." CeCe runs a hand over her belly, which can no longer be hidden by even the bulkiest of sweatshirts. "He's got a job now too. A real job. He tells me he wants to go to a good college and get us a house." She laughs. "Crazy, right?"

"Have you thought more about getting back together?" Hanna asks. "I mean, it does sound like he's trying to turn it around."

"We've been on a couple more dates," CeCe says. "Coffee. The movies. It isn't like before, obviously. We don't make out or fool around like we used to. Just talk." She sighs. "I don't know. His parents help out a lot and send money. They even stop by the house sometimes to check on me. Part of me feels we kind of have to get back together eventually. Or at least try for the kid."

"Well," Hanna says. "You don't have to make any big decisions just yet."

"I don't know what I'm going to do," CeCe says. "I'm still figuring it out. I mean, my first job is to be a mom now. I'm way more worried about that."

"It's not like you have to do it alone." I squeeze her hand. "We'll help."

"I know." CeCe smiles. "They say it takes a village to raise a child. You're my villagers." She glances down at her stomach. "I think this little one's going to be special."

I laugh and place a hand on her belly to see if I can feel anything. CeCe reported to us when she felt the first kick, but we're yet to be able to feel it from the outside.

"You had a good shot as a midfielder," Hanna recalls, running her palm over CeCe's middle. "I'll know when the kick comes."

"If you do, the baby's Cristiano Ronaldo's," CeCe jokes. "If you feel it running away from you, it's Erik's."

All of us laugh. Barely tilting my gaze, I see Chaz break away from Reece and put his arm around her, drawing her in protectively. CeCe turns to me, reading my thoughts.

"Did Chaz lie?"

"I'm beginning to wonder," I say, thoroughly creeped out.

"Um, he better not have." Hanna shudders. "I've changed in front of him. He's seen my boobs. Tomorrow, he'd better be making out with Phil, or I'll castrate him."

CeCe busts up laughing, but I feel uneasy. The old Chaz would've found that hilarious, but now I don't know. As Reece and Chaz walk out of the cafeteria with linked arms, I realize more and more that CeCe might have a point. Knowing Chaz, he'll call again tonight, which means I've got to be the one to find out.

***

"So yeah. We go out sometimes. It's nothing serious."

"Really? You two are always together," I say, twirling the phone cord around my finger. "The whole school saw the two of you at lunch today playing a competitive game of tonsil hockey."

I've vowed that tonight's the night I'm going to finally get it out of him. It's Friday, which would ordinarily mean Hanna and I would be hanging out, but she had plans with her sisters. CeCe's pulling a little extra cash working a late shift, and Nick's at Frankie's, leaving me at home with my mom, who's somewhere on the other side of the house. Chaz sounds upbeat this evening, and I'm glad because I'll be bringing the hammer down on him hard.

"I mean, it's mostly because we're doing the play together, and we hang out with the same people," Chaz says, pointedly ignoring my remark about what we witnessed at lunch. "She's nice, though. Easy to talk to."

"Are you attracted to her?" I ask bluntly.

Chaz pauses for a moment. "It's hard to explain. Yes. And I'm mostly interested in men, but there's something about her I like. I mean, it's kind of how I liked her as a person, as a friend, and I guess it kind of grew into something more."

"I thought you said you didn't know," I say, feeling slightly relieved. "Remember?"

"That's something else," Chaz says. "And it's a lot harder to verbalize." I can hear his breathing quicken over the phone. "I'm still trying to make sense of that."

I shift in my seat. "I talked to Aracely today." I didn't, but I did talk to her last week. She called to check up on us and thank us for the box of goodies we sent her as a thank-you. What I'm also not telling Chaz is how she repeatedly asked how he was specifically and asked me some other questions about him I didn't know the answers to, almost as if she knew something went on but didn't want to allude to specifics.

"Really?" Chaz's voice wavers. "What'd she say?"

"She wanted to know how you were," I say, wondering if he'll suspect anything.

"I'm super."

"You know," I begin, choosing my words carefully, "we never really got to debrief about your morning out."

"There's nothing to debrief about," Chaz replies swiftly. "We went out, talked, I had some questions, I met some people. That was it."

"Like, you guys just went around, talked, and that was it?"

"Yeah, basically," Chaz confirms. "I'm glad I did it, though."

"You're glad?"

"Yeah. It really put everything out in the open."

"Okay, so what were they like, though?" I press. "I mean, I talked to them at the apartment, but it was really brief. You know, small talk. Did you guys get along, or was it kind of like, I don't know…"

"They were awful," Chaz says quietly.

I freeze. "Yeah?"

"I didn't want to say anything because, well, it would've sounded bad. I even replayed it in my head for hours afterward to see if maybe I was the problem, or I was reading into things too much."

My heart is beating fast. "Wow. I—I'm really sorry, Chaz. I'd have never—"

"No!" He cuts me off. "That's exactly why I didn't say anything. Just hold on. I'm trying to think how to explain this."

A while passes before he speaks. "You know how people bullied Edgar and me when the picture went around and for weeks afterward?"

I sigh. "How could I forget?"

"Yeah. It was bullying. It sucked. I felt like shit. But you know what the good part was?"

"What?"

"Everybody was open with it. There was no hiding. There were no whispers. People would come up to my face and say something mean, or shove me, or hit me with silly string when I was at the urinal. They'd just straight up do it."

Nick, Emilio, and I discussed this one night, not long before Emilio was taken away. Nick said that as awful as bullying was, he preferred when people said things to his face as opposed to going behind his back. "That way," he said triumphantly, "you can see them coming."

"It's true," Emilio agreed. "Know your enemy. Always know your enemy and watch out."

I've gotten my fair share of bullying too, but the thing about girls is that everything they do is underhanded. It's a psychological manipulation game, usually done by small cliques of three to four girls, to psych you out. Whispers. Stares. Giggling. Body language that makes you feel like you're dirt on a shoe. Getting up and walking away from you as a group. It doesn't end in a bloody nose or a black eye, but the damage can be devastating.

"When we left Aracely's, they took me to a coffee shop," Chaz says. "And at first, it was fun. Willie was funny for, like, the first ten minutes. Then he got old. The entire thing was about him. He'd get all put-out and snippy and disinterested if the attention moved to anybody else for a long enough period of time. I'd be talking about something, or asking something, and he'd manage to direct everything back to himself."

"Wow. Seriously?"

"And the others would go along with it. Elaine would roll her eyes, but she'd enable it, and Theo would do just about anything to keep the peace."

Oh, group dynamics.

"Everybody at the coffee shop knew each other," Chaz continues. "I guess it's their local hangout. People would come by our table, or nod at us from the line. When they would go, Elaine would tell me if they were gay, or lesbian, or bisexual. It was always about their junk and where they were putting it—nothing else. It wasn't like they talked to me. No one introduced me to anyone who came up to the table. They'd just act like I wasn't there if they wanted to say something, and that was it."

"That's gross," I say. "Did you ever introduce yourself?"

"Yeah, a few times," Chaz says. "And, of course, they would say something back. Then they'd go on to basically ignore me. It wasn't like their discussions were deep or personal. Everything was superficial. After a while, I gave up and waited for it to be over." He pauses. "Everybody looked the same. No variety. I'd always heard about how colorful and vibrant gay people were, but these people were boring and cookie-cutter as shit." An edge has crept into Chaz's voice. "You should've seen it, Roxie. After a while, I couldn't tell any of them apart."

I'm at a loss for words. I don't know what bombshell I was expecting Chaz to drop, but this certainly wasn't a possibility I'd considered. I feel ill knowing I facilitated this entire meeting.

Chaz draws in a shaky breath. "And that was just the first part. Afterward, we packed it up, after barely having talked or anything, and decided to go for a walk. We got to this park that was in the same area. Finally, we got to have our discussion, and I got to ask some questions. I kept it simple because I kind of felt like I didn't want to hear the answer from them, you know?"

"What did you guys talk about?"

"Well, I started by asking them about when they realized they were gay. Willie, of course, hogged that conversation and gave way too many details. Elaine talked about coming out freshman year of college. But Theo was the weirdest. He said he didn't come out until about a year ago and that he sleeps with women sometimes. Like what? That doesn't make any sense."

"How could he be gay?" I ask. "He sounds like he's bored. Or maybe he just didn't have a lot of success with women."

"I was confused, too. But when I asked him about it, they all gave each other looks. So I dropped it." Chaz clears his throat. "From that point on, I didn't want to talk, but figured we'd come all this way, so I wanted to get some things cleared up. But everything I said seemed to be wrong." He coughs. "A little time goes by, and they start asking me questions. What do I do in my free time? Am I crushing on anyone? What do my parents do? Where do I live? What are my political views?" He pauses. "The entire time, they're giving each other these judgmental glances. Elaine just about had a heart attack when I told her my parents are Republicans. After that, it was over for me. They just kept looking at me like I'd killed Matthew Shepard and barely said anything or acknowledged me from that point on."

I bark a laugh. "How's that for acceptance?"

"But get this. I was telling them about my dad's best friend in the Coast Guard. He's basically an uncle to me. At one point, I said, 'he's this big, Black dude,' and everybody got quiet. Then Theo started lecturing me about how I'm a white male and how I should strongly consider using different language in the future because some non-whites might find it offensive. I thought he was kidding at first and looked over at him, but he looked upset. Theo's white, in case you forgot."

I gasp. "No."

"But here's the kicker. We go over by the fountain at the park, and there's this older Black man sitting on a bench. Homeless, maybe, but not on drugs. He asks us if we can spare any change, and I reach into my pocket to see if I've got anything, and you know what? The three of them are smiling these big, nervous smiles and huddling like he's going to murder them. None of them say anything. They just nod over at him, with these huge, plastered grins until I slide him a couple ones and go."

"So let me get this straight," I say, shaking my head in disbelief. "You can't say 'black,' but you can fear any walking Black male and assume he's dangerous…as long as you don't say anything offensive!?"

"That's the message I was getting. Afterward, they seemed embarrassed, especially Elaine, who started blaming the city of Seattle for not taking care of its homeless and basically being racist." Chaz sighs. "Even after something like that, she still didn't get it."

I snort. "Yeah, I can see that."

"She would just project everything onto everyone else. Especially Theo. Remember how she was when we first met? Back at the apartment?"

"'I'm sorry about the boys. They're inept,'" I mimic. Chaz laughs dryly.

"She didn't say anything, either! You're the one who had to break the ice. They would've just stood there gawking if you hadn't introduced yourself." He chuckles quietly. "But it actually gets worse. After getting back to our useless conversation, I had to piss. The three of them stayed outside. I knew they'd be talking about me, so I went inside but didn't come out right away. I went around the side of the building and listened in on their conversation. The things they said about me," he chokes. "Everything about me, they picked apart."

"Oh, Chaz," I gasp. "Chaz, I'm so sorry."

"Everything, from my parents that they've never met, to how I knew nothing about all things gay, even my fucking NASCAR shirt. They totally trashed me. They barely even know me, and they're making a judgment call. Someone used the word 'ignorant.' Oh, then Willie says, 'Are you even sure he's gay?' That fat fuck! If I ever see any of them on this side of the Cascades, the last thing they'll see is a Confederate flag and a pitchfork."

"Now you sound like Nick," I say, trying to inject humor into the conversation.

Chaz chuckles sadly. "I wish your brother would've been there. He'd have handled them."

I'm fuming. The thought of Chaz being hurt like this has sent every drop of blood pulsing through my body like a steroid. I'm about two seconds away from calling up Aracely and telling her what I think of her friends, and she'll feel awful, but not as awful as I do. I didn't have to do this. I didn't have to drag Chaz along on a journey he might not have wanted to take. I didn't have to take him away from everything he ever knew and drop him in unfamiliar territory, foolishly assuming everybody was like us or that all gays were like him. Transformations are personal. I wouldn't want Hanna or CeCe or Chaz to shepherd me along my own grief process dealing with the death of my father. It's something I have to do alone, and they respect that. Did Chaz get that respect? Did I consider, for a moment, he might not actually want to come out? Or did I think this was going to be some fun, easy adventure with a big, happy Walt Disney ending?

"Are you there?" I ask, so softly I can barely hear myself.

"I'm here," Chaz replies. "I'm sorry. Was that a lot to take in?"

"No," I breathe. "I get it now. I totally get it." And I do. Distancing himself from us. Scrambling to get into a relationship with a girl.

Hanging with Phil and the guys. Spending as much time as he can in the drama scene—a place where heterosexuality and gayness can coexist and sometimes blur. He's trying to remake himself, and I don't blame him, given what he's just told me. I try to imagine for a second what it would be like to be rejected by the very people everybody pushed me toward. Given how terribly it went, Chaz has handled it with strength and grace.

"But you know," Chaz says. "I kind of feel sad for them, you know?"

"Why's that?"

"Because they think they're super enlightened and evolved. Like somehow, their way of life is the right way, and everybody else is an idiot."

"Kind of sounded like that, yeah," I say, readjusting the phone against my ear.

"Like, at one point, we get to the topic of religion. They're badmouthing it and talking about how much they can't stand Christianity and how Christians are stupid and how much better Eastern religions are. But the funny part is, they're the same way! They're right, and everybody else is racist or uneducated or is the problem. Only them, and people who think the way they do, have the answer." He pauses. "They surround themselves with people exactly like them because deep down, they don't like diversity. It scares them. They talk about 'breeders,' and bigots, and homophobes, but they're just as bad. Stuck in their own way of thinking and trapped by ideas that don't make sense. They're not really living. What they have is not real."

"Oh, it's real," I argue. "But only to them. Theo might have been wearing some beat-up overcoat, but when he sat down, his sleeve rode up, and I saw he was wearing a freaking Patek! You know how much those run for?"

"He's from some powerful political family," Chaz replies. "Elaine's another trusty. There's the class factor. I mean, my family's solidly middle. Your family is pretty much the same, and CeCe's family's got a little less, but we're regular America, you know? These people were loaded. And they pretended like they weren't."

"Fake all the way," I say, my voice dripping with contempt. The more I think about them, the more I hate them.

Chaz laughs. "You sound pissed."

"Oh, beyond pissed." I heave a sigh. "I wonder what the hell Aracely sees in them."

"I wondered that too," Chaz says. "She was so cool. Real, too."

"Emilio was right," I say quietly as the memory comes back to me. "He was dead on."

"What do you mean?" Chaz asks. "Right about what?"

"You went home that night," I recall. "But he actually said what you said. About people, about human nature. He said something about how societies are formed by people who have the answer. The truth. The only truth. And those who don't share in the view or question it are not only liars. They are the lie."

"Wow," Chaz says. "I couldn't have put it any better. That's exactly what happened to me. I was the lie. It doesn't matter that I'm one person. A scared, confused teenager trying to find sense. They couldn't understand me and didn't want to, so I was out. And I was rejected. Dismissed."

"I'm so sorry," I say softly. "I wish it could've been different."

"I don't," Chaz replies. "I needed to see what it was. It's like Nick said. It's better to be hurt by the truth than comforted by a lie."

"My father," I laugh. "That was his favorite saying. It became Nick's, too."

"What do you think, though?" Chaz asks. "About all that?"

"I don't know," I say. "And I'm done thinking about it." I've got so much I want to tell him, to discuss with him in person, but somehow, I'm not ready yet. The gravity of the conversation is beginning to wear on me, and I realize I've been sitting in the same position for over two hours. Rising to my feet, I try to get some blood flowing while cradling the phone to my ear.

"I need some time," Chaz says, reading my thoughts. "You know?"

"Take it." Fatigue is beginning to creep in. "Please. And call me tomorrow if you need anything else."

"I'm sorry," Chaz breathes. "For everything. What I did was so lousy."

"Yeah," I agree. "It was. But I understand why."

"No buts," Chaz laughs. "Please, no more butts. At least for right now."

I giggle. "Roger."

"I'm gay," Chaz declares. "Always was and always will be. But right now, I need time to think. To lie low. Maybe fake it for a bit. That last thing, it messed me up. It made me question everything. Where I fit in, where I'm supposed to be. But I see it now." He hesitates. "You, Nick, Hanna, CeCe, and Emilio, if we'll ever see him again. You guys are my people. It's not about the differences. It's about what you have together. Yeah, Phil and the drama crowd are cool. They're nice, down-to-earth people. But they're school friends. We've never hung out outside of school. We probably won't. My place in the world? It's on your street. In your house. Any of our houses, actually. You guys are my rock. That's not going to change."

The last of the mountain moves off my chest, and relief floods through me. With everything explained, the last several weeks now make total sense. I've always been intuitive, and I knew there was a reason Chaz was doing what he was doing, but I needed to hear it from him directly. Now that he's told the truth, I can rest easy, knowing I've still got Chaz Humbert in my corner, even though my gut told me he never left.

"Don't worry, hot stuff," Chaz says with a light laugh. "I'll be seeing you soon."

"Okay, Fabio," I chuckle. "See you in Milan."

"For real, though." Chaz snorts. "Get Donatella on the phone. I'm a hunk now. Owen's going to miss the popcorn again if he sees me."

"Jesus, Chaz!" I shriek. "Do you still have a thing for him?"

Chaz groans. "Hell, no. And I don't know how long I'm going to be able to keep this hetero charade up. Reece and I went roller skating together the other day. As far as beards go, she's Bin Laden. She's into me, but she'll figure it out eventually. I'll slip up sometime."

"Tell her you're waiting for marriage," I suggest. "Tell your mom to get you a purity ring."

Chaz sighs. "It's too late."

"Wait, what?"

"Reece's parents are going out of town in, like, two weeks," Chaz says. "She invited me to spend the night with her. I said yes."

"Well, there's got to be a way out of it," I reply. "Make something up. Mom's prosthetic went out again. Blaze needs a sponsor at an AA meeting. I don't know. You're a smart dude. Think of something."

"And then what?" Chaz sighs. "She'll just want to do it some other time. The girl is *wild*. I can't keep holding out."

"Well, this definitely complicates things," I say, fully awake now. "I don't know what to tell you. I haven't been on one date to date. I'm not exactly a wellspring of advice."

"Do you think she'll be on to me?" Chaz asks. "That I'm not into women?"

"I don't know," I say earnestly. And I truly don't. Throughout history, men have lived in the closet: fathering children and living into old age fooling everyone. It's not unheard of. Maybe it'll be good for Chaz to find out beyond a shadow of a doubt that he is indeed gay. He'll just be another notch in Reece's bedpost, he seems to be semi-attracted to her, and I hardly think she'll be torn up if she finds out that he likes men. She'll probably end up liking him even more.

"Oh, God," Chaz croaks, his voice sounding unlike anything I've ever heard.

"What?" I ask, feeling panic bubbling in my chest.

"It's my dad," Chaz chokes, barely audible. "He heard everything."

***

An hour in, I can't sleep. How's Blaze going to take this? He can be unpredictable sometimes, and Chaz told me he's got an awful temper. What if he loses it? Would he hurt Chaz? It's hard to picture jovial, booming Blaze as violent, but who really knows what could set him off?

Nick predicted Blaze wouldn't be the problem, that it would be Mrs. Humbert who would go apeshit, but things have become more and more confusing in the past few weeks. It could easily be the inverse. Mrs. Humbert does dote on Chaz, and while I've had to deal with the less pleasant side of her, she's the motherly type. Chaz told me once in confidence that despite being a loving dad, Blaze was hard on him growing up, and this might be something he can't and won't accept.

I climb out of bed and flip on my bedside lamp. I don't risk opening my drawers in case the noise wakes someone up. Instead, I pick up my sweats from the floor and slip them on. Even though the weather's been getting warmer, it's still chilly at night, and I don't want to catch a cold or get caught in a night shower coming back.

Chaz only lives a mile or so away, but at nighttime, everything seems further. I don't get scared easily, but something about this time of night is eerie. The cul-de-sac is at a complete standstill, and aside from a couple of dimly lit rooms, it's lights-out in Chester. I start with a brisk walk, then a canter before breaking into a full sprint. I'm faintly aware of my heart pounding in my ears, but aside from that, I can't hear or clearly see a thing. By the time I round the corner onto Chaz's street, I'm almost out of breath. From the road, I can see that Chaz's bedroom light is on, so I tread cautiously along the sidewalk, hoping I'll be able to remain undetected.

Crouched in the bushes, I can spy Blaze sitting on the bed and Chaz slumped in the desk chair across from him. He's a wreck. I feel broken just looking at them. I can faintly make out their mouths moving, and Blaze seems intensely focused on something because he keeps talking with his hands and making these dismissive gestures. I sit on the curb and stay for a while longer, trying to assess the situation, but everything looks surprisingly normal. Blaze isn't reacting the way I feared he might at all. In fact, he appears calm and in complete control of the situation. Chaz is the one who really looks out of it, but who could blame him?

From what I can tell, it's all good, so I rise off the curb and head back home. Chaz will probably call me first thing tomorrow, and I want to hear everything without fatigue clouding my focus. I don't know where any of this is going, or what the outcome is going to look like, but as I walk home in the cold night air, I begin to feel hopeful for the first time in a while.

Chapter 19

"Can you meet?" Chaz demands into the phone before I've even had the chance to say hello.

"Where?" I ask. "When?"

Still on an energy high from last night, I rolled out of bed already dressed and came downstairs to eat. I'm ravenous. I check on my Pop-Tart and poke at it with a fork. Still cold. Deflated, I go to the fridge and pour myself a glass of milk.

"I don't know," Chaz says hurriedly. "The park, maybe?"

"Way to be vague," I grouse. "There are, like, five within walking distance. Pick one."

"The one we always go to," Chaz says breathily. "With the stone animals."

The toaster sounds, and my Pop-Tart flies up in the air like shooting clay. I toss it on a plate and take a gulp of milk, grateful for its creamy sweetness.

"Are the girls able to come too?"

"That's a tall order," I say. "They don't even know if you still like them. Maybe we'd better save that for another day."

"No," Chaz insists. "I gotta clear things up. Today. Any longer, and they'll never forgive me."

"Okay, fine," I grumble. "Give me an hour."

***

"As if!"

"Hanna," I plead. "Come on. Don't be like that."

"Be like what?" Hanna makes a face. "Sorry, I don't want to see him. If he wants to come and make up, he's got my number. He also knows where I live. In fact, he used to hang around outside with his shirt off all summer posing outside my window." Hanna rubs her temples. "And now he's calling a meeting? Eff that."

"I don't want him near me," CeCe says, her nose pinched in disgust. "He's about to hit a home run with Reece after pretending to like men because he wanted people around him. What an ass." She rolls her eyes. "I can't believe we fell for it. I feel like an idiot!"

"He's gay," I say firmly. "I heard it from his own mouth last night. He's got his reasons for what he's doing, and we need to respect it. Maybe not enable it, but respect it."

"That could be true," Hanna says, pursing her lips. "But he didn't have to ditch us with no explanation. That was sucky."

"Yeah, it was. And he's sorry." I flop down on the couch. "And I'm not going to talk for him or say anything else about it. He wants to apologize in person." I trail off, unsure of where I'm going with this. "We just need to see him, that's all. Just trust me on this."

"Okay, fine," Hanna relents. "I'm only agreeing to it because I know you're not going to let us out of it. Five minutes. That's it."

"I want to hear it from him, though," CeCe says. "Why he did what he did."

The girls and I pass the two stone lions at the park's entrance and wait for Chaz. Even though it's a little past ten in the morning, a couple of families have already arrived and are pushing their young kids on the swings. After around five or so minutes, I spot Chaz way in the distance, carrying something shiny in his left hand. His head's down, and he's walking slowly, and for a second, I get nervous again.

The closer he gets, I can see he's just really tired. He looks up, and I wave, which breaks him into a trot, and, as he crosses the street, he runs towards me.

"I missed you so much," Chaz says, bending over and setting down a foil-wrapped baking dish. Coming towards me, he swoops me up in a hug, and my feet lift off the ground. He's stronger now, and his shoulders have broadened noticeably. I find myself surprised at how much he's matured in such a short time.

"Wow," I say, as he lowers me back down to the ground. "From fatass to badass."

Chaz laughs. "Feels good."

"The gym?"

He nods. "Never miss."

"You look older, dude," I say, studying him.

"Yeah, you, too," he replies. "Not that you look old."

"If I did, it's from running after you," I complain. "God, you had me worried."

Chaz lowers his voice. "I talked to my dad last night after we got off the phone."

I try to act like this is news to me. "Yeah?"

He swallows sharply. "I'll tell you about that some other time."

"Chaz!" Hanna cuts in loudly. "What a surprise! I didn't know you were still local. I was scared Brennan and Spencer latched you to a pommel horse in the basement of a pawn shop somewhere, but then I saw you ramming your tongue down Reece Margolis's throat at lunch instead. What's changed? Did you suddenly remember we actually exist?"

"Hanna!" I look at her in bewilderment. "What the hell?"

Hanna decompresses and steps backward. "Sorry. Hi, Chaz."

Chaz looks unnerved. "Uh, hi, Hanna."

"Miss us?" CeCe cocks an eyebrow. "Finally figured out we're kind of cool?"

"Oh, I know you're cool," Chaz replies. "The coolest girl gang Chester High School's ever seen, hands down. I'm the one who's not cool. I freaking suck. I baked lemon bars for you guys, but those suck, too."

CeCe smiles slightly. "I'll be the judge of that. I'm not too picky these days." She rubs her belly.

Chaz takes a deep breath and faces the girls. "Roxie and I talked every night for weeks, on the phone. She didn't say a word to you because she wanted me to tell you this in person. That morning in Seattle where I was supposed to come to terms with my gayness and understand myself? It was bad. Really, really bad. Willie, Theo…the lesbian…they decided I didn't belong there and didn't accept me. CeCe, your cousin is amazing. Like, one of the coolest people I've ever met. She makes me proud to be gay. But the others? They made me stop. For a few weeks, anyway." He laughs weakly. "You know what? Maybe those three should open a gay conversion therapy center."

"Hey," I say, pointing at him. "Stay on topic."

"Right." Chaz pauses. "When I came home, I was a mess. I felt alone. I strongly considered hurting myself. I wanted to be somebody, anybody else. Anybody but me. So I turned into someone new. I started pumping iron. I got a fresh haircut. Became a muff tease. Hung out with people who didn't know what I'd been through. Who I'd been. Who I was. It was easier that way, but the truth was I was so ashamed to face you guys because you knew the real me. And I'm so, so sorry."

Hanna looks down at her feet. CeCe does the same. Then, in synchronization, they step forward and hug Chaz. None of us say a thing, but instead just hold each other there, kind of swaying back and forth for a minute.

At last, Hanna tousles his hair. "I forgive you."

"I had no idea," CeCe says, looking stunned. "If I'd known what those people were going to be like, I wouldn't have taken you anywhere near there. I didn't even know Aracely was going to send you with them alone."

Chaz shakes his head. "It had to happen," he says. "Like I told Roxie, this needed to be. It's like going to school for the first time. Not everybody's going to like you. Not everyone's your friend. That's it. Aracely liked me. They didn't. Maybe Seattle's just a cold place with boring gays. That doesn't mean Frisco's like that. Maybe Palm Springs is better. I'll have to find out for myself."

"One size doesn't fit all," I agree. "Some people love a place. Other people hate it. Some fit in. Some don't. I'm just glad I'm young and have a lot of time to find my place."

"I want you guys to meet my new friends, though," Chaz says. "They're really cool. I think it would be a good match."

"Sure," I say. "I'm down."

"Why not?" Hanna shrugs. "I mean, they look nice enough."

CeCe nods. "Yeah. I'm in."

"Monday then," Chaz says. "If I don't see you before, which I probably will. And we're going to have to have a long gossip sesh so y'all can fill me in on what I missed."

None of us wanted to leave the park. But Hanna has plans with Cynthia, CeCe's spending the afternoon with Erik, and Chaz also has somewhere to be, though he didn't say where it was. We tried Chaz's lemon bars, and while Nick would classify them as fowl feed, they weren't too bad. After eating a couple each, we passed the rest out to a few families by the slides. Once we dropped CeCe off at the bus stop, Chaz broke off at the intersection, and Hanna and I took a long way home so we could talk.

"What happened?" Hanna asks. "With Chaz? What did you guys talk about? Why didn't you at least tell me that you were in contact with him? I could've rested a lot easier and not hated him as much."

"It's complicated." I shove my hands into the pockets of my sweatpants. "He didn't want me to tell anyone we were talking. So I respected it. I didn't understand, but I do now, if that makes sense."

Hanna frowns. "Understand what?"

"He'll explain it," I say. "Trust him. Life grew him up big time, and he just needed some time to process."

"Okay." Hanna nods. "I guess that makes sense."

I glance at her sideways. "Blaze knows."

Hanna gasps. "How?"

"It seems he's cool with it. I guess he walked in on our phone call last night and overheard Chaz talking about being gay. He didn't throw him out or beat him up or anything, which was my big fear. He's okay."

"Well, that's good news," Hanna says. "I really didn't think he would, though."

I chew my lip. "Yeah, me neither. But you know how I worry."

Hanna nods. "Yeah. You know, Seattle was cool and everything, but if I had to pick, I think I'd choose here. It's home. Something about that place seemed too big to really be anyone there, you know?"

"I get it," I say. "Say I'm crazy, but I don't hate Chester. Like, it's got its problems, but it's home. People our age always want to get out and see new places, but I don't mind staying here for a while. I mean, everything I want right now is here, so why mess up a good thing?"

Hanna laughs. "Quit while you're ahead?"

"I wouldn't say I'm ahead," I reply. "But I kind of want to take my foot off the gas for a little bit. Just enjoy where I'm at."

Hanna digests this for a moment. "Totally. I get it. And for me, it makes sense because, like, I'm Kelsey and Brooke's sister. I'm a Gilbert girl. That name will always carry weight around here, for better or for worse. In a way, it makes me feel secure, knowing I've got something like that, even if I don't end up using it for anything."

"Makes sense to me," I say. "Life is hard enough as it is. Why pooh-pooh the legacy?"

Hanna smiles. "Word."

***

We reach my place first, and I give Hanna a hug before going inside to get started on my homework. Tuttle went easy on us this week, but Burke's basically making us split atoms by Monday, so I get started on the science and turn off my phone to avoid distraction. The work is impossible, but I manage, and switching between the textbook and Google, I'm making decent headway. Nick's in his room probably doing the same, and my mom's doing the weekly shopping, so the house is pretty quiet. After a couple of hours, my brain's drained, so I throw on the first shirt and pants I can find and head outside.

Locking the door behind me, I check it twice and start down the driveway. The sun's a lot stronger than it was this morning, so I cross the street to the shady side. In the distance, I notice a dark-colored diesel truck speeding toward me. Figuring it's some reckless teenager based on how fast they're driving, I move further away from the curb. As the truck draws closer, I realize it's Blaze's unmistakable forest-green Dodge. Well, that's creepy. Now that he knows the truth about Chaz's sexuality, there's no reason he should be on my street. I'm getting ready to run when the Ram pulls onto the curb and screeches to a stop.

"Got somewhere to be?" Chaz hollers at me from the passenger's side window. I shake my head.

"Then hop in," Blaze commands, gesturing to the backseat with a beefy arm. "We're headed to see Cousin Brandt."

"So," Blaze says as soon as we get onto the highway. "Chaz told me. We're all on the same page, here. Just thought you ought to know. In case you thought you still needed to keep up the girlfriend act." He chuckles.

"I know," I say, declining to mention I crept past his house in the dead of night to make sure he wasn't burning his son at the stake.

"It was a surprise, honestly," Blaze admits. "I can't say I saw it coming. Not that it's a bad thing," he says quickly. "I mean, hell, I love hanging with the boys, and Chaz does take after his dad." He hoots. "He just likes 'em a bit more than I do."

"So where are we going?" I ask, wondering about the urgency with which Blaze is driving.

"A little ways out," he responds. "You're going to be meeting Chaz's cousin, and my nephew, who I love more than anything in the world. He's basically everything I'm not. Smart, cultured, empathetic." Blaze laughs. "So that's why we're headed out. I mean, my family goes back generations in these parts, while Prudence's folks all live out in Massachusetts. And stay there, thank God." Chaz snickers quietly. "But yeah, I've got people all over this side of Washington. Some in Chester, too, actually. And as for you, Roxie? Where do your people stay at?"

"My mom's from California," I say. "Most of her family still lives there."

"Whereabouts?" Blaze asks. "If you don't mind me asking."

"San Bernardino," I reply. "And a few people up in Sacramento."

"Right on." Blaze flicks his turn signal. "I love the Golden State. Tried to play college ball for UC Berkeley but was a mess during try-outs." He rubs his chin. "Couldn't kick. Couldn't pass. I found my way, though. Got settled. Couldn't do it, so I taught it instead." Blaze chuckles, seemingly lost in his thoughts. "It ain't easy, those young years. Even if you look like you've got it together."

I nod, unsure of what to say. We're out of Chester now, and without the shadows thrown by street trees or developments, the sun is brilliant and eternal. Chaz has been uncharacteristically quiet during the ride, but he always gets quiet around his dad. It dawns on me that as animated and lively Chaz is around us teenagers, I've always seen him subdued around adults.

"Were you listening to our conversation?" I ask before I can stop myself. Chaz tenses up in the front seat. Blaze looks a little taken aback, then confused.

"What do you mean?"

"Last night." I swallow. "I mean, I was on the phone with him, we were talking, and then Chaz totally went dead. He said you'd heard everything we'd been talking about and then hung up."

"Oh. I was actually on my way over with the laundry," Blaze replies. "Just took a basket out of the dryer and I heard Chaz talking. I didn't listen to the entire thing, but I heard the last few bits by chance. Purely by chance." He signals into the exit lane and swings right off the highway. "Chaz wasn't himself and hadn't been for some weeks. Thing is, when you're a parent, you gotta notice when things don't add up like normal. I was fifteen once. I remember how I felt. And even now, I struggle with depression. I'm not exactly a modern dad, you know, in touch with my emotions and crap, but I couldn't live if something happened to Chaz. Ever since that college tour in Seattle, he'd been off. I worried it could be drugs or something like that." He glances up at me in the rearview. "I don't know how much you know about me, but I've been around young people for decades now. I'm a coach. Part of my job is to watch my players, watch out for signs, in case, you know…" Blaze trails off. "I've seen things. I've lost people. Times I should've been looking closely and wasn't. People I should've caught." He coughs and shakes his head from side to side. "So I was watching him like a hawk. And I just happened to come upstairs exactly when I was supposed to."

***

Chaz's cousin Brandt is an attractive specimen, somewhat on the smaller side, who looks to be in his thirties. He's dressed for work, either ranching or breaking horses, and kind of reminds me of the Marlboro Man, only more boyish. He's waving to us from a little further up on the driveway. Blaze kills the engine, and the three of us step out of the car. Brandt and Blaze reach each other first, grabbing each other in a bear hug, each trying to lift the other off the ground.

"Don't go all fruity on me now," Brandt mutters, and the two of them laugh. "It's been a minute, Uncle Clint."

"Oh yeah," Blaze sighs. "Lot's gone down. Some of it is not so pretty. Prudence still wants me impaled on London Bridge. Her people have been giving me the shoulder too." He shrugs. "Still don't know what I did." He stops talking soon as Chaz catches up to us. "Anyway."

"And Blaze is still dominating the conversation," Brandt observes, but his eyes glimmer fondly. He turns his full attention to me. "Brandt."

"Roxie," I say. Brandt takes my hand with a firm grip. I don't know why I trust him, but I do. He feels sturdy.

"Damn," Brandt announces, looking over at Chaz. "What happened to my little cousin? You know, the little piglet with no fashion sense?"

"Shut up," Chaz grumbles, but the two of them embrace like they've been separated since birth. "Good to see you, dude."

"Well, I could give you the tour," Brandt says, looking over at me. "But I'm afraid it ain't much these days." He wipes his face with the back of his hand. "Got about thirty acres here. It's small but works just fine for me." He glances down at his watch. "We've got plenty of light left."

"I'd love to see it," I say, some part of me sensing Brandt wants to show it off.

"Well, then." Brandt beams. "Off we go."

I've taken farm tours before, but never from the back of an ATV. My arms are wrapped around Chaz's waist. Neither of us are wearing helmets, and we're rolling at least forty. Brandt's up ahead on his own quad, while Blaze brings up the rear on a battered dirt bike Brandt won in a poker game.

"Faster," Blaze screams, revving on our left. "On we go!" He accelerates and flies up ahead of us.

"Is Blaze drunk?" I shout into Chaz's ear, leaning into him.

"Wouldn't be the first time," Chaz laughs. "But no. He's just had a hell of a weekend so far. This is how he lets off his stress."

"Yahoo!" Blaze yowls, nearly plowing into a barbed-wire fence.

Wherever I look, pastureland goes on for miles. A few brown cows dot the landscape, while way in the distance, a weather-beaten chicken coop stands alone. The property is only partially fenced, making it difficult to figure out how far Brandt's land goes.

"Did you spend a lot of time here growing up?" I ask.

"No, not actually," Chaz yells over his shoulder. "Brandt bought the place when I was ten. So I guess, yeah, I spent time here, but as a young kid, I spent summers on a ranch near Walla Walla. My grandpa owned it, and my grandma still lives out there. Nice place, huh?"

"Yeah." Something about the farm just feels free and infinite. I never pegged myself as a country girl, but after today, I don't know if I'll ever feel liberated again unless I'm way off the beaten trail. It would make sense, though. The first house Nick and I lived in was on three acres, far off from everything. Nothing but sky and dirt roads.

Brandt revs his engine and pulls a sharp turn, and Blaze does the same. Chaz follows suit, and we hurtle past another barn, this one smaller than the one by the front of the house. I can see the outline of several horses inside the barn and a couple of rusted plows stored along the barn's left side. A few minutes later, though, the tour comes to an end, and the four of us roll up to the main barn adjacent to the house. Chaz kills the engine, and Brandt dismounts his quad.

"Where do I park?" Blaze hollers over the buzz of his dirt bike. Brandt shrugs and points off in the distance somewhere. "Wherever."

"You've got a great place," I tell Brandt. "Really. I'd never leave."

He chuckles. "Thank you. Yeah, it's more than enough to keep me busy. I run a small egg and dairy operation. It keeps me fed and outside longer than I want to, but hey, it's my farm." He turns to Blaze, who's trying to figure out how to turn off the bike, and cups his hands around his mouth.

"Hey, it's not that hard. Yo, Blaze. *Blaze*!" Brandt turns to us apologetically. "Chaz, what the hell's with your dad?"

Chaz lowers his voice. "He's kind of got a lot on his mind."

"Really? Blaze actually thinks?" Brandt goes to help Blaze with the bike while Chaz and I walk towards the front porch. "You kids go on inside," he instructs. "Get a pitcher started."

Chaz and I kick off our shoes by the door and step into the front room. On the outside, the home looks a little worn for wear the way houses get after a few too many winters. The inside, though, is beautiful. Elegant in a rustic way, the interior was obviously put together by someone who knew their stuff. The downstairs has been done up in a ranch style, and an old-style American flag hangs framed over the couch in the living room. A rag rug, possibly the largest I've ever seen, covers most of the birch floor, while the walls are dotted with pictures of smiling, related-looking people who I'm guessing are Brandt's extended family.

"Neat place," I remark as we step into the kitchen.

"Right?" Chaz opens the fridge. "You ready for the best lemonade money can't buy?"

I rub my hands together. "Hit me."

Chaz retrieves a pitcher from the cupboard, fills it with ice, and grabs two large glass bottles of raspberry lemonade from inside the refrigerator. He pops the tops and pours. I can hear the ice crackle and suddenly realize how thirsty I am.

"It's divine," Chaz sighs, looking down into the jug. "Brandt makes it himself. My grandma invented the recipe but only passed it down to him. She said he was the only one who could do it." He nods towards the cupboard. "Grab another two glasses, would you?"

I pull the glasses out of the cabinet and place them down on the counter. "Your cousin's really cool," I say. "Good energy."

"Brandt's the best," Chaz agrees. "We're not close enough in age to be friends. I have to respect him and stuff, but he's always treated me like a little brother. Back when my brother was with us, Brandt always made sure to pay attention to me. After Darren left, he helped our family in ways we can never pay back. Kind of took his place, in a weird way. My dad loves him like a son."

"He is really nice," I say. "Warm."

"Brandt likes everybody," Chaz says. "But he doesn't just let anybody in. He knows who you are, though."

I laugh. "Does he think…"

"No. I just told him you're the person who saved my life. That's it."

"You want to take these out to the porch?" I ask, gesturing to the glasses. "Or did they want to drink this inside?"

"Porch," Chaz says. "Let's go to the porch."

***

"So," Brandt begins. "What brings y'all to my place?"

Blaze clears his throat. "Family's important," he says. "It's been a little while since we've all seen each other, and I figured it was time you met Roxie. She's Chaz's closest friend, despite a…history. I guess Chaz used to bother her and her friends back in the day, you know, before he finally came out, I mean, came around, and they've been close ever since."

"Mm." Brandt takes a sip of his lemonade. "Chaz? You haven't said much."

Chaz gulps his drink before looking up at his cousin. "Yes. Roxie's my number one. Next time, I'll bring the rest of the gang so you can see the craziness up close."

"And you know each other from school?" Brandt asks, studying me.

"Yeah," I say. "Known each other for years."

He nods thoughtfully. "How is the high school these days? Is it any better than it was back when I was there?"

"Eh." Chaz shrugs.

"No." I shake my head.

"Figured." Brandt stirs his lemonade with a rhubarb stalk and clinks his ice cubes before taking another sip. "That place is dookie. Subpar education. Mouthbreather students. Tests that don't prove anything.

They should just teach farming. Or insurance sales. That's what ninety percent of them are going to end up doing after graduation anyway."

"That ain't true." Blaze wipes a dribble of lemonade off his chin. "In my gym, we build winners. I've got two boys headed to the pros."

Brandt coughs. "Is that before or after the drug test?"

"Do you have to be such a smartass?" Blaze complains. "Why can't you just play along?"

Brandt mockingly raises a hand. "Because we're best friends?"

Blaze shrugs. "Fair enough."

"So you two are just friends then," Brandt clarifies, looking at Chaz and me. "Not like boyfriend-girlfriend or anything like that."

"No," I say, shaking my head. "Not at all."

"Hm." Brandt scratches his cheek. "Edna stopped by not long ago. Told me she saw you with a girl at dinner a few months back."

Chaz's eyes bulge. "Did she?"

"Yeah," Brandt says. "Said she saw you with a head-turner. That she was super into you, and you guys seemed to be serious. I was just wondering if that was you," he says, turning to me. "You look to fit the description pretty well."

"Well, thanks." I stare at my shoes, blushing from the compliment and the heat. "I don't know about that."

"Edna doesn't give out compliments," Brandt chuckles. "And she doesn't like just anybody. The first time I brought a girl to a family barbecue, Edna took one look at her and said, 'Take a plate for yourself and the mare to the stable.' Should've seen her face."

Blaze frowns. "Which one was that?"

"Annabelle. You remember her, right?"

"Oh, Annabelle!" Blaze says, eyes bright. "I don't know what Edna was on about. If that's what a horse looks like, someone get me the reins!"

Chaz cringes. "Dad, no."

"Sorry, sorry." Blaze takes a swig from his glass and sets it down beside him. "Memories."

"Yeah," Brandt says. "We didn't last that long. Couldn't keep faking it forever."

"Why didn't it work out?" Chaz asks, raising his glass to his lips.

Brandt leans back in his chair. "Because I'm gay."

Chaz almost spits his lemonade out all over the porch. I'm equally shocked. Blaze and Brandt share a look before the two of them laugh hysterically and high-five across the bench.

"Oh, that was good," Blaze crows. "Should've seen their faces."

"Get a load of Chaz," Brandt chortles. "He almost swallowed the glass after that one."

"Ha-ha," Chaz laughs. "Good one. Well played."

Brandt stops. "I'm not playing."

I study Brandt's face. "You're serious?" I ask before I can stop myself.

"Yeah," he replies calmly. "I'm gay. Have been my entire life."

"Woah," Chaz says. "Okay. Slow down. Why do none of us know this?"

"Whose business is it?" Brandt asks.

Chaz hugs his arms to his chest. "Nobody, I guess."

"You're damn right nobody," Brandt replies. "I mean, I'm sure some people suspect it. It's not like people haven't asked. I've dated several women in the past, even got engaged once. Just never worked out for me."

"Wow." Chaz's eyes are still huge. "I just—I never really figured."

"So you can't tell, then?" Brandt asks.

"No," Chaz says. "Never would've guessed."

"Good." Brandt finishes the last of his lemonade. "Guess I'm doing something right."

"Okay, wait." I stare at Brandt. "Do you not want people to know?"

"If they ask me, I'll tell them," he replies calmly. "If they don't, it doesn't need to be addressed. It's just a part of who I am. A small part, really. I don't tell people I throw boomerangs, or that I met President Musharraf when he came to the White House, or that I know how to ride a horse with no hands. It's something you learn about me as you get to know me. If it ever comes up at all."

Chaz turns to his father. "You knew this?"

Blaze nods. "I did."

Chaz frowns. "For how long?"

Blaze looks at Brandt. "Do you want to?"

"I knew when I was about thirteen," Brandt says. "And I know it ain't easy nowadays either, but you should've seen it back then. People think the seventies and eighties were all about new ideas and whatnot. But they weren't. Not out here in the boonies, at least. Maybe in the cities, it was different. But around these parts? You were as good as dead."

Chaz bites his lip. "I would think so."

"So I hid it," Brandt continues. "I knew my pops wouldn't understand. Heard enough from him about what he thought about all that. My ma? I don't even think she really knew what that was. My brothers sure had some opinions, so I knew never to let anything slip to them. And I hid it. I did all the sports. Heavy farm work. Played baseball and football all through high school. Dated plenty. Of course, I never lasted long with any girls, but I could put up enough of an act to keep everybody fooled."

"Was it hard?" Chaz is on the edge of his seat. "Being around all that? Living around people who wouldn't accept you?"

"At first," Brandt replies. "Some days, I would just want to vanish off the face of the earth. I would see couples out together or just regular straight guys walking around with their guy friends looking good and loving life. Not a care in the world. I wanted so badly to be them, think like them. That's how it is as a young person. There's some of us who play it cool, hang on the sidelines, drift into the 'out there.' But most of us want to belong and fit in. I don't know what went on in their lives. I'm sure a few of them were going through what I went through. But you don't see it that way when you're young. You think the world's collapsing in on you and that everybody else's got it together, and you wish you knew the way before the time clock runs out forever."

"Jeez," I say. "Doesn't sound that different from today."

"It's not," Brandt laughs. "Being young is tough. Being young and gay is even tougher."

"Life is tough," Blaze agrees. "My father raised me with a belt. 'Course, people say that's how it was back then, but it didn't have to be like that. Amos was born in a house with no running water. He didn't have a father, period."

"My dad's friend," Chaz says to me quietly. "The one I told you about."

"So, I ran," Brandt continues. "Joined the Merchant Marines. Saw the world. Learned to speak different languages. I got away from this place the only way I could. It was good, though. It helped to open my eyes to other perspectives, ways of life, and whatnot. When I finished up with them, I spent some time on the East Coast. New York, mostly. Philadelphia for a little while. And then I came home."

"Why'd you come home?" I ask.

"Because home is where the heart is," Brandt says, his mouth twitching. "I heard this saying once when I was docked in Bahrain. 'Everywhere you go, the sky is blue.' Nothing is truer in my book. Wherever I went, I found the same problems. Same issues. Yeah, some places were better. Others were worse. But people are people, no matter where you are. Why not be close to the people I love and the land I love the most?"

"My father used to say that," I say quietly.

Brandt smiles at me. "Say what?"

I look down at my hands. "That the sky is blue everywhere you go."

"It's a saying from around those parts," Brandt says. "Old cultures can be very wise sometimes. Very stubborn, but wise nonetheless."

"Are you glad?" Chaz asks him. "To be back, I mean?"

"Happy as I'd be anywhere," Brandt responds. "What's not to love? Clean air. Fresh milk. Wide-open spaces. No gray-haired Berkeley kook next door telling me my guns are evil or that Denver omelets are destroying the planet. It's home."

Chaz purses his lips. "What do you think about Seattle?"

"I go to Seattle for two reasons only," Brandt says. "The Seattle Seahawks and Dick's."

I choke on my lemonade, and Chaz doubles over laughing.

"The burger joint," Brandt says exasperatedly, staring at us. "Jeez, get your minds out of the gutter. Dick's Drive-In. Been around since forever. Still tastes the same after all these years."

Chaz grins. "Dick's in Capitol Hill. Who would've thought?"

Brandt chuckles. "I don't go for those. That scene, that money. It ain't me. I did spend some time there years ago. Tried to get into real estate investing. I knew some guys who had a good thing going. It was iffy, though. I didn't trust the people I worked with."

"You lived there, though, right?" Blaze asks. "If I recall correctly."

"Yeah," Brandt says. "Used to rent a place down the street from the community college. I took some night classes there, just for fun. Sociology, political science. A little bit of philosophy. They had good teachers there; it was a cool mix of people."

Chaz scrunches his face. "Is it just me, or does community college sound like a better gig than a four-year? Maybe I should just stay local."

"It's a hell of a lot cheaper, that's for sure," Brandt says. "College nowadays is ridiculous. I don't know how people afford it." He turns to his uncle. "How much did you pay? Tuition-wise?"

"I had a scholarship," Blaze replies. "So nothing. But if I didn't… shoot, I don't know. Could've paid my tuition on a part-time job back when I went."

Brandt shakes his head. "Affordable education. Used to be what made this country the best place on earth."

"It still is," Blaze shoots back. "Expensive college makes people work harder. I don't believe in free rides. We're still the top dog."

"This country's going down," Brandt says, turning to Chaz and me.

"You don't need to be a rocket scientist to see it. My guess is there'll be a crash. A big one. After that, it'll never be the same. Saturated job market due to for-profit universities. Debt we can't pay off. Military bases we can't afford to run." He winces. "I feel for you kids. You'll never really know what this country felt like before 2001."

"Okay, enough of that." Blaze bats his hand impatiently at his nephew. "I came here to have a good time. I don't need to hear Comrade Brandt and his doomsday prophecies."

"Yes," Brandt intones. "Give Blaze his bread and circuses and he'll never revolt."

"I love the circus," Blaze laughs. "And everybody needs bread to survive. I consider beer bread, should any of you be confused."

***

They say food tastes better on a farm, and by tonight, I'll know whether that's the truth or not. After shooting the breeze for a while longer, Brandt tells us to get up and roll up our sleeves. Dinner here is served at 1800: no earlier, no later.

"Everything is fresh out here," Brandt says. "So we start early and eat plenty."

"Works for me," I say, my stomach gurgling in anticipation. "What are we having?"

Brandt nods at his cousin. "Chaz knows."

The way Chaz tells it, Brandt grills the best ribeye in two counties. Back when he lived on the East Coast, Brandt worked part-time as a short-order cook in a fancy hotel, and while he knows at least a dozen dishes by memory, the Humbert clan refuses to try anything else he makes.

"It's a rare treat," Chaz tells me as the two of us walk to the greenhouse to gather ingredients per Brandt's instructions. "We only come out to the farm for dinner maybe twice a year. Most of the time we just meet at Applebee's or at the mall for some late-night shopping. But once you take that first bite, you'll never eat it anywhere else."

"Well, now I'm pumped," I say, patting my belly. "What's his secret?"

"Only he knows," Chaz answers as we step inside. "I have the list here, but I don't know what goes where. He's kind of possessive with recipes. Him and Grandma."

I examine a sprig of oregano. "What's with grandmas and recipes?"

"Beats me," Chaz replies. "They're like old dragons hunched over a trove of gold. You have to slay them to learn the secret of pecan pie."

I giggle. "At least we have Nick. He's pretty open with his recipes."

Chaz smiles. "Can Nick follow directions, though? He's not really focused. Or organized."

"You know him too well," I laugh. "He's a taste cook. If it tastes good, he eats it. If it doesn't…well, I've seen him chuck a Thanksgiving roast out the window. He's very particular."

Working our way down the list, Chaz and I snip off sprigs of this and that. Oregano, thyme, basil, rosemary. The list seems to go on for a while, and the greenhouse is only so large.

"Is everything really in here?" I ask.

"No," Chaz says, tossing some parsley into our plastic bag. "This was just our first stop."

Between two different greenhouses, our bag of herbs is noticeably heavier by the time we return to the house. On the back deck, Blaze and Brandt sip beers and tend to the grill, poking at briquettes and lifting the lid every so often. While it's still warm out, the temperature's dropped a bit, and I realize I've barely eaten all day. Next to the grill, four raw slabs of steak lay on a bed of marinated vegetables. Chaz tosses Brandt the herbs.

"You get everything?" Brandt asks, palming the plastic baggie. "I don't want to have to go out again."

"It's there," Chaz insists. "The whole list. Didn't skip a thing."

"Roxie?" Brandt asks. "Ever been to Ruth's Chris?"

"Can't say I have."

"Good." Brandt smirks. "Don't waste your time. The Capital Grille?"

I shake my head.

"That's what I like to hear." Brandt snaps his tongs. "This is where steak is made."

"Oh, hush," Blaze says. "Your steaks are just all right. Last time there wasn't enough marbling, and I had to chew a little more than I'm used to."

Brandt grabs one of the steaks and rears back like a major league pitcher. "Want to eat in the field tonight?"

Blaze sips his brew defeatedly. "No."

Brandt tosses it back on the plate and opens the bag. Holding it up to his nose, he sniffs and closes his eyes.

"Smell that?" He passes Chaz and me the bag. "Homegrown, organic. Been growing my own herbs and spices since I bought this place."

"Do you ever sell this stuff?" I breathe in the heavenly aroma. "People would pay a lot for these."

"I do," Brandt says. "People mostly do farm visits when they want to buy. I have a stand at the farmer's market, as well as a few restaurants in town I supply to. My eggs and milk, mostly. The majority of my spices go to a taverna in Spokane."

"That's what I figured," I say. "You seem to lean towards Italian herbs, don't you?"

"Oh yeah." Brandt takes a swig of his beer. "Actually, the best food I ever ate was in Lebanon. Anything with lots of olive oil and garlic, I love. Try as I might, I can't quite get it the way it is out there. Haven't given up, though."

"You want me to season those steaks?" Blaze asks, a glint in his eye. "Or is rubbing the meat your thing?"

Brandt rolls his eyes. "I think you do a lot more of that being married to Prudence."

"Uh," Chaz mutters uncomfortably. "I'm, like, right here."

"Yeah, Brandt," Blaze scolds, shooting him a look but unable to keep from smiling. "That's his mother you're talking about."

We decide to eat inside, mainly because it's still too warm out on the porch to be able to eat anything off the grill. Brandt put Blaze on grill duty and raced Chaz and me back to the kitchen to whip up a salad. Currently, he's hard at work slathering garlic butter on thick slices of French bread while yelling directions at his uncle through the sliding door.

"I try to keep it simple," Brandt laughs. "Doesn't always pan out that way."

"This is simple, huh?" I look at the elaborate salad Chaz is putting together. "What does complex look like?"

"Usually six courses," Brandt says. "I've put on a few of those in the past. It can take a day, not counting prep. This is just a family dinner."

"Hey, Brandt," Chaz calls. "Walnuts or no?"

"Walnuts," Brandt confirms. "Without it, the salad is just glazed lettuce."

"The steaks are done," Blaze hollers from outside. "Want me to bring them in?"

"Do it," Brandt answers. He turns to us with a grin. "You two ready?"

"Hell to the yes," Chaz says, drizzling balsamic dressing over the salad and tossing it with a pair of tongs. "Let's eat."

There's good steak, and then there's Brandt's steak.

For the first fifteen minutes, none of us said a word. My cut was gone in five bites. Blaze finished shortly after I did, and Chaz, savoring his piece, tried to fill up on bread and salad. Brandt is pacing himself well, alternating between food groups and small sips of lemon water.

He sits back in his chair at last and eyes the table. "Well?"

"The best," I say, resisting the urge to lick my plate. "Best I've ever eaten."

Brandt nods humbly. "Thank you."

"You outdid yourself." Blaze rubs his stomach appreciatively. "Mine was perfect."

"Lived up to the hype, huh?" Chaz spears a bit of potato and chews thoughtfully. "I could eat this every night."

"I cook other stuff too, you know," Brandt says. "I've even tried my hand at a few vegan dishes. Come help me run the farm this summer. I'll cook for the two of you."

"I'd love that." I smile at him. "We could work something out."

Chaz opens his mouth to say something but changes his mind.

Blaze glances sideways at him. "Everything cool?"

"Yeah," Chaz says quietly, dropping his gaze.

Brandt and Blaze pick up an earlier discussion on last season's NFL draft, and I place my knife and fork on my plate. Something about Chaz's behavior is off. He keeps pressing his hands together and then squeezing before releasing his grip. I watch him do this for a little longer before nudging him with my foot.

"You okay?" I say under my breath. Chaz nods and lets his hands rest at his sides.

"How did my dad find out?" he asks at last, addressing the table. The other two stop their discussion.

Brandt frowns. "Find out what? Me being gay?"

"Yeah," Chaz breathes.

Brandt massages his temples. "Oh, man."

Blaze looks towards his nephew solemnly. "You don't have to."

Brandt takes a sip of water and leans closer to us, looking a lot older than he did only seconds before.

"Right after my engagement fell through," he begins. "I was lost. I'd been hiding for so long, I didn't even know the first thing about who I was anymore. Did I ever? Do any of us? You couldn't have said that to me then, though. The last hope I had at appearing normal, and she'd broken it off just like that."

Brandt bites his lip, deep in reflection. I feel almost guilty for sitting here at this table, being present for such an intimate conversation.

"Looking back, she was right," he continues. "I wouldn't be shocked if she even had figured it out. Of course, I was just as much to blame. I wasn't present, emotionally. It wasn't natural for me to hug or kiss her. I loved her, but in that way? I was just going through the motions."

Brandt toys with his glass. "Two weeks went by. I waited for the pain to get better, but it didn't. The clarity never came. I didn't have anybody I could talk to. I felt guilty, like the whole thing was my fault. Yet another failure to add to the list. It was tough being around my family. Even seeing families around in public was hard. They looked so normal, so happy. I wanted so badly to join them, step into Dad's shoes for a day. See what it would feel like. When Carly ended things, that dream left with her. I knew it would never happen. And I was done.

"Uncle knew something was up," Brandt says, nodding his head at Blaze. "He kept calling me. I was supposed to help him design some activities for a camp or daycare program. But that night, I didn't want to hear from anyone. I was helping out at the ranch. Grandpa had gone to bed, and I was alone in the barn. Clint knew I was at the ranch because I'd told him to come by after work, that we'd sit down and figure out the game together. But I forgot all about it. Instead, I loaded a bunch of guns, grabbed a bottle of whiskey from the cabinet, and just drank in the barn. I didn't know what I was planning on doing. I don't remember any of it."

"We talked that night," Blaze breaks in. His normally jolly face is clouded with emotion. "There were guns all over the place, and you were blasting music, drunk off your ass. You didn't do things like that. I was scared. I saw those Remingtons and thought something drastic. You were high, too, if I remember. I talked you down. And that's when you told me everything."

"I know that part," Brandt says. "I vividly remember waking up the next morning and somehow recalling what I told you about me. That bit managed to stick."

"And do you remember what I told you?" Blaze asks, rubbing his chin.

"Yeah," Brandt says, staring at the ceiling. "'Get out.'"

"Get out," Blaze repeats. "Get out of here. Looking back, I'm not sure that was the best advice to give somebody in your situation. But hell, it worked."

"It did," Brandt says with a light laugh. "I took drastic action. Signed up with the merchant fleet and shipped out a month later. Didn't come home for years."

"I remember what I also told you," Blaze says. "And it wasn't just about not being straight. You were always different, Brandt. Since you were a kid. You say you wanted to fit in and conform, but I know that's not true. You marched to the beat of your own drum, as corny as that sounds. Never listened to teachers, coaches. Did shit your way. You paid for it, but it was yours."

Brandt laughs. "Yeah. Guess I didn't change that much."

"Prophets are never accepted in their hometown," Blaze says knowingly. "Don't know where I heard that bit of wisdom, and it's about as wise as I'll get, but it's damn true. Been alive a while now. And you? Head and shoulders above these people in every way. Small towns, small minds. But not your mind, Brandt." He wags a finger at him. "You were born for bigger things. That's what I told you that night."

"And here I am." Brandt leans back in his seat, stretching his arms above his head. "Back home on the farm."

"You chose to come back," Blaze replies, waving Brandt's words away with a dismissive hand. "Lot of others don't have that choice. Some people out here have never left. And if you want to come back to it, that's okay. This place? It's good for me. I don't want much else out of life. But you needed to see what was out there."

"I'm glad I did," Brandt says. "I met interesting people. I fell in love. Learned Arabic. I can hold a conversation in Spanish. I'm written into someone's will, and I now have a shack close to Santorini. But out here? I can just be Brandt from the farm and sell my eggs and milk and work on acrylic murals and blues guitar riffs in my free time. But I had to do all that to come back, you know?"

"I know," Blaze says. "And you grew up. Became a better Brandt. The boy came back as a man. But you'd never get it unless you left."

"So Blaze kept your secret?" I ask in disbelief. "All those years?"

Brandt smiles. "He did."

"It seemed hard, keeping it in," Blaze remarks. "I was glad he shared it with me. At first, I was surprised. And, I'll admit, uncomfortable. But I love Brandt, and he is the way he is. God must've made him that way. He's never hurt anyone and the thought of him…" Blaze trails off. "I always wanted him to say it, though. Tell the family. See who was who once and for all."

"I'm afraid I'm still not brave enough." Brandt laughs dryly. "Prefer to stay up in the clouds with the fairies, you know."

"Well, what about God?" Chaz asks. He hasn't taken his eyes off his cousin once throughout this conversation. "And heaven? Do you worry about all that, ever?"

"I did for a time," Brandt says, lowering his eyes. "When I realized for sure, I begged God to change me. To correct me. I felt dirty, even though I was too young to act on anything. I wondered if I deserved this punishment. Then I grew up and went the other way; hated religion and blamed people for dividing themselves. Read a little too much Nietzsche during downtime on the rig. But sort of like the farm, I found my way back to my roots with faith as well."

"So do you go to church?" I ask.

Brandt nods. "Sometimes. There's a cool worship center about ten miles from here called Faith Fellowship. It's kind of a Unitarian type thing. Our preacher, Eoin, used to be a priest. They're nice, accepting people. I try to stop in at least twice a month. I actually did some remodeling for them back when they got the new building." Brandt looks at me. "Are you religious?"

I shake my head. It's a loaded question for me, honestly. I had a lot of faith at one point and received my first communion, much to my mother's delight. After my father's death, I found it impossible to believe in a benevolent God. These days, I see how divisive religion can be, but quietly long for the comfort I felt back when I believed.

I swallow. "Not exactly."

"What about you, Chaz?" Brandt asks, smiling. "Remember your Sunday school readings at dinner?"

Chaz buries his head in his hands. "Yes."

"Who could forget?" Blaze chortles. "Prudence thought he was Billy Graham lite."

"You two should check it out some time," Brandt says. "It's not just old farts like me. There are young people too. Nice kids. Cool group, really."

"Yeah," I say awkwardly. "Might be fun."

Chaz nods his head. "Sure, man."

"And bring the rest of your friends," Brandt says. "I want to meet the crew. If they're anywhere as cool as Roxie, they're welcome here anytime."

***

None of us want to leave, but it's late, and we've got something of a drive ahead of us. We take turns hugging Brandt, and he sees us out to the truck.

"How many fingers?" Brandt asks, waving three digits in front of Blaze's face.

"I'm fine," Blaze grumps. "I can hold my liquor. I'm not some Gerolsteiner-sipping intellectual. I'm a man."

"Chaz," Brandt says. "You're sitting shotgun. If the old man can't keep a straight line, you sit him in the back, got it?"

"Yes, Commander." Chaz salutes Brandt.

"Roxie." Brandt gives my shoulder a squeeze. "It was great meeting you. Thanks for coming."

"Oh, thank you," I say. "For the amazing dinner and conversation."

"Any time," Brandt replies. "And remember, this is a working farm. If any of you kids want to make a little money over the summer, the cages need cleaning and eggs need gathering. I do pay minimum, but you'll get a good dinner. Can teach you a thing or two."

"Definitely," I say. "I'll run it by the group. We all need that college money."

"Well, then." Brandt grins. "I'll be seeing you all some other time."

Blaze fires up the engine and honks the horn twice. We fly forward, and I look through the back window until Brandt vanishes out of sight, swallowed by the darkness.

"Well." Chaz clears his throat. "I wasn't expecting that."

Blaze chuckles. "Thought you were the only one, huh?"

"But him?" Chaz shakes his head. "Brandt always had girls around. And they were hot."

"Can't always tell, can you?" Blaze says. "It's like that, I guess. Just a part of who someone is. Some keep it inside, others don't."

"But what if he doesn't want to?" Chaz sits up straight. "What if he wants to be open with it? Bring a boyfriend around. We'd support him."

"That just ain't his style," Blaze replies. "Brandt's a very private person. It just about killed him to tell me. I don't know what he does with that part of his life. He's never shared any of it with me, and I certainly don't ask."

"Is he, though?" Chaz presses. "Is he actually private? Or is he just worried about being disowned?"

"No idea." Blaze shrugs. "I don't think it's our business to uncover how he feels. Brandt's a diehard Libertarian. He doesn't tell anyone what to do and damn well expects the same courtesy. If he wants us to know, he'll tell us. In the meantime, well. Let's let him decide what he wants to do with his status."

"Oh, totally," Chaz breathes. "I agree completely. I just wanted to know."

"You'll see more of him this summer," Blaze says. "Both of us, actually. I want to start raising horses. Brandt's got the space and the stables. So we'll be over there a lot more. You can ask him then."

Chaz shakes his head. "Like you said, not my place."

"Ask," Blaze insists. "Brandt gets offended at nothing. He's about the calmest person I've ever met. He'll give it to you straight. And it's different now, Chaz. You're not a little boy anymore. You're well on your way to becoming a man. Men talk about these things. And he and I? When I kick the bucket, whatever I have goes to you and him. I ain't leaving a thing to Darren. So confide in Brandt like a brother."

"I didn't want to tell him tonight," Chaz says quietly.

"I didn't expect you to," Blaze retorts. "And neither would Brandt. But when you want to, he's the person to tell. It'll never get past him."

"What if I want it to, though?" Chaz asks. "What if I want to be open with it? Maybe people should know."

"That part of things is completely up to you," Blaze says, changing lanes on the highway. "I'll support you no matter what. If anybody's got a problem with it, they'll be dealing with me next." He flashes us a grin. "But I can't tell you what to do, bud. This ain't my journey. I'm done growin' up. Kind of. All I can do is give you my blessing."

Chaz smiles in the mirror and nods at me. "That's all I ever wanted."

Chapter 20

Monday morning, Hanna, CeCe, Chaz and I meet in front of the flagpole, reunited at school again for the first time in a long time. We fall back into our usual routine within a matter of minutes. CeCe is a lot more upbeat than I've seen her in weeks. Apparently, her weekend date with Erik went smoothly, and they managed to discuss co-parenting methods and how they expect the first few months with the baby to play out. Hanna has a raging headache from spending Saturday and Sunday helping Cynthia prepare Kelsey and Brooke's end-of-the-year party, and of course, Chaz and I told the girls a bit about what we'd been up to, though we didn't give all the details.

"Brandt sounds really cool," Hanna comments as we head to our respective periods. "I hope we all get to meet him this summer."

"You will," I say. "He's the nicest guy. Super down to earth. I'm glad Chaz has him in his life."

Hanna nods. "What's the deal with lunch?"

"What?" I ask. "Today? Chaz wants us to meet the new kids. Says he's going to put the tables together and everything."

Hanna smirks. "Front-row seat to the drama?"

"Oh, just you wait," I giggle. "Reece is going to scream like Liza Minnelli when Chaz drops the gay bomb."

"Yup." Hanna shakes her head. "There you go again, Miss Sensitive. She's really into Chaz. Maybe even in love with him."

"Oh, come *on*," I huff. "That girl's the Carrie Bradshaw of the eleventh grade. There'll be plenty of others after him. And they're not in *love*. They've been together for, like, two seconds."

"I guess." Hanna shrugs. "What happened, though? At the ranch? Like, what did you guys talk about? Chaz barely said anything."

I pause. "That's for another time. We covered a lot of ground. But I don't know what's allowed to leave and what stays, if you know what I mean."

"I get that," she replies, nodding. "It's crazy, though. Like, Chaz was gone for so long, and now he's back."

"It really wasn't that long," I point out. "Just felt like it. He's a big part of things."

"CeCe seems happy," Hanna remarks. "I guess the Erik situation turned out okay after all."

"As okay as it can get," I say. "I mean, come on. Her life will never be the same once that baby's born. Plus giving birth…" I wince and shake my head. "My mom told me you want to die."

"Yeah, but that's your mom," Hanna laughs. "She also refuses to buy food that isn't organic and thinks aspirin kills people. Didn't you tell me she refused painkillers during your delivery?"

"Only because there wasn't enough time," I reply. "I popped out in under an hour. They couldn't have given them to her even if she wanted them. She refused them for Nick. Apparently, he was easy."

Hanna cracks up. "Oh, really, huh?"

"What's so funny?" I demand. "I'm easy. I'm a good kid. I don't give anybody trouble."

"Uh-huh."

"Okay, you know what?" I shake my head, fighting a smile. "I'm done with you. See you at lunch."

***

"So," Chaz says, wringing his hands. "Introductions…"

At the lunch bell, the girls and I scooped Chaz up and the four of us went straight to the drama table. Besides Reece and Phil, who we've already met numerous times, three other students make up the main drama clique, though other kids do come and go from time to time. Andy, Kris, and Donovan, collectively referred to as The Three Tenors, appear easygoing and welcoming.

"I'm Andy," a wiry boy with stark blue eyes pipes up first, nodding at us. "What's good?"

"Kris." A blond kid with ruddy cheeks grins. "Welcome to the A-List."

"And that's Donovan," Chaz says, pointing to a boy whose back is to us. "Donovan!"

"Oh, hi," Donovan says, suddenly realizing there are other people around. "I'm Donovan. Nice to meet you." Donovan promptly goes back to doing whatever he was doing before and tunes us out.

"And, of course, you know the girls," Chaz continues, gesturing to us. "They really don't need an introduction."

"Oh, yeah," Andy laughs. "The regulators of Chester High."

Hanna smiles. "So you guys were there."

"I was," Phil says. "Donovan took a tray to the face. Andy stabbed Victor in the hand with a plastic butter knife. Kris was the one who tried to shoot a war film."

"Hey," Kris argues, holding up his hands. "It was good footage. Don't devalue the evidence."

"I saw what happened to you," I say to Phil. "That face punch."

"Uppercut." Phil nods, wincing. "That one hurt like a bitch. Even my chiropractor was surprised."

"Fritz is such a tool," Andy complains, shaking his head. "He doesn't even play lacrosse. His brother was the star, like, four years ago. He just rides his coattails and wants to fight all the time."

"Okay, okay," Reece interrupts, waving her hands. "Enough with the violent talk. Something happy, please?"

Phil slumps in his chair. "Okay."

"I just wanted to say thank you for sending us Chaz," Reece says, interlacing her fingers with Chaz's and smiling at me. "He told me the play was your guys' idea."

"Yeah." I produce a tight-lipped smile. "He's definitely a treasure."

"Isn't he?" Reece beams. "He's perfect. He understands girl stuff, he's stylish as hell, listens to me, and he's *so* in touch with his feelings. He's a breath of fresh air."

Unable to contain herself, CeCe shrieks and starts laughing, her face growing rosier by the second. Hanna and I gape at her. Chaz forces a grin, but his eyes are darting from Reece to CeCe in sheer panic.

"I'm sorry," CeCe gasps finally, fanning her face. "Baby hormones, you know? Got me acting a little kooky!"

Reece smiles serenely. "How's that going, by the way?"

"Good!" CeCe says, taking a gulp of chocolate milk. "So far, so good, I mean."

"Are you going to bring the little one to school?" Reece asks. "I *love* kids. My older sister just had her second. It's so nice, being able to just pick them up and they can't get away." She giggles. "Do you know the gender yet?"

CeCe shakes her head. "I kind of wanted it to be a surprise, you know?"

"Oh, totally," Reece says absently, feeding Chaz a Rainier cherry while massaging his thigh under the table. "I get that. Makes it *so* much more exciting."

"So, how'd you get into acting?" Hanna asks, nudging my foot under the table. "Reece?"

"Oh me? I've always been into it," Reece replies. "I did tons of school plays in elementary, and then CPA, you know, Chester Performing Arts. I just kept going, and after a while it became me, you know? It was my mom, mostly. She used to work in that industry. So she recognized my talent early on."

I nod. "But you're tired of playing Sandy?"

"Oh God, yes." Reece glares. "The Sandy threepeat. Ninth, tenth, and this year."

"I love Sandy," Hanna interjects. "She's my favorite character."

Reece chuckles. "Go figure."

Hanna looks taken aback. "What do you mean?"

"Oh, you know," Reece says. "You're both blond and sweet. Cute with curly hair. She kind of reminds me of you."

"Oh," Hanna laughs. "Well, thanks, I guess."

"But, like, why would they cast me as her?" Reece demands. "I'm not blond. I'm not sweet, and I'm *definitely* not innocent." She wiggles her tongue at Chaz for emphasis. "Do people not know this?"

"But you're acting," I say bluntly. "Playing a part. If you're none of those things, maybe that's why they picked you."

"Hm." Reece contemplates this. "Guess I never thought of that." She turns to face me. "Well, what about you? Like, what do you do?"

"Well," I stop. "Nothing, really. I skateboard sometimes. My brother's the one with all the hobbies."

"I feel that. You just haven't found yours yet."

"Roxie builds furniture," Hanna says abruptly. "For people she loves."

I stare at her in confusion. "Uh, what?"

Chaz glances at Hanna and smiles. "That she does. Quite the craftswoman."

"Oh, well, that's cool," Reece says, even though I can tell she's already bored. "Like what?"

"Closets," Chaz says loudly. "Roxie and my dad built a big one this weekend. But I think they might take it apart after all."

Reece absently traces Chaz's palm, barely listening. "Uh-huh."

"My brother's a carpenter," Phil offers up. "He's got a small business now. He loves it. Says it makes him feel closer to Jesus."

"Oh yes," Chaz sighs, hiding a small smile. "We've all got our crosses to bear."

***

"You guys are *sick*!" Chaz hisses as the bell chimes for fifth period. While he's shaking his head, he can't keep from laughing. "What the hell was that?"

"I'm sorry," Hanna giggles. "I just…I don't know what came over me."

"It was a tense lunch," I say. "That whole situation was a big yikes. Right after Reece started listing your beta boy checklist, I barely held it together. That girl is denser than a brick wall. She's not going to see this coming."

"The best way to hide something is to put it in broad daylight," CeCe puts in. "But you're right. How could she not know?"

"Yeah." Chaz groans. "This is going to be a bitch coming out to her."

"Hey, you don't have to," I remind him. "Nobody's forcing your hand here. If you need more time, so be it. I can always build another closet, you know, with my insane carpentry skills."

"In less than one week," Chaz says, wringing his hands, "I'm showing up at her house. She's going to pull me inside, pin me against the door, and drop her robe. At least, that's what she said over the phone. When mini-me doesn't salute, the jig is up. I've got to come out now."

***

After school, the four of us reconvened in my kitchen. Debating the next move, I'm counting the minutes until Nick comes home so we can consult him because, without Nick, the council is incomplete. As for us? We need advice. With rabid Reece a mere week away, we're going off the wall determining how to keep Chaz from not being up against the door.

"Just do it," CeCe coaches, pointing to the Nike swoosh on her ball cap. "See? The universe is giving you signs."

"I can't," Chaz whines. "Shit. This is so hard."

"It's really not," I say. "Blaze is behind you. Brandt's in. The girls and I are here for you. A couple of weeks ago, you never could've imagined the support you have now." I pause, letting that sink in. "And I'm not saying you have to shout it from the rooftops. Just tell Reece privately and you can go back to keeping a low profile."

"If I tell Reece, I might as well put up a banner with my face on it in the lunchroom that says, 'I'm gay,'" Chaz says, rolling his eyes. "Not kidding. She talks nonstop to anyone who will listen. She'll let it slip or tell someone, and then what?"

"You really think that?" Hanna looks startled. "I mean, she seems to care about you. I don't think she'd let it slip if she knew how much you didn't want to come out."

"I *want* to come out," Chaz insists. "But at the same time, I don't. I'm so mixed up. Some mornings, I wake up saying today's the day. This is it. I'm finished with the back and forth. And then by the first bell, I want to hide from everyone."

"Damn, dude." I throw up my hands. "I don't know what to tell you. This is all you. We're just here to help the process."

While I understand Chaz's hesitancy, I honestly believed as we left Brandt's that the most difficult parts of his journey were in our rearview. Now, as I see him agonizing over how to break the news to his second fake girlfriend of the year, I realize the road ahead is just as bumpy.

"When's Nick coming home?" Chaz asks. "Maybe he'll have some words of wisdom for us."

"Soon," I say. "But he'll probably just tell you what we did. I mean, none of us have been in your shoes. I don't want to give you the wrong advice."

"What wrong advice?" CeCe sounds exasperated. "There is no wrong advice. There are two choices here. Either come out and face reality or don't come out and face reality."

Chaz chews his lip. "Now, when you put it that way..."

"These people are your friends," I say. "The boys, The Three Tenors? The other dude, too. The mime?"

"Yeah." Chaz smiles. "And don't take Donovan personally. That's just his way. He's brilliant on stage. Sounds a little like Elaine Page. When he sings, anyway."

"He's a safe bet then," I say. "He won't tell."

"He'll probably just forget," Chaz agrees. "And the others? Yeah, they won't say anything. But I know for a fact Reece will slip."

"Why don't you just break up with her?" I suggest. "People do it all the time. Just tell her it's not working or you need to take a break. You're an actor, Chaz. Act."

"Because I like her," Chaz says. "As a friend. Plus, we have the lead roles in the play. A breakup will ruin everything for everyone. People say we've got chemistry onstage, and it's too late to find replacements if we can't work it out. Not just that, but if we both nail this, there's a chance we could get noticed for bigger things. The drama club here? It's launched a few well-known actors. Some dude on *Lost* used to be in it years ago."

"Okay," I say, throwing up my hands. "Then it looks like coming out is the only way to avoid swiping your V-card at Reece's register in six days. Do it."

"I know that," Chaz murmurs, nodding his head slowly. "Trust me, I know."

***

"And the leather jacket looks *great* on Chaz," Reece says loudly, squeezing Chaz's shoulders. "Doesn't it?"

"Totally," Andy enthuses.

Phil nods. "It's a look."

Down at the other end of the table, Hanna crumples up her lunch sack in her fist. She's been unusually quiet since we sat down, and I can't quite figure out why. Though we've never explicitly discussed it, I can sense she's not a fan of Reece, but then again, I'm not either. It's not that Reece is mean. Not at all, in fact. Outgoing, friendly, and definitely a people person, Reece is a nice enough girl. But she isn't deep. Or really interested in anyone around her. Of course, the obvious exception is Chaz, with whom she's infatuated. Perhaps the most irritating thing about her, however, is her need to dictate the topic of every discussion. Having only been seated here five minutes, it's clear that whatever Reece wants to talk about is what everybody talks about.

"It's got a good cut," Donovan calls from some far corner of the galaxy. "Like the one Dennis Hopper wore in *Easy Rider*."

"What about platform shoes?" I ask. "Gel?"

Chaz laughs quietly. "That was so last year."

"Lots of gel," Reece says, mussing his hair. "Lots."

"So, Reece," CeCe cuts in, clearly having heard enough. "You're an eleventh grader, right?"

"Yeah," Reece replies. "I got bumped up a grade, though. Live fast, die young, am I right?" She smiles and nuzzles Chaz's neck.

Phil nudges me. "They make a cute couple, huh?"

"For sure," I say in what I hope is a convincing manner. "They seem super comfortable."

"Hey, Roxie," Kris says from across the table. "You aren't related to Nick Nazari, are you?"

"He's my brother," I reply, sitting up straight. "Why?"

"Is it true he almost got lynched at the Cobra Cove?"

"Uh," I falter. "Well…"

"Did someone attack him with a dookie?" Phil inquires. "I heard something wild went down on the way out."

"Is it true he's in a gang?" Andy interrupts. "People are saying he got killed by The Swindler, and that's why they aren't around anymore."

I laugh. "Don't believe everything you hear, guys. Nick's fine."

"How come he doesn't go here anymore, then?" Andy asks. "Is he in witness protection?"

"Well," I sigh. "That. It's a long story."

"I'm just curious," Kris presses, pushing his hair out of his eyes. "You know, stuff goes around the rumor mill. I just want to know if it's true or not."

"What kind of stuff?" I ask, trying not to bristle. I can't help it. Anytime Nick is mentioned in even the slightest negative light, my back is up.

"Oh, you know," Kris says, sensing my irritation. "Stuff. It's probably bullshit."

"Well, try me," I say. "You've got my attention now. What is it?"

"People are saying he went crazy." Kris chews his lip. "That he's on a watch list or he got sent to Guantanamo Bay. I mean, I never believed any of it. But people still talk about him here."

I roll my eyes. "That's it? Don't people have anything better to talk about? And why do you want to know?"

"'Cause Nick's a G," Kris says. "He was always chill to me. I was getting roughed up once in middle school, and Nick randomly stepped in to help me. He came flying out of nowhere with a football jersey on and a bandana and was all like 'where you from,' and the bullies scattered. They just about shit a brick."

I crack up. "Was it a New York Giants jersey, by any chance?"

"Yeah!" Kris laughs. "Like, three sizes too big. He rocked it, though."

"I didn't know that," I say, smiling at the imagery. "He never told me."

"He just did stuff like that for people," Kris says. "Never asked for anything back. Those guys were big fuckers, too. Eighth graders. There were like four of them, but he didn't care. Didn't ask for a thank you, nothing. Just kept on walking."

"Nick's good," I tell him. "He's at community college now getting his associate's. He got a job. He's okay."

"Good." Kris sits back in his chair. "That's the thing. People still talk about him here. I guess he was kind of a legend."

"He still is." I take a swig of my orange juice. "I'll tell him you said 'hey.'"

"Yeah, definitely." Kris smiles. "Tell him Kris says what's up."

"Earth to Kris!" Reece yells, snapping her fingers in front of his face. "Don't you think Chaz and I would make good-looking kids?"

Chaz forces a grin. CeCe and Hanna exchange annoyed looks. I ignore her, but The Three Tenors nod in unison.

"Totally," Phil says heartily. "Guys?"

"Oh, yeah," Andy agrees. "I can definitely see it."

Kris frowns. "You aren't expecting, are you?"

"No, no," Reece says, swatting her hand at him. "Don't be lewd, Krissy." She turns to Chaz and blows him a kiss. "Well, not yet anyway."

"Uh," I say, standing up. "I've gotta bounce."

"So soon?" Kris asks, looking disappointed. "Everything good?"

"Yeah, yeah," I say. "Everything's great. Just got to get some studying in before fifth."

"Roxie and I both do, actually," Hanna says, jumping out of her chair. I can tell she also wants to get away from this circus as fast as she can. "Finals will be here before we know it."

Chaz laughs and pokes my arm. "Since when do you study?"

"Since I decided I don't want to spend my entire summer in this hellhole," I retort. "See you after school?"

"For sure." Chaz nods. "Well, I'll see you guys in a few hours then. Are we meeting at Roxie's?"

"Um, Chaz?" Reece scrunches up her face. "Did you forget already?"

"Ah," Chaz slaps a palm against his forehead. "Right. Can't today. Got to go over my lines."

"Well, we'll see you some other time then," I say, slinging my backpack over one shoulder. "Adios."

I wait until we're a good distance away before exhaling dramatically.

Hanna makes a barfing motion. "Raise your hand if you hate her."

CeCe's hand shoots up. "What the hell?" she says. "Who is this bitch? Where did she come from? How long has she even known him?"

"There's more to the story there," I say. "There's gotta be. I don't know all of it. But it's obvious she's got him now."

"I hate how she speaks for him," CeCe spits. "He doesn't have rehearsal today. We were supposed to go to your place and help Nick wash the Impala. We needed that extra set of hands."

"I can tell Chaz is overwhelmed." Hanna grits her teeth. "He's stuck."

"Yeah," CeCe says, rolling her eyes. "Stuck to Reece."

"I know," I sigh. "But even if he really was into her, I don't like it. I don't like her, and I definitely wouldn't like her for him."

"She's a walking headache," Hanna gripes. She's really worked up now. "You got to talk to the guys at least, who seem all right. I was stuck down at the other end with her and Chaz. It was exhausting. When she's not talking about herself, which she does like ninety percent of the time, it's all about him. Kissing him, fondling him, doting on him. It's insane." A muscle jumps in Hanna's jaw. "I don't understand. He doesn't even talk about himself that much, so why should she?"

"Because he's an extension of her now," I observe. "At least, in her mind."

CeCe nods. "That's definitely true."

"I really wanted to like her," Hanna sighs. "But I just don't."

CeCe takes a compact out of her bag and inspects her makeup. "Has she asked you guys anything about yourselves? Like, to get to know you better?"

"Nope," I say. "She hasn't. Instead, she surrounds herself with a gaggle of nerdy boys who worship her. She can't talk unless it somehow ties back to her or what she wants to talk about. And this thing with Chaz? *She* wants to be in charge. *She's* the man in the relationship. It's like he's the starry-eyed freshman girl getting to date the football star."

"Well, that's sexist," Hanna laughs. "But not untrue. She's the matriarch. The queen bee. The boys are nice, don't get me wrong. But it's football and deadlifts around here. Drama club doesn't exactly equal popularity. She's probably the only girl they talk to."

CeCe crosses her arms over her chest. "I don't want to sit here and bash her, but what the hell, Chaz?"

"Creative types can be really self-centered," Hanna says. "At least, that's what I've heard."

"He's got to come out," I declare. "Like, now. It's gone on too long, and she's digging her heels in. The longer he keeps up this charade, the harder it'll be once he breaks the news."

"I know," CeCe says, snapping her mirror shut. "It's got to happen. Like, this week."

"It's like Chaz said," Hanna says. "There's no choice. He's got to do it to save the play. So we have to trust he knows better than anyone."

"Exactly." I nod. "When Chaz put it that way, I got it. And even though I can't stand her, I still want him and Reece to stay friends. I don't want to control him. We're too much like the mafia as it is. No outside friends. Code of silence. Extortion."

"That's not true," Hanna protests. "We all just happen to live close to each other. Plus, you're kind of a lot to take in for new people."

"So?" I shrug. "Who cares? You guys are the only ones I want to see. Everyone else is just white noise."

"I just want things to go back to normal," Hanna sighs, rubbing her eyes. "You, me, CeCe, and Chaz. It's a good balance. No fights, no drama. The thing that almost tore us apart was Chaz leaving, and that was mainly because we had so much fun before he left."

"It'll all work out," I say. "Trust me. And as far as his other group goes, the boys are kind of cool. But Reece?" I shake my head. "That girl's in it for herself."

***

"So, let me get this straight." Nick smiles. "Excuse the pun. But he's *still* in the closet? Even after everything with his dad played out well and the nice dinner with his cousin?"

The two of us are embroiled in an intense game of chess, which has been fueled by some blueberry muffins Nick pulled out of the oven a half-hour ago. I've just finished giving him the latest on Reece. As expected, it didn't take long for Nick to join the "Reece sucks" camp—especially when I informed him of Hanna's vehement dislike.

"Oh yeah," I say, taking one of Nick's pawns with my rook. "He's still Rock Hudson. Honestly, between you and me, I'm not confident he's actually coming out."

"Yikes!" Nick's eyes go wide. "No, he's got to do it soon. Otherwise, he's going to be in too deep."

"Literally," I snort. "Deep is coming. His first time's slated for this weekend. He'll be really fucked after that."

"Can you not?" Nick says, grimacing. "I really don't want to think about Chaz in that way. And watch your language. It's unbecoming."

"Unbecoming?" I raise an eyebrow. "Please leave the dad card on the table. And I've heard you plenty of times, and nobody likes a hypocrite." I move my queen to put Nick in check. "Plus, I'm older now."

Nick inspects the board. "I guess."

"'I'm a young woman now,'" I say, imitating Mom.

He laughs. "But not a lady."

"Oh no," I agree. "Definitely not."

Nick moves his king. "What about Reece is so terrible? Besides the fact she's taking all Chaz's attention?"

"Oh lord," I say. "Where to begin? She's annoying. Loud. Self-absorbed. And she surrounds herself exclusively with people who enable her selfishness."

"Mm. A real drama queen."

"Oh, her life is a never-ending drama," I say with relish. "It's the Reece show. And we're stuck in the audience, at least until Chaz comes out and things can go back to normal."

"Why don't you guys just sit somewhere else?" Nick asks. "It's not a POW camp. Get up and leave."

"I wish. But Chaz wants us there right now," I sigh. "It's hard to explain."

Nick laughs. "Why are you enabling him?"

I smile. "Because you can't come to school with me. I need someone to take care of."

Nick chuckles and advances his pawn. "Fair enough."

"Oh, I almost forgot." I slide my bishop across the board. "Do you remember a dude named Kris? Short kid, with blond flat-ironed hair?"

Nick frowns. "Sounds familiar. Why?"

"You saved him from a group of bullies. Like, two or so years ago?"

Nick's face breaks out in a grin. "Oh, yeah. I remember him. Good kid."

I laugh. "He says what's up."

"Tell him what's up back," Nick says. "How do you know him?"

"Reece's entourage," I explain. "He's one of the Three Tenors."

"Ah," Nick chuckles. "He's under her spell too, then?"

"They all are," I say. "It's so weird. Like, she'll say something, usually something pointless, and they answer like a barbershop quartet. And it's always with the answer she wants, which I'm guessing is the only acceptable answer. Like a call and response."

"Terrifying." Nick shudders. "I'm all for strong women, but that's just weird. They're young dudes. Doesn't she have anybody her own age to hang out with?"

I nod my head vigorously. "Right?"

"But," Nick continues as I block his rook with my knight, "at the end of the day, it isn't your business what Chaz does or who he sees. Friends, girlfriends, boyfriends, or otherwise. You need to live your own life. That goes for CeCe and Hanna, too. Chaz can handle his own stuff. He got over that Seattle trip just fine, and he can do this. If he wants to keep living this way, it's up to him. If he wants to jump on the table naked waving a pride flag when he comes out, more power to him. But it's his choice, Roxie. It's his choice."

"I know," I say, shifting in my chair. "And I agree. It's just hard. He's one of my best friends. I don't want to see him fall."

"He can always say no to Reece," Nick points out. "Girls do it to guys all the time. They make the guy wait. Sometimes for a few months, sometimes for years. Or they don't have sex at all. If Reece really likes Chaz, she'll understand."

"There's where you're wrong," I say. "Reece is a special case. What Reece wants, Reece gets. Why else would she hang around a bunch of younger boys who worship her? It's who she is. An egomaniac."

"Then he needs to come out," Nick says firmly. "I don't care what the story is. Peer pressure sucks. There's nothing cool about it. If he keeps going through the motions, this is going to set the tone for his whole life. He'll never be happy."

"Exactly!" I nod. "Now do you see why I've been pushing this? I think I know him well by now, and it's the only way. It's frustrating to sit on the sidelines and watch this happening."

I look down at the board and contemplate my next move. "He doesn't have choices," I say, mostly to myself. "This is his choice."

***

"Right there," Reece says, clapping her hands excitedly. "Hold it. Tighten it. Boom!"

A quarter bounces off Chaz's abdominals before dropping to the floor of the lunchroom. Chaz pulls his shirt back down and sits up straight again, his face flushed.

Reece slams the quarter on top of the table. "Tails."

Chaz turns to face Hanna and me. "I mean, five hundred crunches a day. I've got to have something to show for it, right?"

"Water," Reece says, pushing her stainless-steel bottle at him. "Drink up."

Chaz takes a sip and passes it back to her. "Thanks."

Lunch again. For some reason, this one's been hard to bear. I haven't looked forward to a bell ringing this much since detention, but we've got a ways to go. Around us, our classmates are chatting with friends, catching up on the latest gossip and generally enjoying their break. I wish I could join them. But instead, I'm forced to endure another half hour of pointless banter between Reece, Chaz, and the Three Tenors.

"You're so different from most freshman boys," Reece murmurs, squeezing Chaz's bicep. She slides her fingers just beneath the arm hole of his T-shirt. "You're a lot more mature, like physically. How tall are you, baby?"

"I don't know," Chaz says. He wriggles his arm away from Reece's fingertips. "It's been a while since I had a checkup."

"I'd say five eight. Maybe five nine?" She laughs. "Not that it matters. I'm not big on height."

"Brennan's tall," I say before I can help myself.

Reece smirks. "Not where it counts."

"Well, that's good to know," Chaz says, forcing a laugh. "I totally needed that bit of info."

"What? It's tiny!" Reece shakes her head. "It's probably why he is the way he is. Aggressive. Rude. Homophobic." She shudders. "Thank God he's a thing of the past."

"Yeah," I interject. At least this conversation has taken a turn for the interesting. "I kind of had a feeling. Just couldn't confirm. Thankfully."

"And, like, the whole gay thing," Reece continues. "Where did he come up with that?"

"The poster," Andy cuts in. "Remember? The one that went around at the beginning of the year?"

"That was so fake," Reece says dismissively. "Whoever made it did a terrible job. Amateur."

"I don't know about that," Phil starts. "I mean, people did think…"

"Shush, Phillip!" Reece rotates in her seat and puts her back to him, as if to punish him for speaking. "It's, like, the dumbest thing I've ever heard. Chaz is handsome and strong. Sexy, passionate. You can't fake that."

Hanna locks eyes with me and tries to hide a smile.

"Why bring it up now?" I ask, stretching my legs under the table. "Kind of a random topic."

"Well, you brought up Brennan," Reece says. "Which got us here, so, yeah."

"So gay people can't be handsome?" CeCe asks, abandoning her yogurt cup to join in on the discussion. "Or passionate? Or strong?"

Reece exhales dramatically. "Of course they can be. I'm just talking about the vibe Chaz gives off. The way he carries himself. He doesn't fit the bill, even a little bit. So it was dumb to make someone like Chaz the center of a silly rumor."

"I think that's kind of generalizing," I say. "Some people, you really can't tell which way they go. Not everyone wears their sexuality on their sleeve."

Reece smirks. "Do you even know any gay people, Roxie?"

"Actually, yeah," I say, my irritation rising. "I've known several. Still do, actually."

"Well, yeah, and me, too," Reece says quickly, as if we're neck and neck in a competition for who has the most homosexual friends. "I mean, hello? Theater person, here. It's practically impossible for me not to know any. And I agree with you. But my point is..."

"Pointless," Chaz says abruptly. "Your point has no point."

Reece's eyes bulge. "Um, what?"

"Roxie's right," Chaz says. "There are people who live a lie their entire life. Nobody knows who they are. Sometimes they get married and hide out. Stay on the down low. But not every gay man walks around in tight jeans and works as a makeup artist in SoHo. You can't always tell just by looking at somebody."

"Sometimes people are open with it," Hanna adds. "Some aren't. For a lot of people, that's their entire identity. For others? It's just a piece of a way bigger puzzle."

"Well, it sure sounds like you all know someone," Reece says, folding her hands into her lap. "Who?"

Chaz takes a breath. "Me."

Chapter 21

"Yeah," Chaz says. "I'm gay."

The table is silent. Hanna's eyes are closed, her expression unreadable. CeCe catches my eye and looks at me as if to ask what's next. The Three Tenors have stopped their chatting and are wearing the same surprised expressions. But Reece? She's turned to stone.

"Fuck yeah!" Jerome yells from one table over. "Atta boy, Chaz!"

"I'm gay," Chaz says again, relishing uttering the words out loud. "My whole life, I have been gay. I've known. I've felt. I am. There's no denying it. I don't need to hide it because I'm not ashamed of it. I'm not embarrassed by it. I don't even want it to go away because there's nothing wrong with me. Good? Bad? Neutral? Depends on who you ask. But me? I'm done asking."

"Chaz," Reece gasps. She drops her head. I'm not heartless; I feel bad for her. But this moment isn't about Reece. It's about Chaz and Chaz alone.

"Reece," Chaz says, looking her in the eye. He touches her hand gently. "You're beautiful. And there's nothing wrong with you. I'm the piece that doesn't fit. I can't. Even if I wanted to."

"So, you're gay?" Kris says, scooting closer as not to be overheard. "Like, really gay?"

"Yes," Chaz says simply. "And glad to be out."

"Wait," Andy says, scrunching his face. "So that whole poster thing? With Edgar?"

Chaz laughs, shaking his head. "That wasn't real. Like Reece said, it was a fake. Made by somebody who rightfully hated me after years of me being an…oh man, a terrible person. But I got over it. And I came out the other side a better person. A new person. And in ten lifetimes, I'll never be able to repay the people who helped me get there."

"Well, what does it mean?" Phil asks, his forehead creased.

Chaz frowns. "What does what mean?"

"Gay? Being gay?" Phil shrugs. "I mean besides the obvious, I don't really know. I mean, like, I've heard about it. My dad has some interesting opinions about it. My reverend condemns it. But, like, what does it all mean?"

"Honestly? I don't know either," Chaz says. "I wish I could tell you. Like Hanna said, it means different things for different people. But for me, right now? It's just what I'm attracted to. That's it."

"Oh." Phil nods slowly. "I get that. I just need a little time to kind of wrap my head around it, that's all."

Chaz smiles. "Couldn't imagine it, huh?"

"No," Phil replies. "Honestly, no. Like, sometimes you'd get a certain way on stage, but I just thought you were a good actor. Well, you are. You should win an award for fifteen years in the closet."

Chaz hoots. "Oh, that flick was way overrated."

Kris smiles and pats Chaz's shoulder tentatively. "I support you, man."

Chaz bows his head. "Thanks, Kris."

"Same," Andy says. "But it figures. Seriously, guys, how else could he hang out with three hot girls all the time?"

"Right?" Chaz runs a hand through his hair. "I get all the honeys."

"Plus, Chaz is just cool like that." Jerome has ventured over from a table away and slides into a vacant spot next to Chaz. "Get to know him, guys. He's a lot of fun."

Hanna gives him a small wave. "Hi, Jerome."

"What they said," Phil adds, nodding at his friends. "I'm glad you feel you can share with us."

"Thank you," Chaz says. "I mean it. You guys are cooler than you'll ever know."

"Yeah," I chime in. "Ten out of ten."

Hanna smiles at Kris. "A-list."

"But now that you've told us…" Kris leans forward. "What do we do next time somebody makes fun of you or starts shit up?"

"Tell them." Chaz shrugs. "If people ask, confirm. Have them come to me if they don't believe you. I really couldn't care less."

Kris nods. "Got it."

"People will talk," Chaz says. "Some will make jokes. A few people might not even like me after this. But like a mentor of mine once said, it all comes out in the open. And that's more than fine with me."

"I feel that, dude," Andy says. "Sometimes, it's better to just know."

Reece stands up. I think this is the longest I've ever seen her go without talking. Her face is stricken. She quickly wipes at her eyes with the back of her hand. Black eyeliner streaks the side of her face.

"I'm sorry," she gasps. "I just can't do this." Turning her back to us, Reece grabs her purse and storms out of sight.

***

"Well. If someone told me when I woke up this morning all that was going to go down, I definitely wouldn't have believed it."

"Yeah," Chaz agrees. He's been walking on air for the past thirty minutes. Each step he takes seems lighter than the last. "Me, either."

The two of us skipped fifth period to have some alone time together. Out wandering the periphery of the campus, Chaz and I haven't talked much, and truthfully, there's not a lot to be said. If you ask me, Chaz couldn't have come out more gracefully. I'm so immensely proud of him, not to mention relieved at the way the drama guys took the news, that I feel some type of celebration should be in the works. But at the same time, today is so unremarkable in every other way that it's difficult to believe such a momentous event took place.

The ground's slick from a spring shower, and I can taste the dampness in the air. When I go home, I'll probably make myself a mug of chamomile tea and sit by the back deck to admire the color of the wet earth before getting started on my homework. Nick will either be home or on his way, and we'll catch up the way only we do. I'm excited to report to him that Chaz successfully came out. But what will Chaz do when he gets home this afternoon? Will he tell his mother? Could Spencer or Brennan heckle him on the way home? Or will everything be fine, and there really is nothing to fear but the fear itself?

"I feel bad for Reece," Chaz states after a long silence. "I can't help it. I just do. I've probably ruined the play, and she's been good to me. I feel like I screwed her over."

"Reece will recover," I say. "I don't care about her right now. My only concern is you. Life's going to be different for you, and we don't really know what it's going to look like yet. And what about your mom?"

"I'll tell her tonight," Chaz says firmly. "I mean, I already came out at school. It's only a matter of time before the news makes its way to her. My dad and I were actually talking about it last night. He said he'd tell her privately if I wanted, but I know I've got to do this. Blaze isn't coming out. I am."

"He just wants it to be easier for you," I say. "Being hard enough as it is."

"It wasn't, is the thing." Chaz looks over at me. "There was nothing hard about it. I had more anxiety and fear thinking about it every waking minute than admitting to a table full of teenagers that I'm gay. I didn't plan it. I just did it."

"And how do you feel now?"

He grins. "I feel free. Calm. Like I don't care what happens next. It needed to happen, and I think it happened at the right time. I'm not scared or worried. What'll be will be."

"That's a good attitude," I say, smiling. "From one anxiety case to another."

"You get anxious over other people," Chaz replies. "But do you get anxious over your own things, too?"

"Oh, God, yeah," I say. "I just have learned how to hide it."

The corners of Chaz's mouth turn down. "You can bounce stuff off me, you know." He squeezes my hand. "I can be a good listener."

"You're great," I affirm. "And it's not just one specific thing. It's just this cannonball chained to my leg that I can't step away from. A constant feeling, more than a concrete reason."

"I know what you mean," Chaz says. "Anxiety for anxiety's sake."

"Yes!" I squeeze my eyes shut and reopen them. "Why?"

"We're smart, deep-thinking people," Chaz says, laughing. "If there isn't something to worry about, our brains will create it."

I sigh. "A damn shame."

"But cut the weight loose for a second." Chaz stops in his tracks and turns to look at me. "I finally came out. Nick's holding down a job and seems well-adjusted. Owen's out of the picture. Erik's back in CeCe's life and finally manning up. My dad, my cousin, and my friends love and accept me unconditionally. Our little group is back to normal, and our bond is stronger than ever. Of course, I could go the other way. I could talk about what happened to Emilio, or how my brother won't see the outside world for some-odd years. I could mourn the fact I'll never get to meet your father and tell him you're my hero. I haven't even told your mother yet. Hell, I don't tell you enough. But come on, Roxie! The world's a dark place. Try to enjoy the stars."

"You're right," I say, feeling overwhelmed. "You're totally right. It's just really, really hard sometimes."

"I know." He brings me in for a much-needed hug. "But as corny as it sounds, try to just live. It's all any of us can do."

***

"So he did it?" Nick asks. "Cold turkey?"

"Yup," I reply. "We definitely weren't expecting it. It wasn't a planned thing. It just happened. It was such a Chaz way to come out. I wish you could've been there."

"Eh." Nick shrugs. "I know the dude. He's kind of just radical no matter what he does. Plus, I need to start planning the menu for his coming-out party. When is it?"

"I don't know," I say. "We've got to at least hold something here at the house to honor him. I'm thinking around the end of the month."

"Cool." Nick nods. "School won't have much going on. I can finally break out the torch for soufflés."

"Just remember to point the torch away from you this time," I chuckle. "We can't risk another Iwo Jima for the sake of fine dining."

"Trust me," Nick says. "I won't make that mistake again. If Jerome's in attendance, I'll just point it at him."

I frown. "You will *not* singe Jerome. That fight was ages ago. It's time to move on."

"Irrelevant," Nick seethes. "The ungrateful pleb isn't fit to even *point* at my accordion. I don't want him to come."

"*Anyway*," I say breezily, "we can hold the party here in the dining room or on the back deck if the weather's good. We'll have cake, of course. Maybe some appetizers. Mom might let us break out the champagne for a toast or something."

"Who's coming?" Nick asks. "Besides the obvious?"

"Phil. The Three Tenors." I tick them off on my fingers. "They're good friends of Chaz's now. I doubt Reece will show."

"Frankie can probably stop by on his way to work," Nick says. "That means we've got to prepare for around ten guests. How are we on funds?"

"Everybody pays their way," I say. "I'll start collecting the cash once we nail a date down."

"Is there a theme?" Nick raises a brow. "Should we invite the cast of *Queer Eye?*"

I smile. "Let's just keep it local."

Nick takes a medium-length blade out of the knife drawer and starts cubing tofu while oil spits in a pan. Mom's coming home early tonight, which is nice because we rarely eat dinner as a family anymore. I'm eager to tell her about today's events.

"You know," Nick says quietly. "I really wish Emilio was here today."

At the very mention of his name, my heart sinks. Even now, Emilio's deportation still gets me the way it did when I first found out. I can't really describe it, but it's kind of like the sharp stab I feel whenever somebody mentions my father.

"I know," I sigh. "Everything is finally starting to work out, and he's missing it. He taught us so much."

"He's a giver." Nick gets to work mincing a handful of garlic cloves. "Some might call him a taker. A leech. Somebody who makes ends meet by doing anything. But us? We saw a different side of him. I've never met anybody that selfless."

"Especially after I heard that last part," I add. "About him counseling Erik. He didn't have to do that. There wasn't anything in it for him. He did it truly because he cared."

"Emilio made a lot of mistakes in his life," Nick says, looking up at me. "We talked about it a bit. He's no saint, and he'd be the first to say it. There are things he's done that he's not proud of, and I understand why." He pauses. "But when I knew him, he was really trying to get right with himself. He wanted to see us succeed, to not make the same mistakes he did. It's so easy to get off the straight path, especially when you're figuring it all out. I know I almost did."

"I just hope that he's okay," I breathe. "That he's safe. I know he's smart and savvy and all that, but I still get worried about him."

"I know," Nick agrees. "It's hard to think about him on his own. After everything he did for us, we can't do a thing for him in return. It's one of the worst feelings you can have."

I shake my head. "Amen to that."

"But we can't give up hope," Nick says. "He could come back. Or maybe life in Mexico is what he's looking for after all. Emilio did tell me that he was ready for a change. Think about the major changes we've all gone through this past year. Things, people. They take you to different places."

"Jenna Carmichael," I say immediately. "In a roundabout way, she's the reason Chaz and I became friends. CeCe, too. Emilio. Aracely. It all happened for a reason."

"Right?" Nick shakes his head. "It's so weird, this life journey we're on. We never see it while it's happening, but months or years later, you take a step back and all the pieces click together."

"That it does," I say. "This needed to happen. Some people say we've got free will. Other people think there's destiny and that you've got a path." I stare at the ceiling, collecting my thoughts. "I'd like to believe we all have free choice, that we can choose the lives we want to live. But after this? I think there's a reason we're all here. And we journey through life putting the pieces together as we go."

"Here we go with the esoteric stuff," Nick laughs. "This was supposed to be a light discussion."

"It's us," I chuckle. "And there's you. You've got the dorkus touch. Everything you touch turns intellectual."

"The dorkus touch." Nick smiles. "I like that."

"I do too," I say. "Accept it. You're grown up now. It's not going away."

***

Dinner was great. Mom came home about an hour after I debriefed with Nick, and fried tofu with broccoli in garlic sauce is now in my top ten. We all helped clean up, even though Nick and I tried to make Mom sit down and let us do the heavy lifting. After cleanup, Nick brought out some homemade shortbread he'd been saving and put the kettle on for tea. We hadn't done something like that in ages, maybe even years, and it felt so good to finally sit down like a family again. When I told my mother about Chaz coming out at lunch, she was surprised but agreed with me that it was time. With his friends behind him, he'll be A-okay as far as the social scene at school goes.

"But do you think he'll *really* be okay?" I ask her. "Before, people just heard rumors. Now, it's real. Wouldn't that give them more fodder for bullying?"

"Some will be jerks," Mom says, stirring some creamer into her mug of Earl Grey. "They'll say things. Maybe heckle him physically. But Chaz is bigger and stronger now, and honestly, you kids give me hope. Not just your friend group, but kids your age in general. At least with this stuff. Young people these days are a lot more accepting about things like sexuality than my generation ever was."

"She's right," Nick says. "My friends and I actually talk about this stuff all the time. You know, with the whole gay rights movement going on right now, a lot of people are coming around and seeing that other perspective. Besides, people our age are tired of the division. They're sick of the war. The Muslim hate. The gay hate. Racism. They want change, not just for them, but for everybody."

"We need it," I agree, breaking my shortbread square in half. "In politics, in society. I saw how Chaz's new friends took the news. It was nothing to them. They just nodded and went along like normal."

"And that's what I'm saying," Mom says, reaching for the honey. "Kids are a lot more open-minded. At least, some of them can be. Chaz's sexual orientation is his own business, and that's that. You can all still be friends."

"Why can't everybody be like that?" I ask. "Just chill. Relaxed. Accepting."

"Some will come around eventually," Mom says. "A lot of people just need to live a little. Grow up. Maybe meet somebody who alters their perspective. It happened to me, you know."

Nick nibbles his shortbread. "What do you mean?"

"I mean with your father," Mom replies. "Growing up, I'd always assumed I'd eventually marry somebody who looked like me. Someone who came from my culture, who was part of the church. I didn't really look at foreign men, not because I didn't like them, but because I never really thought we'd have anything in common. When I met your father, things changed. I changed." Mom's eyes are bright; I can tell she's reminiscing. My heart pangs. "And no, things weren't perfect," she continues. "Far from it. But I grew and saw another way, saw another perspective. And he was good for me in that way. The inverse was also true."

Nick and I nod.

"Of course, our families weren't as open-minded," Mom remarks. "His or mine. But they came around eventually. Some of them even still talk to this day. And both of them love you two, so there's a commonality right there."

"I never thought about it like that." I look down at my hands. "I just figured it was always that way. It sounds dumb, but I thought in our family everybody was cool with each other and got along from the beginning."

"And someday I hope it's like that with everybody," Mom laughs. "Gay people included. It's no one's concern what consenting adults do behind closed doors, gay, straight, or otherwise. They're not affecting anyone. I, for one, have enough on my plate as it is without worrying about two men eloping."

The doorbell rings.

Nick knits his brow and rises from his chair. "This late?"

Mom turns to me. "Are you expecting somebody?"

"No." I shuffle towards the door, wondering who it could be. Deliveries never come past six, and it's a weeknight. The porch light isn't on, so I can't see who it is, but I unlock the door anyway and open it.

"Hi, Roxie." Chaz is trying to smile, but his voice cracks. Behind him, Blaze looks years older than he did when we were all at Brandt's just days ago. He manages a tired wave but is uncharacteristically silent. The truck sits in the driveway, glossy under the street lamps.

"Chaz," I say. "Blaze. What's going on?"

Chaz exhales. "I told my mom."

My heart thrums loudly in my chest. "You know what, guys?" I say. "Come on in. Mom!" I yell behind me. "Nick! We've got company."

"So what happened?" I demand as soon as Chaz and I are upstairs. Blaze and my mother are sitting downstairs in the front room with Nick. I took Chaz up to my room to give him privacy.

"Oh, man," he breathes, wringing his hands. "It was *bad*. I'm glad you weren't there. It's a funny feeling when your friends who hated your guts just a few months ago accept you, and the woman who gave birth to you doesn't."

"So, she's not okay with it?"

"Oh no," Chaz says. "I knew that after I came out today, at school, I had to tell her tonight. She was bound to hear it anyway. You know how news spreads. So I told her an hour ago, and she's still crying. Well, now she's crying. At first, she was screaming bloody murder. She threw the book at me. The Bible mostly, but there was some other stuff in there, telling me why I shouldn't feel this way and how she's already lost one son to sin, and all she has is me and how I've gone and broken her heart and all that."

I close my eyes. "We knew this could happen." I take his hand. "But I'm so sorry that it did."

"Oh, I was prepared for the worst. But you can imagine how my dad reacted to that. When he heard that last bit from her, he went *off*. Told her she was full of shit and that I was going to have a hard enough life with people like her out in the world. And my parents don't talk to each other like that. I've never heard that from either of them."

"Blaze is honestly amazing," I say, feeling a surge of love toward a man who was once just Chaz's pervy dad. "At first, I was worried he'd be the one to react like that. It's usually dads who have a harder time with stuff like this."

"Yeah," Chaz agrees. "I could see how you'd think that. But Blaze is a teddy bear. There's no malice in him. He might not go to church, and he drinks too much and adores Hooters, but he lives closer to the book than she does. I really think he tries his best to love everybody."

"So what does this all mean?" I cross my arms over my chest. "What's going to happen?"

"I don't know," Chaz says earnestly. "We definitely didn't leave on a good note. Like, she calmed down a little bit after a solid twenty minutes of screaming and sobbing. It's never easy seeing your mom cry like that, even if the reason why is total bullshit. But all she kept saying was that I need help. That's all I heard until we left." He shivers. "It's gonna be a while before I get that out of my head."

"It's hard for her," I say, leaning against the bed frame. "We can't change that. But it's not up to you to change. Only she can do that."

"I know she'll tell our pastor." Chaz shakes his head, looking nauseous. "They talk about everything. They'll want to stage an intervention. He's done it to other gay kids who were part of our parish. Somebody knows Dean Foote from Covenant Church, and he's a big name around here. If he's doing a conversion workshop, she'll try and make me go."

"She can't!" I exclaim. "You're not a boy. You're almost a man. You *are* a man. It's your life, Chaz, and only yours."

"My dad wouldn't let her anyway," Chaz says. "He thinks those things mess people up, and he's right. I've heard all sorts of horror stories, like they make you have sex with women or scare you with tales of eternal damnation and AIDS. I don't know if I believe in any of that stuff anyway, but still. I'm already feeling exposed. I don't need anything else worrying me."

"No, you don't." I pat his leg. "And all of us are here for you, but you know that. I'm sorry, Chaz. I'm really, really sorry."

"I am too," Chaz says. "And it's weird, but I'm mostly sad for my mom. She won't be able to hug her older son for at least the next five years. Every time she sees him, he'll be behind a glass. If she really believes everything Pastor Willard with the fitted suits, pouty lips, and mysterious limp has to say about gayness…well, I'm as good as dead to her."

"Mothers love their sons," I say firmly. "And you're the apple of her eye. She'll be upset, and there'll be tears and probably anger if she really thinks the way she does. But you're her son, Chaz. Her child. Did Darren's sentencing stop her from loving him? Of course not. And this is a lot better than…whatever he did."

"Scamming old people," Chaz says listlessly. "Robbing houses. Somehow, he broke into an upscale care home and dropped a deaf phone on his foot. He was so high he didn't even remember going there. Regardless, she still loves him. If she can't love me for being a good son who just happens to be gay…well, fuck her, then."

"She does," I say. "I can almost promise you. And you're a great son."

"That's what Blaze said," Chaz mutters, tucking his knees under his chin. "He told me if she doesn't come around and accept this, we'll go get a place of our own."

***

"I would've taken him to Brandt's, but he's out of town," Blaze explains as Chaz and I pull a couple overnight bags out of the backseat of the truck. "He gets back next week. Your mother's kind enough to let Chaz stay here for a few days while I get things sorted at home."

"Chaz can stay as long as he wants," I reply, hoisting Chaz's duffel over my shoulder. "Don't even worry about it."

"Thank you," Blaze says, giving my shoulder a squeeze. "For saving my son."

"Chaz saved me," I say firmly, looking Blaze in the eye. "We all saved each other. It's who we are. The scariest thing in life, to me anyway, is not having what we have right now." I slam the car door shut. "We're all lucky, I think."

"What she said," Chaz says. "And what you said. She did save me." He points at me with two fingers. "Don't even say it isn't true."

Blaze lays a hand on Chaz's back. "Got everything you need, kiddo?"

"Yeah," Chaz says quietly. "And—I'm sorry."

Blaze frowns. "For?"

"Ruining what's left of our family," Chaz chokes out, refusing to look at either of us. "Everything's already so tense between you and Mom. Ever since Darren got in with that crowd. Things were never the same at our house, and now I've just messed up the rest of it."

"Hush," Blaze orders. "Enough of that nonsense. What goes on between your mother and I has nothing to do with you. Darren, maybe. We both play that blame game. But you are my *son*. Nothing will ever change that, and I'm proud of the man you're becoming. And I don't care that you can't go long, or learn trick plays, or even watch a whole game with me. I love you, and I love who you are."

"I love you, too, Dad," Chaz says, his voice hoarse.

"Don't forget to call," Blaze says gruffly, prodding Chaz in the chest. "I mean it."

"I won't," Chaz says. "Promise."

***

"So Chaz spent the night with you?" Hanna giggles the next morning before school. "Oh, man, if you would've told me that back in sixth grade."

"Life is weird," I reply. "You really never know where it's going to take you."

Chaz shrugs. "What's the big deal? She's my hero. And her floor is uber comfortable."

CeCe pulls her water bottle out of her bag. She's been especially quiet this morning. "So what does this all mean?"

"I don't know," Chaz admits. "It was bad. I mean, we're all lost. But at the same time, I'm seeing everything clearly for the first time, if that makes any sense. I don't want it another way. I know my mother still loves me, that this is hard for her. But I've done some reading and watched some videos, and this is how some people react, I guess. She is who she is. I'm not counting on her changing her mind."

Hanna folds her arms. "How long are you staying at Roxie's?"

"A couple days," Chaz replies. "At least. Brandt gets back in town next week. I'll stay with him as long as I need to if the home situation is still toxic."

CeCe passes me her bottle and I take a sip. "Any news from Reece?" Chaz shakes his head.

"Give it time," Hanna says. "And try to understand. You really are amazing, Chaz Humbert. She'll be hard-pressed to find a replacement."

"Remember what Andy said?" Chaz laughs. "About how else could I be surrounded by hot girls? That was literally the best part of the whole conversation."

"I know!" I exclaim. "No wonder Reece keeps him around. I totally get it now. He's good for the ego."

"Andy's really cool," Chaz says. "I can't wait for you guys to get to know him better."

"They're all cool," I reply. "And you need guy friends as much as they need you."

"I do," Chaz says. "And you three are my besties, but I'm still a dude. Gotta have my wolf pack."

CeCe sucks in a lungful of air and spreads her fingers out on the tabletop. "Something came in the mail."

I swivel in my chair to give her my full attention. "Does it have to do with...?"

"Yeah." CeCe swallows sharply. "Are you ready to see what it says?"
Hanna clasps her hands. "I'm ready."

Chaz looks at me. "Roxie?"

"Yeah," I say, my heart thumping in my ears. "Let's open it."

To my five deep crew,

Hola! Long time no talk. Let me just say I'm doing more than okay down here in sunny ___________. It's great. The beach is filled with beautiful women, and the beer is cold. But this is not forever. And I don't want it to be.

The day I got deported, I was at the grange. It's a bad place, and don't let no one tell you differently. Nobody wants to end up in a place like that. When ICE arrived, I was there bringing antibiotics to a sick kid who couldn't afford the stuff or even get it. His family was coming from El Salvador, fleeing gang violence and political persecution, but didn't get asylum status. I don't know where he is now, and I never saw him in the detention center. I can only hope he's okay. Sometimes in the detention center, I wanted to be back at the grange. It was that bad. I still can't get it out of my head and have nightmares that I'm still there. While I was there, I thought about a lot. My old life, mostly. When I got off the plane in Mexico, I was scared. I didn't really know anybody and wasn't sure my family would remember me or accept the life I'd lived up north. But they welcomed me, and it's starting to feel like home here. But it'll never be home.

You kids were the best part of living in El Norte. In my line of work, you have a lot of associates, but that's it. Like Carlito Brigante says, "there are no friends in this shit business." And we know what happens to him. But you guys? That was a trip! That day we drove to Elderwood, I saw loyalty. Real loyalty. Not Omerta but people who care. And that's real.

Nico, your quick thinking will serve you well in life. I'm hoping you got my lowrider out of there before asset seizure, which is why only you were given a spare key. As I can't use it right now, I'm having Diego put you all on the title so you can use it as you will. Cars are meant to be driven, and you haven't lived until you've driven a Chevrolet SS with the top down in mid-June. I hope you'll have fun this summer.

As for me? This dumbass is back in school! Sounds crazy, but John from

Elderwood managed to recover my transcripts. He sent them to the high school down here so I could come in as a senior. I graduate winter semester, and you're welcome to attend the ceremony if you feel like coming down. John has since left Elderwood and now teaches at Gonzaga. He said he'll put in a word for me if I choose to apply, and I'm going to. I'll have to wait a while for my student visa, and there might be complications since I was deported and everything. But John's word goes far, and if Gonzaga wants you, Gonzaga gets you. Go Spike!

I was born in Mexico, as were my parents. My blood is Mexican. But I can never be from here, if you know what I mean. It's time to come home.

Best wishes and see you soon,
Emilio Sanchez-Cruz

***

By lunchtime, it's public record. Chaz Humbert, reformed sex predator and one-time pinup boy, is gay. What's most surprising, though, is the quiet. A few people stare at him whenever we walk together, and he told me a couple boys goaded him in passing, but overwhelmingly, the response has been neutral. The teachers, who pretend not to know anything about what goes on (but undoubtedly know by now), have been treating him exactly the same. All in all, it really couldn't have gone better. It seems all that stress was for nothing.

"I mean, time will tell," Chaz says as he dunks a carrot stick in a packet of ranch at lunch. "But so far, so good."

"Humbert."

Brennan and Spencer loom over us, arms folded. The girls and I look up, as do the Three Tenors. Jaw clenched, I prepare for whatever storm is coming.

Chaz nods coolly. "Boys."

Brennan clears his throat. "We heard the news."

Spencer bobs his head. "We did. And, uh…"

"It's not like we didn't know," Brennan breaks in. "We did. But we're not going to stop bullying you."

"Because it's homophobic," Spencer adds. "It would be homophobic not to bully you. Because that would be treating you differently based on your sexual preference which is, like, technically discrimination."

"So we have to," Brennan reasons. "Plus, it's fun."

"You've got a week," Spencer says, giving Chaz a curt nod. "Grace period. After that, game on, Chaz-gender."

"Can't wait," Chaz calls after the apes. "I'll be waiting."

I roll my eyes. "Seriously?"

Hanna sighs. "They could just stop."

"Nah." Chaz shakes his head. "I owned them the last time. They'll never be able to top that one. This was to save face."

"Well," I say. "I guess that's as bad as it's going to get around here. Looks like we're home free."

"I saw Reece between classes," Chaz informs us. "She apologized. For how she reacted. She told me she'll support me no matter what, but she's going to be out of my life for now. That she needs time to process."

CeCe pats his thigh. "It'll be good for both of you."

"Still." Chaz looks conflicted. "It won't be the same."

"She was crazy about you, man," Kris says. "I'd never seen anything like it."

"Yeah," Phil agrees. "You were kind of a big deal."

"Well, one more thing I screwed up," Chaz laughs. "There I go again, being a selfish jerk. At least I won't do that ever again."

"Guys," Andy says, rolling his eyes. "Come on. Reece is a cougar. She was on the prowl for a mate, and she found Chaz. There'll be more where that came from."

"Andy!" Phil widens his eyes at his friend. "Look, man, don't talk about her that way."

"It's fine, Andy," Chaz says with a chuckle. "And Phil? Buddy, it's your time to shine."

"Hey. Chaz."

Stephanie Quayle plants herself in front of our table, snapping her bubble gum loudly. She tilts her head at Hanna and me. "You two are amazing. Or batshit crazy. Way more forgiving than I'd ever be."

"Hi, Stephanie," Chaz says. "Care to join us?"

Stephanie grimaces. "Not really. I mean, maybe if you weren't here, but you are, so I won't stay." She pauses. "I just want to say you've got balls. Coming out and everything. Especially after what happened. It takes a lot."

"Well, thank you," Chaz says, smiling slightly. "And I'm sorry about everything. The harassment and stuff. I really am."

Stephanie gives him a stiff nod. "I forgive you. God knows you went through a lot."

"I heard you started an outreach," Chaz says, sitting up straight. "For LGBT kids. How's it going?"

"Oh, yeah," she laughs ruefully. "That. Well, uh, that was kind of just a joke I had going on when you…"

"No, let's do it," Chaz says, a smile playing at the corner of his mouth. "'Quayle for Queers' has serious potential."

"Are you serious?" Stephanie snorts. "Well, I guess it couldn't hurt."

"Let's stay in touch," Chaz says. "There may be others. Let me be the pitchman."

"Hired," Stephanie laughs. "See you around, creep."

"Bye," Chaz calls after her.

"Stephanie?" Hanna shakes her head in amazement. "Didn't she take out a hit on Chaz at some point?"

"We tried," I tell her. "Emilio turned it down. No women, no kids."

"Never saw that coming," Chaz chuckles. "I figured she'd have had a field day with this."

"Oh, she did," I say. "And that intercom announcement she made was money. But people grow. And you took a lot of heat those weeks. She probably figures the score is even now."

Chaz wipes his brow. "Boy, did I."

"Seems like so long ago," Hanna remarks. "Can you believe the school year is almost over?"

I shake my head. "Unreal."

"Yeah," CeCe says. "Hanna's right. We're coming up on eight months since starting high school. Erik and I were madly in love. Chaz was a serial sex offender. Life sure was different."

I close my eyes. "And I never want to go back."

Acknowledgments

Not unlike Roxie, I'm truly blessed to be surrounded by some incredibly unique, funny, talented, and caring people. *Finding Chaz* was a daunting, almost decade-long endeavor that couldn't have happened without the support and assistance of several individuals. I'd like to acknowledge their contributions here.

First, and most importantly, my brother Kian. Without your support, creativity, and belief, *Finding Chaz* would still be rotting, unfinished, on a 2008 iMac in the garage. Thank you for loving this story and its characters as much as I do. I could not ask for a better best friend and creative partner, and I can't wait to share our future collaborations with the world.

Mom. You are my voice of reason (I know you find that ironic) and my rock. Thank you for always supporting my dreams. I love you.

Boo: You were not only my favorite teacher but the most influential one. Finding me again, reaching out, and gently encouraging me to keep writing was pivotal to my becoming an author. I couldn't wait to get the finished manuscript to you.

Tina, you with your magical artwork captured the vibe of the book and Chaz's essence in a way nobody else could have. You created a cover I am so proud to have my name on. You're truly the best.

To my trusted first readers who read *Finding Chaz* as a choppy, gruesome mess and still had positive feedback and words of affirmation: you are my heroes. Your input and observations were vital to making *Finding Chaz* reach its full potential.

And finally, to the entire team at Paper Raven Publishing: you guys rock. Thank you for calming my anxious brain and making my author journey painless, exciting, and fun.

Free Reader Bonus

Thank you for buying *Finding Chaz*. I have a free bonus chapter for my readers! Just visit the url below to get your copy.

https://www.anisaashabi.com/finding-chaz-bonus